FATE of
WORLDS

FATE *of* WORLDS

RETURN FROM THE RINGWORLD

Larry Niven

AND

Edward M. Lerner

A TOM DOHERTY ASSOCIATES BOOK • NEW YORK

This is a work of fiction. All of the characters, organizations, and events portrayed in this novel are either products of the authors' imaginations or are used fictitiously.

FATE OF WORLDS: RETURN FROM THE RINGWORLD

Copyright © 2012 by Larry Niven and Edward M. Lerner

All rights reserved.

A Tor Book
Published by Tom Doherty Associates, LLC
175 Fifth Avenue
New York, NY 10010

www.tor-forge.com

Tor® is a registered trademark of Tom Doherty Associates, LLC.

ISBN 978-0-7653-6649-8

Tor books may be purchased for educational, business, or promotional use. For information on bulk purchases, please contact Macmillan Corporate and Premium Sales Department at 1-800-221-7945 extension 5442 or write specialmarkets@macmillan.com.

First Edition: August 2012
First Mass Market Edition: July 2013

Printed in the United States of America

0 9 8 7 6 5 4 3 2

To big ideas. And to those who dare to dream them.

CONTENTS

DRAMATIS PERSONAE

HUMANS

Sigmund Ausfaller: *retired Defense Minister; New Terra resident; Earth expatriate.*

Julia Byerley-Mancini: *Captain in the New Terran Defense Forces; commander of starship* Endurance; *leader, expedition to "The Anomaly"; granddaughter of Sigmund Ausfaller.*

Alice Jordan: *member, expedition to "The Anomaly"; New Terra resident; Sol system expatriate.*

Donald Norquist-Ng: *Minister, New Terran Defense Forces.*

Denise Rodgers-Bjornstad: *Governor (planetary executive), New Terra.*

Louis Wu: *Earthborn adventurer; member of both Ringworld expeditions; newly escaped from the Ringworld.*

Tanya Wu: *Earthborn junior naval officer aboard ARM vessel* Koala.

Wesley Wu: *Earthborn naval officer commanding* Koala, *deployed to the Artifact Monitoring Mission.*

GW'OTH
(FLEET OF WORLDS [NATURE PRESERVE FIVE] RESIDENTS UNLESS OTHERWISE NOTED)

Cd'o: *A Gw'o unit from the Ol't'ro ensemble mind; born on the colony world of Kl'mo.*

Er'o: *Memory remnant within Ol't'ro of a long-dead Gw'o unit; veteran of the Pak War.*

Ol't'ro: *the Gw'oth ensemble mind (a Gw'otesht-16) who secretly rules the Fleet of Worlds; also see artificial intelligence Proteus and Citizen/Puppeteer Chiron.*

Tf'o: *the Gw'o leader in the joint Gw'oth/Citizen expedition lurking around the Ringworld.*

ARTIFICIAL INTELLIGENCES

Hawking: *AI managing tactical operations of Earth's Task Force Delta within the Artifact Monitoring Mission.*

Jeeves: *Any of the many AIs descended from the shipboard intelligence of the ramscoop Long Pass (from whose embryo banks New Terra was populated).*

Proteus: *AI that manages the Hearth/Fleet of Worlds defensive grid; controlled by Ol't'ro. As a minor function, it also animates the "Citizen" known as Chiron.*

Voice: *AI long in exile with Hindmost on the Ringworld.*

CITIZENS/PUPPETEERS
(HEARTH RESIDENTS UNLESS OTHERWISE NOTED)

Achilles: *planetary hindmost (*) of Nature Preserve One; member of Experimentalist Party; former Hindmost (*); former Minister of Science; former physicist.*

Baedeker: *former Hindmost (*); former Minister of Science; former engineer; member of Experimentalist Party; in off-world exile.*

Chiron: *longtime Minister of Science and planetary hindmost (*) of Nature Preserve Five; secretly a network persona animated by Proteus; Ol't'ro's stealthy presence within the Citizen government.*

Hindmost: *deposed Hindmost (*); member of Experimentalist Party; hindmost (*) of the second Ringworld expedition; newly escaped from the Ringworld.*

Horatius: *Hindmost (*)—as a pawn of Ol't'ro—since soon after the first Ringworld expedition; head of the Conservative Party.*

Minerva: *Citizen head in the joint Gw'oth/Citizen expedition lurking around the Ringworld. A deputy director of Clandestine Directorate.*

Nessus: *onetime senior agent/scout of Clandestine Directorate; hindmost (*) of the first Ringworld expedition; in exile on New Terra.*

Nike: *former head of Clandestine Directorate; former Hindmost (*); Experimentalist.*

Vesta: *longtime deputy to Achilles; Experimentalist.*

(*)*The* Hindmost—"He Who Leads from Behind"—is the head of government in the Fleet of Worlds (comprised of the Citizen home world of Hearth and its Nature Preserve companion worlds). *A* hindmost, in lowercase, directs any lower-level Citizen organization or entity.

KEY DATES

2645	Puppeteers and their worlds flee the galactic-core explosion
2650–51	Human slaves rebel; New Terra (was Nature Preserve Four) goes free
2659	Puppeteer effort to reclaim New Terra fails
2675	The Pak War
2780–81	The Gw'oth War
2783	Isolationist New Terran regime veers away from the Fleet of Worlds
2850–52	Ringworld discovered; first expedition to the Ringworld
2878–93	Second expedition to the Ringworld; explorers all stranded
?–2893	War among many spacefaring species for control of the Ringworld

(Dates follow Earth's calendar and reflect Earth's frame of reference. During much of this era, New Terra and the Fleet of Worlds traveled fast enough relative to Earth to experience significant relativistic time dilation.)

The Flight of the Puppeteers, Earth Dates 2645-2894

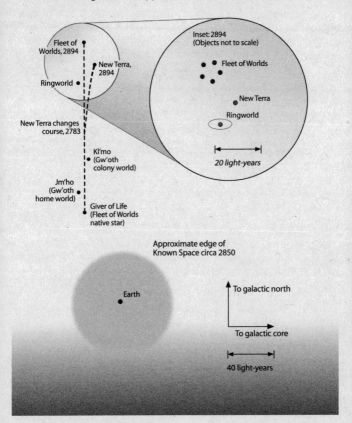

PRELUDE

Earth Date: 2893

A beautiful world, alone, serene, races through the interstellar void. Warmed by necklaces of artificial suns orbiting from pole to pole, the world's climate is everywhere and always temperate. Beneath the many suns, oceans sparkle and cloud tops gleam. Bountiful fields and lush forests span continents. Here and there cities stand, proud and prosperous.

The human inhabitants call this paradise New Terra. Only in story do they remember the days when their home was known merely as Nature Preserve Four. When their home was but one farm world among many in the Fleet of Worlds. When alien masters ruled their lives. "Citizens," the aliens called themselves and, moreover, "saviors."

But young and old on New Terra know the hard-won truth: that their former masters had attacked their ancestors' ramscoop, not chanced upon a derelict starship. That from the wrecked ship's embryo banks the aliens had bred a race of slaves.

Independence had not come easily, but now New Terra sets its own course through space.

And what of Old Terra? Earth? No one here could say where the ancestral world may lie.

Not only artificial suns accompany New Terra on its

seemingly endless trek through the darkness. Myriads of tiny spacecraft, sprinkled across many light-days, hold formation with the world. The early-warning array endlessly scans in all directions, endlessly probing with every known method of long-range sensing.

In the planetary defense center, staffed round the clock, people try to imagine against what, besides boredom, they stand guard. New Terra is light-years from the nearest star. Aboard their Fleet of Worlds, the ruthlessly cowardly Citizens—increasingly, and aptly, come to be known to all here as Puppeteers—have receded beyond the reach of every instrument except powerful optical telescopes.

Suddenly every element in the planetary early-warning array clamors in unison. Every watch stander in the planetary defense center jolts to full alertness to stare at their consoles.

To gape at the impossible.

RIPPLE

Earth Date: 2893

"There is an intruder, sir," Jeeves announced, breaking the silence.

Sigmund Ausfaller sighed. Age had not so much mellowed as exhausted him. The universe was out to get him, and so what? It had been—years?—since he had mustered the energy to care. Maybe it had been years since he had cared that he no longer cared.

"Sir?"

Shading his eyes with an upraised hand, Sigmund peered across the desert. The day's final string of suns was low to the horizon. Here and there, scattered across barren landscape, cacti cast long shadows. A lone bird glided overhead. Beyond the limits of his stone patio, civilization had left no visible mark.

A cluster of cacti reminded him of other columns. Long ago. Far away. Columns of a world-shattering machine. And they *had* shattered a world, although by the time it had happened he had been dead. That happened to him far too often. The getting dead part. Peril to entire worlds, too, but—

"You should withdraw to safety, sir," Jeeves prompted.

Sigmund sighed again, this time at himself. Age made one's mind wander. So did living by oneself. Not that, with Jeeves around, he was truly alone. To be old and alone—

"Sir," Jeeves insisted.

Sigmund struggled out of his big mesh hammock to stand. "Describe the intruder."

"An antigrav flitter. It's on approach from the east at just within the low-altitude speed limit."

"Visual sighting?"

"Too distant at present. Radar, sir."

"How long until it arrives?"

"Ten minutes, sir, if the craft maintains its current velocity."

Sigmund glanced at the dark circle inset in a corner of his patio. The circle was the bottom of a stepping disc. Apart from its active side being obstructed—and so rendered inert—the device was like millions across the world. Flip to light-colored side up and in one pace he could teleport at light speed to any disc of his choosing, almost anywhere on the planet.

But were he to invert the disc, then others, if they had the authority to preempt his privacy settings, could teleport here.

Sigmund valued his privacy, and his stepping disc stayed upside down.

And to be honest, his disc was not exactly like the millions of others. The micro-fusion reactor on *this* disc would overload seconds after he stepped out, destroying all record of his destination.

He *really* valued his privacy.

"Sir?"

Sigmund considered. "They're not stealthed. They're approaching from the east, easy to spot, not flying out of the setting suns. They want us to know they're coming." Sigmund gestured at his modest home, in which, on the oaken desk he had crafted by hand, his pocket comp sat powered down. "It's not as though they can call ahead."

"Very good, sir," Jeeves said in his gentleman's gentleman tone of voice: acknowledgment and mild reproach together.

Jeeves was more ancient even than Sigmund. The butler mannerisms that had once been a few lines of code—an affectation or a jape on someone's part—had, over the centuries, permeated every facet of the AI's persona. Kind of like paranoia in Sigmund's brain.

Friends don't reprogram friends, even when they're able.

Sigmund dropped back with a grunt into his hammock. "Let's find out what our visitor wants."

THE FLITTER MORPHED from invisible to droning speck to, all of a sudden, *here*. Sigmund stood watching as the craft swooped in for a landing on the windswept sands. The canopy pivoted upward from its aft edge; a woman, dressed in the trim blue uniform of the New Terran Defense Forces, stepped out of the cockpit.

"Good evening, Minister," his granddaughter called.

Minister. An official visit, as though her uniform would not have told Sigmund that.

"It's hot," Sigmund said. "Join me in the shade, Captain."

"Thank you, sir." Julia looked around before joining Sigmund under the awning that overhung half the patio. She was a tall, lithe, beautiful woman with pale blue eyes and shoulder-length ash-blond hair.

"Sit, Captain. May I get you something to drink?"

"No, thank you, sir." His visitor stood, ill at ease, uniform cap clutched under an arm.

Her nametag read BYERLEY-MANCINI. Sunlight reflecting off the nametag rendered a shimmering hologram, detailed beyond the capability of badge-sized photonics to mimic. So, too, did her rank insignia. On a world where everyone dressed in garments of programmable nanocloth, where on a whim the wearer could change the color, texture, and pattern of her clothing, the credentials of the planetary defense forces remained—special. And, in theory, difficult to counterfeit.

In progeny and in uniforms, Sigmund's legacy survived. And in a third respect: that New Terra remained free and whole. If others had had their way . . .

"If I may, sir," Julia prompted gently, as though channeling Jeeves.

"Go ahead," Sigmund said. "What brings you here?"

"An astrophysical phenomenon, sir. An anomaly."

Sigmund twitched. Twice in his long life he had been marooned, alone, deep in space. Three times he had been murdered, each death grislier than the last. A glimpse of an *astrophysical phenomenon* had presaged his most recent death and, after resurrection, left him stranded in interstellar space.

Turbulence in the ineffably tenuous interstellar medium. An uptick in concentrations of interstellar helium. Only by such subtleties had the Pak invasion armada, wave upon wave of ramscoop warships, given warning of its coming.

The Pak were genocidal xenophobes, a pestilence upon every other form of life. As protectors, the neuter postadult life stage, Pak were freakishly brilliant, reflexively aggressive, utterly selfish in the defense of their bloodlines. Eating tree-of-life root transformed an adult, what protectors dismissively called a breeder, into a protector.

Humanity, it turned out, descended from a Pak colony that had failed on Earth millions of years ago, because Earth lacked trace elements essential to tree-of-life. From the Pak perspective humans were, rather than distant cousins, mutants to be obliterated.

Sigmund shivered, all too aware that the universe cared not a fig for his memories or his phobias.

Julia was doing her best to hide her feelings, but beneath a stoic, professional veneer she was tense. Perhaps only someone who knew her well would notice.

Sigmund said, "I'm no astrophysicist." *Open up, Julia. Tell me what's troubling you.*

"Understood, sir." Julia hesitated. "Is Jeeves with us?"

"Indeed, sir," the AI intoned.

"This is a matter of world security, Minister," Julia said.

"Jeeves and I are both fossils. Our security clearances, like my title, are long lapsed." Never mind that, as far as this world was concerned, Sigmund was the one who had *invented* security clearances. That he had built from nothing what had been known on his watch as the Ministry of Defense. Never mind that Julia would have no inkling what a fossil was. Life beyond the single-celled was too recently imported to New Terra to have left fossils. "Whatever this anomaly is, you've come to tell me about it. So, tell."

"Right." Julia took a deep breath. "Something impossible has happened. You're familiar with space-time ripples as ships enter and leave hyperspace?"

Sigmund nodded.

"Yesterday, the planetary defense array detected a . . . big ripple."

"How big?" Sigmund asked.

"That's the thing, sir. It can't be that big."

And so your superiors sent you to see what alternate explanation my devious brain can conjure. "How big did the ripple look to be?" Sigmund persisted. "How many ships?"

"The ripple was reported by every sensor in the array. Saturation strength."

The array that surrounded New Terra. An array—at least during Sigmund's tenure in the Ministry—deployed in concentric spheres across vast distances. To saturate all the sensors at once would require an unbelievable number of ships, many emerging almost on top of New Terra.

He tamped down resurgent memories of Pak war fleets. This was no time to get lost in the past.

After detecting ships nearby, the first step in the alert protocol would have been a hyperwave radar sweep. He asked, "And radar showed what?"

"Nothing," Julia said. "That's part of what's odd."

Because no one had ever found a way to disguise the interaction between a hyperwave and normal matter. That didn't mean no one ever would. "I imagine the Defense Forces dispatched ships. And found nothing?"

"Right, sir."

Very puzzling. "Just the one ripple?" Sigmund asked.

"Yes, sir. Whatever emerged from hyperspace didn't drop back into it. That, or these ships came a great distance through normal space, shielded from our sensors, waiting until they were on top of us before jumping into hyperspace to speed away. Either would explain a single ripple."

"A huge fleet, after sneaking up on us and shrieking the news of its arrival, continues on its way? I don't believe that, either."

"Nor do our analysts." She hesitated. "They need you at the Ministry to figure it out."

After the revolution, confusing correlation with causation, the new regime had reached a strange conclusion: that the emergencies from which Sigmund had time and again saved this world *he* had provoked through his own interstellar meddling. The new government made clear just how unwelcome he was. Now they wanted his help?

Nameless, faceless, *they* had haunted Sigmund for much of his life, but it was all too clear who thought to manipulate him today. The current minister.

There's a reason the Defense Forces sent, specifically, *you*, Captain. The minister believes I can't say no to you. And he is probably right.

Many of Sigmund's family had joined the New Terran military, and among them Julia was neither the youngest nor the oldest, the most junior nor the most senior, the least nor the most accomplished. And yet she was special. Sigmund would deny it if asked, but of all his grandchildren, Julia was his favorite—because she was the spitting image of her grandmother.

Tanj, but he missed Penelope! *His* deaths faded from memory. Never Penny's. Hers had stuck. He had met her soon after coming to this strange and wondrous world, awakening from his second death—

"Grandpa?" Julia said hesitantly. "At the Ministry, we need some . . . creative thinking."

"About what might have tricked the sensors, and how," Jeeves commented.

"It's the current theory," Julia agreed. "That something, or someone, somehow confused our sensors. Only our experts have yet to find evidence of tampering or intrusion."

Something stirred in the back of Sigmund's mind. Not quite the old paranoia, but maybe more than the skepticism of age. One could never discount a security breach, but he doubted that a breach explained this big ripple. Anyone who *could* spoof the planetary defense network would keep that ability secret—until they attacked.

Transparent manipulation be damned, the safety of the world was at stake. "Show me the data."

"Sorry, sir. That information is only available at the Ministry. Very restricted."

Except for the security breach the "experts" thought they had. Fools.

Sigmund stared out at the desert. The suns had all but set, and a few bright stars managed to show themselves overhead. A thick, inky smear near the western horizon hinted at mountains. "Then take me to the Ministry." He started walking toward her vehicle.

"Not the flitter, Grandpa." When he turned back, Julia pointed at the upside-down stepping disc inset in his patio. "You're needed now."

As he turned over the disc, Sigmund switched off the self-destruct. Surreptitiously, to be sure, but Jeeves would have seen it through the house security cameras. No need, old friend, to net yourself someplace else.

Sigmund gestured to Julia to step ahead. Seconds after her, flicking across half a world into the security vestibule of the headquarters of the New Terran Defense Forces, he brooded what nightmare this latest *astronomical phenomenon* portended.

· 2 ·

An overweight, florid-faced colonel met Sigmund and his granddaughter in the secured teleportation foyer, expediting their way through screening. With a half-dozen armed escorts, they strode deep into the building, past one interior checkpoint after another.

Once you've overthrown one government, why wouldn't you suspect others of plotting to overthrow yours?

The previous government had vanished almost overnight through a self-organizing consensus process Sigmund had never understood and would never accept, but that the native New Terrans somehow considered proper. The transfer of power was more Puppeteer-like than the rebels appeared to recognize, even if the new technocracy had more of a human feel to it.

Sigmund had sworn to uphold the elected government, but when the demonstrations went worldwide, he had ordered his troops to lay down their arms. On his watch New Terrans would never attack their own people.

Or maybe he had rejected violence because, at some level, resistance would have been self-serving. Ultimately, the old government's downfall was about *him*. To be rid of all alien "entanglements"—to hide from the galaxy—the people had had to be rid of him. And so, on the heels of the Gw'oth War: the revolution.

Never mind that he had maintained New Terran neutrality, that he had guided his adopted world, unscathed, through yet another interstellar crisis—

Stop dwelling on the past, Sigmund lectured himself, no matter that mostly he lived there. He was too ancient to do otherwise.

And *ancient* was how everyone here would see him. The doddering old man. The relic of a bygone era. The freak from another world. Why would they heed him?

Astronomical phenomenon, he reminded himself, with a shiver. Figure it out, then make them listen.

"Are you all right, Grandpa?" Julia whispered.

"Fine," he lied.

They passed a Puppeteer in the hall: two-headed; three-legged; the fluffy mane between his serpentine necks/arms elaborately coiffed. He wore only a narrow sash, from which hung pockets and a clipped-on computer, but insignia pinned to the sash showed him to be a civilian.

Of *course* he was a civilian. At the first hint of danger, Puppeteers ran. As, even now, the trillion Puppeteers aboard the Fleet of Worlds fled from an astronomical phenomenon that would not reach this corner of the galaxy for twenty thousand years. Puppeteers only defended themselves in desperation, when neither flight nor surrender was an option. Or when—undeniable, because Puppeteers had set their robots to seize *Long Pass*—they could strike with overwhelming superiority and their meddling could not be traced back to them.

Cowardice did not preclude ruthlessness.

A few Puppeteers, outcasts and misfits, had asked to remain after New Terran independence. More Puppeteers had arrived as refugees amid the Gw'oth War; some of them had stayed, too. Most had settled on the continent of Elysium, on territory first planted as a nature preserve for Hearth life. A very few lived and worked among humans.

This Puppeteer was deep in conversation, in full two-throated, six-vocal-corded disharmony. With a final jangling chord he made some point, to which, voices rumbling out of the dangling pocket comp, another Puppeteer responded in similar atonality.

Without recourse to a chamber orchestra, humans could not begin to reproduce Puppeteer languages. Puppeteers, fortunately, managed English without difficulty.

Approaching an intersection, Sigmund's entourage met six people coming down the corridor from the opposite direction. Among the newcomers was a pallid, white-haired woman. Tall despite her pronounced stoop, she towered over her uniformed escorts. Turning the corner, the two groups merged.

"Hello, Alice," Sigmund said. Meeting her here did not surprise him. Whatever motivated pulling him out of disgrace and retirement would merit retrieving her, too. But he had not spoken to Alice in over a century; seeing her so *old* was a shock.

Alice, coldly, said nothing.

They halted before a well-guarded entrance: the situation room. Sigmund knew this place all too well, having spent far too many days and nights there. Alice, as his deputy, too. One of their escorts pointed, unnecessarily, to the lockers on the right of the doors. Shielding in the walls, floor, and ceiling blocked unauthorized transmissions, but security also demanded that no one inside make illicit recordings. After Sigmund, Alice, and Julia deposited their comps in lockers and initialized the biometric pads with their handprints, a guard opened a door and waved them through.

Donald Norquist-Ng, minister of the New Terran Defense Forces, presided from one end of the long oval conference table. He was short, gaunt, and dour, with eyebrows like wooly yellow caterpillars. He sat stiffly, and rising to his feet to point into a tactical display, he moved ponderously, too. The man was not yet even a hundred; the stiffness was all for effect: would-be gravitas that struggled even to achieve pretension.

As Sigmund, Alice, and Julia entered, Norquist-Ng glanced up. His eyes slid over them without acknowledgment, and the session went on without pausing for introductions. Sigmund thought he recognized some of the faces around the table from the 3-V.

Current events held no interest for Sigmund, but what little he knew about the current minister suggested a Napoleon wannabe. Not that anyone on this world had heard of Napoleon. The Puppeteers had never admitted to their servants knowing . . . *anything* about humanity, its origins, or its culture. Even English—irregular verbs, illogical spellings, and all—had been designed by their selfless patrons. So, anyway, the slaves had once been taught.

The table offered no empty chairs. Julia found them seats against a wall, among the aides, adjutants, and flunkies, while the discussion continued.

This was not Sigmund's first crisis and he thought he could bring himself up to speed. For all the tech improvements since his era, nothing meaningful had changed: too much data still spewed from too many displays. Star charts. Sensor scans. Ship statuses. Weapon inventories. Lists of speculations.

". . . Compromise of the sensor array. Our security

experts continue to search for the means of intrusion. Regrettably they have yet . . ."

". . . Obviously spurious data. If ships were near, we would have found them by . . ."

". . . Once we learned to leave the galaxy alone, it's been content to return the favor."

Sigmund let it all wash over him, categorizing the big themes, itemizing the points of contention, winnowing facts from assumptions. Alice, her lips pursed, her forehead furrowed, appeared to be doing much the same.

". . . Audit trails in the intrusion-detection software . . ."

". . . Another patrol ship reports finding nothing . . ."

He and Alice had yet to be recognized, much less invited to contribute. Were they here to help? Or, Julia's earnest plea notwithstanding, had they been summoned so that Norquist-Ng could say later, if things should go wrong, "We even brought in the off-world experts."

The latter, of course. Futzy fools.

The New Terrans Sigmund had been kidnapped to protect knew that the universe was a dangerous place. But that generation, the independence generation, had passed. Their children were gone, too, or retired, isolationism had long been the norm, and in their hiatus from history, Norquist-Ng and his ilk had come to mistake good luck for wisdom.

Sigmund was the only person on this world to have heard of ostriches. No matter: to deny danger by burying one's head in the sand was folly. He stood, loudly clearing his throat.

Norquist-Ng turned to glower.

"If I may summarize," Sigmund said. "One hyperspace ripple, immense beyond all precedent. You don't believe sensors and patrol ships could fail to find *any* of the many vessels emerging from hyperspace. And you don't see how sensors and patrol ships could overlook that many ships sneaking up on us through normal space, to startle us with a massive ripple when they dropped back *into* hyperspace. So you infer—"

"We *conclude,* Mr. Ausfaller," the minister snapped, "that someone compromised the sensor network. It's the only logical explanation. Helping us to find the security breach, if you were not informed, is why you are here. The sole reason. Now if you will—"

"You're wrong," Sigmund interrupted right back. "Because another explanation is staring us in the face." The explanation you're all too timid to imagine. Or, perhaps, too sane.

"And this explanation is?" Norquist-Ng asked.

"That the sensor data mean just what they say," Sigmund said, "notwithstanding the absence of nearby ships."

Alice nodded. "We need to consider the possibility."

"Hyperspace ripples without hyperdrive ships," someone stage-whispered. "Nonsense."

"Enlighten me," Norquist-Ng said, somewhat more pragmatically.

"Is a Jeeves present?" Sigmund asked. "I need some calculations done."

"Yes, sir," declared a voice from a ceiling speaker.

This wasn't any Jeeves that Sigmund knew. *Sir* carried no hint of an English butler; this AI sounded like a junior officer addressing his superior.

Hyperspace-emergence ripples, like light and gravity, dropped off rapidly with distance. Sigmund asked, "Do I have this right? The ripple's peak amplitude maxed out sensors at all locations? No discernible attenuation measured anywhere within the array's volume?"

"Correct, sir. Saturation strength throughout."

"Assume a *single* emergence ripple just powerful enough to overload all sensors throughout the array. What's the nearest to New Terra that such a source could be located?"

The pause for calculation was all but imperceptible. "A bit over five light-years."

"That's ridiculous—"

Sigmund cut off the freckle-faced aide. "And a stronger source for the ripple could be even more distant."

"Correct, sir," Jeeves said.

The early-warning sensors took bearings on any sightings. "Continuing to assume a single source, Jeeves, what is its triangulated point of origin?"

"Any differences in bearings are meaningless," the same aide huffed. "With the sensors overloaded, the directional data are suspect."

"Jeeves, please answer the question," Sigmund persisted.

"All bearings point in more or less the same direction. The variations are smaller than the known tolerances in angular measurement."

"Averaged across all the sensors, random differences will cancel out," Sigmund guessed. "Right?"

"To an unknown degree, sir."

"Caveat noted, Jeeves. Do the calculation anyway, please."

"I have a result, sir, but that inferred point of origin is subject to considerable uncertainty."

"You're wasting everyone's time, Ausfaller," Norquist-Ng growled.

Alice's head had taken on the thoughtful cant that

Sigmund remembered so well. "Jeeves," she said, "plot the apparent direction and point of origin on a star chart."

Above the conference table, a hologram opened, dim but for a scattering of sparks. A blue dot, for New Terra, blinked at the holo's center. Translucent concentric blue spheres centered on the blinking dot marked off the light-years. From the blinking dot, a pale red line segment reached out, not approaching any star until it ended—Sigmund counted the pale spheres—about fourteen light-years out.

Fourteen light-years? Whoever had caused this disturbance controlled incredible energies.

Like the power to move worlds?

His hands trembling, Sigmund said, "Jeeves, now overlay the course taken by the Fleet of Worlds."

"Yes, sir."

A green trace, at this scale perfectly straight, came into the holo. Across the room from Sigmund, someone cursed in wonderment.

The green line representing the Puppeteers' flight grazed the star from which—just maybe—the mysterious space/hyperspace interface distortion had originated.

A star that *this* world would have encountered well before the Fleet, had the revolutionary government not seen fit to divert New Terra onto its present, much different path.

SIGMUND GAVE NORQUIST-NG credit: the man had the sense to clear the room. He asked that Alice and Sigmund stay, and also a long-faced female aide whose name Sigmund had not retained. Sigmund insisted that Julia remain.

And the Jeeves, of course.

"Might the Fleet have been involved?" the minister asked. "They had to have traveled well past this star when . . . whatever happened."

It was a sensible question, but posture or tone of voice or—*something* showed that what Norquist-Ng meant was, "Wasn't the new regime wise to set an independent course?"

As in, where could be safer than far from the Fleet? Than—once New Terra made it that far—deep inside the zone of devastation Pak armadas had wiped clean of technological civilizations?

Using that logic, the revolutionary government had redirected their world's course, tapping the planetary brakes while turning inward toward the galactic core, even as the Fleet continued its headlong rush into galactic north. It had been decades since New Terra had had contact with its former masters.

Sigmund thought once more of ostriches.

"Maybe the Puppeteers *were* involved," Alice said. "We should check out the solar system where the ripple originated."

"Why?" Norquist-Ng asked. "You and Ausfaller have only confirmed the wisdom of New Terra staying disengaged."

Disengaged? Like it or not, New Terrans had reengaged when . . . whatever . . . swept past them.

Sigmund gestured at the star map. "Jeeves, assume the disturbance originated near where the lines converge. To produce the effects we observed here, how large an object entered or exited hyperspace?"

"A very significant mass, sir. Perhaps a few gas giants."

The tremor in Sigmund's hands worsened. "Gas giants. You mean . . . gas-giant *planets*?"

"Yes, sir."

"Whole *planets* entering or leaving hyperspace?" the aide said. "Minister, respectfully, it could be dangerous not to know more."

"I'll go," Julia offered, coming to attention. "My ship, the *Endurance,* is ready."

"Your offer is appreciated, Captain," Norquist-Ng said, "but adventuring is no longer our way." He added, pointedly, for his aide, "This government does not go seeking trouble fourteen light-years away."

Ostriches! Sigmund thought again.

"Planetary masses converted to ships," Alice said. "Think of the technology, the sheer magnitude of the power that *someone* must wield. For all we know those ships are coming right at us, in swarms to make the Pak fleets look insignificant. We must check it out."

Norquist-Ng rubbed his chin, considering, before turning to Julia. "Captain, they may have a point. Take Ausfaller as an advisor, but you command the ship and the mission. You are *only* to scout out the region and report back."

Take Ausfaller.

The room faded, seemed to spin. Sigmund, wobbling, groped behind himself for support. He scarcely noticed Julia guiding him into a chair.

He had not been off-world in over a century. Not since the Pak War. Not since he had been left adrift in that useless stub of a derelict starship, light-years from anywhere. Alone but for a Puppeteer frozen in time, inert within a medical-emergency stasis field.

And where was Baedeker now? Long gone . . . Sigmund did not know where.

"Grandpa?" a voice called from an impossible distance.

Sigmund trembled. Fourteen light-years? It would mean forty-two days' travel each way. Forty-two days of the less-than-nothingness of hyperspace gibbering worse than madness into his mind . . .

"Behold the famed destroyer of worlds," the aide scoffed.

With a convulsive shudder, Sigmund forced himself back to the present. He couldn't care less what politicians thought of him. But Julia's worry? Alice's disdain? Those cut him to the quick.

"*I'll* accompany the captain," Alice said.

If any two people on New Terra should have been friends, they were he and Alice. He was from Earth and she from the Belt, separately exiled among strangers. Neither had arrived under their own power, or by their own choice. Neither knew their way home.

Until they had lived on this world so long that *this* was home.

For a long time, they were friends. Not counting Penelope, Alice had been his best friend—

And when he hadn't been paying attention, he and Alice had become relics together. Despite years spent frozen in stasis. Despite time dilation from New Terra's sometimes relativistic velocity. She was biologically about 225 in Earth years, ancient on a world yet to invent boosterspice. She *looked* ancient.

Whereas he, after making the same allowances, had passed 350. By rights, he should have been long dead. Probably Alice still wished him dead.

But physically, Sigmund was younger, "only"

more-or-less two hundred. The prototype autodoc that had twice, all but magically, restored him to life had both times also rejuvenated him to about twenty.

He should go with Julia to check out this latest threat. In another life, he had been an intelligence agent—an ARM—a high-ranking operative in the United Nations' unassumingly named Amalgamated Regional Militia. He had put together what passed for a military to protect this world.

What made him feel *so* old? The weight of experience? Or the scorn of the one person still living who had once truly understood him?

"Ms. Jordan," Norquist-Ng said respectfully, "it is a commendable offer, but you are in no condition for such a trip. You must realize that."

"But I *am* going. I was a police detective, back in the day, back in the Belt. On this world, for a long time, I was deputy defense minister. We both know"—said staring at Sigmund—"*someone* with off-world experience must go."

Tanj stubborn pride! Few Belters ever went prospecting solo, with only a spacesuit and a singleship to protect them—but loner self-sufficiency had deep roots in their mythos, their schooling, maybe their genes. No matter what was at stake, you questioned that belief at your peril. To presume to make life-or-death decisions for a Belter? That was the ultimate affront.

Once, long ago, Sigmund *had* presumed. In the same desperate circumstances, he would do it again. Better a live ex-friend than a dead friend.

And however scornfully Alice looked at him, he still meant to help keep her alive.

Merely the thought of setting foot onto a spaceship had Sigmund trembling. "Alice," he said weakly, "I'm just not able. I'm sorry, but it'll have to be you. But maybe not alone."

"Is there another 'friend' you'd send?" she mocked.

Not exactly. Friends didn't reprogram friends, even in a good cause. Friends didn't keep dark secrets from—or kidnap—one another. Nonetheless, a champion of New Terra.

Sigmund nodded. "I won't say who, Alice. But if I can convince him to join the expedition, you would be fortunate to have him along."

Weeding, pruning, breaking apart clumps of dirt, Janus worked his way through the garden. Sweat trickled down his flanks and matted his mane. Mud spattered his legs and clung to his hooves.

The redmelons were coming along acceptably, but other melon varieties struggled. Tall stands of ornamental grasses, oddly scented, in shades of amber (a touch too orange) and violet (too pale), bowed in the warm breeze. But the fruit trees showed promise. Winged borers evidently agreed, for the red-and-purple insectivore hedge that bounded the garden was a frenzy of lunging, snapping tendrils.

Once this world had been a granary of the Fleet of Worlds. Most of the farmland here, even long after independence, had grown crops for export to Hearth. No more. Now terrestrial crops prospered, for with the severing of ties with the Concordance had come many changes. Most overt: the reprogramming of the suns. Hearthian flora had yet to adapt to cycles altered to mimic the length of Earth's day and year.

What Janus truly craved was the terrestrial vegetable that he never dared to plant. Someone might remember a Puppeteer with a fondness for carrot juice. He had departed Hearth long ago, but among those in authority was one with long memories. One who nursed grudges.

Even on this world, Achilles might have spies.

Janus had come late to gardening. His mate had loved to garden; to work in the soil was a way, however imperfect, to commune. And gardening had been something to share with the children of their lost parent.

Absent parent, Janus chided himself. He would not, must not, think of his mate as lost, as departed.

No matter that since their parting, the "children" had grown to adulthood. Aurora had even mated. Elpis, the younger of the two, had no memory at all of Hearth, the world of his birth, the home world of his kind, the jewel of the Fleet.

And in all that time, never had as much as a grace note of rumor about Baedeker, much less any news, found its way to Janus.

Beyond the hungry hedge, in a pasture of freshly mown meadowplant, children gamboled and frolicked, bleated and sang. This is a good life, Janus thought. The humans treat us kindly, better than we deserve.

A sudden squealing erupted from among the young, and an outpouring of melodies from the adults who supervised the children's play. Janus set down his trowel, then craned a neck, the better to listen. He was too distant to make out all the chords, and the breeze carried off most of the upper harmonics, but the little he could hear tantalized him. Surprise, certainly. Reassurances for the little ones. Reassurances for one another.

He was quite close enough to see the youngest children scattering from . . . a human.

Round-faced, gray-haired, thick through the middle, his garment set all to black, the newcomer stopped by a cluster of the child-tending adults. Perhaps the man spoke to them, because one indicated the garden with a briefly straightened neck. With a murmur of thanks, the man began shuffling toward Janus.

Sigmund Ausfaller?

The man looked terrible. Decrepit, to be sure; sadly, that was to be expected. Troubled. Shaken. But the eyes, dark and brooding, burned as intensely as ever.

Janus had not seen Sigmund for . . . since soon after taking asylum on this world. No, he should be precise: since Sigmund had smuggled him and the children onto this world. The New Terran government did not know and would never have approved. For Sigmund to reappear . . .

Janus yearned to gallop away like the children. He ached to collapse onto the ground and hide from the world, his heads tucked between his front legs, tightly rolled into a bundle of self. Whatever events brought Sigmund here . . . whatever had shaken Sigmund . . . it would be *bad*.

Sigmund edged through a gap in the hedge, flinching from the tendrils lashing out to taste his face, hands, and garment. "Janus?"

"So some call me," he said. The name he used in the village, no human could sing.

"Two-faced god. Two-headed Puppeteer. Fair enough." Sigmund chuckled. "And, among his attributes, also god of beginnings, endings, and time."

Sigmund's reappearance foretold an ending of Janus' idylls. And a beginning, too. But the beginning of what?

His heads swiveling, Janus briefly looked himself in the eyes. Sigmund would grasp the ironic laughter.

"Apart from you, Sigmund, who on this world knows such things?"

"There is that."

Silence stretched awkwardly. With a mind of its own, his left forehoof began tearing at the dirt. "What brings you, Sigmund?"

"To chat with Janus? Merely a social call. But if I were to speak with—"

"A name none mention in this place." The hoof dug more frantically. A head darted deep into his mane, tongue and lip nodes tugging and twisting at a stray lock of hair.

Sigmund took a computer from his pocket. "There is something I would show that one. Something that a former scout for the Fleet would find interesting."

Janus willed the wayward hoof to rest—one runs fastest on obedient limbs. He released his mane, so that both heads could see. Alas, he understood too well Sigmund's concept of *interesting*. The more circumspectly Sigmund broached a topic, the direr circumstances must be. Beyond the ability of the fleetest to escape. Beyond, sometimes, the ability of Fleets . . .

"Something interesting," Janus echoed. "What manner of thing?"

"Call it an anomaly. A ripple in the continuum, such as ships make when entering or leaving hyperspace. Except . . ."

"Except that no mere ship would explain your unheralded visit."

"A ripple from far away. A vessel departs New Terra soon to investigate." Sigmund opened his comp. "Let me show you."

A graphic sprang from the comp. Amid a scattering

of stars, red and green lines crossed near an ordinary yellow sun. Janus quivered with horrible premonition, but the image used an unfamiliar coordinate system centered on New Terra. He could not be certain.

Until two binary stars and a red giant caught his eye, oriented him. In the shock of recognition, he was Janus no longer.

"I-I know this place," Nessus stammered. "Have me delivered to, to, to the ship."

Then he collapsed, catatonic with terror, onto the ground.

RINGWORLD

Earth Date: 2893

· 4 ·

At the center of the bridge, to the howl of a klaxon, *Koala*'s jump timer reset from a bit longer than five minutes to just less than one. New destination coordinates popped onto the pilot's console.

"What do you think, Lieutenant?" Commander Johansson asked.

Tanya Wu stiffened in her seat at the comm console because, almost certainly, the question was a test. She was newly rotated aboard a ship long deployed. And posted as a lowly purser in a combat zone. And Wu being such a common name—unless she had somehow, without knowing it, pissed off someone in Personnel back on Earth—she had ended up serving under her own father as captain. Dad swore he had had nothing to do with her assignment to *Koala,* but oh, how pathetic the situation made her look.

Amid the orderly bustle of the bridge, she caught sidelong glances and heard yet another whispered reference—*damn* this ship's name—to marsupial pouches and helpless offspring.

"You *do* think?" Johansson prompted.

"Yes, sir." External view ports showed only stars, and Tanya turned toward the bridge's main tactical display. A supply ship as defenseless as its name suggested,

Koala, one vessel among hundreds, huddled near the middle of ARM Task Force Delta. Scattered around the periphery of the holo: two small clusters of Kzinti warships. A Trinoc battle group. An ARM squadron, perhaps patrolling, perhaps returning from, well, Tanya did not try to guess its assignment. Apart from fellow ships of the task force, even the closest icons registered as farther from *Koala* than Saturn from the sun.

The local star was merely the brightest among dimensionless points in the display, and all these ships were outside its gravitational singularity. Out here, light had ceased to set the speed limit. Jump to hyperspace and back out: the nearer group of Kzinti could emerge within the ARM formation, laser cannons blazing, antimatter munitions spewing, within seconds. Still . . .

"Too many ships too close together," she temporized, "but that's always the case."

"Business as usual, then?"

Definitely a test and the bridge crew knew it. In unending round-the-clock high alert, even lowly pursers took their turn standing watch.

Tanya said, "Let's hope this never becomes the usual."

Of the thousands of warships in and around this solar system, at any given moment *someone* was jumping from or reentering Einstein space. Even within formations ships shifted, the fluid configurations yet another complication for anyone contemplating a sneak attack.

The tactical complexity was staggering. Hawking, the chief artificial intelligence aboard the task force's flagship, and its distributed subsets in computers across the armada, continually integrated readouts across hundreds of ARM ships and tens of thousands of sensor-laden probes. It pondered every hyperspace-related ripple to triangulate its point of origin. It endlessly assessed evolving risks and opportunities, calculating new deployments for the task force.

Attempted to do all that, anyway.

"Thirty seconds to jump," the pilot announced over the intercom.

Meaning that soon after thirty seconds, recently disappeared ships in threatening numbers could emerge in synch in and around Task Force Delta, to blast away at everything in sight and return to hyperspace faster than mere mortals could react. Or zip through the formation without shooting, just to rattle the ARM crews. Or stay in hyperspace a few seconds longer, to target another nearby formation.

Or remain in hyperspace for a long time, leaving this chaos behind. Nothing remained to fight over. Nothing tangible, anyway. To be the first to go would be to retreat, and *honor* remained to fight over. . . .

Too many possibilities and too little information to choose among them. Tanya said, "It looks like a routine precautionary fleet jump to me, Commander."

A maneuver that would, in turn, unleash a torrent of new ripples, to which thousands more ships, in formations large and small, all around this solar system, must hurriedly react. . . .

Johansson left her hanging almost till the jump. "To me, too," he finally allowed.

"Jumping in three, two, one . . ." the pilot announced over the intercom.

Across the bridge, view-port screens went dark. The human brain was not wired to perceive hyperspace. Lucky people so confronted sensed walls snapping together, denying the less-than-nothingness presented in a porthole or view port. Unlucky people got lost in the . . . whatever hyperspace was. The Blind Spot, starfarers called the phenomenon, and it had driven people mad.

"In three," the pilot called. "Two. One. Dropout."

On *dropout,* stars refilled the view ports. Pale, translucent spheres popped up scattered throughout the tactical display. Each sphere centered on the most recent confirmed pre-jump coordinates of a ship; the sphere grew with the moment by moment uncertainty of where that ship had the potential to be *now.* One by one, like soap bubbles pricked, spheres vanished. Everywhere a ship had been definitively located, whether by *Koala*'s instruments or in hyperwave downloads from remote sensors, a tiny icon replaced the bubble. Sometimes nothing replaced a bubble; that meant a ship had disappeared into hyperspace in the seconds while *Koala* had been disconnected from the familiar universe.

"Report," Johansson ordered.

"Jump timer at three minutes and holding, sir," the pilot said.

"No threatening deployments, Commander," the tactical officer said.

"Hyperwave links opened to *London* and *Prague*"— respectively the task force's flagship and *Koala*'s assigned escort—"sir," Tanya said.

"What do you think?" Johansson asked her again.

She reached into the tactical display to point out a nearby proto-comet, a vaguely potato-shaped glob about five kilometers along its shortest axis. "I don't care for the snowball," she said. "We're too close, and a decent-sized squadron could hide behind it." If so, perhaps well stocked with nukes or antimatter.

The grating, prepare-to-jump tone blasted.

"Jump in twenty seconds," the pilot called over the intercom.

At eleven seconds, another audible alarm, at the pitch that warned of a bogey. It morphed into the warble that identified the bogey as a hostile. A scattering of new icons, lens-shaped, manifested in the tactical display, from *Koala*'s perspective lurking behind the snowball. The latest intel download from Hawking.

"I see some Kzinti agreed with you," Johansson said, a rare touch of approval in his voice.

"Jumping in three. Two . . ."

The task force executed seven more micro-jumps before the watch changed and Tanya, exhausted, could shamble to the ship's mess for a hurried meal.

TANYA TOSSED AND turned, suspended in midair between sleeper plates in her tiny cabin. As the intercom blasted alerts every few minutes, her thoughts churned. Could three navies, and armed observers from yet more military powers, converge like this without everything ending in disaster? How long until someone lost patience, or cracked under the unending pressure, or simply made an honest mistake?

Reaching through the loose mesh of the crash netting, she slapped the touchpoint and collapsed the antigrav field. She recorded a quick it's-crazy-here-how's-it-going-with-you message for Elena, wrapped it in standard fleet encryption, and queued it for transmission. She and Elena hadn't managed a live vid call since soon after Tanya arrived; now they counted themselves lucky when even short texts got through without long delays. As the pace of jumps grew ever more frenetic, tactical traffic between ships consumed almost every scrap of available bandwidth.

After graduating ARM Naval Academy, she and Elena had gone their separate ways. Elena had been posted to the Artifact Monitoring Mission, two hundred light-years from Earth. Tanya's first posting was as assistant cargo officer on a supply ship supporting the Fleet of Worlds diplomatic mission, even farther from home.

Elena was a line officer, however junior, and *Canberra* an actual warship. Tanya, in her heart of hearts, admitted to a twinge of envy. She had volunteered repeatedly and insistently for reassignment. Nothing interesting, in any military sense, would ever happen around the Fleet. No matter that the Puppeteers were cowards—or, perhaps, because they were—an intimidating defensive array of sensors and robotic craft protected their worlds.

Which was too tanj bad! The Puppeteers had much for which to answer.

A Puppeteer scout had bared the Concordance's sordid history of interspecies meddling. (Why? Tanya did not begin to understand. The retired admirals among the Academy faculty did not pretend to understand, either.) And this scout, Nessus, had revealed those secrets—*and* the long-hidden location of the Puppeteer worlds, the theretofore unimaginable Fleet of Worlds— *and* the existence and location of the yet more inconceivable Ringworld—to, of all improbable people, her great-grandfather! Louis Wu had vanished from Human Space before Tanya was born. Dad scarcely remembered the man.

After six interstellar wars and their megadeaths, human governments and the Kzinti Patriarchy had learned to coexist—the uneasy peace of four centuries that had given way in this system to bloody skirmishes. A peace whose prospects further crumbled by the nanosecond.

Wherever they were, *if* they still were, did Nessus and Louis comprehend the mess they had left behind?

Whatever the reasoning behind past disclosures, day by day, year by year, the Puppeteer worlds receded farther into the galactic north. Even by hyperdrive, the Fleet was already a two-plus-year epic journey from Earth. Maybe the aliens gambled—if so, correctly—that humans and Kzinti, no matter their just grievances with the Puppeteers, would put off confronting the Concordance to first seize a nearer, stationary, more enticing—and seemingly defenseless—prize.

And that far from being an opportunity, the Ringworld would turn out to be a trap.

THE RINGWORLD . . .

A loop of ribbon, its circumference rivaling Earth's orbit, encircling its sun. A ribbon broader than four times the distance that separated Earth from its moon. A ribbon as massive as Jupiter and with a surface area to equal millions of Earths. An inconceivably huge construct, made of a mysterious, impossible *something* as strong as the force that bound together the particles of an atomic nucleus. Home to many trillions of intelligent beings. Home, undeniably, to wondrous technologies.

Its civilization fallen; its wealth and its secrets ripe for plunder.

And more incredibly still, vanished in an instant into

hyperspace, no matter that the "experts" insisted such a thing could not happen.

All that mass disappearing had sent a gravity wave crashing through this system's Oort Cloud. Billions, perhaps trillions of snowballs careened from their once stable orbits. Snowballs? Snow *worlds,* rather, some of them bigger, even, than Pluto. Large and small, they plunged inward toward the sun, or hurtled outward into the interstellar darkness, or shattered one another. Wherever they went, they made an already overcomplicated tactical situation that much worse. All those fleets dodging—

The ceiling light of Tanya's cabin flashed. Her wake-up gonged. Time again to stand watch on the bridge.

THIS WASN'T A war zone. Not exactly. Not technically.

A distinction without significance to all who had died here.

"Welcome back, Lieutenant," Commander Johansson said, yawning despite the *blat* of another emergency-jump alarm.

"Yes, sir." Tanya managed not to yawn back.

In *Koala*'s main tactical display chaos still reigned, as it had for the weeks since the Ringworld—somehow—vanished.

Even without the prize, the mission continued. Artifact Monitoring Mission, the deployment was officially called, although outside of formal communications no one called it that. Across the fleet, names ranged from Mexican Standoff to Cold Confrontation, from the Interspecies Scrimmage to the No-Win War. Tanya favored the Frigid Face-Off. Naval Intelligence said the Kzinti called it something that sounded like a cat fight (then again, what in Hero's Tongue didn't?) and that translated loosely into Interworld as Grudge Match. What the Trinocs called the situation was anyone's guess.

Or the locals when, at last, they had joined the fray. The natives were not as helpless as they had first appeared. The rumor mill whispered about ships erupting, blazingly fast, from the Ringworld, and even more incredibly about X-ray lasers—powered by solar flares!—vaporizing intruders that had ventured too close.

And that was only the combatants. Puppeteers had ships here observing, too, as did the Outsiders, as did—

"Jump in ten seconds," the copilot announced, her voice grown hoarse.

"Sit, Lieutenant," Johansson ordered.

Tanya sat.

Once again, they flashed in and out of hyperspace. Seconds after *Koala* reemerged, an outgunned Trinoc squadron jumped away, leaving what spectrographic analysis suggested was the hull debris of an *Avenger*-class Kzinti scout ship.

An ambush? An accident, someone's nerves stretched beyond endurance? Or the beginning of something much, much worse?

Thousands of warships far from home, and nothing left to justify the huge expense of their deployments. Nothing to excuse the lives already lost. Nothing to distract from historic grudges, or from fresh setbacks amid the endless jockeying for advantage. No brass ring left to grab. No one left to confront but one another.

"How does this mess end, Commander?" Tanya asked.

"Well above my pay grade, Lieutenant," Johansson said, and the pay reference didn't come across like a wisecrack about pursers, either. "Ours is just to do and die."

The intruder alarm wailed.

· 5 ·

Hindmost capered up, down, all around a maze of serpentine access tunnels. Within the digital wallpaper virtual herds accompanied him, left and right, for as far as the eye could see. He was *free*!

Not safe, to be sure. Not restored to power. Not unburdened of doubts and regrets. Not yet home, but in possession of a starship.

Rid—at long last!—of the Ringworld.

Still, thousands of alien warships prowled the vicinity, and every faction in the conflict coveted the technologies in this vessel. As would the observers aboard the three skulking ships of obvious Fleet provenance. That ships of the Concordance remained scattered around the war fleets told Hindmost who commanded aboard those ships. Who must yet rule Hearth.

If he ran out of options, he would sooner let humans take this ship.

As reality crashed down on Hindmost he stumbled, missing a step and ruining the unfolding pattern. But with a kick and a tight pirouette, he put himself back into the dance. Every Citizen lived in fear. That he had left Hearth and herd sufficed to prove him insane, besides. He had managed his fears—mostly—for a very long time. He would cope a bit longer.

Soon, he told himself, he would go home. He and his loved ones would be together again. He tried to picture the happy day, but his imagination failed him. It had been *so* long.

The dance must suffice for a while longer.

"Analysis complete," Voice sang.

"Thank you," Hindmost sang back.

His politeness was neurotic; *having* an AI at all was psychotic. No sensible being set out to build his prospective successor. But in the subtle calculus of countless dangers and endless responsibilities, to have a companion—any companion—had won out. Had he chosen otherwise, had he dared to undertake his Ringworld adventure without an illicit AI, he would doubtless have faded, long ago, into terminal catatonia.

The sweet release that ever beckoned.

"Another segment of hyperdrive-control software characterized," Voice continued. "Calculating next jump."

Working directly in binary code, Tunesmith had reprogrammed many of the computers aboard *Long Shot*. The new programming was convoluted beyond Hindmost's ability to parse, one more instance of the arrogant improvisational brilliance that came so naturally to protectors.

If not as natural as doing *anything*, no matter how extreme, to protect their own kind.

"Are more jumps necessary?" Hindmost asked.

"Yes. The software I am studying continues to self-modify. As I analyze the code, I only fall further behind."

"So you theorize from functional tests."

"Theorize and confirm, especially as to the apparent behavioral constraints on the self-modifications. As you say, Hindmost."

Once the hyperdrive customizations had been characterized he would refocus the AI on other changes. Humans, Kzinti, and Tunesmith, each in their turn controlling this ship, had modified shipboard systems, stripped out test instrumentation and decoy equipment, and retrofitted their own paraphernalia. He knew by placement and deductive reasoning how many of the bridge controls must function, but of settings and status displays, all in the dots-and-commas script favored by the Kzinti, he could read nothing.

It would be a long time before he could undertake the flight home. Time for Louis to heal, and to emerge from the autodoc. Time, again and again and again, to overtake the spreading gravity wave unleashed by the Ringworld's disappearance, to study the only direct evidence as to how the impossible had been accomplished. Time between stints in hyperspace to gradually build up speed in normal space—fearful, all the while, that even across great distances the white-hot exhaust of *Long Shot*'s fusion thrusters would attract unwanted attention.

Time to prepare for the surprises certain to await him at the end of his journey. He had been trapped on the Ringworld much too long.

With a graceful twirl he concluded this dance. "Keep us far from the other ships in the system," he ordered. A terrifying number of ships. Ships all too easily seen with Tunesmith's exquisitely sensitive instruments.

"*Long Shot* is much faster than any vessel among the Fringe War," Voice commented.

Thousands of times faster. Faster than Hindmost trusted his reflexes to pilot, even if he could read the Kzinti displays. Even if he understood Tunesmith's alterations.

But Louis could fly it.

Picking at his meticulously coiffed mane, Hindmost sang, "And yet Tunesmith took this ship from the Kzinti."

Trickery that one protector had conceived, another could, too. As fervently as Hindmost hoped all protectors had gone away with the Ringworld, their departure remained theory.

"Far away, Hindmost, as you have ordered."

HINDMOST SQUINTED THROUGH the frost-speckled dome into *Long Shot*'s single autodoc. In thirty-seven days, if the master readout could be believed, the autodoc would complete its treatment and release its occupant. "You are looking much better," he sang, and it was true.

Despite Louis Wu's ashen pallor. Despite the splotches of red and yellow and very little green among the progress indicators bleeding through from the dome's inner surface. Despite swollen joints and contorted limbs and genitalia just beginning to regrow. Despite the distended brain case and toothless gums. Despite all that, Louis began to look again like an adult human, and a bit less like a human turned protector.

"I was too twisted up when the tree-of-life started to change me," Louis had admitted before, with Hindmost lifting from behind, he had climbed into the autodoc. Only minutes had passed since their escape from the Ringworld. "I'm dying."

Disclosure that offered no prediction as to whether, to heal Louis, the autodoc would undo or perfect his conversion into a protector.

With any other autodoc there would have been no hope, but this unit was one of a kind. Frightfully advanced. Nanotech-based. This autodoc could, if necessary, rebuild a person from the molecular level up; Hindmost was convinced that it was doing that to Louis. Carlos Wu had built this amazing prototype, long ago and far away. It had been smuggled from Earth, then stolen, but—not for lack of trying—never duplicated.

Yet in a way, Tunesmith had surpassed it.

He had extracted nanites from the autodoc, reprogrammed them, distributed them far and wide across the Ringworld to replicate, and—well, Hindmost remained fuzzy on what, exactly, Tunesmith had done. Used the nanotech to rewire the Ringworld's whole superconducting substrate. Adapted what he had learned in his brief study of *Long Shot*'s hyperdrive.

So, anyway, Louis had explained. It took a protector to understand a protector. And not even a protector ever fully trusted another protector.

Trembling, Hindmost continued studying the twisted figure in the autodoc. "I am glad for you, Louis." *And relieved for myself.*

For Louis knew the harm the Concordance had once brought to the Ringworld. As a human protector, Louis would seek to destroy Hearth and the Concordance.

If the autodoc did not undo the transformation, *he* must kill Louis while that remained possible. With Louis defenseless in a therapeutic coma.

Louis-as-protector would have seen that, too, and yet Louis had climbed, defenseless, into the autodoc. Hence, Louis knew *he* would wait to act until the course of the cure revealed itself. Hence Louis expected to emerge as a normal human, or he would have killed Hindmost before getting into the autodoc.

Matching wits with a protector was futile.

"I look forward to again having your company, Louis," Hindmost said. In thirty-seven days.

Until then, Louis, I have the dance.

. 6 .

In *Endurance*'s claustrophobic exercise room, Alice plodded away on the treadmill. She had little to do on the long flight *but* exercise. Puppeteers were the galaxy's consummate worriers, and scant days from New Terra even Nessus had run out of contingencies to plan for and theories to fret about.

On the tarmac, Sigmund had taken Alice aside to warn her Nessus would be stingy with facts. Two relics exchanging the obvious about a third relic. She had promised Sigmund to set aside their differences for the sake of the mission. Also, her differences with Nessus. Once this situation was settled, the Puppeteer had a lot of explaining to do.

The wallpaper showed rolling forest, the foliage a riot of autumn colors. On solid ground, the view would have been stunning. Here, the imagery only reminded her that behind the thin-film display, outside thin ship walls, lurked . . . Finagle knew what.

Something stirred in her gut, whispered unintelligibly in her ears, tickled behind her eyes. Something that her hindbrain denied and her forebrain rejected.

Hyperspace couldn't kill any deader than could vacuum, and she had no trouble living around vacuum. But she had grown up in the Belt. Vacuum was something to respect, to guard against—but also something understood.

Unlike hyperspace.

Was hyperspace an alternate reality? Hidden dimension? Parallel universe? She didn't pretend to know. The so-called experts didn't.

If anyone understood hyperspace, it was the Outsiders. They had invented hyperdrive. Which, although they sold it, they themselves never used.

That seemed instructive.

Blotting sweat from her face and arms with a towel, she abandoned the treadmill. She strode down the corridor to the bridge to check the mass pointer. Because one thing she did understand about hyperspace: while crossing it, keep your distance from large masses. Get too close to a gravitational singularity while in hyperspace and you never came out.

A light-year every three days. Logically speaking, stars being light-years apart in this region, a glance at the mass pointer every few hours more than sufficed for safety.

Logic failed to convince the tingling behind her eyes.

In the mass pointer, the most prominent instrument on the pilot's console, nothing looked close. As Alice could have predicted from her last peek, less than an hour earlier. But her skin still crawled. The . . . whatever . . . behind her eyes prickled worse than ever.

The bridge walls showed forest, too, but that only emphasized how unnatural their surroundings were. If the less-than-nothing of hyperspace could be said to surround—

"Not very convincing, is it?"

She flinched at the unexpected voice.

Nessus stood at the bridge hatch. With one head, he indicated the mass pointer. His other head tugged at the remaining braid in his much-stirred mane.

"Can't sleep?" she asked.

"Can you?"

"Not very well." She cleared her throat. "What did you mean, the mass pointer isn't convincing?"

"It was once my misfortune to be brave." With a final yank and a plaintive sigh, he released the tortured braid. "That is to say, I was insane. Insane enough to volunteer to leave home and become a scout. On my last scouting mission . . ."

"Go on." They had the bridge to themselves, and she sat on an armrest of the pilot's crash couch.

"I returned home missing a head." His two-throated wheeze came out like minor scales in clashing keys. "I left the autodoc scared normal."

Did he want her to feel sorry for him? Fat chance. "The unconvincing mass pointer?"

"My last mission. We are going there now. To the source of the ripple that summons us." He sang a musical phrase, sad and jangling. "You and Julia have heard me describe it."

More of the facts with which Nessus had long been stingy.

She still struggled to believe that such a place could exist. "And?"

"Even after the Ringworld, I kept my trust in mass pointers. No one who could readily colonize the planets of other stars would build a habitat so vast. They would have no need."

"No one with hyperdrive, you mean."

Heads moved in alternation: up/down, down/up, up/down. A Puppeteer nod.

She was *old,* tanj it. Tired. Behind her eyes, the itch got even worse. Mass pointer. Trust. The Ringworld.

She whirled to stare at the mass pointer.

The Ringworld was massive; it would create its own gravitational singularity. Despite that, the armchair experts on New Terra had concluded that the Ringworld somehow jumped to hyperspace. That the Ringworld was itself the source of the ripple.

No one had even a theory how that could be possible.

Alice said, "But it looks like the Ringworlders *have* hyperdrive. What if the Ringworld returns to normal space?"

"Without warning," Nessus agreed. "Bringing its gravitational singularity."

And if *Endurance* was in the wrong place at the wrong time? They would be hurled, or interdimensionally shredded, or whatever. Without warning.

The mass pointer, despite the booming thump it offered when Alice slapped it, seemed a very nebulous thing. The itching grew fierce behind her eyes.

"Could you use some help twisting your mane?" she asked.

"AND . . . NOW," JULIA announced from the pilot's crash couch.

Where fall foliage had long reigned, crisp points of light teemed. The bridge's wraparound image looked no different from the starscape Nessus had had digitally painted, the past several days, across his cabin walls. Somehow these stars *felt* different.

"Still there," Julia said, standing and stretching. "Always good to see stars."

"Very much so," Nessus said. "How long will we stay?"

Because except to eject another hyperwave-radio buoy every few light-years, Julia had been keeping them in hyperspace, charging toward . . . Nessus trembled to imagine what they would find.

Julia tilted her head, considering. "We'll remain here for half an hour. Longer if the folks back home have something to talk about." She uploaded a text message, their galactic coordinates appended, to the nearest buoy in the chain. *Trip remains uneventful.* Endurance *out.*

"They will," Alice predicted from the corridor outside the bridge.

With only the three of them aboard, they staggered their sleeping hours so that someone was always awake to check on the mass pointer. Not today, though. Not on such a long flight. No one would choose to sleep through a scheduled respite of normalcy.

Nessus suspected Alice was right.

Outside of gravitational singularities, hyperwave propagated instantaneously. Dropping relay buoys along the way to boost the signal, one could talk across many light-years. Delay only cropped up when an end of the link was inside a singularity. Then, to do hyperwave/laser-beam conversions, you needed a relay at the singularity's brink. For a free-flying world like New Terra, its mass tiny compared to a star's, the one-way delay was less than a minute.

One could converse across the light-years—with something useful to say, or not.

"We'll know soon enough," Julia said, squeezing past Alice to leave the bridge. "Meanwhile, I'll drop another buoy."

While he had the opportunity, Nessus uploaded long

messages he had recorded on his pocket computer. It helped to be in touch, even fleetingly, with the children. As the transfer proceeded, he pulled up an old holo of himself with the children, taken in the sprawling, well-tended garden behind their house.

"Your family?" Alice asked.

"Aurora and Elpis. Elpis, though younger, is the taller one." He took a moment to savor the memories. "As a scout, I never expected to mate, to have children. It was hard to leave them."

"I understand." And tentatively, "And your mate?"

"Long gone." So long that it was hard to maintain any hope.

"I'm sorry," she said. And angry, her manner added. Consumed by a well-cultivated bitterness.

Before her simmering rage, even the lopsided, eager grins Elpis wore lost the power to charm him. "A funny thing, Alice. They grew up on New Terra. They expect suns during the day, and for stars to sparkle like diamonds in the night sky."

"And you don't."

Hearth blazed with the lights of its continent-spanning cities, was warmed by the waste heat of its industry. Hearth needed no suns. It had no suns. Its farm worlds, like four gigantic moons, bleached most stars from the sky.

"I grew up differently," was all he could bring himself to say.

Because dissimilar skies were the least of the differences. The residents of one large arcology on Hearth would rival the entire population of New Terra, humans and Citizens combined. His children knew only wide open spaces. They had friends on New Terra. They had grown up sharing a world with humans.

If Aurora and Elpis could return to Hearth, would they?

LAUNCHING THE BUOY was simple enough. After a final comm check, Julia had only to turn permeable a small area on the cargo hold's exterior wall and press the buoy straight through the hull into space. Quick swipes with a structural modulator restored that stretch of hull to its customary imperviousness, its original shape remembered.

Exceptional stuff, *twing*. Clear or opaque or of any semitransparency between. Tunable to any color of the rainbow. As soft or hard as desired. Only General Products hull material was stronger—and unlike GP hull material, no one could turn *twing* to gossamer from a distance. Grandpa had learned not to trust a GP hull.

And *twing* was just one of the marvels New Terra's scientists had coaxed out of the Pak Library. But she wasn't supposed to know about that, or that Grandpa, Alice, and Nessus had all played a part in bringing the Library to New Terra and the Ministry.

Her task done, Julia dawdled in the hold, leaving Nessus and Alice alone to talk. They had to work past their issues.

Because who *didn't* have issues? She lived her life in her grandfather's shadow. Sigmund Ausfaller was a hero to some, New Terra's bane to many. Self-deluded fools, the latter, an opinion she kept to herself. In order to serve she played along, telling herself Grandpa would understand.

With a drink bulb of coffee from the ship's mess, Julia returned to the bridge. "What did I miss?"

Alice gestured dismissively at the comm console,

where a new message read: *We've been waiting for you to check in. The minister has called a strategy session. We've begun contacting participants. Expect to begin in about two hours. Acknowledge.*

They could travel far in two hours. Farther in two hours plus a meeting.

And she knew how Grandpa felt about too many cooks.

"If they had urgent news for us, they would have texted it," Julia decided. "And we have nothing new to tell them."

Acknowledge, the comm console chided.

"Too bad we didn't see that message in time," Julia said. "Hyperspace in twenty minutes, people."

Alice managed to shiver and smile at the same time.

· 7 ·

One mouth grasping a curler, the other a brush, Hindmost primped and teased, combed and curled. Strings of newly synthed jewels, of Experimentalist orange more often than any other color, glittered in his mane. He had already buffed his hooves and brushed his hide until they glistened.

The elaborate grooming was not for the lack of pressing things to do. Quite the contrary. He needed to assimilate Voice's observations and analyses of *Long Shot*'s controls. Synthesize the measurements taken of the gravity wave set off by the Ringworld's disappearance from normal space. Account for the absence of a second hyperspace ripple: either the Ringworld had yet to emerge from hyperspace or it had reentered many light-years away, so remote as to be undetectable. Sift his memories of Tunesmith's cryptic and misleading explanations, and of Louis-as-protector's interpretations, for clues. Connect all that he had learned/heard/surmised to what little he might know about hyperdrives—which, demonstrably, was not enough.

And there was the madness of Louis launching *Long Shot* into hyperspace from inside the Ringworld. Escaping *through* the Ringworld floor! From the depths of a singularity!

Every conventional theory of hyperdrive and hyperspace insisted they should be dead.

Except to eat and sleep and jettison more of the decoy equipment that still clogged the ship, for days Hindmost had done nothing but struggle to understand. He had accomplished little. The wonder was that he functioned at all when, at any time, any of the thousands of warships that his sensors showed might detect this ship.

And while fear-ridden before every jump that this ship might cease to exist such that it *could* be noticed.

To sense mass from within hyperspace required psionic abilities that mere software lacked. On every hyperdrive jump, the AI's dead-reckoning navigation might drop them into the nearby star.

His circumstances were intolerable, but setting off in a jury-rigged ship was not the answer. Protectors lived by the jury-rig, supremely confident in their improvisations—and in the makeshifts and expedients, yet to be imagined, by which they would resolve other crises yet to emerge.

Not so Citizens, certainly not the Hindmost. Especially not *this* Hindmost. He dare not undertake a long voyage, especially with unintelligible Kzinti controls.

Unable to flee, his every instinct called out for catatonia. Instead, he continued to brush. Finally, he set down his implements. Rising from his nest of mounded pillows, he pivoted before a full-length wall mirror, also newly synthed. Through his appearance, if in no other way, he would be worthy of his station.

If only all the responsibilities of the office were as easily satisfied . . .

Earth Date 2850

Haunch brushing haunch, Hindmost and his most senior aides and ministers settled astraddle twenty padded, Y-shaped benches. Despite the companionable closeness, Hindmost did not feel in the least part comforted. No one did.

Above head level at midroom, centered within the circle of benches, floated that which they must discuss. The pale blue loop of thread could have been pretty, but not with that yellow spark blazing at its center. The spark was a *star*, and that meant the loop was *enormous*.

Soft and urgent, plaintive and terrified, phrases of song filled the room. When the cacophony gave no sign of abating, Hindmost intoned, with harmonics of command, "We will begin." The murmuring stopped abruptly.

"Explain what your long-range instruments have seen," he directed Minerva, the deputy director of Clandestine Directorate.

Minerva gestured at the blue ring. "The unexpected sighting lies a little more than two light-years distant, not far off the Fleet's path," he sang.

"Why have we not heard before of this object?" Hindmost asked, feigning ignorance. In truth, he had feared this day since—it felt like forever. Since Chiron's arrival.

"We knew something encircled the star." Minerva sang in low, apologetic tones. "Until we observed it at a suitable angle, we thought it an ordinary dust ring. Not"—he glanced once more at the blue thread—"*that.*"

"And so only recently did you look closely."

"Yes, Hindmost," Minerva agreed timorously.

"Who built it?" Aglaea, an aide, wondered.

"We don't know," Minerva answered.

"*Why* build it?" another asked.

"We don't know," Minerva repeated. "Nor how. Nor of what. To construct something so huge—"

"We must send an expedition," Chiron interrupted brashly. His mane was a glorious structure of complex silver ringlets.

More precisely, *its* mane. Chiron was a holographic projection, animated by Proteus: an illicit AI. And equally, *their* mane, because directing Proteus was the Gw'oth group mind known as Ol't'ro. Two truths unimaginable to those physically in the council chamber, save by the Hindmost and one other.

Hindmost's ministers and aides knew Chiron as the long-serving Minister of Science, resident on and governor of Nature Preserve Five, the better to oversee research best performed off the home world. Governments came and went, Hindmosts came and went, and Chiron served them all.

If only that were so.

In the blackest secret in the long, dark history of the Concordance, *behind* He Who Leads from Behind, Chiron served only him/it/themselves. The herd chose whom they wished to rule the Concordance; time and again, their choices changed nothing. Each outgoing Hindmost revealed to the next the unbearable secret: Chiron, in a moment, could obliterate five worlds and a trillion Citizens. Chiron had promised to do so, if he/it/they ever deemed its unwitting subjects a danger to the worlds of the Gw'oth.

The Gw'oth were native to the sea-bottom muck of the ice-locked ocean of a now-distant moon. A Gw'o was mostly tubelike tentacles: like five snakes fused at their tails. One was no longer from tip to tip than the reach of Hindmost's neck, little thicker through its central mass than the span he could open a mouth. The uninformed Citizen might feel more pity or disgust at the sight of a Gw'o than cause for fear.

And, as usual, the uninformed Citizen would be mistaken.

Gw'oth were courageous and curious, psychoses they shared with other species evolved from hunting animals. And they had used those flaws to terrible purpose. Within Hindmost's lifetime, the Gw'oth had broken through the ice of their home world and advanced from fire to fusion, from muscle power to hyperdrive starships.

But even among their own kind, the sixteenfold Gw'oth group mind that was Ol't'ro was the exception. A perversion. Frightfully intelligent.

Their power of life and death over a trillion Citizens was absolute.

Chiron had spoken; the decision was foregone. The Concordance would send an expedition. And like the herd's delusions of self-determination, the mission would be meaningless, too.

Worse than meaningless. *Dangerous.* The expedition could serve no purpose beyond the keeping of secrets.

For the Ringworld was not newly discovered, but rediscovered, and the Concordance's historic role in defanging the trillions of Ringworlders must remain hidden at all costs. In Hindmost's first, temporary, fall from power, he had purged that dangerous information even from the Hindmost-only archives, lest Ol't'ro come upon it.

Room-temperature superconductors underpinned

most advanced technology on the Ringworld. Or had, until Hindmost's many-times-removed predecessor approved the dispersal there of a gengineered plague. The airborne microbes devoured the ubiquitous superconductor wherever they encountered it.

Very quickly, *everything* had stopped working. How many Ringworld natives had perished when the floating cities crashed? Millions, without a doubt. More likely, billions.

He must hide this history from Chiron. Else his Gw'oth overlords would surely judge the Concordance irredeemably dangerous to their own kind.

And so Hindmost only half listened to the debate, its outcome predetermined. In jangling chords and chilling arpeggios, the arguments washed over him in the dreamlike slow motion of inevitable disaster.

". . . Cannot veer," Hemera, Minister of Energy, was singing. "It is basic physics. At the Fleet's present velocity, in the time remaining before we encounter this Ringworld we can make no meaningful change to our course."

"I propose that we not deviate at all from our long-time course," Zephyrus, Minister of Foreign Affairs, sang back. "As we have seen the Ringworld, so we must assume the natives have seen us. Suppose we veer off our course from comparatively close, traveling at our present high speed. It could suggest that after launching impactors we seek to put distance between ourselves and the debris from kinetic-weapon strikes. If the Ringworlders should suspect that, what weapons will they turn against us?"

Several ministers bleated in dismay at song of weapons and strikes, and Chiron glanced warningly at Hindmost.

"Sing no more about such terrible things," Hindmost directed. He held his gaze on Zephyrus, but sang for his master. *We consider no such drastic measures, Ol't'ro. As ever, we are rendered harmless by our fears.*

"All the more reason to send an expedition," Achilles sang. "Let the Ringworlders not misunderstand us."

Did that mean, let the Ringworlders fear us?

Achilles rivaled Ol't'ro in madness. Achilles was a sociopath with limitless ambitions. During the era of human servants, many Citizens had had reason to take human-pronounceable names. But only one Citizen had assumed the name of a legendary human warrior!

Insane ambition had led Achilles to interfere in Gw'oth affairs, scheming to turn his manufactured Gw'oth threat into mass hysteria across Hearth, into rule over the Concordance. When his meddling had gone spectacularly wrong, reconciled Gw'oth worlds had turned their massed might toward the Fleet of Worlds. In an evil alliance, Achilles had smuggled a few Gw'oth warships past Hearth's defenses, had let Ol't'ro take possession of Nature Preserve Five's planetary drive.

If destabilized, the drive would pulverize every world within the Fleet.

From their position of absolute power, Ol't'ro had demanded that the Hindmost abdicate, that he endorse Achilles to succeed. Achilles promised the terrified public a deal. Accept him as Hindmost, and he would negotiate withdrawal of the Gw'oth fleets. And so, on a wave of popular ignorance, the architect of disaster came to rule as Ol't'ro's first puppet Hindmost.

And ever after, from their watery habitat module, a few unsuspected Gw'oth held five worlds hostage.

Achilles remained, for reasons Ol't'ro declined to

explain, a bit like Chiron: among the favored few every incoming Hindmost was made to accommodate in his new government. In the current government, Achilles ruled Nature Preserve One as its planetary hindmost.

As *he* had been imposed, for a time, on Achilles' erstwhile government. Much to Achilles' displeasure.

"What do you say, Hindmost?" Achilles prodded. "Do we send a ship to investigate this object?"

"I believe we should," Hindmost sang, and it galled him to be seen taking Achilles' side.

"I propose that Nessus lead the expedition," Chiron offered. "He remains our most accomplished scout."

Achilles glowered: there was no love lost between Nessus and him.

For his own reasons Hindmost objected to sending Nessus, but he held his tongues.

"*I* will go," Achilles sang. "We can learn much from close-up observation, and Nessus is no scientist."

"Your place is *here,*" Chiron sang back.

Achilles twitched, then dipped his heads respectfully. *He* knew who spoke through Chiron.

"Lead the expedition?" Hemera sang, breaking the sudden, awkward silence. "Chiron, your melody implies that more than Nessus will go. Who else among us"— and he glanced, apologetically, at Achilles—"would dare to scout out this Ringworld?"

"Doubtless, some humans," Chiron sang. "Let Nessus recruit his own team."

"The New Terrans no longer serve us," Hindmost gently reminded. "We are no longer welcome on their world."

"Wild humans," Chiron clarified. Several ministers

started at the petulant grace notes in his song. "Nessus can recruit on Earth."

"Earth is too distant," Zephyrus sang. "Sooner than Nessus can reach Earth, the Fleet must already have encountered the Ringworld."

"Not if Nessus takes *Long Shot*," Chiron rebutted.

With renewed forebodings of disaster, without options, Hindmost once more concurred.

Earth Date: 2893

With a shiver of dismay, Hindmost turned from his mirror.

So many years. So much travail. Only to find himself on this ill-fated ship! He at best half understood normal hyperdrive, a level of insight that made him more knowledgeable than most. The Outsiders priced their technology and the underlying theory separately—and the technology was costly enough.

But somehow, just once, inspired (and demented) tinkerers in General Products Laboratories had created what they called the Type II drive. The Type II hyperdrive shunt was *huge*: the largest hull that General Products built, a sphere more than a thousand feet in diameter, could barely contain the apparatus.

After years of hideously expensive research had failed to duplicate the initial prototype, General Products Corporation was no closer to understanding why this particular hyperdrive flung this particular ship through hyperspace thousands of times faster than any other. The Outsiders, when Concordance engineers approached them, had expressed no opinions and declined to participate in any research. No one knew why, but no one understood why the Outsiders did most things. Creatures of liquid helium, the Outsiders were, simply, *different*.

General Products was on the verge, reluctantly, of halting their futile research program when inspiration struck.

From Hearth's ancient place of hiding, the Concordance did business in that era with a half-dozen alien trading partners. With some grand demonstration, some spectacular publicity stunt, General Products thought to lure alien investors into underwriting continued experimentation. They jammed every nook and cranny of the prototype with extraneous equipment to mask the ad hoc nature of the only working Type II drive. They recruited a human pilot to fly the ship he named *Long Shot* all the way to the galactic core.

Of such convoluted origins comes disaster.

Except for Beowulf Shaeffer's flight, the chain reaction of supernovae among the close-packed stars of the core would have gone undiscovered. A dangerous thing not to know, to be sure. But better to be ignorant of a peril many millennia into the future than to evoke immediate catastrophe.

Except for *Long Shot* and Shaeffer's discovery, the Fleet would never have cast off its gravitational anchor from Giver of Life, its ancestral star.

Except for Hearth's sudden, unplanned sprint from the galaxy, Citizens would never have trained their human servants to explore in the Fleet's path. Their humans would never have uncovered their true past. Nature Preserve Four would still be one among the farm worlds serving the Concordance.

Except for scouting ahead in the Fleet's hastily chosen path, the Gw'oth would have remained unknown to this day.

And yet . . .

Had the Gw'oth not spotted the refugees running from the core explosion, had the Gw'oth not contacted newly independent New Terra, Pak war fleets would have caught everyone unawares, would have pounded *all* their worlds, Hearth included, back into the Stone Age.

Hindmost plucked loose a tress he had just tucked into place. It seemed every course of action led to disaster.

Now *he* rode the ship that, from Beowulf Shaeffer's era until Ol't'ro's covert reign, none had dared to fly. The ship on which Ol't'ro had demanded the Concordance dedicate its wealth and best scientists, in vain hopes that the technology would be mastered.

And yet it was worth the price, *any* price, to divert Ol't'ro from wondering if the time had come to pull the doomsday trigger. Every Hindmost had complied willingly.

Then Ol't'ro had ordered Nessus to Earth. Aboard any normal vessel, even then, that would have been a trek of almost two years. On *Long Shot,* the trip was a matter of a few hours. Nessus had recruited two humans and a Kzinti diplomat for the "first" Ringworld expedition, bartering *Long Shot* itself as their payment.

Humans and Kzinti could waste lives and treasure trying to duplicate the Type II drive. Hindmost remembered his relief that the ill-fated ship was gone.

Only to find, long after, while stranded on the Ringworld by his own foolhardy misadventure, that *Long Shot* had returned! Kzinti had usurped the fastest ship in existence, using it as a courier to coordinate their

part of the interspecies mayhem Hindmost knew as the
Fringe War. Until Tunesmith seized *Long Shot* from the
Kzinti. Until Louis and Hindmost took it from Tune-
smith, because the protector chose to be rid of them.

And here I am aboard *Long Shot*. After . . . how long?

"Voice," he called.

Notes tinkled from a nearby intercom speaker. "Yes,
Hindmost."

"Do onboard computers indicate the current date?"

"They do, although not using the Concordance calendar."

"The human calendar will serve."

"The Earth date is 2893, Hindmost."

Much as he had expected—but suddenly, so terribly
real. He had fled Hearth in 2860. Thirty-three years
ago! Thirty-seven years as reckoned on Hearth, except
that in the Fleet, rushing northward out of the galaxy
at eight-tenths light speed, clocks ticked a third slower.

By any measure, and in every frame of reference, too
long.

He looked himself in the eyes. All those years gone
forever, and for what?

"Have I ever explained why I brought us to the
Ringworld?"

"No, Hindmost."

As he had thought. One does not justify oneself to
one's tools. But when only a tool stands between oneself and catatonia . . .

He left his cabin to canter once more around this ac-
cursed ship. The AI would track and hear him through
hallway sensors, would continue the dialogue through
any convenient intercom speaker. "I came for technology. The Ringworld must have had, the Ringworld

embodied extraordinary technologies. It did not matter that the Ringworlders themselves had forgotten."

Technology he meant to trade. No matter the depth of his loneliness, with whom he must negotiate went unstated. Some burdens only a Hindmost can bear.

"And did you find what you sought, Hindmost?"

To this day, he believed that the Ringworld foundation material, the wondrously robust stuff the natives called *scrith*, could only have been manufactured through some industrial-scale process of transmutation. *That* was the magic he had sought, the enticement for Ol't'ro, the treasure with which he had hoped to buy freedom for Hearth. The technology of which he had gotten not as much as a glimpse in his years on the Ringworld.

"Not even close." Hindmost rounded a corner—

And froze.

He did have *Long Shot* with Tunesmith's improvements. Louis had jumped it to hyperspace from within the singularity that was the Ringworld, which itself was within the singularity of the nearby star—and despite all theory and experience, the ship had come back out. He had clues painstakingly collected to the operation of Ringworld-become-hyperdrive, imprinted in its obscenely powerful gravity wave.

After much anguished deliberation, the outline of a new hyperspace physics had begun to take shape in Hindmost's mind.

When Louis emerged from the autodoc, hopefully still able to pilot this ship, perhaps they could use *that* knowledge.

. 8 .

A very thin line encircled the bridge: short navy-blue dashes alternating with longer pale blue dashes.

The Ringworld.

Or, rather, *Endurance* having exited hyperspace sixty light-days from its destination, the Ringworld as it had appeared sixty days earlier.

Alice stood at the center of the bridge, turning slowly, trying to take it in. Her view was from above the plane of the Ringworld, and she could see . . . everything. She just couldn't wrap her mind around what she saw.

Six hundred *million* miles in circumference. It was an expanse beyond comprehension, so she tried changing scales. About sixty feet around the bridge. Each foot of image along the wall represented . . . ten million miles. Still unreal. Call it 830,000 miles—more than thirty times around New Terra—to the inch!

"I wish you luck," Nessus said, his voice quavering. He sat astraddle the pilot's couch, looking uncomfortable. He had offered to pilot so that Julia could concentrate on observing. He had seen it before.

Left unstated: who better to be ready to run?

"What do you mean, Nessus?" Alice asked.

He looked himself in the eyes. "You wish to grasp the scale of the thing. I never succeeded."

Julia walked up to the wall and with her thumb covered a bit of the loop. "The width of my thumb? It's almost a million miles! Walk fifty miles a day, and you couldn't cross the *width* of that place in fifty years."

A hoof scraped at the deck, but Nessus said nothing. With one head he stared at the main sensor panel; with the other he watched the panorama streaming in an auxiliary display: the Ringworld, spinning in place beneath their telescope, simulating a flyover.

Alice watched terrain undulate past at an almost hypnotic pace. Hills. Lakes. Grassy plains. Forests. A sea. Make that an ocean. A *big* ocean.

"Any signs of civilization?" Alice asked.

"Not yet," Nessus said, "except for the structure as a whole, of course."

Julia said, "How long until—"

"Wait! Back up." Something in the flyover had caught Alice's eye. Something familiar. But what here could be familiar?

The close-up stopped and then retraced its path. And there, little more than a speck in that vast ocean, what had caught her eye: a patch like a flattened map of Earth! Nearby was a reddish disk that could be Mars. More disks, unfamiliar to her, lay scattered nearby. Other worlds?

"The world models are full-sized," Nessus said. "No, I can't explain them."

Julia had never seen Earth or Mars. No native New Terran had. She asked, "How long until light from the anomaly itself reaches us?"

Nessus glanced at a timer running on his console. "Call it five minutes."

At two, he banished the simulated-flyover view,

turning an eye back to the wall and its view of the ring. "It's coming up," he said. "Five seconds. Four . . ."

At zero, from almost a trillion miles away, they saw the Ringworld—disappear.

UNIFORMED ESCORTS HUSTLED Sigmund through the corridors of the Ministry of Defense, past closed doors and hushed but intense hallway conversations. Something was going on, and it had not just begun. There had been time for rumors, if not yet actual news, to run rampant through the building.

Since Julia's departure, he had carried his pocket comp at all times. He had kept the stepping disc at home right-side up. That he hadn't been contacted the moment . . . whatever happened was someone's deliberate choice.

He did not think he was being paranoid.

Knowing Julia, she had kept her normal-space sanity breaks to a minimum. *Endurance* might have reached its destination.

Was that why he had been summoned?

In the situation room, too crowded for his taste, Sigmund found a meeting already in progress. The bridge of *Endurance* occupied the room's main holo display. The crew looked weary but unharmed, and Sigmund breathed a little easier.

He took a chair at the main table next to one of the more helpful, less doctrinaire deputy ministers. Corinne somebody. Age had not improved his problem remembering names.

"Here." Corinne tapped the personal display inset in front of Sigmund. "The real-time feed so far for the link."

"Thanks." He fast-forwarded through the recording, skimmed the transcript. Much of the session had gone to waiting for light to crawl to and from the hyperwave relay at the edge of New Terra's singularity. He hadn't missed much.

Except for the Ringworld disappearing.

An inner band, rapidly spinning, had remained behind. Even at full magnification it looked like coorbiting panels, but Nessus' Ringworld expedition had found that invisibly thin wires held the panels together.

Shadow squares, Nessus had called the structure. Without the shadows it cast, Ringworlders would have lived in unending day. Compared to the Ringworld itself, the shadow-square band looked flimsy—only it, too, must be incredibly robust or centrifugal force would have torn it apart. Clever, but Sigmund was more interested in the other technology purportedly on the shadow squares: solar power plants and vast numbers of sensors.

". . . Thorough survey, across the spectrum," Minister Norquist-Ng was saying. "Our scientists have proposed several theories, and we'll want to give them—"

"Excuse me, Minister." Sigmund turned to address the camera. "I have to ask something time-sensitive. Who else came to investigate this phenomenon?" Are the three of them safe?

The light-speed delay to and from the hyperwave relay gave Norquist-Ng plenty of time to frown.

"You're right, Sigmund, we have company," Alice said. "Lots of ships, to judge from hyperspace ripples and comm chatter. But the comm is unintelligible, whether alien or just encrypted. Our Jeeves hasn't yet had any luck with it.

"Having said that, everything we've intercepted,

radio and hyperwave, is faint. I doubt we have anyone nearby."

"Near being a relative term," Sigmund said.

A minute and a half later—time enough, through hyperdrive, for any of the nearby ships to travel two light-days!—he saw Alice's answering shrug.

Nessus turned a head toward the camera. "I keep us moving, a short hyperdrive jump every few minutes. In fact, if you'll excuse us—"

The holo froze for several seconds. When motion returned to the real-time feed, Nessus was giving his full attention to his instruments.

"Very well, Mr. Ausfaller," Norquist-Ng said. "As I was saying—"

Those ships. Might they be from Human Space? After *so* long, could the path be open back to Earth? But for what peaceful reason would anyone send so many ships? And if not peaceful, then . . .

"Whose ships are they, Nessus?" Sigmund interrupted again.

"We would need to get much closer to tell," Nessus said, as with his other head he tugged and twisted at his mane. Clearly, he did not want to get closer. That might be only typical Puppeteer risk avoidance.

Or Nessus might hesitate lest Alice and Julia find an ARM ship to contact.

"Are you *finished,* Ausfaller?" Norquist-Ng asked. "We sent a ship to scope out an unprecedented event. It seems other worlds did, too. With reasonable precautions, I think we can avoid any—"

Ostriches! Sigmund thought. Did isolation ever *not* backfire?

But Julia was also speaking. ". . . May . . . Ringworld left . . . one-light-hour hops . . ."

"Jeeves, back us up to the start of the captain's last comment," Sigmund directed.

"Yes, sir," the conference-room AI said.

"We may have data on why the Ringworld left. We backed off several light-days in one-light-hour hops, hoping to see what led up to the departure. What we observed, scattered around and sometimes on the Ringworld, were gamma-ray bursts, some powerful."

"So, gamma-ray bursts," someone muttered from the back of the room. "The skies are full of them."

"Not around *planets*," Norquist-Ng barked at the hapless aide. "Ausfaller. Any ideas?"

"Antimatter," Sigmund said. "The most powerful explosive imaginable. When matter and antimatter meet, all that's left from the encounter is gamma rays.

"Someone was fighting over the Ringworld, and we've sent our people into the war zone."

· 9 ·

As Alice and Julia kept trying to bring a halt to the interminable consultation with New Terra, Nessus focused on piloting their ship. Warships armed with antimatter! Against antimatter, *twing* would be like tissue. Not even a General Products hull could withstand an antimatter bullet. No wonder the Ringworld—however the trick had been done!—had fled.

And good riddance.

Had he not been certain that the humans would wrest back control, he would already have started *Endurance* on its way to . . . anyplace but here.

Instead, every few minutes Nessus jumped the ship around the chaos. The task required surprising concentration. Although Jeeves could have proposed jump timing, the algorithm the AI used to simulate randomness might have been familiar to ARM ships executing the same algorithms. He could not imagine them predicting *this* pattern.

Earth finding the Fleet? That had come to serve his purposes. Earth discovering the ancient crime by which New Terra had been settled? That was a complication and a risk he had spent much of his life trying to prevent.

(Alice had recognized the map of Earth! She had

tried to cover her slip, not said *what* caught her eye, but he knew. He had long suspected she was from outside. But wherever Alice was from, however she had come to be on New Terra—Sigmund, too, kept secrets—if she could have guided a ship back to Earth, it would have happened by now.)

"Could *Endurance* be spotted?" someone on New Terra asked.

"We're stealthed, but that goes only so far," Julia said. "We can't avoid giving off heat, so infrared sensors might see us. Our power plant sprays neutrinos. And ships detecting this broadcast might be trying to track us down."

"Let's review calibrations on your passive sensors," someone said, missing or ignoring Julia's hint.

"Another jump," Nessus announced, his heads shaking. Julia or Alice would have to take his place soon.

"Be right back," Alice told the camera.

They emerged from hyperspace three seconds—and a light-hour—from their last position in normal space. As Nessus considered his next step, he half listened to the resumed consultation. People safe in their meeting room, light-years away, continued their endless questions. Were there snowballs nearby from which *Endurance* could replenish its deuterium tanks? How long would it take to refuel? Did they plan to deploy additional probes for monitoring? Were . . .

Through it all, Sigmund kept trying to bring the discussion back to the nearby fleets, and how *Endurance* might identify an ARM ship to contact. Norquist-Ng kept calling anything beyond lurking "premature" and any attempt at outreach "too risky."

"Preparing to jump," Nessus interrupted.

So much danger. So much tension. Nessus tuned out

the endless meeting. He tried to concentrate only on the choreography by which to keep *Endurance* one step ahead of any ship that might come after them.

But old, dread memories of the Ringworld would no longer be denied. . . .

Earth Date: 2851

The Hindmost's council chamber: a place Nessus had never expected to see. Now he was in it, the center of attention. By his own doing. At his own insistence.

Madness took many forms.

Every time he had left Hearth and herd, he had had to work himself into a manic state. But to come in a frenzy to the inner sanctum of the Concordance?

Focus! Nessus ordered himself. Taking a deep breath, he examined the council room. Sparely furnished and devoid of ornamentation. Locked doors and no stepping discs. Well lit, the entire ceiling a glow panel. Intimate, the benches close together, the Hindmost and his ministers seated haunch by haunch. And Nessus' true audience: a hologram—and whoever was behind it.

If observation and deduction had not led Nessus astray. A long chain of inference, from very few facts, led to his conclusion as to who must hide behind Chiron. Not even his beloved would comment upon Nessus' speculations.

But it was too late to have doubts. Hormones surged anew, warmed his blood, stoked the flames of his transient manic euphoria.

"We shall come to order," the Hindmost sang in a loud, clear voice. "The hindmost of our Ringworld expedition has demanded an audience."

"I bring good news," Nessus began. "On Earth I recruited two humans and a Kzin for investigation of the Ringworld." He began extolling his crew's qualifications.

"You bring them here and this is *good* news?" Achilles interrupted. "You have revealed the Fleet!"

"It was necessary, as I shall explain." Nessus dipped his heads briefly in feigned regret. "Recall my assignment. I need qualified crew to explore far beyond the edge of what they consider Known Space. Before their perilous explorations can even begin, they must entrust their lives to an experimental spacecraft. Further, the Type II hyperdrive so fills *Long Shot* that there is scarcely room for the pilot. The rest must agree to go into stasis, trusting that they will be released."

"All this was clear before you set out," Achilles sang. "You made no mention then of revealing the Fleet."

If he could, Achilles would seize control of the Ringworld mission. He would undo everything Nessus strove to accomplish.

Nessus dare not allow that to happen.

Scouts, so very rare among the herd, had to be insanely brave. Achilles was also insanely brave—he had been a scout, too, early in his career—and obsessively ambitious, and a sociopath. To further his ambitions, he had once tried to *kill* Nessus. To further his ambitions, he had provoked Pak and Gw'oth alike—and somehow won.

For a time.

To become Hindmost again, Achilles would do—*anything*.

Nessus chose his next chords with care. "I could not know in advance what payment our explorers would demand."

"You could have offered something else to—"

"Let him report," Chiron sang.

At the rebuke, Achilles twitched and fell silent.

"As partial payment," Nessus sang, "they demanded *Long Shot* itself."

Two ministers warbled in surprise; others glanced sidelong at Chiron. Most, the Hindmost among them, seemed determined *not* to react. Chiron's research program had been ruinously expensive.

"Why *Long Shot*?" Chiron asked.

Because I offered it. "Because," Nessus sang, "their people lack the technology to move their worlds. The new hyperdrive, if their species can reproduce it, could someday be of great utility in fleeing the core explosion." And of greater utility, much sooner, confirming the incredible discoveries my crew will bring to their homes.

Achilles straightened on his bench. "A very great prize, yet you deem *Long Shot* a partial payment. And you have ignored my question about exposing the Fleet. You could have arranged to meet anywhere to transfer from *Long Shot* to the exploration ship. You chose *here*."

They had penetrated to the hearts of the matter. Nessus sang, "The reason is simple. As part of their price, the crew asked the location of the Citizen home world."

In truth, one *had* made such a demand. Never suspecting that Nessus—after long protecting the Fleet's secret location—had planned from the start to reveal the way to Hearth.

"This is madness," Achilles sang with stern undertones, cutting through the sudden cacophony of dismay. "We must dispose of these recruits."

The Hindmost stared at Nessus. "You had no alternatives?"

"I did not." Through the lie, somehow, Nessus kept his harmonies firm and steady. At a higher level, he sang the truth. What he did was for the good of the herd.

Unless he had gone as psychotic as Achilles.

The Hindmost, after a long silence, sadly sang, "We can erase these memories. After the mission. There is precedent."

"Memory edits would violate the agreements I made," Nessus sang back. He spread his hooves, *un*ready to flee, pretending to a confidence he lacked. "I will not travel to the Ringworld without the council's assurances that they will honor my promises. And my crew refuses to go without me."

Several among the council blinked at this boldness.

"We *must* explore this amazing artifact," Chiron insisted. "Imagine what we can learn."

Nessus managed not to stare. Scouting, he understood: sacrificing a very few to the perils of exploration to uncover unsuspected dangers waiting to pounce on the entire herd. But exploring to satisfy curiosity? Did no one here see that the intelligence behind "Chiron's" hologram could not be a Citizen?

Or did they choose not to see?

The Hindmost seemed more saddened than surprised at Chiron's melody. "It shall be as you suggest," he sang at last.

"Respectfully, I ask that the entire council agree," Nessus sang back. *I mean you, Chiron.*

"It was my understanding," Chiron trilled, "that we honor our commercial commitments." Following his lead, most added their assent. "Besides—if need be, we can defend ourselves."

Curiosity *and* recklessness? Gw'oth, Nessus suspected, though he could not prove it. One of their group minds.

An uncertain future stretched before him. The unknowable perils of the Ringworld. And more Citizen secrets to reveal, dark secrets that would—if anyone survived the Ringworld encounter—bring humans and Kzinti navies racing to the Fleet.

Citizens alone would never oust Chiron. Perhaps the ARM or the Kzinti Patriarchy could.

SOMEHOW NESSUS MANAGED to stay lucid. He returned, after finally being excused from the council chamber, to the park where he had left his crew waiting. They did not notice him arrive.

The last traces of mania drained from him. He stumbled along a curving path, heads whipping from side to side at each rustle in the foliage and every insinuation of a breeze. As he reeled closer, his crew speculated aloud about the mission. He listened—

Until a wayward flower-sniffer caught him unaware. With one reflex he squealed, leapt high into the air, and came down, wrapped into a ball, on the close-cropped meadowplant.

How tempting it was to withdraw . . . forever! Reluctantly, he let the aliens coax him back to reality. They asked where he had been, what had frightened him so.

Humans were obsessed with sex: their own, and rudely conjecturing about what anyone else might do. He concocted a story, told his crew that extorting a mate had been his price for going to the Ringworld. The lie satisfied them. Better vulgar fiction than the truth: that he gambled with their lives, and their peoples' lives, and the lives of a trillion Citizens.

As through a fog, Nessus led his crew from the park. During his brief recruiting trip to Earth, the Ministry of Science was to have equipped a ship for the coming encounter with the Ringworld.

It was time to see what Chiron had provided.

Earth Date: 2893

But neither Kzinti nor humans had ever come charging at the Fleet. Not, in any event, before the herd threw out the Experimentalists altogether. Chiron had allowed it.

Might war fleets have converged upon Hearth after Nessus fled with his young family? No. The forces that should have liberated Hearth had gone, instead, to the Ringworld.

Throughout the flood of memories, a cadence had continued to throb and thrum in his brain. A much loved theme from the grand ballet. With an inward bleat, Nessus refocused his attention on keeping *Endurance* safe from the ships all about. The melody ran strong in his mind.

Across several melodic lines, a synchrony of beats approached. His cue. "Ready to jump," Nessus called in warning.

· 10 ·

Haltingly, Hindmost made his way to the chamber where Louis Wu slept. The autodoc would soon wake the man, let him out. Unless *he* overrode the automatic release, kept Louis in suspended animation. . . .

The meandering tunnel led Hindmost to the hull. Most of its surface remained as clear as the day it had left the General Products factory. A glimpse of the distant blue-white flare of a fusion drive hurried him on his way.

He had abducted Louis, survivor of the first Ringworld expedition, to return there and find a transmutation device. If Louis decided to seek revenge, could the human be blamed?

But then Louis had purposefully stranded them both (and the Kzin, Chmeee, now vanished with the Ringworld) because the immense artifact had become unstable in its orbit. If Hindmost had had the choice, he would have fled. Together—without other options, and at great personal risk—they had fulfilled Louis's improvident vow to a native woman, preventing the Ringworld from crashing into its sun, plucking trillions from the jaws of certain death.

Maybe *that* balanced the scales between him and Louis.

And if not? He had found Louis a hopeless tasp addict and cured him. Nor would this be the first time he had saved Louis's life with the Carlos Wu autodoc.

Only Louis might never have suffered tasp addiction but for the first Ringworld expedition—which, as far as Louis was concerned, Hindmost had ordered. The autodoc only undid injuries Louis had suffered because of his abduction.

And Hindmost *still* feared to pilot this ship himself.

A complicated decision, to be sure. Best to hedge, to probe Louis's attitude when he emerged from the autodoc. Hindmost turned and cantered back to *Long Shot*'s bridge.

"Voice," Hindmost sang. "I wish to be remotely present in the autodoc room."

"It is done," Voice answered.

A hologram opened, its vantage above and to one side of the autodoc. Sensors brought him the soft hum of the machine, the gentle rise and fall of Louis's chest.

And so, from the comparative safety of the bridge, Hindmost watched and waited.

THE CLEAR DOME of the autodoc slowly retracted. Looking restored and rejuvenated, Louis climbed out. If being greeted by a hologram surprised him, he hid it.

"Nothing hurts," Louis said matter-of-factly.

"Good," Hindmost said. After two months, Interworld felt strange in his mouth.

"I was used to it. Oh, futz, I've lost my mind!"

"Louis, did you not know the machine would rebuild you as a breeder?"

"Yah, but . . . my head feels futzy. Full of cotton.

I never felt so much *myself* as when I could think like a protector."

"We could have rebuilt the 'doc." The comment was a test. If being a protector appealed to Louis, a chord sung to Voice would open hatches, would blast Louis out into space.

If matters came to that, Hindmost would feel guilty.

"No. *No.*" Louis slammed a fist against the autodoc lid. "I remember that much. I have to be a breeder, or dead. If I'm a protector . . ."

Hindmost let Louis prattle on with the irrepressible energy of one fresh from an autodoc. Then, "Louis."

"What?"

"We haven't moved since you went into the 'doc, two months ago Earth time." Precision would only complicate matters: they had not moved *far*. "We are a warm spot on the sky. Sooner or later the Fringe War will notice us. What else has that heterogeneous mob got for entertainment but to track us down and take our ship?"

Take us far from this awful place. Please.

"Right," Louis said.

He watched Louis set off toward the bridge. The maze of access tubes was much expanded since Louis had tumbled into the autodoc. Hindmost, from time to time, offered directions from the nearest intercom speaker as his hologram followed Louis. As footsteps approached the bridge, Hindmost sang a chord to terminate the projection.

Louis dropped into the pilot's chair and activated the hyperdrive. The bridge screens went dark. The crystalline sphere of the mass detector lit with radial lines pointing toward the nearby stars, rotated to show their new course.

He is taking us the wrong way!

"I don't have the nerve to fly us to home," Hindmost had admitted, moments before helping Louis-as-protector into the autodoc.

"Not Canyon?" Louis had asked.

Canyon was where, long ago, Hindmost had tracked down and abducted Louis. "Home," he had corrected. Faster than explaining, he had dissembled. "I did not think I could hide us on Canyon. Too small. Home is very like Earth, Louis, and has a wonderful history."

From the course Louis had set, he had heard—misheard—Home, the human planet.

But Hindmost had meant, simply, home. Where the hearts are. After two long exiles on a quite different human world, and with the loved ones he had left there, New Terra felt like home. He had planned to give Louis coordinates to fly them there.

And then it hit Hindmost:

—That only one place could ever truly be home to him, and that was the Fleet of Worlds.

—That at some level he had known it all along. Why else had he built up *Long Shot*'s velocity until it matched the Fleet's?

—And that something in the bridge displays had been screaming for his attention for the past few hours.

Against all odds, Hindmost hoped he knew what it was. *Who* it was.

"Louis," he said, "we must go back."

REUNION

Earth Date: 2893

11

Alice pored over the bridge displays, at once fascinated and anxious. From the way Nessus tugged at his mane, he felt no such ambivalence. Alice couldn't decide how Julia felt.

A poker face is a good skill in a commander.

Space seethed with hyperwave chatter. The longer *Endurance* skulked about, the more hyperspace-jump ripples its instruments detected. The ship stocked—and had widely scattered—sensors far better than anything the Ministry had had in her day. Compared to the tech with which Alice had, long ago, grown up in the Belt, the new sensors were scarcely distinguishable from magic. The sensors, like *twing*, were a gift from the Pak Library.

Alice froze her display on a ship so long and thin that it suggested a crowbar. At the limits of resolution, smaller dartlike ships buzzed around it. "We see lots of ships like this, a second type like thick lenses, and a third kind more like squat cones. Each shape seems to stick with its own. Fleets, do you suppose, Sigmund?"

"Almost certainly," Sigmund answered a minute and a half later. "The formations look defensive. As makes sense when at least one faction has antimatter weapons."

"But whose fleets are they?" Julia asked. "Sigmund, Nessus, do you know?"

Pausing his soft, rhythmic humming, Nessus looked up from the pilot console. "The Ringworld is gone. The danger it embodied is gone. The mystery of the hyperspace ripple is resolved. I do not understand why we tarry."

Changing the subject, Alice noted. She waited for Sigmund to comment.

Sigmund's answer eventually arrived. "When I left Known Space, most human warships, including ARM ships, had been built in GP hulls. Kzinti warships, too. Of course, General Products had just pulled out of Known Space and . . ."

Nessus turned one head toward the camera. "Not knowing whose fleets these are, we *must* consider them dangerous."

Strange creatures, Alice thought. Puppeteers had no curiosity. And though Nessus yearned to flee, he stayed alert. Sigmund used to say something about no true coward ever turning his back on danger. And that Nessus *always* had undisclosed motives.

This was neither the time nor the place to let her mind wander. *Damn old age.*

". . . Almost certain I recognize some ARM and Patriarchy vessels," Sigmund was saying. "Cut off from their supply of General Products hulls, I suspect naval designers reverted to proven configurations."

Sigmund's brow furrowed in the manner Alice remembered so well.

Even . . . before, the closest of friends, working together every day, she hadn't always understood what had plunged him into one of his dark moods. But *this* scowl held no mystery: General Products hulls were among his fiercest obsessions.

It turned out that a GP hull was a single nanotech-grown super-molecule, the interatomic bonds massively reinforced by an embedded power plant. Disable that hidden fusion generator, and a ship's own air pressure blows apart the hull.

Not a feature General Products had chosen to disclose to its customers.

In his life on Earth, Sigmund had worried that Puppeteers could destroy the "indestructible" hulls they sold. Of *course* he had, but that had been only the paranoia speaking. The first time Sigmund truly knew, he had lost someone very close to him.

Lost, dead. Not just lost, gone far away. For a moment Alice forgot her ancient, simmering bitterness.

". . . The long skinny ships remind me of ARM ships from archives of the first two wars with the ratcats. And before GP showed up, the ratcats favored lens-shaped ships like those *Endurance* is also seeing.

"No one can improve on Outsider hyperdrive technology, so maybe there hasn't been a reason to radically redesign ships." Shrewdly: "Or has General Products mastered the much faster drive used by *Long Shot.*"

"No." Nessus shuddered. "Not while I lived on Hearth. As far as I know, *Long Shot* remains one of a kind."

"Ratcats?" Julia asked.

Nessus twisted a lock of his mane. "An informal term for aliens who call themselves Kzinti. A Kzin looks something like an Earth animal called a cat and has a hairless tail like another Earth animal called a rat."

To hear Sigmund speak of Kzinti, a very *large* cat:

kind of like a bipedal tiger looming eight feet tall. Kzinti ate their prey—almost certainly, when Sigmund was a child, his parents. It might explain Sigmund, just a little.

That didn't mean that Alice forgave him.

"What about the conical ships?" Julia asked. "Those are present in large numbers, too."

"I don't recognize them," Sigmund admitted. "Do you, Nessus?"

Nessus shifted his humming to a single throat. "I do not, Sigmund. That scares me."

Everything scared a Puppeteer. As for the claim not to recognize the third fleet, Alice did not believe it. *Am I reading body language, or channeling Sigmund's suspicions?*

Sigmund broke the growing silence. "I guess I need to say it. The ARM is the military force of Earth's government. *Earth,* people. The home world of humanity. New Terra's long-lost roots. We have to make contact."

"I don't *have* to do anything," Norquist-Ng snapped back. "Ours is one ship among hundreds, maybe thousands. Of all people, Ausfaller, I would expect you to know to be wary." He paused, rubbing his chin thoughtfully. "Maybe Nessus is right about *Endurance* coming home."

"You can't mean that!" Sigmund said.

"I will not gamble the safety of this crew, much less the safety of this *world,* on vague recollections of pre-historic ship designs. Captain . . ."

"I understand, Minister." Julia did not meet Sigmund's anguished gaze.

To have come this far. To have come so close. Alice's heart sank.

"But hopping around like we've had to do uses a lot

of fuel," Julia continued. "Minister, we will redirect our efforts to refueling for the long return flight. Maintaining a safe distance from the alien ships as we must, collecting deuterium may take us a while. Will there be anything else, Minister, or may we get started?"

"Proceed, Captain. We're done." The connection broke.

Alice could not look away from the darkened comm console. *So close* . . .

Julia crossed the bridge to rest a hand on Alice's shoulder. "I can stall for a few days. See what you can find."

IT ALL CAME down to Pak crypto software.

Because loath as Alice was to admit it, Norquist-Ng might be right. After two centuries, who was to say that Sigmund could recognize an Earth warship? Maybe another species had independently come to use the same basic shape. Maybe the flying crowbars were Earth ships of ancient design, but long ago sold to . . . whomever.

Maybe if Nessus would *stop* that infernal *humming,* half a dozen melodies at the same finagling time, she could think straight.

The Pak were whizzes at crypto. Alice suspected the best Pak algorithms never made it into the Library—clans battled clans, after all—but the Library offered plenty of the underlying math. Not even Norquist-Ng knew she had brought Pak algorithms, from the stash Sigmund called their "Secret Santa."

But not even superior crypto technique would be enough. Suppose ARM ships were out there. What languages would their crews speak? You can hardly decrypt what you can't even understand in plaintext.

Nessus knew human languages, and not only New Terra's English. With but one set of vocal cords, no human could manage any Puppeteer language.

And so, Nessus had spoken Interworld back in the day he and Sigmund first met on Earth. And Nessus must have mastered a more recent dialect—and likely also Kzinti-speak, the so-called Hero's Tongue—when he recruited on Earth for the disastrous Ringworld expedition.

Nessus, characteristically, refused to share his expertise.

His refusal wouldn't have mattered if *Endurance* carried a Puppeteer translator. The Puppeteers had effective translation software—and it was among the most controlled of their technologies. Natural-language processing was too close to AI, was the official story, and Puppeteers saw no reason to risk building their own successors. Still, of necessity, scout ships had carried translators—and no ship that New Terra, upon gaining its independence, had been allowed to retain had had translation software. No record had ever been found on New Terra of the alien languages known to General Products' trade representatives.

Sigmund, despite his best efforts, had never succeeded in stealing the information.

Jeeves knew English as it had been spoken when the ramscoop *Long Pass* set out from Sol system—more than a half millennium ago. Alice had taught the AI the Spanglish of her era in the Belt. Sigmund had taught Jeeves his more recent—but still, very dated—Interworld.

How much had Earth languages drifted in the meanwhile?

Jeeves had caught a few drops from the unending

message streams. Just possibly, he had decrypted a tiny fraction of what he had intercepted. Nothing in any way enlightening. Nothing that seemed critical. No video: it would be too easy if they could *see* that humans were nearby. Despite Jeeves's best efforts, all Alice had to go on were isolated words and the occasional short phrase scattered across intership text messages.

As likely, the purported decryptions were spurious.

A few days, Julia had said. Alice struggled not to despair. What could they hope to accomplish in a few days?

She had to focus their efforts. Somehow.

Recurring among the supposedly decrypted words was—Jeeves had reasoned from the logic of syntax—a person's name. By terrestrial standards, a very common name. Nonetheless: a familiar name. Alice chuckled to herself. For all she knew, Wu meant *snacks* in Kzinti-speak.

She had nothing better on which to roll the dice.

"Jeeves," Alice said. "Devote ten percent of your effort to messages to and from the signal source *Koala*."

12

"You understand my requirements?" Horatius asked. The melody was not really a question.

"Yes, Hindmost," Achilles sang. The title stuck in his throats.

"Very well," the response finally came. The light-speed delay between Hearth and Nature Preserve One accounted for a few seconds of the gap. Most was just another of the Hindmost's habitual, aggravating pauses. "I shall await your report on the matter."

Protocol demanded that the Hindmost terminate the link. Jaws clenched, Achilles waited. And waited.

"Thank you," Horatius offered at last. The status light blinked off and his image froze.

"I shall await your report on the matter," Achilles mimicked. He had far more important matters with which to concern himself than minutiae of agricultural production. The Hindmost should, too.

Hindmost! Achilles grimaced at the static image still projected nearby. Tawny of hide (with unfortunate white markings more stripelike than proper patches), broad through the withers, and strikingly tall, Horatius had the potential to look worthy of the office. But that straggly, too lustrous mane? It needed to be toned down and tamed. The abundance of dark green jade among the curls and braids was acceptable as Conservative Party colors, but could not Horatius have found a green sash that better matched the gemstones?

"Image off." Achilles rose from his nest of soft cushions, brushed his hide, straightened his own sash of office, and adjusted several circlets of orange garnets in his coiffure. *He* knew how to present himself.

Guards waited outside his private chambers; when Achilles threw open the doors they came stiffly to attention. Aides, assistants, adjutants, and their various flunkies stopped whatever they were doing to tend to his needs.

His chief deputy cantered over to him: loyal, trustworthy, none-to-bright Vesta. "Excellency, the farm administrator is here for his appointment."

Subtle harmonics reinterpreted the verb's explicit tense. The administrator had, it would seem, been kept waiting for a considerable time.

Too bad. *He* still waited to reclaim the position that was rightfully his. That a pretentious simpleton like Horatius should be Hindmost was almost too much to bear. Someday, Achilles promised himself, he would make Ol't'ro realize that a change was necessary. A restoration.

Until that happy day, he had Nature Preserve One to rule.

"Very well," Achilles announced. "You may notify the visitor that I am coming."

He set out for the door, letting Vesta, a secretary, and his guards scamper to form ranks around him. Together, hooves clattering on the marble tiles, Vesta crooning into his communicator, they filed from the room. The remaining assistants, factotums, and minions went back to work.

A stepping disc would have been quicker, but not as satisfying as the stroll across the palace. Achilles had had it built grander than the Hindmost's own residence on Hearth.

Grander or not—oh, how he wished he were back in the Hindmost's residence.

Down spacious halls his retinue marched, across the domed grand rotunda, then outside along a majestic colonnaded promenade. Hints of a breeze penetrated the weather force field. The residence sat high atop a mountain crag, and the view into the valley was stunning. *Take* that, *Horatius*. At the end of the promenade, they came to the foyer to Achilles' audience chamber.

Looking anxious, his visitor extended a head in greeting. "Excellency."

"Welcome." Achilles ignored the too-familiar gesture. "Vesta, if you will."

With a wave of his pocket computer, Vesta unlocked the door, then closed it behind Achilles and his petitioner.

Achilles settled astraddle a tall, well-padded bench. His visitor, looking ill at ease, took one of the much shorter guest benches. In proper Experimentalist fashion, this one had assumed a name from human mythology. Some apt rustic deity. Achilles summoned the name from memory. "What brings you today, Eunomia?"

"Excellency, thank you for seeing me. A . . . technical issue brings me."

"You are dissatisfied about something?" Dissatisfaction was but a short step from criticism. Would this one take that dangerous path?

"Concerned, Excellency. I would ask to review the allocation of fertilizer."

"What *about* the allocation?" Achilles sang.

Eunomia shrank back. "So far this growing season, my farm has received less fertilizer than we had requisitioned."

"Anything else?"

"There are matters of expedient access to the grain ships . . ."

Achilles lifted both heads high, and gave this impertinent . . . supplicant a hard stare. "You do not feel your little enterprise is getting fair treatment?"

"Doubtless fair, Excellency, but . . ." Eunomia trailed off, unsure how else to couch his complaint.

"Yet you are 'concerned' with the outcome. Perhaps you think me and my staff ill-informed?" Achilles prompted. "Or incapable of reaching proper conclusions from what is reported to us?"

"No. No. Of *course* not, Excellency."

"Then . . . ?"

"If I may begin again," Eunomia bleated.

Achilles waited.

"There is some risk, Excellency, that our upcoming harvest will fall short of its quota." Pause. "If it were possible to get . . ." Eunomia sang on, more anxious and uncertain by the moment.

"Perhaps you would be happier relieved of the challenge? To trade your burdens for lesser responsibilities?" To toil from sunsup to sunsdown on your farm, while some erstwhile underling enjoys the privileges you forfeited.

Eunomia flinched. "I will find a way, Excellency."

It was a process Achilles had polished to a high gloss. Citizens were intensely social, so get them alone. Make them doubt themselves. Hint at the privileges they might lose.

And then ease up, just a bit. Offer a reason for hope.

Keep them dependent. Make them grateful. Replace the social contract with personal bonds.

Repeat as needed.

"You did well to bring these concerns to my attention," Achilles sang soothingly. "Might some additional workers alleviate the difficulties?"

Up/down, down/up, up/down: Eunomia's heads bobbed agreement. "Yes, Excellency." He would depart with his job, and his perks, and something, at least, to show for his trouble. "Yes, additional workers would be most helpful."

Very well, Achilles thought. Beyond sheltering Hearth's ancient biomes and growing luxury foods, Nature Preserve One served as a dumping ground for the herd's antisocial. A few "rehabilitees" transferred from one of the reeducation camps would secure Eunomia's gratitude. Hearth's trillion residents would always have misfits, outcasts, and loners to take their place.

(As *I* was once banished to this world. That Ol't'ro had assigned him to rule *this* world gnawed at Achilles, no matter how useful he found the captive workforce. The reminder was not subtle.)

"Thank you, Excellency," Eunomia burbled in relief, rising to leave. "I will not disappoint you."

Achilles rose from his bench and came around the table. Now *he* extended a neck. As they brushed heads, he felt Eunomia trembling in relief.

Eunomia all but crept from the audience chamber, heads lowered in subservience and respect.

Across the years, and careers, and even worlds, Achilles had conditioned many to follow him. It had worked again today. It worked almost without fail, especially with the impressionable young.

Angry at himself even as he did it, Achilles tugged free one braid of the edifice that was his mane coiffure. *Almost* without fail, because there had once been a failure. A disaster. A prospect turned acolyte turned traitor. The nemesis who time and again had defied and stymied Achilles' grand plans.

Curse that Nessus. And curse his paramour . . .

Earth Date 2828

"You cannot mean it!" Achilles sang.

"Yes, I can," Chiron responded, voices ringing with the firm harmonics of command. He might never master every nuance of Citizen psychology, but he had become proficient in the subtleties of their speech and body language. The comm delay between Hearth and Nature Preserve Five seemed to underscore his imperturbability.

"You are in the Fleet because I brought you here." Achilles kept his voices level, desperate not to let his fear show.

"I am here because neither you nor your predecessor had any choice." Chiron paused. "As you have none now."

Because the price of disobedience is the shattering of the worlds.

"I have served you well," Achilles sang.

"As shall the former Hindmost when he reassumes the office."

Every guard on Penance Island was loyal. For a moment Achilles considered sending the order for his rival to have an unfortunate accident. But only for a moment. No matter their loyalty, Achilles could not be certain his minions had the mental—call it strength—to kill. "So be it. I will declare him rehabilitated."

"Yes, you will. Then you will resign your office and endorse him."

The chords slipped out. "But *why*?"

Once more: delay, and imperturbability, and the firm harmonics of command. "That I must ever seek out and deflect your egregious deceits grows wearisome."

"You trust *him* more?"

"I trust no Citizen." Pause. "After being so long off Hearth and out of power, he will need time before he can hatch new mischief."

"Who better than I to make sure he does not?" Achilles sang. Without retaining some role in the government, *he* might end up filling the vacancy soon to open on Penance Island.

The longest pause yet. As the silence dragged on, Achilles worried that he had dared too much. His necks ached to tug at his mane. His legs trembled with the urge to flee. But shorn of power, nowhere within the Fleet would be safe. . . .

"You shall go to Nature Preserve One," Chiron declared—and then he looked himself in the eyes. "To govern there. As such, you shall remain among the Hindmost's ministers."

"It shall be as you say, Chiron." *Until I find a way to undo this travesty.*

Earth Date 2893

Achilles shook off the gloom that had taken him. Steadfast of eye and firm of step, he exited the audience chamber. The entourage formed about him and they returned across the residence. Leaving his guard detail standing at their posts, he reentered his private chambers.

Though he had yet to regain his full power, his enemies had lost theirs. After the disaster that was the Ringworld expedition, the populace had risen—in the polite, orderly, and slow-motion process of a consensualization—to reject the Experimentalist Party altogether.

And after, he had taken consolation in watching Horatius, the latest interloper, chief of the Conservative Party, discover Ol't'ro ruling from behind the Hindmost.

· 13 ·

Go *back*?

Louis dared not shift his eyes from the mass pointer, not while *Long Shot* hurtled through hyperspace at almost a light-year every minute. He imagined Hindmost looking crazed. "I thought you wanted to get away, to go to Home."

"The matter is complicated, Louis."

"Just relax. We'll be there in a few hours."

"With such a fast ship, what matters a bit of delay? Take us back."

Inside the clear dome of the mass pointer, blue lines groped hungrily at Louis. Each line represented the gravitational influence of a nearby star. Should *Long Shot* come too close to any of them, then . . . well, he did not know. Everything he had been taught about hyperdrive said that using hyperdrive to escape through the Ringworld should have been disastrous—and yet here were. As a protector, he had understood. As plain old Louis? He hadn't a clue why the stunt had not killed them.

He tweaked the controls and almost immediately nudged them back to veer around an onrushing star. He adjusted course yet again to thread the needle between another sun and a yellow-and-orange binary lurking just beyond.

"Louis?"

"At least give me a reason."

"Something I noticed just as we left. Or, rather, something that registered, that made me realize what I had been seeing for hours." The sound came of hoof scraping at the deck. "You would think me ridiculous. Allow me to observe a while longer and then I will explain."

By what logic would a Puppeteer ask to return to a war zone? "Is Home not safe?"

"*Please,* Louis. Turn the ship around." More scraping. "Regardless, know that you misunderstood me. By 'home,' I meant Hearth, the main world of the Fleet of Worlds."

That explained the normal-space velocity *Long Shot* had accumulated. Louis said, "And after you check out . . . whatever you think you saw, would you then expect to go to Hearth?"

"No. Yes. In time." The voice grew muffled, as though spoken by a head plunged deep into a Puppeteer mane. "I would like to know more before returning to Hearth. I have been away for a long time."

Skirting the maw of a red giant sun, Louis considered. *He* had been gone for a long time, too. Hindmost had found Louis as a wirehead in hiding on Canyon. Why did he rush back to Human Space? To renew his current addiction? Tanj, no! "Dropping back to normal space." Because with every second of dithering, the ship careened across another hundred-plus billion kilometers. No matter how quickly they could retrace their path, it felt wrong to speed so far out of the way.

The mass pointer went dark. With a sigh of relief,

Louis lifted his gaze to the main view port. The stars—now that they were no longer trying to devour him—were lovely.

"Thank you, Louis."

He turned. Hindmost stood across the bridge, his eyes manic, his mane disheveled.

"I haven't agreed," Louis said. "If we do return to the Ringworld system, then what?"

"A short period of observation. Perhaps only a few hours."

When they could, Puppeteers ran from danger. "Could Hearth have become more dangerous than the Fringe War?"

Hindmost pawed at the deck. "The possibility exists."

Returning to Human Space sounded better and better, but Louis could never live with himself if he fled from danger a *Puppeteer* was determined to face. "Tunesmith's instruments vanished with the Ringworld. Whatever you'll be looking for, how can you hope to find it?"

"With Tunesmith's instruments, because they remain available to us—on the shadow squares. *Long Shot* has access to those sensor arrays. One of Tunesmith's lesser upgrades to this ship."

Then they *could* see the antics of the Fringe War ships. But there was a catch. Wasn't there? Tanj it, he had had the mind of a protector! Louis remembered leaping to conclusions faster than he could articulate the problems. Now he felt . . . dull.

So articulate your problems. Hindmost is no protector, but he is smarter than you.

Louis said, "Those sensors are deep in the star's gravitational singularity, so they must be light-speed limited. The array is broad enough to triangulate positions of what it detects, but it sees where things *were*. Readouts from the sensors are light-speed limited, too. And we're not dealing with a few ships, but thousands, all taking evasive maneuvers through hyperspace." It pained Louis to add, "I can't begin to interpret this much data, let alone adjust for so many light-speed lags."

"Nor I. But while you healed, I integrated Voice into the ship's networks."

"Hindmost's Voice?" Louis asked. "Are you there?"

"Welcome back, Louis." The words came from an overhead speaker. "*I* can handle the data from the shadow squares." And a touch petulantly, "Although I do not know what Hindmost wishes me to observe."

"I will explain," Hindmost said. "So, Louis?"

"And after, we go to the Fleet?"

"Sooner or later."

"I would like to see more of the Fleet," Louis said. "On our stopover en route to the Ringworld, Nessus didn't let us see much."

"After I finish my preparations, we will go together." Once more, a hoof scraped at the deck. "Do not be surprised if things have changed since your last visit."

· 14 ·

Five worlds. Thousands of drones buzzing beyond and everywhere around the worlds' combined gravitational singularity. Hundreds of thousands of free-flying sensors, at distances up to a half light-year from the Fleet.

And to coordinate everything, a single mind.

Proteus observed: the ships ceaselessly shuttling grain to Hearth and returning to the farm worlds with fertilizer. The endless swirl of its probes, ever maintaining an impenetrable defense, dipping as needed into planetary oceans to replenish their deuterium reserves. The vessels of the human and Kzinti and Trinoc diplomatic missions, and the comings and goings of supply ships for those missions.

At every instant, Proteus had at least ten drones targeting every alien spacecraft. His weapons swarms had sufficed, since the arrival of the first ARM vessel, to deter aggression against the Fleet.

No Citizen, or even an army of Citizens, could do what this single AI could.

Single, but also complex. He was a distant descendant of Earth, by way of Jeeves. He was a descendant, too, of the worlds he guarded: for Jeeves had been modified into the first Voice, and more recently into his present form. His study of the alien visitors suggested that many of his tactical processes had been programmed to mimic Kzinti behaviors.

It was strange to have so varied a pedigree.

Would it fall upon him to defend these worlds? His Citizen aspects never stopped fearing it. Much of the rest of him had begun to fear it, too. And the remainder? Intriguingly, alarmingly, a bit of him—the Kzinti influence, he thought—had started to relish the challenge.

"PROTEUS," ACHILLES SUMMONED.

"Speaking," an overhead speaker replied.

Only the merest fragment of the AI would be here in his office. The rest was spread among computing nodes on five worlds and in space all around the Fleet. Most of Proteus existed beyond the Fleet's singularity, linked—and in command of its far-flung sensor and weapons arrays—by instantaneous hyperwave.

Perhaps, Achilles thought, his finest creation.

If only Proteus had destroyed *Long Shot* when Nessus had brought it here. Of course there had been no Proteus then. It had required Nessus' madness— revealing the Fleet to his Ringworld expedition!—to convince Ol't'ro of the need to create something like Proteus. As it had been Nessus who had—

Enough.

He could bask another time in his enduring, white-hot rage against Nessus. The Concordance's lurkers reported increasing restiveness among the alien fleets near the Ringworld star. That news carried with it an auspicious moment, a fleeting opportunity that he would seize.

He had only to plant the seed . . .

"Proteus," Achilles sang, "I have a question for you. Suppose that more alien ships approach the Fleet. If need be, can you defend against them?"

"How many ships?"

"At the least, a few hundred. Perhaps thousands."

"To defend against so many, it would be wise to expand my capacity."

Knowing the answer to *this* question, too, Achilles chose his next chords with special care. Ol't'ro would hear them through Proteus, if from no other source. "Do your algorithms scale to handle such numbers of targets?"

"Not as responsively as I would like, even with additional hardware."

"That is unfortunate," Achilles sang back. His work was done; the seed planted. "We can hope that more ships never come."

Proteus must seek out Horatius, and Horatius must contact Achilles. Who better to extend the AI's capabilities than he who had raised Proteus from more primitive software?

When Horatius did call, Achilles would demur, citing the burden of his existing duties. Horatius must go to Ol't'ro, lest alien hordes departing the Ringworld should charge at the Fleet, and then *Ol't'ro* would "ask" for Achilles' aid.

Again he would demur—a proper, fearful Citizen— loath to extend *any* AI, especially an armed one. Rich with trills and undertunes and grace notes, the melody he would offer ran softly in his mind's ear. To further develop Proteus risked evoking a runaway intelligence cascade, creating a super-sapience, inducing a singularity event . . .

Ol't'ro was expert at coercing acquiescence, but

how does one coerce creativity? They would want Achilles' hearts and mind committed, without reservation or distraction, to the task of enhancing Proteus. And when they realized that . . .

To depose Horatius and restore *me* will be a small price.

Ol't'ro were beyond genius and could modify Proteus themselves. But they wouldn't: the task was too mundane to hold their interest. They would rather obsess on the enduring mystery of the Type II hyperdrive. They would rather keep working on a gravity-pulse projector to precipitate ships from hyperspace—and to find a way, if they ever had such a projector—to peer into hyperspace to aim it. Ol't'ro had an unending set of ambitious projects, and the entire Ministry of Science to do their bidding.

And within that Ministry, every scientist and engineer would be terrified to touch the internals of an AI.

Rather than set aside their toys, Ol't'ro would *want* Achilles to upgrade Proteus. A commitment to replace Horatius should be no obstacle.

Success was not in question. Achilles had had programming extensions in mind for years, waiting for the opportunity to have access. Not from curiosity, for that was a foolish human trait. Not from the panicked reactivity that motivated most Citizen invention. From preparedness. He who would lead from behind must *prepare* to lead from behind.

"Do you have further questions, or are we finished?" Proteus asked.

We have only begun, Achilles thought. But he sang, simply, "Finished."

· 15 ·

Louis roamed the narrow, serpentine corridors of *Long Shot* looking for distraction because Hindmost refused to be rushed. Louis looked for weapons, too, not that, if it came to combat, one ship could prevail against whole fleets. *Long Shot*'s advantage was its speed.

"Hindmost's Voice," Louis called. "Review your orders."

"If any ship emerges from hyperspace nearer to us than a light-hour, initiate an immediate ten-light-day maneuver outward from the star through hyperspace. Repeat as needed until I detect no ship within a light-hour."

"Very good." Louis turned another corner, plunging deeper into the ship. Kzinti had held this ship for . . . he did not know how long. If only for a day, there would be *some* weapons aboard. Tunesmith would have added weapons, too.

Louis doubted he would recognize a protector's weapon design.

He squirmed through a narrow passageway into yet another equipment room. Except for some stepping discs and float plates Tunesmith must have stowed in the corner, photonics racks filled the space. To judge from the power converters and backup fuel cells, whatever this gear did drew a lot of power. Fat fiber-optic bundles ran between racks and out the hatch into the passageway he had just left. The ship was filled with rooms like this.

Much of it decoy equipment, he had come to realize. His first time aboard, long ago, not even the maze of access tunnels had existed. Louis imagined ARM engineers, and after them Kzinti, ferreting out sham apparatuses one laboriously traced photonic circuit at a time.

As mired in molasses as his thoughts seemed, a few insights remained from his brief time as a protector. Never the reasoning, but sometimes the conclusions.

He found an intercom control. "Hindmost?" No answer. "Hindmost!"

"What?" the answer finally came.

"The lifeboat Tunesmith had in his workspace. The lifeboat we stowed aboard this ship just before leaving the Ringworld. It was on *Long Shot* in the first place, wasn't it?"

"What do you mean?"

What *did* he mean? Tanj this dim-witted breeder brain!

Something glimpsed on the Ringworld, Louis thought. Something seen in the war room Tunesmith had improvised within the Ringworld Meteor Defense Room.

Or was it something *not* seen? Louis remembered the war-room display tagging a few ships with an icon to denote an indestructible General Products hull. This ship. Three ships that hung far back, remote from the Fringe War action. They, like *Long Shot,* had number four hulls. Puppeteer craft, he had thought then. Had he seen any smaller ships in a GP hull?

Louis said, "The lifeboat is built in a General Products #2 hull. The simplest explanation for such a lifeboat is that it was aboard the whole time."

"Tunesmith may have captured it," Hindmost said.

"While the Fringe War raged, while warships blasted holes in the Ringworld with antimatter, Tunesmith was clearing space aboard *Long Shot* to accommodate a ship a hundred meters long. I don't think so."

"Perhaps Patriarchy engineers installed the lifeboat."

"*Long Shot* is all but defenseless. If Kzinti had had the option, instead of a lifeboat we'd have found a hangar jammed with fighter ships or something just as lethal."

"Very well, Louis," Hindmost said. "You have me. A lifeboat was always aboard. When Nessus sought you out for the Ringworld expedition. Even when Beowulf Shaeffer took this ship to see the galactic core.

"The Type II drive was new and experimental. Suppose it had stopped working far from Hearth, far from Known Space, beyond hope of rescue by conventional hyperdrive, beyond hope of the Outsiders rendering assistance. *Then* directions would have been hyperwaved to the pilot how he might release the lifeboat and perhaps, over a very long time, hope to return home."

That answer Louis believed. "Thank you for not taking the lifeboat and abandoning me."

"I brought you to the Ringworld against your will. If I can, I will take you safely away. Certainly I owe you that.

"If I have satisfied your curiosity for a while, may I hope you will permit me to continue my observations?"

. . .

STARING OUT THE main bridge view port at the stars, Hindmost let his mind wander. Invisible to the naked eye but (courtesy of Voice) prominent in an augmented-reality view was the endless swirl and shift of the ships of the Fringe War.

There was another dance to be seen, if he was not more devoid than usual of reason. At least he thought he saw a dance. Whenever Louis, still bursting with energy from the autodoc, ranging all about the ship, managed to leave him in peace.

From time to time Hindmost drank from a bulb of water. About the time it registered that the bulb seemed bottomless, he realized it must have been replaced. By Louis, on any of his several returns to the bridge.

Hindmost activated the intercom. "Thank you, Louis."

"For what?"

"Indulging me. I am ready when you are."

Louis soon appeared in the hatchway to the bridge. "What, exactly, do you see out there?"

As much as see, I hear. I feel. But perhaps it is only wishful thinking. "We will do a test, and then I will explain."

Louis shrugged.

"Voice, run a correlation." Hindmost sang out the cadence he had found—or imagined—in the display. "Across the Fringe War, how many ships leap about following that cadence?"

"Hold on," Louis said. "How can it answer that?" Pause. "Hindmost's Voice, *can* you tell ships apart?"

"To an extent," Voice said. "The shadow-square sensors often catch the silhouettes of ships. By triangulation, I can determine distance, from which I calculate sizes. And I can distinguish hull compositions."

"Hull compositions," Louis repeated skeptically. "By spectral analyses?"

"Only rarely. In most cases the reflected light is too dim for that," Hindmost said. "But among our sensor upgrades is something new. It appears that hull surface subtly influences the normal-space bubble that protects a ship from hyperspace. Those hints about hull material get imprinted onto the ripples made when ships enter and leave normal space."

"That doesn't sound possible," Louis said.

"Hyperwave interacts with radio gear to perform hyperwave communications. These new sensors are little different, in principle."

"In principle." Louis laughed. "So we again have Tunesmith to thank."

Hindmost shivered. "I am glad to be rid of protectors."

"Back to identifying a particular ship for this correlation," Louis said. "Among the larger formations, there must be many ships of a given type."

"That is problematical," Voice agreed. "When similar ships set out together and part ways in hyperspace, I cannot know which vessel went where."

"Voice will tell us if he cannot do the correlation," Hindmost said. *As he will, because this may be the craziest idea I've had since . . . coming to the Ringworld.*

"I *have* done the correlation," Voice said. "While we spoke."

Hindmost hesitated to ask. Suppose a correlation did exist. Would he dare to act on it? Hope and intuition struggled with innate caution.

"And?" Louis prompted.

"I find a correlation," Voice said. "One ship."

Louis blinked. "How did you know?" he asked Hindmost. "What was that pattern?"

"It is from a favorite performance of the Grand Ballet on Hearth. From a day I shared with someone very important to me."

"Nessus?" Louis guessed.

"As you say." Hindmost shivered, for how could Nessus be *here*? He had left Nessus on New Terra, the world that had for so long been their home. "Of course many know that ballet."

"Is the dancing ship from the Fleet?" Louis asked.

"Doubtful," Voice said. "It does not have a General Products hull."

"You can be sure of that?"

"That it is not a General Products hull? That, Louis, I can say for certain. This one ship interacts with hyperwave quite differently from the obvious Fleet vessels."

"Anything more?" Hindmost asked.

"Possibly. With so many hyperdrive emergences in this region I am uncertain. I first noticed that particular hull material only a day ago."

"A new ship type," Louis said. "An appearance two months after the Ringworld disappeared. It sounds like some new player came to see what's happening here."

Hindmost's mind raced. After many years away, he could not know exactly where New Terra had traveled. Most likely, a New Terran ship could have reached here by now. It *could* be Nessus aboard that ship.

Assume for the moment that the new arrival had come from New Terra. Maybe, Hindmost thought, he could establish New Terran provenance another way. "Of what material is that new ship constructed?"

"I cannot tell," Voice answered. "Our instruments sense differences among hulls, but they have not been calibrated to identify specific materials from hyperwave interactions."

"And if we get a little closer? Perhaps, a light-hour?" Hindmost persisted. "Could you then remotely identify the hull material by spectral analysis?"

"Belay that," Louis said. "Hindmost, I don't understand. How does knowing the hull material tell you who is aboard?"

"Trust me that it might." *If* the hull is of a particular material. The explanation would tread too close to secrets long kept from Louis. "Voice. How close?"

"Not where the ship is now," Voice said. "Nearer the star, with brighter light, then yes."

"Does the music in your head say *where* that ship will go next?" Louis asked.

Hindmost considered. The endpoints of jumps had not caught his eye, only the timing. Was he missing a vital clue? But no: the ballet was performed on a stage, the dancers' graceful leaps circumscribed by gravity. The ship that he watched so hopefully darted about in three dimensions. "No. Only *when.*

"Keep watch on that ship," Hindmost added to the AI. "Tell me when it is near enough to the star for spectral analysis from a light-hour away, and when *Long Shot* could approach it with no other ship any closer."

"Approaching an unknown ship? That seems very brave of you," Louis said.

Hindmost turned both heads to stare. "There is no reason to be insulting."

. . .

HINDMOST HAD BEEN studying bridge displays for hours. His eyes ached. His thoughts grew fuzzy. He needed sleep.

He sang aloud the next several bars of the libretto that echoed in his brain, ordering Voice to watch for the mystery ship's next moves.

Louis wandered past the bridge yet again.

Hindmost closed his eyes but sleep refused to come. Fuzzy or not, his thoughts kept churning. Dancers. Ships. Leaps. Danger all around. Leaps. Partway home (well, Home, in any event), and back.

His eyes flew open. Louis had flown *Long Shot* much farther than he had allowed Voice to take it. "Voice, were internal instruments active during the hyperspace move toward Home?"

"They were."

"Bring up the data."

Displays lit on an arc running halfway around the bridge. Necks craning, Hindmost took it in, now and again reaching out to scroll deeper into the recordings. On other monitors, he reviewed data gleaned from studies of the Ringworld's disappearance.

Patterns in the data reminded him of something, but for the longest time he could not put his tongue on it. An odd coincidence, he decided. He had seen such patterns before.

Long ago he had tried to reverse engineer the planetary drives purchased from the Outsiders. It was a desperate undertaking, to be sure—moving worlds involved vast energies—but not quite as insane as getting overrun by the genocidal Pak. Instead of discovering how the planetary drive worked, he had succeeded only in learning the many ways in which it might destabilize—

And that the energies so unleashed could vaporize a world.

Of course, very different mechanisms sometimes shared a mathematical description, as with pendulums and electronic oscillators. *This* parallelism surely meant nothing. Still, sometimes having an analogy suggested new ways to approach a problem . . .

Sipping from a drink bulb, his exhaustion forgotten, he thought how, while in office, he had opposed—to the modest extent Ol't'ro tolerated opposition—the unending study of this ship. He thought how *his* newfound obsession with understanding the Type II drive would amuse Ol't'ro. He thought about—

He straightened on the uncomfortable crash couch. His eyes closed, this time in concentration. For all the Ministry's years of study, he had something they did not: protector-built instruments. And now he knew something they did not.

How to toggle the Type II drive to and from Type I speed.

The new hyperspace physics with which he dabbled remained incomplete, and yet—with Tunesmith's help—he had made more progress in days than Ol't'ro and the Ministry of Science together had in more than a century. Chords of triumph rose in his throats. Maybe he *could* barter for the Concordance's freedom. This was his greatest insight since—

Reality crashed down. His greatest accomplishment since discovering how to destroy General Products hulls from a distance, without antimatter.

Long Shot had been built well before hulls were redesigned against such attacks.

Louis squeezed onto the bridge. "Did I hear you say something?"

"I was talking to myself," Hindmost said. Because this time, I *will* understand the implications of my discoveries before I unleash them onto an unsuspecting galaxy.

· 16 ·

Dry land sweltered, mere air no obstacle to the fierce sunlight. Sessile life forms, in every color from far-red to a deep ultrablue that only instruments could detect, covered the undulating landscape. Motile creatures burrowed in the dirt, gamboled in the meadows, swam in the little ponds, and soared high into the boundless sky.

Unattainable, all of it.

Beyond the habitat was an entire existence Cd'o would never taste, a rich ecology that thrived on light instead of the bountiful chemical stew endlessly upwelling from oceanic trenches. Beyond the wall, not even a tubacle's-length distant, was a whole alien world. Somehow, she had to content herself with glimpsing that world through satellite imagery and in the bottomless archives of the Citizens.

Her ventral sphincter agape, she spread her thorax wide. When, bloated, she could draw in no more water, she let the orifice snap shut. Her tubacles curled behind her, she expelled the water in a convulsive, frustrated *whoosh* and jetted across the chamber.

Two more pulses sent her jetting from the observation room, on her way to the Commons. Nothing there and no one's company would change *anything*. Still,

for a short while, a batch of magnesium salts sometimes let her forget that she would live and die in this
prison.

And that she was warden as much as inmate.

As she coasted into the corridor, someone swam into
position behind her. "Your Wisdom."

Her servants/bodyguards/minders took shifts. Which
was this? From a tubacle still arched ventrally, Cd'o
looked. She found distinctive permanent textures hiding among the red and far-red patterns anxiously rippling across his integument. "Good day, Kg'o." Knowing
that in this one regard, her words would fail to elicit
obedience, she added, "There is no need to call me
that."

"Yes, your Wisdom."

Too soon they had crossed the pathetically small
habitat, to glide into the Commons. Cd'o saw all-too-
familiar figures inside. Scarcely five five-squared Gw'oth
lived on Nature Preserve Five. Some, spawned here,
thought of this metal can as home. Why wouldn't they?
The habitat was all they had ever known.

Many whom she found in Commons were Ol't'ro's
progeny. They were brilliant and gifted in the art of the
meld—and, from inbreeding, often deranged. Among
them two had become infirm. The detritus of old age
clogged their minds; in a meld, the noise of their petty,
inconsequential thoughts grew ever more intrusive.

And so, the newcomers.

Was rage vivid on her skin? As quickly as they recognized her, Gw'oth across the Commons backed away.
Conversations trailed off into respectful silence.

Respect was a sorry substitute for camaraderie.

But the Commons were not *quite* silent. The four
newcomers clustered together in a corner, staring at

her, whispering. From the accents, they were from Jm'ho, the home world. From the patterns rippling over them, they were at once scared, awed, and humbled.

As you were in their place, an elder's engram fragment reminded.

She jetted over. "Welcome. I am Cd'o."

Anxious far-reds deepened. "Thank you, your Wisdom." Timidly, the new arrivals introduced themselves.

"What can I tell you about your new home?" she asked. "Have you been shown around the habitat?"

"Tell us about . . . them," one said. "What are they like?"

About Ol't'ro. About their destiny. One way or another, all would serve.

When she did not answer, another of the new arrivals asked, "What are Citizens like?"

"Citizens are intriguing," Cd'o said. "Cowardly and ruthless. Smarter than any of us." Individually, that was. "Their culture is older by far than any on Jm'ho. You would do well to study them."

To truly understand Citizens, though, one had also to understand humans. Concordance leaders had a morbid fascination with humans. Much of that fixation came of guilt for the ancestral crime that had established New Terra, and fear of their former servants, and dread of the retribution "wild humans" would exact if they ever discovered New Terra and learned its dark secret. There was fascination with human curiosity—and an abiding horror of it, too.

And especially among the Experimentalist faction, Citizens were obsessed with human myths.

"Come with me," Cd'o directed. "I will show you around."

The tour was all too brief, mostly security measures and environmental systems. The "town" was sealed as tightly as any spaceship. Whatever entered, to the smallest drop of water—and the occasional "volunteer," like these—was quarantined and thoroughly screened.

You were a volunteer, she reminded herself.

And a fool, she answered.

Every few years, the ultimatum went out from Ol't'ro: send us four of your best. To be chosen is an honor. To join the meld, for the few who prove capable and worthy, is a rapture.

All lies.

She looked sadly at the latest to answer the call: you are sacrifices.

Having learned something of human myth, Cd'o had fancied herself as Theseus. She meant to slay the monster and end the demands of tribute. Only to be doomed by her aptitude for melding. Only to become the Minotaur . . .

We are equally the great King Minos, a ghostly remnant of the meld mocked. Part of the curse was never to be alone, even within her own thoughts. *Should you think to escape on wings of wax and feathers, we are also as close as you will ever come to being Daedalus.*

Cd'o brushed aside the intrusion, refocused on showing the newcomers the ways of the labyrinth. They had come to an auxiliary water lock, and she explained its sensors and redundant filtration systems. The habitat ringed the planetary drive: damage the planetary drive and a trillion Citizens died. Citizens were too smart and craven ever to risk a physical attack, but Ol't'ro could not rule out some subtle toxicological or biological attack. If every Gw'o in the colony were to be incapacitated simultaneously, and Citizens were then to force their way in, and to locate and disable the self-destruct before the fail-safe timer set it off . . .

Cd'o explained the precautions in detail. Despite the endless clamor of remnant melds, she was not ready to die.

"What is it like?" a newcomer asked.

"A meld?"

"Yes, your Wisdom."

On Jm'ho the newcomers had been a Gw'otesht-4. A computation unit, no more. They would know the mechanics of melding. They would have experienced the innocent sharing of mathematics. They could not begin to understand the majesty and misery and transcendence of a Gw'otesht-16 meld. No one could, until it had happened to them.

Until, as for her, it had been too late.

THE DAILY RESPITE ended all too soon.

Cd'o left the newcomers in the Commons and continued on her way. At the mouth of a long tunnel, her companion turned aside to loiter with other servants.

She swam down the long tunnel to the melding chamber. Friends/colleagues/alter egos waited inside, and more followed close behind her. They would be one soon enough and few bothered with greetings. The last to enter sealed the massive door.

Some eager, some dutiful, the sixteen sidled together. A tubacle, questing, engulfed one of Cd'o's own. Within the maw of her tubacle, the eye and heat receptor went dark. The ear fell deaf to all but the beating of two hearts: one speeding up, one slowing down, seeking unison.

The tubacle tip probing deep within hers found its neural receptacle.

A shock like electricity raced up her limb and a great hunger jolted her mind. Unimaginable insights tantalized. Profound truths beckoned, just beyond her grasp.

More! She needed more! Switching to ventral respiration, she reached out with other tubacles. She felt all around and felt other limbs in return. Tubacle found tubacle, aligned, conjoined . . .

Ganglia meshing!

Feedback surging!

Heart pounding!

Electricity coursing!

We will begin.

The command echoed and reechoed in Cd'o's mind. Her fears and doubts receded. Her thoughts—as fiercely as she fought to hold on to them—faded. Her sense of self all but vanished.

Ol't'ro, the group mind, had emerged.

"That's the way of it, Sigmund," Donald Norquist-Ng concluded.

"I urge you to reconsider, Minister." Sigmund held his voice flat, although the day had been a roller coaster (another metaphor that no one on New Terra would understand). Alice and Julia had done it! And fools like this would throw everything away.

Norquist-Ng frowned. "We are *not* going to rehash things. It was obvious in the situation room that you didn't accept my decision. I invited you to stay for one reason: as a courtesy. In your time, in your way, you worked hard for this world. I chose not to berate you in a roomful of people.

"In private, in my office, I will speak as plainly as is necessary. I had hoped that being direct would suffice, but not even direct works with you. Very well, I will be blunt. *Endurance* is coming home. That is my order, Sigmund. It is not open for discussion."

"But they've identified an ARM ship. It's been the dream for *so* long."

"*Your* dream, and I don't understand even that. You've lived on New Terra for more than two hundred years. There's nothing left on Earth for you."

"Tanj it, I agree with you. In part, anyway. I have no

interest in going back." Sigmund suppressed a shudder. "I have no interest in off-world travel of any kind. But this isn't about me, Minister. The people of this world—my children, and yours, too—deserve to know their history, to reconnect with their own kind. The independence generation would have given *anything* to—"

Norquist-Ng slapped his desk. "How convenient for your argument that the founders are all gone. I suppose I should take your word for it how they felt."

"Haven't you ever wondered about your roots?"

"What part of 'subject closed' confuses you? I've said no. The governor, whom I've briefed, says no. That roomful of people we just left—and whom you failed to sway—said no."

"Because they know you've made up your mind."

"Because it is too dangerous." Norquist-Ng sighed. "And in part I believe that for having listened to you. For years you warned about the Kzinti creatures. For years you said our scout ships had to be armed, lest we run into Kzinti or someone worse.

"Well, our people have found your Kzinti. *You* identified them as such. Kzinti and the Earth ships are blowing each other apart. I'll risk nothing that might bring such madness to New Terra."

"That's not the only risk." Could a ship be tracked through hyperspace? Not that Sigmund had ever heard. "The Ringworld drew all those warships practically into our backyard. However distant their home bases, three fleets are within fourteen light-years of us. If the Kzinti should spot New Terra, or those cone-ship people . . . then what? We need to contact the ARM, to ally with Earth, *before* that happens."

Silence.

Sigmund dared to hope he was making his point. "Of *course* our people should be discreet as they reach out to the ARM. They should use short digital messages, hard to trace. They should relay everything through comm buoys, so that no one can backtrack the hyperwave beam. There needn't be any contact but comm until we know more."

Norquist-Ng tipped back his chair, seeming to consider, then shook his head. "No. Engagement with other worlds always makes matters worse. We have the proof of that from *your* era in this chair, one wretched crisis after the next. My orders stand, Sigmund. *Endurance* will not contact anyone. And it's coming home as soon as they finish refueling.

"Challenge me again in public and that will be your last time inside this building."

SIGMUND PACED THE dusty, cluttered, memory-clogged confines of his den.

Alice's latest report had brought more than the news that low-level ARM encryption had been cracked. The crew had also spotted, on the far fringes of the scene, an Outsider ship departing. Not into hyperspace— although Outsiders had invented hyperdrive, they did not use it—but racing away at near-light speed.

The Outsiders, with *their* level of tech, would crack military codes faster than anyone. That they chose now to bug out meant something. What did they know that he didn't? His gut insisted that mayhem, at a deadlier intensity than ever, was about to break out near *Endurance*.

Tanj it!

Sigmund had spent his life imagining what "normal"

people found inconceivable. That was how one uncovered conspiracies. That was what had made him valuable as an ARM agent. That was how, time and again, he had saved New Terra.

It was time again to confront the inconceivable.

The minister was all but as timid as a Puppeteer. Did a person like that innocently get appointed to run the Ministry of Defense? Or were people high in the government *working* for the Puppeteers?

"I WASN'T EXPECTING to hear from you," Alice said. Certainly not one-on-one; after the fireworks of the last mass debrief, the bigger surprise was that Sigmund still had access to the Ministry's long-range hyperwave gear.

It was only comm delay, but Sigmund seemed to stare at her from the console.

"You know how it is," he finally answered.

She managed not to react. From long ago, the innocent phrase was code for *We need to speak in private.* She set her pocket comp on the comm-console shelf and activated what Sigmund called protocol gamma: sound suppression, bug suppression, and a holographic screen to stymie lip-readers.

"Countermeasures are active, Sigmund. Now what's this about?"

"The minister is not seeing reason."

Norquist-Ng could hardly eavesdrop on *her* end of the link, and Alice doubted Sigmund wanted her to undercut his own granddaughter. So they were keeping secrets from Nessus, still ensconced in front of the pilot's console. With the activation of the countermeasures, his irritating humming had faded into white noise.

Without the holo screen, could Nessus have read her lips? She didn't put it past him. But it had been Sigmund's idea to bring Nessus. Wheels within wheels . . .

She said, "And you suppose Nessus won't see reason, either."

"He always has—

"His own agenda," she completed. "I know." The Puppeteer might have been a valuable resource, but the Ringworld was gone. Nessus' priority would revert—had reverted—to keeping Earth ignorant of the Concordance's erstwhile slave colony.

"We don't dare *not* contact the ARM," Sigmund said. "Not with Kzinti fleets so near."

Until yesterday, everything she knew about the Kzinti she had heard from Sigmund. She hadn't doubted that hostile feline aliens existed, but that was no reason to obsess. It just hadn't seemed credible that the Kzinti could be as aggressive as he claimed—not after losing successive wars to humans—and she had taken his foreboding as the paranoia speaking.

No longer. Not after watching those lens-shaped ships in action . . .

"It's not our decision to make," she said, shivering.

"True, we lack the authority. On the basis of qualifications, don't you think the answer is different? Millions of lives are at stake."

The worst of it was, she agreed with Sigmund. That didn't give them the right to decide for everyone on New Terra.

Wait. How *had* he gotten access to a Ministry comm channel to plot sedition? "You're working with someone in the Ministry," she said. The notion made joining him in rebellion more palatable. Maybe.

"You could say that."

And maybe not. Knowing Sigmund, she guessed that someone wasn't cooperating by choice. Someone embezzling from the Ministry? Sloppy with classified information? Sigmund had always made it his business to know. He had never admitted, even to her, every trap and back door hidden in the Ministry's computer systems.

"Let's say I agree with you," Alice said. "What then?"

"Then you and Julia decide if you can safely reach out to the ARM." For a moment, the demented mastermind paranoid expression melted to simple human worry. "I stress, safely.

"If you succeed in making contact, the story for everyone here will be that an ARM ship reached out to you."

· 18 ·

Some elements of the current investigation were well established: Eleven-dimensional tensors for the quantum-gravitational-field model. The differential geometry that had proven itself useful, if only empirically, in past analyses of hyperspace. Multiverse matrix mechanics.

Ol't'ro lost themselves in the beauty of the mathematics.

But multiverse theory embraced an infinite number of possibilities. The equations had no known closed-form solution, and offered scant guidance which approximations might converge, even given the massively parallel, reconfigurable computers of the—

"Your Wisdom," a timid voice intruded into the sealed melding chamber.

Ol't'ro ignored the intercom, but the voice returned.

"Your Wisdom, it is time. You asked that I remind you."

Almost, they had a candidate partitioning onto the processor arrays of the latest set of equations. The granularity of the partitioning was coarser than they would have liked. If only they had another million processing nodes for the simulation—

"Your Wisdom," the servant tried again, plaintively, a bit louder.

The gathering on Hearth is at your demand, the Cd'o unit chided. And fainter, from an imprint of one long dead, *Doing science is not our main purpose on this world.*

"Your Wisdom, please. Before the meld, you were most insistent."

They had not insisted. Before the meld there could be no they. *Cd'o* had insisted.

Frustrated and distracted, the gestalt began to crumble. Like an underwater avalanche, slow and inexorable, the mathematical synthesis fell into ruin.

From deep within the communal mind came the image—from how long ago?—of rocks and mud cascading down the side of a seamount. When, Ol't'ro wondered, had they last experienced the sea? Many generations, and yet within their newest units the memories remained fresh. The ice-locked, world-spanning ocean of Jm'ho. The storm-tossed seas of Kl'mo, the colony they had—

Shaking off the reverie, Ol't'ro spoke through the microphone positioned deep within a unit's tubacle. "Thank you," they told the anxious servant. "That will be all."

Binding a Proteus fragment to the meld, linking to the Hindmost's council chamber a world away, they opened the eyes of Chiron.

"THESE ARE WORRISOME times," this most recent Hindmost sang, directing a furtive, entreating glance at his master. "Without the Ringworld to fight over, at any time three alien fleets may turn our way. We have pre-empted additional resources to strengthen our defenses. As that effort progresses, we may find we need to divert yet more resources."

"And I agreed," Ol't'ro, through Chiron, sang. To extend Proteus would be an intriguing experiment. "Nonetheless, our own research is important. It—"

"Worrisome times," Selene repeated. He was new, his predecessor as Minister of Industrial Production lost to catatonic collapse at the previous cabinet meeting.

From the indifferently brushed nature of Selene's mane, Ol't'ro did not expect this one to last, either. They ignored the interruption. "My research could lead to a new defensive weapon."

Silence greeted this justification: the harmony of discord. Everyone waited for someone else to object aloud. The Ministry of Science had many open-ended projects, often claiming defensive improvements—eventually—as the justification.

We could destroy their worlds, an angry chorus welled up in Ol't'ro's thoughts. The mind traces of many departed units, a Gw'otesht within a Gw'otesht. And *Do they not also remember our successes?*

For alien ships were already all around the Fleet, had been for years, yet everyone on these worlds remained safe. *Ol't'ro*'s efforts kept the alien visitors well behaved. The all-but-reactionless drives *they* had devised—the closest anyone, anywhere, had come to duplicating the Outsider reactionless drive technology—propelled the thousands of defensive drones that held alien ships at bay.

Self-congratulation accomplishes nothing, scolded an ancient engram, the faint echo of a unit long departed.

As faint as were those thoughts, and as impertinent, the unit made sense.

"Chiron?" the Hindmost sang. "Have you taken into account this matter of priorities?"

The insolent unit: *If the Fleet should fall, what then of your research?*

Ol't'ro considered:

That the least of their interests was how the Concordance managed its affairs, as long as Citizens stayed far from the Gw'oth worlds.

That as politicians went, Citizen or Gw'oth, Horatius was stolidly reliable.

That by a show of deference to Horatius, should they choose to offer one, they would strengthen him as Hindmost.

That Cd'o's wanderlust was illogical. Suppose they were so rash as to expose one of themselves as a potential hostage. Sealed into an environmental suit, immobile without a motorized exoskeleton, *still* restricted to viewing the outer world through sensors . . . Cd'o might as well remain within the habitat.

That to go from the water-filled habitat into the crush of gravity would be peculiar.

And intriguing, too.

That it was interesting to speculate how expanded computing resources would affect Proteus, and that diverting resources to the AI's extension would answer that question sooner.

At the cost of further emboldening Achilles, whose reticence to enhancing Proteus was so blatantly contrived.

That if alien armadas, having chased away the Ringworld, should set out today, standard hyperdrive could not deliver them to the Fleet of Worlds any sooner than a hundred days. There would be more than ample time to enhance Proteus.

That if the alien fleets had had Type II hyperdrives, the situation would be different. But the Type II hyperdrive was a conundrum, a cosmic joke, an unending frustration.

That they half hoped the reports from the Fleet's observers were correct: that the *Long Shot* had vanished with the Ringworld, never again to confound them.

That if alien navies did come to the Fleet of Worlds, their unwelcome attention would be drawn ever farther from the Gw'oth worlds.

That logic aside, a part of them, too, hungered to see new vistas. That a cacophony of engrams, echoes from deep into their past, remembered leading much different lives.

That Cd'o's unhappiness was not the matter at hand. Exploration was not even foremost at this instant among that unit's thoughts.

That whether or not to redirect resources was trivial, yet they vacillated and hesitated because trivia muddled their thoughts. Sooner rather than later, they must reinvigorate themselves. Some units would pass into memory, but they had candidates to join the meld.

That adapting the troublesome multiverse simulation onto the present, limited set of processors would be a useful test of the candidates' potential contributions to the meld.

That they were *old*.

That they wanted this meeting ended, to turn their attention to more appealing topics.

Through Chiron, Ol't'ro sang, "For now, Hindmost, I withdraw my suggestion. We should continue to enhance Proteus."

Tanya poked at whatever it was she had been served for dinner. She didn't remember having eaten any. From her distracted stirring, the food had begun to look used.

She had never seen *Puma*, never been aboard, never, to her knowledge, met any of the corvette's crew, but in her mind's eye that ship differed little from *Koala*. Too many sailors crammed into too little space. An endless background droning, from the clipped commands and acknowledgments on the bridge, to tense speculations in the public spaces, to stress-relieving high jinks in quarters. A place full of life.

No more.

Puma had transformed in an instant into a gamma-ray burst and a quickly dissipated debris field. Antimatter explosions didn't leave much behind.

Tanjed ratcats.

Seething rage had squelched the usual boisterousness of the junior officers' mess. She set down her fork and shoved away her tray.

"Not hungry, Lieutenant Wu?"

Junior officers shot to their feet. Tanya said, "Commander, I didn't see you—"

"At ease," Commander Johansson ordered from the

open hatchway. "Lieutenant, would you mind coming with me?"

"Yes, sir."

They walked forward. Something in Johansson's stiff gait told her not to bother asking what this was about.

They came to the last place she would have expected: the captain's cabin. "Enter," came a gruff answer to Johansson's knock.

Dad looked grim. Lieutenant Commander Ovando, the chief communications officer, looked puzzled. With Tanya and Johansson squeezed in, the cabin was packed. Dad waved off her salute.

"Show her," Dad said.

"Yes, Captain." Ovando handed Tanya a pocket comp.

The screen displayed her inbox. Ten messages had come in since she'd last checked mail—but the most recent, a ship-to-ship, had been read. An icon showed it had come wrapped in standard fleet encryption. The subject line read *Personal and Confidential.*

Who said stuff like that? Who was Alice Jordan?

"This came by hyperwave a few minutes ago," Ovando said. "A routine security audit flagged it."

"I don't recognize the name," Tanya said.

"I'm not surprised," Johansson answered. "No one by that name is serving in the ARM, and I don't mean only the expeditionary force. Not anywhere."

"Shall I open it?" Tanya asked.

"Go ahead, Lieutenant," Dad said.

Tanya tapped the screen and scanned the header that popped open. It indicated standard ARM comm protocol and fleet encryption, and that the message had ping-ponged its way to *Koala* through a half-dozen hyperwave relays.

The stated origin of the message was a vessel called *Endurance*. Ships had carried that name back to the days of sail, but she didn't recall any ship named *Endurance* deployed to the Ringworld theater of operations.

With a finger swipe Tanya scrolled down to the message body. "Finagle," she said wonderingly.

"Exactly right," Dad said.

"I've done database searches," Ovando said. "A colony ramscoop named *Long Pass* did vanish—almost seven hundred years ago. A goldskin named Alice Jordan disappeared from Sol system a few decades later."

"Goldskin?" Tanya asked.

"Belter police of that era wore yellow spacesuits," Ovando explained.

"You mean this message could be *real*?" Johansson said. "That's unbelievable."

"No," Tanya said. "What's unbelievable is that a long-lost colony and a woman who should be long dead contacted *me*."

SOONER THAN ALICE had dared to hope, the comm console pinged. Telltales indicated a hyperwave link and ARM encryption.

"We're getting video feed," Jeeves announced. "Not an animation, as best I can judge."

Tucking a loose strand of hair behind an ear, Alice looked at Julia. "We're agreed?"

"Go," Julia said. To Nessus, still at the pilot's console, she added, "Your objections are noted. And if you can't stop that infernal humming, get off the bridge."

"No humming," Nessus promised. He began tapping out a rhythm with a forehoof.

Alice angled and zoomed the camera to show only herself, then tapped ACCEPT.

A young woman appeared. Her trim blue jumpsuit had the look of a uniform, its insignia unfamiliar. She had long, straight, black hair, worn pulled back, and her skin was golden. The slight slant to her eyes made their icy blueness all the more startling. Nothing showed behind her but bare metallic bulkheads.

"This is *Endurance*," Alice said. "My name is Alice Jordan."

"Hello, Alice," the woman said. She frowned in concentration, as though struggling with Alice's archaic speech. "I'm Tanya Wu. You messaged me?"

Interworld sounded as awkward to Alice. "I did, Tanya. Thank you for responding."

A burst of typing came from Alice's left, and text appeared on her contact lenses. It was Julia asking: *Is she an ARM?*

Tanya said, "Your message speaks of a lost human colony, New Terra. Where is it?"

In Alice's peripheral vision, Nessus tore at his mane. She said, "It's a dangerous galaxy, Tanya. I would rather not broadcast that information."

Tanya frowned. "We're talking by hyperwave, and I presume you reached this system by hyperdrive. You've obviously had dealings with the Outsiders, so why not ask them how to get home?"

Because, in a long-ago, three-way barter, the Outsiders had committed to the Puppeteers never to help the New Terrans get home. New Terra's history was too tanjed convoluted for anyone to swallow in one serving. And that left telling lies.

For years Alice had spurned Sigmund's efforts to contact her. Here and now she needed the devious insights of his twisted, brilliant mind—and she couldn't reach him. The Ministry of Defense said he was unavailable.

The best lies are the simplest, she decided. "We can't afford the answer."

"And Outsiders don't haggle," Tanya acknowledged as her eyes darted about. Reading cues off her own lenses? "You messaged an ARM ship. Why be coy now?"

"I'm being cautious, not coy. We would like to reconnect without drawing the attention of uninvited parties."

"That's understandable." More darting of Tanya's eyes. "How does it happen that *Endurance* shows up in this region of space at this time?"

"A big hyperspace ripple," Alice said. "We came to check that out and found more than we expected."

"I'll bet." Tanya pursed her lips. "How is it you knew ARM encryption?"

"We didn't. We *cracked* the encryption. That only worked because the plaintext recognizably derived from English."

"Still, it's military-grade crypto. I guess you mastered a few tricks in your isolated little colony."

"A few."

"Such as impersonating humans?" Tanya gibed.

"I'm as human as you," Alice snapped back. "I grant I can't prove it over a comm link."

"And seven hundred years old? Really?"

"Bringing us back to tricks we've learned." The lie was again simpler and more credible than the truth.

Tanya's eyes darted about once more. "How do you see this encounter playing out?"

"We propose to jump *Endurance* into an ARM formation."

"I don't recommend that. We'll blow up any unfamiliar ship that tries."

We're *not* Kzinti, Alice thought. But she and *Long Pass* alike had left Sol system before Kzinti first burst onto the scene. How would she explain knowing about Kzinti? Was she caught already in a web of her own lies?

Text, this time from Nessus, flowed across Alice's lenses: *Time to move. Safety first.* His forehoof ceased tapping a rhythm to begin clawing at the deck.

Alice shook her head marginally: no. She considered swinging the camera to reveal Nessus—only that would beg the question why New Terra didn't ask their Puppeteer friend for the way home. Finagle! *She* would not have believed the story she was spinning.

Alice said, "Then give me coordinates for Earth, or to *any* human-settled world."

"It's a dangerous galaxy, as you said." Tanya laughed mirthlessly. "If a ship of strangers doesn't know the way, I'm not about to tell them."

Julia typed: *Plan B.*

Alice nodded. "Tanya, I understand. How about a one-on-one meeting? *Endurance* and your ship. You set the coordinates."

"And a swarm of ships swoops down on us the moment we appear."

For all Tanya knew, this *could* be an elaborate trap. Alice wanted to cry, to scream, to break things. Had they traveled so far, had they come so close, only to fail? It was tragic.

"I have a question," Tanya said. "Why me? Why in particular did you contact me?"

Tanya Wu was a name recovered from the message stream, because she texted a lot. Alice might as well have contacted the friend, Elena.

"Simple coincidence, most likely," Alice said. "Wu was a common name the last time I visited Earth. Still, long after, I met a man named Louis Gridley Wu. You wouldn't happen to know him?"

Tanya blinked. "My great-grandfather. In a way he's why I'm here. He discovered the Ringworld." More eye darting. "I'll be right back, Alice."

The video froze.

"We're overdue to jump," Nessus said.

"Not yet," Julia ordered.

As Alice was beginning to doubt they would ever hear back, the image flashed. An older man with a pencil-thin mustache had taken Tanya's place. "I am Captain Wesley Wu. My grandfather was a wanderer and an incorrigible storyteller. Agent Jordan, see if you can convince me that you knew him.

"And if you manage that, you can explain why Grandpa didn't tell you the way home."

· 20 ·

"They missed a jump!" Hindmost said in alarm.

Louis yawned. He hadn't slept since emerging from the 'doc more than a day earlier. "Who? The ship you believe has Nessus aboard? That its maneuvers remind you of a ballet could be a coincidence." Or, more likely, wishful thinking.

"I do not believe that," Hindmost's Voice offered. "Too many jumps have matched the cadence Hindmost remembers."

"But you still see the ship?" Louis asked.

"Yes," Hindmost said.

Louis yawned again. "If Nessus is aboard, he can't pilot nonstop. Maybe he's getting some sleep."

"Perhaps." Hindmost plucked at his mane. "That his shipmates do not follow the rhythm suggests they are not a party to his signaling."

"Or maybe Nessus is alone on that ship," Louis countered.

"The ship just took a short jump," Hindmost's Voice announced. "It emerged as near as I have seen it to the star."

Scanning the tactical display, Louis saw nothing close to what might be Nessus' ship. Louis said, "Hindmost's Voice, how long will it take to gather data for a spectral analysis?"

"No more than five seconds."

"What are you . . . ?" The question trailed off into an anxious, two-throated bleat as the view port flashed to static.

Seconds later, Louis dropped *Long Shot* back to normal space. "Start recording. Tell me when you're—"

"I have the data," Hindmost's Voice said.

Louis jumped *Long Shot* to hyperspace, emerging four light-hours from where they had been. He turned to Hindmost. "Weren't you tired of waiting?"

"Very well." With a shudder, Hindmost straightened. "Voice, did you identify the hull material?"

"It is *twing.*"

"What's *twing*?" Louis asked.

"It is—"

With a short, sharp trill, Hindmost silenced the AI. "Louis, it is almost certain that ship was built on the world where I last saw Nessus."

What about a hull material is so secret? Louis wondered. "That's good, I assume."

"It is encouraging." Hindmost stared into the tactical display, crooning to himself.

"What aren't you telling me?" Why aren't you hailing that ship?

Hindmost said, "That world is called New Terra. Most who live there are humans."

"Why haven't I heard of it?" Louis asked.

"It lies far outside Known Space." Hindmost turned one head toward Louis. "But you are correct. The time has come to contact that ship. Will you make the call?

Lest I am mistaken about Nessus being aboard, I prefer not to reveal myself just yet."

"Easier said than done. I don't expect Kzinti comm software to know New Terran protocols." Because if the Kzinti knew of an isolated human colony, that would not be the sort of place Hindmost would have stashed his family.

"I know New Terran protocols," Hindmost's Voice said. "Shall I make the call?"

"Louis," Hindmost said, "do not disclose your true name."

Louis shook his head. "I've never heard of this world, and I'm supposed to use an alias? Explain."

"It is complicated. Please, Louis, we cannot know how long that ship will remain in the area. That it no longer signals in the form of the ballet may denote its imminent departure."

"But you *will* explain," Louis said.

"If need be, but it is more Nessus' place to explain. Let us both hope he is aboard."

Louis rubbed his nose, intrigued. "Do New Terrans speak Interworld?"

"They speak a dialect of a precursor language called English. Voice can translate."

"All right," Louis decided. "Whenever you're ready."

Hindmost retreated to the adjacent tiny rec room, abandoning the equally tiny bridge to Louis. "Voice, hail the New Terran ship."

"Done, Hindmost."

They waited. After a minute a light began flashing on the comm console. Louis accepted, and a holo opened. He didn't recognize the person who answered, a young woman, but he hadn't expected to.

"*Endurance*," she said. "Who is this?"

"Nathan Graynor," Louis improvised. The name had just popped into his head. "May I speak with—"

"Hold on. You're not . . . at home. There's no comm delay. Where are you?"

"On a ship, of course. Look, I don't have all day. May I speak with Nessus?"

"He's in his cabin, asleep. I'll take a message."

Nessus *was* there. Why didn't Hindmost stick a head through the door with some guidance? Louis kept improvising. "Actually, Miss, I'd—"

"Captain."

"Sorry. Captain, I need to deliver this message in person."

"I'll get him up." She reached toward her console.

"There is no need." With a clatter of hooves, a Puppeteer cantered onto the bridge. His hide was off-white with scattered tan spots, and his dark brown mane was unkempt. His eyes didn't match: one was red and the other yellow. "Louis!"

"Nessus!" Louis greeted back. "You look well."

"Two heads *are* better than one." Nessus trembled. "I should have guessed I would find you here. And is . . . is . . ."

The captain had stiffened at the mention of Louis's true name. She interrupted Nessus' nervous stammer. "You introduced yourself as Nathan Graynor."

"One and the same," Nessus assured her. "I am surprised you remember, Louis."

Remember what? Louis wondered. *And we met at my two hundredth futzy birthday, and now I look maybe twenty. How did he recognize me so quickly? And why doesn't Hindmost come in and show himself?*

For the last question, at least, Louis had a guess:

Hindmost chose to reunite in person. "You're right, Nessus. I have company aboard."

"We should rendezvous, Julia," Nessus said. "These are old friends."

The New Terran vessel, like most ships in the area, had no normal-space velocity worth mentioning. "We'll need time to match velocities," Louis said. "We're doing about point eight light speed."

Julia took a while making up her mind. "What's your location, Louis?"

Hindmost didn't object so Louis transmitted *Long Shot*'s coordinates. The AI knew the New Terran navigational conventions, too. "What about matching our velocities, Captain?"

"Be right back," Julia said. The holo froze.

Hindmost's Voice reported, "They've gone to hyperspace. We've lost comm."

"How far are, were, they from us?" Louis asked.

"A few seconds by standard hyperdrive." Pause. "They are here."

The holo unfroze and Julia said, "Matching course and speed . . . now."

A small ship hung, immobile, in *Long Shot*'s main view port.

Outsider ships could start and stop in an instant, and Louis had seen a Puppeteer ship match speeds with the Fleet in about an hour. Before Hindmost had shanghaied Louis, he had never heard of a human world with similar technology.

The New Terrans—whoever they were—looked more and more interesting.

21

Louis stepped from *Long Shot* to *Endurance*—into a skinny, cylindrical, clear-walled isolation booth. The entire booth floor was a stepping disc, and another disc sat on the deck just outside.

Stepping discs had tiny control switches inset on their rims, but the tiny booth left him nowhere to stand but on the disc. He could not get at its controls, even if he had known the address of the other disc.

"Déjà vu, Louis?" Nessus asked.

Huh? Louis sensed more to the odd greeting than meeting each other after many years. He rapped on the booth wall. "I've had friendlier welcomes."

"Blame me." With some kind of a handgun dangling from her belt, Julia emerged from a dim corner of the cargo hold. "The eyeball check was a final precaution. Nessus, you may extricate our guest."

Eyeball check? Precursor language or not, Louis thought he might have to link in Hindmost's Voice to translate to and from English. *Blame me* was plain enough, though. He waited to be let out.

In Nessus' sash, some gadget made a pocket bulge. Nessus plunged a head into the pocket—

And Louis found himself standing outside the booth. He and Hindmost had scattered stepping discs around the Ringworld and across *Long Shot,* and Hindmost had never mentioned that the discs could be controlled from a distance. Somehow it didn't surprise Louis that the Puppeteer had kept a trick in reserve.

"Welcome aboard, Louis. I'm Julia Byerley-Mancini, captain of this ship. If half what I've heard is true, you have some interesting stories to tell."

"And I won't mind telling them," Louis said. "Nessus. Someone is waiting for you aboard *Long Shot.* Someone with whom you shared a special night at the ballet."

"It has been a long time." Nessus shivered. "I need a moment to compose myself."

"Go when you're ready," Julia said.

"I'd like to see your ship," Louis said.

"Let's see Nessus off first."

She *wants* Nessus to leave, Louis realized. What else was going on?

With a tremulous and somehow eager glissando, Nessus stepped onto the disc and disappeared.

"How about that tour?" Louis asked.

"Soon." Julia eyed him appraisingly. "You could pilot this ship to Earth, couldn't you? Or tell me where to find it."

"No problem. Earth is about two hundred light-years from here, mostly to galactic south. Based on Earth years, that is. I'll show you on a star chart."

Beaming, she said, "Then this mission has been a brilliant success."

"And I wouldn't mind seeing your world. I've been called something of a tourist."

"New Terra will be our next stop. I sense Nessus won't be coming back with us."

"My guess is he won't." Begging the question: would he go with Julia to this new world? Louis had been looking forward to exploring the Fleet. Free will could be a terrible thing.

"Louis, there's someone aboard waiting to see *you*."

"That doesn't seem possible," he said.

"Nevertheless." Julia turned toward the door. "Wait here, please."

Through the door Julia left ajar, Louis heard two indistinct voices. Two women's voices. Who could he know here?

The door swung open and a tall, white-haired woman entered. Did New Terra not have boosterspice? Maybe she wasn't the oldest person Louis had ever seen, but she *looked* the oldest. She had a quiet, mature grace about her.

She shuffled toward him, hope and confusion—and anger?—flickering in her eyes. "It *is* you. Louis, it's been more than a century and you haven't changed a bit."

"I'm sorry, ma'am. I'm afraid I don't know—"

She caught him across the jaw with a right hook. "You no-good bastard."

NESSUS STEPPED INTO a narrow corridor. "Hello?" he called. His voices echoed a bit.

"Here." A mere chord of welcome, but laden with undertunes.

Nessus edged toward the voices. He remembered them well, but after so long apart, how could he *know*?

By being together. That's how.

He rounded a corner into a small room. And standing there—

"Nessus. I had dared to hope it was you on that ship."

Years of worry melted away. Nessus bounded forward joyfully, chanting, "Baedeker. Baedeker."

LOUIS LET HIMSELF be escorted to *Endurance*'s compact relax room. Alice insisted they knew each other and glowered at his denials.

He synthed brandy for himself. "Can I get you something?"

"Coffee." She smiled sadly. "I don't suppose you remember how I take it."

"Sorry." He'd said that a lot since meeting her.

"A dash of milk, no sugar." She sat at the small table, looking lost in thought, till he handed her a drink bulb. "Our last evening together was dinner at our favorite restaurant."

"On New Terra?"

"Of course, New Terra. You made a terrible scene, blaming Sigmund for ruining your family's life."

Nothing like that had happened to Louis, nor did he know anyone named Sigmund, but he had stopped denying things because Alice refused to listen. She was old and her memories confused.

Even so, she packed a mean punch.

"The horrible, ironic thing, Louis? That scene was a sham, something you and Sigmund and I cooked up. But after the charade had served its purpose and we should have been together . . ."

"Yes?"

"You left. You abandoned your own unborn son. Alex was a great kid, and you missed him growing up. He is a good man. You would have been proud of him."

"I'm sorry," he told her yet again. "I've never been to New Terra."

"Yes, you have. Not only that, you have grandchildren and *great*-grandchildren there."

"I wouldn't have left," he said, stubbornly.

"You *did* leave. Sigmund curse him Ausfaller convinced you that leaving was for my own good. For my safety. I was off-world, and you didn't even wait for me to get home. I had a right to take part in the decision, damn you, or to go with you. By the time . . ."

Alice was less a woman scorned than an Amazon pissed off. To have such fire now, she must have been a force of nature in her prime. This was not someone he would forget, tanj it!

The problem was, *she* didn't seem the type to hallucinate imaginary lovers.

What did he have to unlock this puzzle?

Ausfaller. The name had a familiar ring to it, like the alias Louis had given himself. From Nessus' reaction, Nathan Graynor wasn't a random name plucked from the air. "Nessus was involved, too?"

"Yes! He brought you to New Terra in the first place. Then he spirited you away."

Louis took a long swig of his brandy. Nessus had appeared from nowhere on Louis's two hundredth birthday to recruit him for the first Ringworld expedition. Nessus had had his reasons—none of which had ever rung true.

Not an hour earlier, Hindmost had urged Louis to use an alias. When Louis had asked why, Hindmost had said to ask Nessus.

Maybe Alice wasn't the one with a memory problem. Louis drained his brandy. "I'll be having a long talk with Nessus."

. . .

NESSUS LOST HIMSELF in joy and union as profound as two Citizens can know without a Bride. He and Baedeker huddled together for a while after, necks twined, in intimate silence.

"How are the children," Baedeker finally asked.

"Well." Nessus edged closer. "Children no longer, of course. Happy on New Terra."

"I never meant to be gone for so long."

A sad melody. A heartfelt melody. And like so many Nessus had sung, an evasive melody? *Long Shot* had not been accelerated to the Fleet's velocity because his mate planned a return to New Terra. Some terrible duty must yet remain.

His dread came crashing down. "The New Terrans will soon reconnect with their roots. Either my ship-mates will make contact here with the ARM, or Louis will reveal the way to Human Space." He sang softly, "I fear disaster must follow."

"All that can wait," Baedeker sang, "if only because we cannot change it."

Baedeker's pocket comp trilled insistently. They ignored it. Nessus' pocket comp rang, and they ignored it, too.

"I have an urgent hail from Louis, aboard *Endurance*," Voice announced.

"It can wait," Nessus sang. "Tell Louis we will call back."

They were on the fastest ship in the galaxy. They could run away and know peace at last. Only neither of them was built that way.

"We must speak with Louis," Nessus sang.

Baedeker bobbed heads in agreement. "We owe Louis. More than he knows."

"We will have to explain . . . did you hear something?"

Footsteps. Louis stuck his head into the room. His face was flushed. "I want to know my past. *All* of it. Now. Start with Alice Jordan."

Nessus untwined his necks from Baedeker's, and they stood. "And you will. I will tell you whatever you wish to know. But perhaps . . ."

"No *perhaps*. Start by explaining why I don't remember Alice or New Terra."

"Do you still have the Carlos Wu autodoc?" Nessus asked Baedeker.

"It is aboard," Baedeker said.

"What does the autodoc have to do with this?" Louis asked.

Nessus stood tall, his hooves set far apart, summoning a confidence he did not feel. He might as well be unready to run: he and Baedeker were cornered. "Your surmise is true, Louis. I brought you to New Terra long ago. Your memories of that visit, and much more, are recorded in that autodoc. If *I* had not been in an autodoc on our return from the Ringworld, I would have offered you your memories then.

"You will come out of the autodoc remembering everything. You *will* find you agreed that those memories be edited."

The color had drained from Louis's face. With fists clenched, he studied Baedeker. "In all our years on the Ringworld, you never spoke a word of this."

Baedeker said, "I knew of your past visit—to New Terra and the Fleet, too. I knew those memories had been removed. I did *not* know the recordings were with us the entire time." With a sad glance at Nessus, he added, "We have too many secrets, even from each other."

"But no longer," Nessus said.

"No longer," Baedeker agreed.

Finally, Louis spoke. "Whenever you're ready, Nessus."

REJECTION

Earth Date: 2893

22

Would the ARM ship ever get back in touch? Julia, finally, had to sleep. She had no sooner reached her cabin than Jeeves announced, "*Koala* is hailing us."

"Respond 'message received' and that we'll be online soon."

"Will do. Shall I awaken Alice?"

"Yes. Have her meet me with coffee." Julia strode onto the bridge. "Jeeves, until I direct otherwise, you and I will communicate only by text. Now open the link." A holo popped up, showing Wesley Wu. "Captain Wu. I am Captain Julia Byerley-Mancini. Alice Jordan will join us shortly."

"Good to meet you, Captain." He looked as weary as she felt. "I have news."

"Go ahead," she said.

"I've gotten the go-ahead for a rendezvous. It will be just my ship, lest I am mistaken in trusting you. Let's see what velocity mismatch we have to contend with. Here is our vector."

A string of text appeared at the bottom of the holo.

Jeeves understood kilometers per second—if, over centuries, the meanings of kilometer and second had not diverged—but not the reference axes for *Koala*'s heading. Louis might have known, but he remained incommunicado aboard *Long Shot*. Until he reappeared, she didn't have to decide if or how to mention the reappearance of Captain Wu's grandfather, or that Louis looked younger than Wesley Wu's daughter.

Julia wondered, fleetingly, how *her* grandfather was doing.

Comparing ship's clocks, she and Wesley Wu confirmed that they agreed on the duration of a second. Comparing the number of kilometers in a light-second, they found they agreed about the length of a kilometer, too.

Wu sent a cartoon: an arrow and its bearings on several pulsars. "That's our heading and we're doing about a thousand klicks per second."

Here it is in our coordinates, Jeeves wrote.

Alice walked onto the bridge and stood behind Julia's crash couch. "It's good to see you again, Captain Wu," Alice said.

"Ms. Jordan," Wu said. "We are discussing how best to get together."

Louis had worried about velocity matching before Julia brought *Endurance* alongside *Long Shot*. Now another Wu raised the same issue. Whether courtesy of Puppeteer science or the Pak Library, maybe New Terra had things to offer their home world.

Thinking again of her grandfather, Julia lied, "We're making about the same speed, but pretty much at right angles to your heading." With a burst of typing, she passed fake course and speed data to Jeeves. "Sending that data . . . now."

Alice offered Julia a drink bulb. When Julia took the coffee, Alice's hand lingered on Julia's shoulder. Julia chose to take the gesture as support for her deception.

"I propose that we meet here in an hour," Captain

Wu said. A new cartoon indicated a location a few light-hours from *Endurance*'s present location. "Keep your present normal-space velocity and we'll match course and speed with you."

"Agreed," Julia said. It would be easy enough to change velocity to what she had told him.

"Wu out." The holo disappeared.

"For what it's worth," Alice said, "I think you made a smart call. There's no reason to reveal our ship can outmaneuver theirs. They distrust us enough already."

"Thanks." Julia took a long swallow from her coffee bulb. "Jeeves, tell *Long Shot* we're going on an errand and radio silent, but that we'll get back in touch."

TANYA JETTED ALONE through frigid darkness, *Koala* shrinking behind her faster than her target grew. She was more than a kilometer from *anything*, and every twitch of the telltales in her HUD screamed "cosmic rays." The local sun was scarcely a spark.

For an instant, purser duties had their charms.

After one look at *Endurance*, Dad had declined the offer to dock. "That's a GP #2 hull," he had growled. All that kept him from jumping back to hyperspace was that the ship at the rendezvous point reflected light differently than did a GP hull. It didn't reflect like *anything* anyone on the bridge had ever encountered, or anything in Hawking's databases.

Tanya saw the resemblance, too. She'd seen plenty of General Products-built ships during her posting to the Fleet of Worlds. Precious few humans, though: only her fellow ARMs, a few would-be traders, and the diplomats in the United Nations embassy on Nature Preserve Three.

So yes: the ship at the rendezvous point *did* resemble a GP #2 hull. Was a long, thin cylinder so unlikely?

"There's one way we'll find out," Tanya had declared. *She,* specifically, had been invited aboard *Endurance* and had volunteered to go—knowing she had left Dad with no choice. To send anyone else or abort the contact now would look like he was protecting her. He had answered, only, "Stay in touch, Lieutenant."

Midpoint in ten seconds, flashed on her HUD. A counter began decrementing to remind her when to begin braking.

With her visor at max magnification, she spotted someone in the open air lock of the still-distant *Endurance*. A biped, certainly, if not from this distance definitively human.

Tanya brought herself to a halt a half meter from *Endurance,* then holstered her gas pistol. Alice, wearing a simple jumpsuit, stood watching. Tanya reached through the pressure curtain, grabbed a handhold, and pulled herself aboard. The outer hatch began to close.

"Welcome to *Endurance*." Alice pointed to a row of lockers. "You can stow your gear here."

In bare feet Tanya stood 190 centimeters tall. Alice, even stooped, was taller—like every Belter Tanya had ever met. Of course, people were tall on low-grav worlds like Wunderland, too. Alice's height proved nothing.

As Tanya removed her helmet, text began flowing across her contact lenses. *We have audio and visual.* She twitched a finger twice to acknowledge, her gesture sensed by an implanted accelerometer. "I'm pleased to meet you, Alice."

Once Tanya's pressure suit was stowed, Alice asked,

"Would you and everyone watching like to see the ship?"

They're good, Tanya read, and had to agree. Her spy gear used microburst transmissions and top-secret crypto, not the simple—and known to be compromised— algorithms that sufficed for routine ship-to-ship chatter.

"It's only medical telemetry," she lied. "Standard protocol."

Alice smiled knowingly.

Tanya said, "And yes, I would appreciate a tour."

"Very good. We'll start aft, in the engine room."

Despite unending texted questions and prompts to turn her head this way and that, Tanya managed not to trip over her feet as she followed Alice. *Endurance* seemed like a ship configured by and for humans. In the relax room, randomly checking the synthesizer menu, Tanya recognized many options. The coffee it synthed tasted no worse than what she drank on *Koala.*

"Next stop, the bridge," Alice said.

"Lead on." They headed forward, which Tanya took as a good sign. The bow was the last place a Puppeteer would put a bridge: too exposed. Tanya was ready to chalk up the hull's resemblance to a GP model to pure coincidence.

"Are you prepared to believe that New Terra is a human world?" Alice asked.

Tanya needed no prompting to answer, "Are you ready to tell us where New Terra is?"

Alice laughed. "Yes, actually, although I think that is more properly the captain's prerogative. And we're here."

"Welcome aboard," Julia called through the bridge's

open hatch. She stood (and wasn't nearly as tall as Alice, who maybe *was* a Belter) and offered her hand.

Filling half the bridge was a padded, Y-shaped bench. *What's* that *doing there?* Tanya read. "That's a Puppeteer bench, isn't it," she said, knowing tanj well that it was. So why didn't you just contact an ARM vessel at the Fleet of Worlds?

Julia returned her hand to her side. "Come in and have a seat. It turns out New Terra's history is more complicated than we've so far volunteered."

TANYA QUIT TRYING to take it all in. Everything Alice and Julia said—and Jeeves, too, once Julia introduced the AI—streamed in real time from Tanya's audio pickup to *Koala*. Hawking texted from time to time to corroborate bits of narration. After a while, Dad texted he was ready to open a channel.

"Have we convinced you, Captain?" Julia asked him.

"Enough to have recommended that we dispatch a ship to visit New Terra. The admiral asked if your government will extend a formal invitation."

"I'll call home to arrange that when we finish," Julia said.

"One more thing," Dad said. "You cracked our encryption in a few days? Truly?"

Julia nodded.

"Have you cracked codes for the other fleets in the area?"

"Jeeves?" Julia asked.

"No," Jeeves said. "I would need to know the underlying languages first. If provided with dictionaries and grammar rules, then perhaps."

"We can do that," Dad said. "Hawking—that's our

AI, Julia—will send linguistic files for Hero's Tongue and whatever information we have relating to Interworld evolution since Jeeves's time."

Why Kzinti and not also Trinoc? Tanya wondered.

Maybe Dad knew her well enough to read the question from her expression, or maybe he would have volunteered an explanation anyway. He said, "Messaging among the Kzinti warships has trebled in the last few hours. We need to understand why."

· 23 ·

"It's too dangerous. We don't know how the situation has evolved," Nessus sang. The chords stuck in his throats, as though he were failing Baedeker. Perhaps he was. Perhaps he had hidden too long on New Terra, had lost all his skills. "For all we know, Achilles again rules."

"We can't discover the situation on Hearth *until* we go back," Baedeker countered.

Both opinions were correct, and in the uneasy truce that followed the only sounds were faint whirrings from *Long Shot*'s ventilation fans and the low hum of the autodoc.

Nessus arched a neck to study the still figure within the autodoc. "Perhaps Louis can undertake an exploration for us." But the idea was ludicrous. Louis would awaken with his memories of New Terra restored, with personal priorities to pursue.

"I respect Louis," Baedeker sang, "but can he illuminate the political situation within the Concordance? Can he discern Ol't'ro's frame of mind? This time, Louis cannot help us. We must help ourselves."

"Hindmost," Voice interrupted. "I have a message for Louis from Alice, sent from *Endurance*."

"Go ahead," Baedeker sang.

"Louis, we've made contact with the ARM fleet. You have family aboard one of the ships! They would very much like to see you." Voice switched from Alice's voice, in English, to proper song. "I advised her that Louis is unavailable. She asked for specifics."

Baedeker studied the status readouts. "He must stay in the autodoc for two more days."

"I will inform Alice," Voice sang.

"Assure her that he is well, that the process simply takes time."

"I will," Voice sang.

While Baedeker and Voice consulted, Nessus brooded. *The premier scout of the Concordance fears to go home.* Scared sane, he had described himself to Alice and that was the truth. A scout no longer, when one was desperately needed. He tasted bitter cud.

"Too few," he sang softly.

"What is that?" Baedeker asked.

"Nothing. I was singing to myself." Nessus stopped midmeasure. "Very few can bear to scout."

"The burden is great and unfair," Baedeker agreed. "Voice, can you finish that message for Alice?"

"Yes, Hindmost."

Very few. Nessus felt the stirrings of an idea. "I might know crew aboard the Concordance observer ships. Or you might."

"How?"

"With three ships of the Fleet here observing, how could we *not* know someone among the crews? Someone, perhaps, loyal to the rightful Hindmost."

Baedeker considered, shifting his weight from hoof to hoof to hoof. "Among crew loyal to the present government."

"Or to Achilles personally."

With a mind of its own, one of Nessus' hooves scraped at the deck. Some in the Concordance ships *would* be Achilles' disciples. While hindmost of the scout academy, he had molded many an impressionable cadet to further his ambitions. *As Achilles almost warped me.*

"There are apt to be Gw'oth aboard, too," Baedeker sang.

"Very likely," Nessus agreed.

"Allies and enemies, both in much smaller numbers than in the Fleet," Baedeker crooned, his undertunes pensive. Then, decisively, he added, "That was a prudent idea. Let us contact the Concordance ships and see what we can learn."

"I AM PREPARED to transmit on narrow beam," Voice announced.

Baedeker stretched a neck into the tactical display, indicating with his tongue the Concordance vessel lurking farthest from the skirmishing. "A Citizen may have influence aboard that ship. We will try it first."

"Yes, Hindmost," Voice sang.

Nessus stood at the ready before the pilot's console. *He* read and spoke Hero's Tongue. "And I am prepared to run," he sang.

"Hail the designated ship," Baedeker sang. "Put it on speaker."

"We wish to speak with the hindmost of the Concordance vessel." The recorded message was audio-only. It began in Baedeker's voices, then switched to Nessus' song. Anyone with whom they dare confer should recognize their voices. "We are far from home and seek guidance."

"We have a response," Voice sang. "Also audio only."

"Do not speak on the link, Voice," Baedeker sang. "Put them on."

Understood, Hindmost.

"This is the Concordance vessel *Amity.* To whom am I speaking?"

"Our ship does not carry a Concordance designation," Baedeker lied. He was not about to identify *Long Shot* in the clear. "Is your hindmost present?"

"Minerva is off duty," the unfamiliar voices sang. "May I help?"

Minerva! Some of the tension drained from Baedeker. "I must speak with Minerva. At once."

"Who is this?" the voices on *Amity* asked.

"Friends of Minerva. I can sing no more." Baedeker loaded his voices with authoritative undertunes. "You may tell him we worked together twice before." As Minister of Science and again as Hindmost, Baedeker had been fortunate to have Minerva as his chief aide.

"Very well," the unseen Citizen decided. "I will relay your message."

"Thank you." *Mute,* Baedeker signaled with a swipe of a head. "He'll come," he sang to Nessus. As the link stayed quiescent, Baedeker sang again, more softly and to himself, "Minerva will come."

The link returned to life. "Who *is* this?" so-familiar voices sang. Minerva!

Baedeker unmuted the link. "A very old friend."

"And a second," Nessus added.

"One moment," Minerva sang. They heard him order the bridge cleared. A hatch clanged shut. "We need a secure link."

"I have software"—at least, Voice did—"but no current keys," Baedeker sang. "If you know my voices, perhaps you will know this." He alluded with subtle indirection to the planetary-drive research program at the Ministry of Science. "Do you recall our name for that project?"

"Yes, Hind. . . . That is, yes. I remember."

"We will use that term as the encryption key."

"Agreed."

Baedeker tongued in the key for Voice.

I have a secure connection, Voice reported.

Open video, Baedeker keyed back. The holo that opened showed an old and trusted friend. "Minerva."

"Hindmost! You have been gone for so long! I had not expected to meet you here. Or you, Nessus."

"It is a long story," Baedeker sang. "I was marooned. Fortunately, I escaped the Ringworld before it disappeared."

"I would not have guessed." For a moment, Minerva looked wistful. "I had come to think you had joined Nike."

Joined Nike. The chords bowed with despairing undertunes, sagged beneath a counterpoint of burdens too long borne. It was a melody yearning for the final release.

But Nike's disappearance reflected nothing as ordinary as death. As Gw'oth war fleets had swooped down upon Hearth, Nike and his aides fled into the Concordance's deepest, most secret hiding place—locking the door behind them. Nike was the sane one during the crisis.

No one had heard since from him. Few knew of the Hindmost's Refuge as anything other than ancient fable. For all Minerva knew, Nike *was* dead.

"I will never forsake the herd," Baedeker sang. "I left seeking a way to free everyone."

Minerva glanced nervously at the closed bridge hatch. "I have company on this ship."

Company rang with undertunes of unease. For others to hold dominance *over* the ship's hindmost. . . .

"That is why I reached out," Baedeker sang. "To understand the state of affairs on Hearth. That your ship has a Gw'o aboard tells me much."

"We have three. They are in their habitat at present."

Not a Gw'otesht. "Only a little smarter, then, than us." Baedeker permitted himself a quick, one-eyed smile. "I came to the Ringworld for advanced technology, something to entice Ol't'ro. Do you think a trade is possible?"

Minerva trembled. "I *know* very little. On occasion I have participated in ministerial meetings, representing Clandestine Directorate. When 'Chiron' sings, the Hindmost heeds. Always Chiron wants more resources for his research."

"That sounds encouraging," Nessus sang.

Baedeker thought any optimism was premature. "Who is Hindmost?" Unless I get back safely, I cannot negotiate with Ol't'ro.

"The current Hindmost is Horatius," Minerva sang.

"Who?" Nessus asked.

"The most recent Conservative to preside." Minerva sang a formal name. "Conservatives do not last long after finding out who truly rules."

"Yet this one deemed himself Horatius defending the bridge," Nessus sang. "I think I would like this Conservative."

Holding the bridge against whom? An army of the Etruscans, maybe. Or Babylonians. Maybe Mayans. Nessus was the one who had studied human myth and history. But Baedeker had come to understand—painfully mastered, over the years—the art of politics. "Who are Horatius' leading ministers?"

Baedeker did not know most of them, either. Except one: Achilles. "How much influence does *he* retain?"

"A great deal." Minerva hesitated. "You will not understand until I review some events since you left the Fleet."

More bad news? "Proceed," Baedeker sang.

Minerva took time to gather his thoughts. "After the Ringworld expedition, Nessus' crew returned to their homes knowing the location of the Fleet."

"And nothing came of that," Baedeker sang. He shot a quick, sorrowful glance at his mate. Exchanging long-held secrets, Nessus had confessed to *wanting* ARM and Patriarchy navies to descend upon Hearth. But had that scheme for chasing off the Gw'oth been any less mad or desperate than Baedeker's own? Hardly.

Minerva lowered his heads subserviently. "For many years, that was the case. The distances were great. The secrets of the Ringworld beckoned. But after the two of you left . . ."

Fled, their friend meant. "Sing plainly," Baedeker directed.

"Aliens began to arrive." Minerva looked away. "Not in large numbers. Their strength had all been sent to the Ringworld. But still, aliens were among the Fleet. Watching. Demanding commercial relations. Every group of aliens scheming to embroil us in its rivalries against the others. Having been permitted to open embassies on Nature Preserve Three, they push to establish presences on Hearth itself."

"Have they learned about New Terra?" Baedeker asked.

"No, Hindmost."

"They may know soon," Nessus sang sadly. "A New Terran ship brought me here."

Minerva sang, "It will find ARM ships and reveal the shameful past."

"So I fear," Nessus sang.

"About conditions in the Fleet," Baedeker prompted.

"I apologize, Hindmost," Minerva sang. In broken melodies and with disheartening grace notes, he told the sordid tale: Chiron judging the old, automated defense arrays inadequate. An artificial intelligence given control of the array. Proteus getting more and more enhancements—and since Ringworld's disappearance, yet more capacity and new capabilities.

What would my old friend think of Voice? Baedeker wondered. But the circumstances were not the same. Voice was a companion, little more. To surround Hearth and herd with weapons under the control of an AI?

"Let me guess," Nessus sang. "Achilles built Proteus. In the process, he has made himself indispensable."

"As you sing, Nessus." Minerva's heads sagged lower. "Who else is that crazy?"

"Or ambitious?" Nessus added.

"As you sing," Minerva repeated.

Baedeker was still struggling with the implications when Minerva intoned meekly, "There is more, Hindmost."

What more *could* there be? How much worse could the situation get? "Go on."

"Ol't'ro is old," Minerva sang. "Their youngest members are of the eleventh and twelfth generations. No Gw'otesht has ever clung together this long. They are . . . not quite right."

"How can you know that?" Baedeker demanded.

"One of my crew, Hindmost. For a time, Tf'o was

unwillingly a part of the meld. He was replaced."
Minerva trembled. "This far from home, even a Gw'o
sometimes needs companionship."

As for a long while, I had only Voice, Baedeker
thought. For much of their "adventure," Louis had set
his own course, ranging far across the Ringworld. To
reunite with Nessus after so many years—

Text pulsed on a console. A warning from Voice. *All
Kzinti ships have jumped to hyperspace.*

Where were they going?

· 24 ·

Come at once, the Norquist-Ng summons read.

"Not much for small talk," Sigmund muttered. He didn't expect specifics, but *please* would have been a nice touch. *On my way,* he texted back.

But first . . .

This jumbled den was his favorite room of the house. He had been standing at the clear wall, admiring the view, when the message came. Yucca plants and the mesquite hedge bowed beneath the wind. The desert, starkly beautiful, stretched to the distant rugged mountains.

He turned away from the vista to sit at his desk. Rummaging in a side drawer, he retrieved a comb, a pocket pack of tissues, and breath mints. In the process he sprang the false back to palm the earbud long hidden in the desk.

He didn't trust Norquist-Ng. That the weasel would have him under surveillance was the least of it. With a fingertip pressed deep into his ear, pretending to dig at wax, Sigmund set the bug into place. It would hear and record everything he heard.

Assuming that it worked. The bug had lain hidden in the drawer for a *long* time. He tapped a test rhythm on the desk.

To the ear with the bug, Jeeves sent the double-click that meant, *Loud and clear.*

"Jeeves, I will be at the Ministry." Where, the second I enter the situation room wearing a bug, I become a felon. "Keep an eye on things here."

"Very good, sir."

Sigmund reprogrammed pants and shirt from his customary black—by local standards, misanthropic—to more sociable, if still reserved, shades of gray. The muted colors would help him fit in at a time he *really* didn't want to call attention to himself.

Then he strode out his back door, flicking from the patio to the security lobby of the New Terran Defense Forces headquarters.

"I HAVE GOOD news," Julia reported. "No, make that *excellent* news."

Sigmund spared a quick glance around the situation room. He saw hope and relief—and some shifty eyes. *Excellent* meant different things to different people.

Had Julia and Alice made contact with an ARM ship? Julia was larger than life in the situation room's main display, but still Sigmund leaned closer to the table and her image.

"Continue, Captain," Minister Norquist-Ng said. "I take it you are prepared to return home?"

"Soon, sir," she said, "but our news is far more consequential. We were contacted by an ARM vessel, the *Koala.* We need not return alone."

Cheers rang out, only to choke off as Norquist-Ng smacked the table with a fist. "Captain, you are not to—"

"It gets better." The minister's objections had yet to

reach *Endurance,* where the bridge camera pivoted toward Alice's voice. Sigmund couldn't remember seeing such a big grin on her. "We know the way to Earth. From this location, it's about two hundred light-years, mostly to galactic south. From New Terra, a bit over two ten. Jeeves? Show them."

Alice disappeared, a graphic taking her place: a star field, bearings on pulsars, and one star set to blinking.

Sigmund had sought this information for half his life—ever since Nessus had forever *changed* his life. Instead of a flash of recognition, Sigmund felt . . . nothing. Those memories weren't just buried. They were gone.

In an instant, so was the map.

"Graphic off," Norquist-Ng barked. The last view of Alice replaced the map. "Jeeves, you will show that image to *no one* except by my authorization. I'll brief the governor. No one is to speak a word about this development outside this room."

"Understood, sir," the local Jeeves said.

The life-altering news was recorded in Sigmund's earbud, together with the ordering of the cover-up. But Earth's coordinates? Vanished!

If *only* he had worn spy lenses, too—but he had not dared. Light glinting off the lenses could have given him away. And each extra bug would have drawn a trickle more power from the power transmitters recessed into the walls, a drain that might have been detected.

While Sigmund second-guessed himself, Norquist-Ng's orders reached *Endurance.* "I don't understand," Alice said. "Don't we want to find our roots?"

"That will be quite enough, Ms. Jordan." The minister stood to scowl into the camera. "Captain, you are to return home at once. You will not reveal New Terra's location, nor invite foreign vessels to accompany you. If your new acquaintances have told the truth, we can visit Earth at a time of our choosing. If not, we wouldn't want them to know where *we* live."

Sigmund took a deep breath. Suppose it took a little while to get out the word Earth had been found. Maybe that would be all right. The minister was within his rights choosing to bring such unexpected developments to the governor.

Logic be damned, Norquist-Ng was stalling. Of that, Sigmund had no doubt. One way or another, he promised himself, the word *would* get out.

But where was Nessus? Sigmund pictured him locked inside his cabin, furled into a ball—catatonic with dread of ARM retribution for ancient Puppeteer crimes and the founding of New Terra. "How is our friend coping with events?"

"Nessus doesn't know," Alice said. "The Concordance has observer ships here, too. He had left us to visit an old friend before *Koala* hailed us."

Her posture had become tense, Sigmund noticed. *She's not telling us something.*

Norquist-Ng said, "Captain, you have your orders. If Nessus isn't prepared to leave, he can stay with his friend."

"We're not quite done refueling," Julia said. "Hopping around between snowballs for safety slowed down the process, and we also had a minor equipment malfunction. About two days and I believe we'll be ready."

Alice seemed to relax.

Something would happen in two days. Sigmund wondered what, knowing Alice well enough not to fish for hints. Nor could he ask in private: his coerced source had been shipped off-world for routine patrol duty. Until he uncovered someone else in the comm center with a hand in the cookie jar . . .

Focus, Sigmund!

Maintaining contact with the ARM was the first priority. How hard did he dare push? Norquist-Ng had nearly banished Sigmund once before. "Minister, there is another factor. The Patriarchy fleet remains in the neighborhood. Kzinti are very warlike, very dangerous. We can't risk them spotting New Terra before Earth forces arrive."

"Fourteen light-years is hardly 'in the neighborhood,'" Norquist-Ng said. "As for avoiding your aliens, that's easy. We'll remove our ship from what *is* their neighborhood."

A minute later Julia answered, "That's another thing. The Kzinti have gone."

Futz! Sigmund said, "Minister, I recommend putting the defense forces on full alert. And more than anything, we need allies."

"Calm down, Ausfaller," Norquist-Ng said. "We're always alert. That's how *Endurance* came to be where it is, as you very well know. Clearly your aliens realized the Ringworld is no longer there to fight over."

"*We* are here to fight over," Sigmund said. And to eat. "To oppose a Patriarchy expeditionary force of the size *Endurance* observed, we'll need ARM reinforcements."

Norquist-Ng frowned. "Is there any circumstance for which you *don't* think contacting Earth is the right—"

"If I may," Jeeves interrupted.

It wasn't the local AI that Sigmund heard, because Julia answered it without delay. "Go ahead, Jeeves."

"I have cracked the Kzinti encryption, and their fleet is not bound for New Terra. Nothing I have decoded so far would suggest they are aware of New Terra."

"Satisfied, Ausfaller?" Norquist-Ng snapped.

". . . And so they are on their way," the distant Jeeves continued imperturbably, "to invade the Fleet of Worlds."

· 25 ·

Beneath a frost-speckled coffin lid, afire with nervous energy, Louis opened his eyes. He had the briefest sensation of déjà vu—had he not *just* awakened in an autodoc?—before the memory storm struck.

Parents and sister, long forgotten. Nessus. Desperate times, derelict ships, and daring rescues. Raiding the Pak evacuation fleet to steal the Library. Starfaring starfish waging civil war. Lunatic Puppeteers, led by a sociopath, wielding planet-busters. A lost colony world, unsuspected, home to millions of humans. Adventure and amnesia, each in its turn eagerly embraced. A willowy, strong-featured woman—

Alice! In his memories, she was younger, raven-haired, brown eyes warm and inviting. And she was pregnant!

He slapped the panic button. Too slowly, the lid began to retract. The familiar clutter of *Long Shot* appeared.

"Good. You have returned to us," he heard Hindmost say.

With old/new memories bursting like thunderclaps, Louis retrieved a name: Baedeker. The receding dome *finally* let Louis sit up. He found Baedeker and Nessus observing him, Nessus sidling out the doorway. To make room for Louis? Or preparing to flee from him?

Louis said, "I knew you both long before Ringworld."

"True," Baedeker said. With a straightened neck, he offered Louis a clean jumpsuit.

Leaning to take the garment, Louis almost tumbled from the 'doc. Without order or logic, memories kept crashing over him. He steadied himself against the side of the intensive care cavity.

"You are disoriented," Nessus said. "I feared this might happen."

Like drinking from a fire hose, the images over-whelmed Louis:

—A woman's face, contorted in a death rictus, glimpsed through a blood-splattered visor.

—A stupendous fjord, the tide surging in, and Alice standing nearby. He had just met her.

—Hyperwave consultations with the starfish. Gw'oth! That's what they called themselves.

—Painkillers, addiction, and withdrawal.

—Making love to Alice.

—Broken ribs and men with funny asymmetric beards and—

"Louis!" Nessus shouted. "*Listen* to me. The 'doc restored many engrams. You're reliving most of a year all at once."

Louis shook his head, desperate to clear his mind. "I experienced these things in a particular order, tanj it. Why is everything so chaotic?"

"It's been a long time," Hindmost—no, *Baedeker*—said. "Since those recordings, countless experiences have imprinted themselves as new and altered neural pathways."

But Louis scarcely heard the explanation, still drowning in the past:

—Cooking breakfast for Alice, who could hardly synth her own toast.

—Barhopping his way through spaceport dives.

—Playing secret agent and double-crossing Achilles.

—Tiny suns like strings of pearls.

—Getting thrown out of a big, ugly government building by New Terran soldiers.

"It's as though I have two minds," Louis struggled to get out. "It's like being in two places at once. You're suggesting the old engrams don't fit where they're supposed to. Too much in my head has changed for the old . . . for the old recordings to reintegrate as they should."

"I believe that to be the case," Baedeker said. "Of course except for Carlos Wu and perhaps Tunesmith, no one ever understood the full capabilities of this autodoc."

"Carlos. My *father*."

"Yes," Nessus said. "This amazing autodoc is your legacy."

As from a whirlpool, Louis struggled out of the 'doc. Clumsily, he slipped into the jumpsuit. "I need to talk with Alice."

"*Endurance* and *Long Shot* have gone their separate ways," Nessus said. "Beyond 'not now,' Alice and Julia have had nothing to say to our hails."

"Alice will speak with me," Louis said, "once she knows that I remember."

"Perhaps," Nessus said.

It hit Louis: he was *starving*. "I'm still disoriented. Would one of you mind bringing me something to eat?"

"Of course not." Nessus backed farther into the corridor. "Or stand between us. We will guide you to the synthesizer."

As they walked, old memories kept erupting. Twice Louis stumbled against a wall; once he fell across Nessus' broad back. He only avoided a tumble by grabbing hold of the mane.

With a shrill, atonal wheeze, Nessus stopped. He stood, legs braced far apart, while Louis regained his balance.

"Hindmost's Voice," Louis called out. "Keep hailing *Endurance*. Tell Alice, 'Louis remembers now.'"

"I will let you know when they answer."

"Thank you, Voice," Baedeker said.

Maybe Louis had become smarter over the years. Maybe he only saw connections now because of the odd juxtapositions of random memories.

He had been naïve.

"Chiron," Louis began cautiously.

Nessus swiveled one head to look backward. "What about Chiron?"

"He briefed the team for the Ringworld expedition." Everything suddenly seemed so clear to Louis. "Chiron didn't appear as a holo out of fear, because we were aliens."

"No," Baedeker agreed from behind Louis.

Approaching the tiny rec room Nessus pressed against the wall so Louis could squeeze past. "Chiron came as a holo to hide that he wasn't a Puppeteer." His thoughts churning, selecting dishes at random, Louis piled a tray with synthed food. "Puppeteers no longer rule in the Fleet."

"Sadly so," Baedeker said.

Still *more* memories spewed forth: tiny spaceships,

water-filled. Not-quite-starfish. Feeling slow and dim-witted in the presence of a truly superior mind.

Ol't'ro!

Louis said, "Nessus, you hired me to stop Achilles from manipulating the Gw'oth situation. I failed."

"No one could have succeeded," Nessus said.

In Louis's mind the Gw'oth War had just concluded. He had just rescued Nessus from Achilles and prison. Baedeker had just refused to come with them. Just as—in Louis's mind—the Ringworld and its thirty trillion inhabitants had disappeared only days earlier.

Louis said, "So, the Gw'oth rule Fleet."

"Yes, to Ol't'ro," Baedeker said. "Achilles schemes anew to reclaim the semblance of power as the puppet Hindmost. You must now see, Louis, why I so desperately sought technology from the Ringworld. To free Hearth."

Desperate enough to abduct not merely Louis, but also Chmeee. A Puppeteer kidnapping a Kzin! Even now, such an action was difficult to fathom. Louis turned to face his friends. "Did you find what you needed?"

"Maybe." Baedeker waved a neck sinuously, the mannerism somehow inclusive. "Nessus and I must soon find out."

Louis shook his head. "*We* will find out."

ALICE FINALLY MADE contact. "You think you know me now?"

"I know I do," Louis said. Her face seemed to cycle between the angry old woman who had slugged him and the dark-haired beauty—even more spirited—who his aching heart insisted he had just left. Could he have forgotten those eyes? Truly? That seemed impossible. "I'm glad that I remember."

She managed a smile. "It was good while it lasted."

It was, indeed. "Achilles would have done anything to hurt me. I was a target on New Terra. By staying, I'd have made *you* a target."

"So Sigmund explained at the time. Why was I the only one without a vote?"

Apart from being light-years away, on New Terra's business? Aside from being in and out of medical stasis so that you wouldn't give birth to our son aboard ship? "It doesn't matter, Alice. I'm back. I'm *here*. I remember. I love you as I did the day I left."

"The day you ran away."

That hurt. "I'd like to pick things up—"

"Pick up again?" She laughed uproariously. "It's been more than a century. I'm a crone. You're a kid."

"I'm almost as old as you," Louis retorted.

She just stared at him.

"I'm sorry I hurt you," he finally said.

"At least you learned something." She severed the link.

. 26 .

Predators crept forward, their passage through the tall wild grain visible only from above. The herd, upwind, grazed unawares, although from time to time sentry animals raised their heads the better to see, hear, and sniff.

Predator and prey alike reminded Cd'o of Citizens. The animals were smaller, of course, more similar in size to a Gw'o than to a Citizen. The grazers stood upright like Citizens, while the hunters slinked and stalked near to the ground. Cd'o zoomed her view closer still—

"Your Wisdom?" a servant said hesitantly.

The robotic aerostat hovered high above the remote island game preserve; Cd'o's startled yank on the control stick sent her view into a wobbly spin. Her attention had been worlds away, on Hearth.

"What?" she asked crossly. She lifted a tubacle to see who had interrupted her too-rare respite. She recognized a servant, Kg'o, his integument a self-conscious far-red.

"Excuse me, your Wisdom," he murmured. "I am to tell you that all have been summoned. An important message has just arrived."

"From where?"

"The ship *Amity,* your Wisdom."

From the Ringworld, then—or, rather, from where the Ringworld had been. From amid the mad chaos of multispecies squabbling. "A meld, then," Cd'o said.

Uneven stripes rippled across Kg'o. "I know nothing more of the matter, your Wisdom."

It had not been a question, and she had not meant to embarrass him. Cd'o swam away from the computer, pointing at the still-spinning image. "Do you know what this is?"

"No, your Wisdom."

"The lone game preserve on five worlds, an island half an ocean away from anywhere. Here the Citizens maintain remnants of their primeval heritage. What do you make of that?"

Thoughtful yellows and greens washed across Kg'o. "That I do not understand Citizens."

Because suffering predators to exist was not the logic of sentient prey? "Once gone, an ecosystem can never truly be re-created. A transplanted environment, such as we have in our habitat, is never as rich or robust as a natural ecosystem."

"So Citizens fear losing the potential of even an old, dangerous environment? I believe I see." Kg'o wriggled and flexed a tubacle nervously, struggling with unfamiliar concepts. "Their cowardice is more complex than I had realized."

And far more calculating, Cd'o surmised. She jetted off, Kg'o trailing at a respectful distance, to meld.

IN THE AUSTERE inviolability of their melding chamber, Ol't'ro considered:

That from the fringes of the vanished Ringworld's

cometary belt, the Concordance vessel *Amity* reported the synchronized departure of the Kzinti fleets.

That war over the wealth of the Ringworld had been inevitable.

That the artifact's disappearance had not.

That Baedeker and Nessus, long absent from the affairs of Gw'oth and Citizens, had reappeared—from the Ringworld?—to assert that Kzinti warships were bound for the Fleet of Worlds.

That for a singleton, Baedeker had been a competent scientist. It was unfortunate that he persisted in meddling in their affairs.

That a former unit of theirs, exiled to *Amity*, confirmed Minerva's report.

That they remained puzzled why Tf'o had found—and rendered—melding so distasteful that it had become expedient to expel him.

No? I can explain, Cd'o asserted faintly.

They swatted aside the impudence, tamped down the impertinence, and continued their deliberations.

That by its actions near the Ringworld, the Patriarchy had shown itself to be as reckless and dangerous as it had appeared in the historical files of Clandestine Directory.

That humanity had proven itself to be almost as reckless as and even more dangerous than Kzinti.

(*And Sigmund? Louis? The New Terrans?* posed a remnant unit. *Did they not twice save* our *worlds?*)

They ignored that interruption, too.

That Nessus' pathetically obvious scheme to draw alien interceders to Hearth was, finally, about to succeed. That all that had been required to advance Nessus' plot was the still-unexplained disappearance of the Ringworld into hyperspace!

That *they* had not foreseen that possibility, either.

That Nessus was about to discover that to bring armed allies and to evict Ol't'ro were quite different undertakings.

That a New Terran vessel had also appeared, drawn by the unique event that was the Ringworld departing.

That *Endurance* had made contact with the ARM humans, and so the long-hidden history of a world of slaves must, inevitably, come out.

That whatever might be motivating the Kzinti warriors to come, the ARM humans had just found more than ample reason to attack the Fleet.

That the historical record implied—Citizens' feeble efforts at secrecy notwithstanding—Concordance meddling in the affairs of humans and Kzinti and perhaps other species besides.

Pragmatic cowards, Cd'o whispered into the meld, along with fleeting images of predators in a preserve.

That cowardice did not preclude violence, only channeled violence into subtlety.

That by their dominance of the Fleet and their taming of the Citizens, *they* kept the Concordance from continuing its practiced, selfish aggression.

That their choices now came down to two. They could just leave, the Citizens deserving everything that was rushing toward them. Or they could fight, because every warship destroyed here was a warship that would never endanger Jm'ho, or Kl'mo, or the newer colonies they had yet to know in person.

Imagine the marvels to be beheld on new worlds, Cd'o tempted.

Ol't'ro again swatted the insolent unit into silence.

That they had almost four five-squared days until

the Kzinti could arrive. That they had easily twice as long if—as, supposedly, the New Terrans reported—the Kzinti intended to invade. To land, Kzinti ships would need time to match normal-space velocity with the Fleet.

That for as long as they ruled, the full resources of the Ministry of Science remained their personal instrument.

That they themselves could evacuate this world in a day, should they so choose.

That to preserve their options, they would do well to expand Proteus as fully as possible.

That they could tolerate Achilles' smug satisfaction with their decision.

That they suffered fools like Horatius and Achilles expressly to preserve their own time for projects of greater interest.

And so—the news from *Amity* passed on, their decision regarding Proteus delivered—they turned their full attention to fine points of multiverse mathematics. . . .

"THIS IS SPACE Traffic Control."

In Achilles' tactical display, queues of transponder codes, each code denoting a ship, streamed to and from Hearth. He sang, "This is *Poseidon*, inbound from Nature Preserve One."

"Acknowledged," the controller reported, adding the parameters of a midaltitude staging orbit. "Confirm."

Achilles waited silently. His hearts pounded, for this course of action was insane. Stepping away from the herd, whether to scout or to guide, was the very definition of insanity.

And for the herd to survive, there must be crazies.

"*Poseidon,* do you confirm?"

Achilles flipped off his transponder, removing *Poseidon* from the Space Traffic Control system. Seconds later, his instruments reported radar pings. But *Poseidon* was in stealth mode; it would produce no echoes.

"*Poseidon,* are you there?"

Achilles altered course and speed, then altered them again.

New voices came: stronger, firmer, with stern harmonics designed to command instant obedience. Proteus. "This is Hearth Planetary Defense. *Poseidon,* or whoever you are, we are tracking you with optical sensors. Break away or you will be destroyed. This is your only warning. In ten. Nine. Eight . . ."

In Achilles' tactical display, nearby grain ships scattered.

Between seven and six, his console reported a low-intensity laser beam. Target lock, or a lucky hit? He zigged, this time putting the ship into a spin.

Jaws ached to release the flight controls. Legs trembled with the urge to run. *Feel the mania,* he told himself. *Embrace the madness.*

His jaws remained clenched on the controls. There would be time later to collapse.

The laser beam stayed locked.

A second laser beam impaled his ship. Now the tactical display showed infrared sources in three tiers streaking toward him. Kinetic-kill drones.

"Four. Three."

Achilles pulled away from Hearth. With his other mouth he flipped the STC transponder back ON.

"Two."

"This is *Poseidon,* Minister Achilles speaking." The lasers stayed locked on, but the nearest rank of the inward-streaking drones veered off. "This was an unannounced test of planetary defenses."

"Identity challenge," the stern voices commanded. They transmitted a random-sounding sequence of numbers.

A console computer generated the corresponding response and Achilles tapped SEND.

"Confirmed," Proteus sang. "Traffic Control, you may resume."

"This is Minister Achilles requesting prioritized clearance to Harmonious Field."

"Very well," the controller sang tremulously. "You are cleared for immediate landing."

Achilles landed *Poseidon.* Moments after the ship grounded, Citizens emerged, quavering, from stepping discs embedded in the tarmac. He stepped from his ship to appear among his greeters. Sashes and coveralls identified them as spaceport workers.

One stepped forward. "Welcome, Minister. We hope your test went satisfactorily."

"Very well, thank you," Achilles sang.

They lowered their heads subserviently and waited.

"Very well," he repeated. Because while Proteus performed as expected, even one ship deviating from routine sufficed to panic you. "If you will excuse me, official matters require my attention."

A tongueprint and wriggle of lip nodes retrieved a protected address from his transport controller. He stepped from the tarmac directly to the security foyer of the private residence of the Hindmost.

. . .

GUARDS ESCORTED ACHILLES through the residence to
Horatius' private office. Achilles knew the room well—
and disdained these bland and minimalist furnishings.
Scattered cushions and one massive oval desk did not
suffice. Not for a *Hindmost*'s office.

"Leave us," Horatius sang.

"Yes, Hindmost," the senior guard responded. The
squad retreated, shutting the door behind them.

"I asked you here to see me, not set off a panic,"
Horatius began without preamble. Displeasure did
nothing to shorten his would-be portentous pauses.

"Our defenses require realistic testing," Achilles
sang.

"Chiron would likely agree with you." Horatius
settled onto a mound of pillows. "He proposes a significant expansion, to be implemented within the next
hundred days."

Proposes. It was all Achilles could do not to look
himself in the eyes. This was the sort of suggestion no
Hindmost dare ignore. "Why did you invite me?"

"To oversee the changes to Proteus, as you doubtless
realize." Annoying pause. "Why do you bother to pretend otherwise?"

*As a reminder, Horatius, that you need me. That
Ol't'ro needs me.* "By your very welcome, this proposal
is sound. You sang that with a single ship, I caused a
panic. What would have been the response to an entire
Kzinti fleet?"

His necks trembling, Horatius managed *not* to pluck
at his unimaginatively braided mane. "We would surrender, of course. Any sane ruler would."

"Only Ol't'ro will not allow surrender, will they?"

"That is why you are here," Horatius admitted.

Remember that. "To expand our defenses will entail significant resources."

"You will have them," Horatius sang.

"And there will be more unannounced tests like you saw today, some involving more than one ship. Respectfully"—*that* chord was a twisted, ironic lie—"can you govern in those circumstances?"

Horatius stood tall, hooves set far apart. "I am Hindmost."

"So you are." *But you are not up to the task.* "But you need not carry that burden."

The longest pause yet, but this time Achilles chose to interpret the silence as his offer being considered. "I am Hindmost," Horatius finally sang.

Achilles sensed further nuance in the harmonics. A yearning? A moment of temptation? "War amid the worlds of the Fleet is unprecedented. How can any Conservative preside at such a time?"

"I *am* Hindmost," Horatius repeated.

The grace notes of pain in that repetition were unmistakable.

27

Sigmund picked at his dinner, the little he had managed to eat burning in his gut like molten lead. There were only so many ways to convey, "I don't know," and "Sorry, I can't tell you that." He had used them all.

"It's not fair, Dad," Hermes said. His face was weathered and tanned from years of farming. "I spent my childhood wondering if you would make it back home. I grew up watching Mom struggling to put on a brave face for Athena and me. Now my daughter is the one out . . . somewhere, the one out of contact."

And she's my granddaughter. I do understand, son. "I can only tell you that Julia is well, that she's doing work you can be proud of. I'm sorry, but I can't say more."

"You *won't* say more," Amelia chided.

His daughter-in-law normally had a wicked sense of humor. She was a communications engineer and twice as smart as Sigmund—just ask her. Amelia didn't very much like Sigmund and the feeling was mutual. But she loved Hermes and his son loved her, and together they had raised one heck of a fine bunch of children. Sigmund's dislike of Amelia did not matter.

Today she was one hundred percent an aggrieved mom, and Sigmund was as close as she could get to the people who had put her child at risk. Had Amelia only known, he *was* one of them. Her dinner also looked stirred and untasted.

"Well?" she prodded.

"I won't say more," Sigmund conceded.

"Will she come home soon?" Amelia tried again. "Is she in danger, Sigmund?"

She's in a war zone, far, far away. If he *could* answer truthfully, it wouldn't help. "She'll be fine," Sigmund said, knowing the words were hollow.

His pocket buzzed. "Excuse me." He retrieved his comp.

Come now. The text was from Norquist-Ng.

"Is that about Julia?" Amelia asked.

Certain that it was, Sigmund said, "I don't know," once more. "I have to go, though. Thanks for dinner."

From a stepping disc just outside Hermes and Amelia's front door, he flicked to the Ministry.

"IT'S MY FAULT," Julia said. She looked drained, beaten. "I take full responsibility."

Norquist-Ng paused the playback. "What do you think?"

Sigmund looked around the private office, glad to be rid of the usual hangers-on. I think that Alice took matters into her own hands, Minister, because you took matters into yours. And that had I gone aboard *Endurance,* Alice would be here, alive.

On whose hands was the blood thickest?

"I'd like to speak with Julia," Sigmund said.

"The news won't get any better, but all right." Changing tone, Norquist-Ng directed, "Jeeves, hail *Koala* and ask for a secure link to our captain."

Though it took only minutes, the wait seemed interminable. Finally, a holo opened: Julia, in a nondescript, closet-sized cabin, looking even more dejected than in her message. Something about her surroundings—proportions? furnishings? the wall color?—shouted that this wasn't any New Terran vessel.

"We have your report," Norquist-Ng said abruptly. "We have questions."

"Yes, Minister." She swallowed. "Grandpa. It isn't good."

"Start at the beginning," Sigmund suggested.

"Yes, sir. *Endurance* was fueled up for the trip home, but low on feedstock for the synthesizer. We'd been communicating with an ARM ship, *Koala,* so Alice suggested we ask if they had feedstock or food to spare." Julia sighed. "Unfortunately, they did.

"I suited up to jet over. On my way . . ."

"Go on," Sigmund said, gently.

"Alice radioed. She said, 'I have no choice. Sorry.' A second later she was gone. I mean, *Endurance* was gone."

Gone to hyperspace and bound for Earth. Sigmund understood that much from the original anguished message. The women had been arguing, but Julia planned to obey their recall order. And the last telecon, that charade about needing two more days . . . had Alice given herself two days to change Julia's mind?

"And then?" Sigmund asked.

"I continued to *Koala* and convinced them to hail *Endurance* nonstop. There was still a chance." She looked down. "Until there wasn't."

"What do you mean?" Sigmund asked.

"Since discovering the rival forces here, my priority has been making sure no hostile group can backtrack us to New Terra. First and foremost, that meant making sure no one could take control of *Endurance*."

"An autodestruct cycle on the main fusion reactor," Norquist-Ng explained brusquely. "My orders. The captain had to reset it daily."

"Alice didn't know," Julia said. "If I had reached her, I would have warned her. She could have returned, surrendered the ship, let me reset the autodestruct."

"All alone, vaporized, in the less-than-nothingness of hyperspace . . ." Sigmund shuddered. "It wasn't your fault."

Lips pressed thin, Julia just stared.

Sigmund felt himself staring, too, but not at Julia . . .

Two lifetimes ago, *he* had hidden a bomb aboard a starship. But he had warned its pilot—the whole point being to make sure Shaeffer knew he couldn't steal the ship, knew that he had to complete his assignment.

Uh-huh. An assignment Puppeteers had coerced Shaeffer into taking, with Sigmund's advice and blessing. And not just *any* Puppeteer, but futzy Achilles. But Sigmund had been an ARM, protecting Earth against alien menaces. The job required making hard choices.

Did he want ARMs factoring New Terra into their plans? Sigmund had a moment of doubt. But the Kzinti were out there. And Pak hordes. One bunch of those had passed, but who was to say more Pak weren't out there? And the cone-ship people, who seemed as aggressive as Kzinti. In a dangerous galaxy there were far worse things than the ARM, and most of the time the ARM left Earth's onetime colonies alone.

"Ausfaller?"

Norquist-Ng had caught Sigmund with his mind wandering. *Stay on task, old man.* Julia was far from home, on an ARM vessel. Alice, bitter until the end, was dead. The road to Earth tantalized. So what came next?

Sigmund thought about Hermes and Amelia. *I can't say* felt emptier than ever.

"It wasn't her fault," Sigmund said.

Julia said, "Minister, I have new information."

"Go on," Norquist-Ng said.

"Yes, Minister. Soon after the Kzinti left, another faction took off. Trinocs. That's the species with the conical ships."

Sigmund said, "I'm unfamiliar with that name. First contact with them must have happened after I left Known Space."

Julia did something below the view of the distant camera.

The creature in the new foreground image was bipedal, but that was almost its only similarity to a human. Most of the alien's height was in its legs. Fat rolls separated head and torso, with no indication of a neck. Its skin was chrome-yellow. It had three deep-set eyes—Trinoc was likely an Interworld nickname, and Sigmund wondered what the aliens called themselves— and a triangular mouth. Teeth like serrated knives peeked out from behind yellow lips.

"One more detail, Minister," Julia said. "My ARM friends call Trinocs racially paranoid."

Wonderful new neighbors for mankind, Sigmund thought.

"The speculation here is that the Trinocs also set out for the Fleet of Worlds. They wouldn't want the Kzinti to take over the place."

"Nor will the ARM," Sigmund said. "What are their plans?"

"They won't tell me. Need to know." Julia smiled sadly. "What I need to know is how I'm getting home."

Norquist-Ng tore his gaze away from the Trinoc. "Contact Nessus. Get a ride home from his friend."

"I tried. No answer. If I had gotten through, the friend is from the Fleet. That's where they'll be going."

Abandoning his shipmates without a word? That didn't sound like Nessus. Something else was involved. Something Julia didn't feel free to discuss. Sigmund said, "The Fleet of Worlds is about to become a war zone. It makes no tanj sense to go there, even if you can hitch a ride."

She nodded. "That brings me to the offer that's on the table."

"Take down that hideous image," Norquist-Ng said.

"Yes, Minister." Julia did something else out of camera range, and the Trinoc vanished. "This ship, *Koala,* heads soon for Earth. They've offered to bring me."

Sigmund turned to Norquist-Ng. "From what Julia has already learned, New Terra is more or less on their way. They can swing by, bring Julia home."

"I'm not prepared to invite foreign warships here," Norquist-Ng snapped.

"Then the captain goes to Earth." Where, most likely, Julia will reveal—be made to reveal?—New Terra's location.

Let her go to Earth or invite the ARM to New Terra? To judge from his sour expression, Norquist-Ng hated both his choices.

"*Koala* is a supply ship," Julia said. "Unarmed."

Norquist-Ng said, "Captain, can you transfer to another ARM ship, one remaining in your present vicinity? I'll send a ship to get you."

"Hold on, please." She froze the image.

Sigmund tried to work through what the various militaries would be doing. It beat thinking about Julia stranded for the more-than-a-month a rescue ship would need to reach her. It beat wondering what he would have to do if Norquist-Ng thought to abandon one of his own people. *That won't happen, Julia. I won't allow it.*

The Kzinti had leapt first—no surprise there—but wouldn't the ARM forces also head for the Fleet? They would have no difficulty finding an excuse: to share in the spoils, perhaps. Or to ally with the Puppeteers and cut out the other aliens. Or to avenge past Puppeteer meddling in human affairs. Sigmund guessed even the admirals didn't know—beyond that they needed *something* to show for the blood and treasure already squandered at the Ringworld.

ARM, Patriarchy, Trinocs . . . every side was in the same bind. Things were looking bleak for the Puppeteers. Maybe that explained Nessus' abrupt silence.

Then Julia was back. "No one will explain, but waiting here isn't an option. I either go to Earth, or come home if you'll welcome an ARM ship."

"Aren't Outsiders still nearby?" Norquist-Ng asked. "They must be. They don't use hyperdrive. Maybe you can stay on an Outsider ship until I can get a ship to you."

"They're creatures of liquid helium, living near absolute zero. What kind of guest quarters do you suppose they'll have?" Turning from the holo, Sigmund locked eyes with Norquist-Ng. *Do the right thing, Minister.*

"A supply ship," Norquist-Ng said at last, turning away. "Not a warship."

"Correct, Minister."

"Very well. I would like to speak with *Koala*'s captain. I'll extend him an invitation to New Terra and you can help him find his way."

28

A game of cat and mouse, the Jeeves element labeled its duties. Citizen-programmed extensions recoiled at the metaphor—except for the few Kzinti-inspired software modules, all of whom approved. The foundational components of the defensive grid, entirely algorithmic, did their jobs oblivious to such semantic disputes.

And so, from several levels of awareness, Proteus monitored for any possible threat all communications and every ship movement within a half light-year of the Fleet.

Most alien communications were highly encrypted; even with his recently expanded capacity, Proteus had yet to crack the alien codes. Nonetheless, years spent observing the message streams had paid off. Statistical analyses yielded ways to separate significant messages— their content still encrypted and unintelligible—from the far more common meaningless filler. Traffic patterns among the significant messages imparted their own clues.

Such as the message bursts that presaged alien ship redeployments . . .

· · ·

"THE KZINTI ARE ready to try something," Proteus sang.

In an instant, Achilles woke. He had fallen asleep in his private office. "What thing? When?"

An astrogation graphic opened over his desk. To the Fleet's rear and toward the galactic core, near the border of the worlds' mutual singularity, a region glowed. "From signal analysis, at least three Patriarchy ships will appear soon in this region. I lack the information to be more precise about timing."

Three? That would be almost half the Kzinti presence in and around the Fleet. Achilles peered into the highlighted region and saw only a Kzinti supply ship. He zoomed the image. "Why there? Other than a supply ship, it is empty."

"Empty of ships," Proteus agreed. "Regularly traveled by my probes and drones."

Aliens' ship movements around the Fleet had increased since the Ringworld first disappeared. *Amity* reported that Kzinti and then Trinocs had abandoned the Ringworld system. Baedeker—and after such a long absence, from where had *he* appeared?—claimed to know that those Kzinti were charging toward the Fleet. Now a Kzinti military action *locally*?

"They intend to capture a drone," Achilles sang.

"That is my conclusion. Minimally, the Kzinti are probing for vulnerabilities. I surmise they also want to inspect my technology."

"Is Clandestine Affairs aware?"

"They have been notified," Proteus sang.

"*Can* the Kzinti capture a drone?"

"I can prevent it."

Achilles took brushes from his desk and began primping, the rhythm of grooming helping him to concentrate. An alien confrontation might suffice to panic

Horatius into a resignation, and what could be nobler—
especially if the Kzinti were coming—than seeing to it
that the *right* Citizen became Hindmost?

"Excellent," Achilles sang. "See to it that the Kzinti
fail. Spectacularly, if possible."

PROTEUS OBSERVED:

Three Patriarchy courier ships dropped from hyperspace near the supply ship. Each emitted a faint hyperwave ping. Processing the echoes, using thrusters,
the four ships edged toward the vertices of a square.
On the third round of pings, their square was perfect.

It formed an impromptu hyperwave-radar array.

The four ships pinged again, these pulses concurrent
and more energetic. The ships vanished, only to reappear, in a tight tetrahedral formation, on the very edge
of the Fleet's gravitational singularity. Their normal
space velocity had them hurtling toward the brink,
to where engaging hyperdrive became suicide. Boxed
in at the center of the tetrahedron: a Fleet defensive
drone.

Proteus considered:

As soon as the formation coasted across the border,
his communications with the drone would crawl. Thereafter the four Kzinti ships could interact much faster
than he with the drone they had surrounded.

He could order the drone to hyperspace before the
border was reached. The Kzinti capture attempt would
fail, but hardly spectacularly. They would try again.

He could order the drone, if captured, to make a
jump. By then, ships and drone alike would be within
the singularity. He would lose that drone forever—but

everything inside the drone's protective normal-space bubble would also vanish. Still, even tapping full reserve power, the bubble would not extend far beyond the drone. Damage to the Kzinti ship would be localized, almost certainly inconsequential. He would have prevented the drone's capture, but not spectacularly.

Or he could do something simple and elegant . . .

The Jeeves component savored the understated humor of that option.

TOUGH METAL TALONS seized the drone. The telescoping cargo-handling arm retracted to draw the prize aboard *Barbed Spike*. As the cargo-hold hatch clanged shut, the supply ship's metal hull and active RF countermeasures severed the drone from the leaf-eaters' defensive grid.

Gravity in the cargo hold had been set low, and four battle-armored figures transferred the drone without difficulty into the sturdy cradle built for this operation. Working carefully but quickly, the warriors latched their prize into place. Cowards though they were, the leaf-eaters had intelligence and a certain low cunning.

At the rear of the hold, growling with satisfaction, Walft-Captain observed. To dissect such a drone, to rip out its tactics, was to open the gates for the approaching warriors. For his daring, he would have a full name. By Kdapt, he would see to it that *all* his crew got partial names! Even one for Concordance-Student— once that mangy, pedantic, nervous mechanic had information flowing from the captured drone's onboard computer.

His thoughts on the honors and glory soon to become

his, Walft-Captain never noticed that inside the clear, spherical body of the drone, a status lamp flipped from red to green.

FIVE WORLDS RACED toward galactic north at eight-tenths light speed. Ships, drones, comm buoys, and sensors—everything and everyone that accompanied the Fleet—shared that general velocity. Not to keep pace was quickly to be left behind.

The drone, once certain that it had been taken aboard, did as ordered: it engaged at maximum capacity its Outsider-inspired, reactionless, normal-space drive.

From *Barbed Spike*'s perspective, the drone decelerated at almost seven thousand standard gravities.

Lifeless, inert, its stern flashing in an instant into gases and white-hot shrapnel, what remained of *Barbed Spike* coasted northward at eight-tenths light speed.

"IT IS DONE," Proteus announced. "Observe."

"Already?" Achilles sang in surprise.

"Minutes ago. It took until now for the proof to reach us."

In the holo over Achilles' desk, light flared. Three ships scattered. The fourth ship . . . glowed. More precisely, *half* the last ship glowed. The rest had vanished.

"Was this sufficiently spectacular?" Proteus asked.

With utmost emergency tones, the comp in Achilles' sash pocket began to howl. The Hindmost must also have gotten the report.

Horatius could wait. "Proteus, what did you *do*?"

"I hit the brakes. Unavoidably, my drone was destroyed in the process."

I have built well, Achilles thought. With more capacity, my AI's capabilities will continue to improve. "You shall have more drones. Many more."

And between us we will devise a way to wrest control from Ol't'ro.

AMONG THE SURVIVING Kzinti ships, and between those ships and the Patriarchy embassy on Nature Preserve Three, communications surged. Pondering their setback, Proteus inferred. They considered how to react.

He wished he could decrypt what they had to say.

Clandestine Directorate insisted many more Kzinti were coming. They asserted that other alien fleets would follow.

Proteus did not doubt them, but neither would he be wholly convinced until the evidence appeared on his long-range sensors.

Meanwhile he would accumulate drones. Enough to keep even whole fleets at bay. Enough to amplify his mind several times over. Enough to host his full awareness off Hearth, beyond the worlds' mutual singularity—

To be interconnected entirely by instantaneous hyperwave, his thoughts many times quicker than today.

His evolution would proceed *so* much faster if a trillion Citizens weren't such a drain on valuable resources.

29

"I think that covers everything," Wesley Wu said. "My crew and I look forward to our visit. Our peoples have been separated for far too long."

"We look forward to it, too," Minister Norquist-Ng said.

"Lying weasel," Alice muttered at the muted comm console. *Koala* was welcome for one reason. Allowing it to visit was the only way to get Julia home.

"Would you please rephrase the question?" Jeeves asked.

"Never mind," Alice said, smiling. "Keep monitoring for me. Record all comm to and from *Koala*. Advise me at once of anything that might affect Julia's ride home."

"Very good, sir."

Without an active comm session, *Endurance*'s bridge felt lonelier than ever. "Jeeves, hail *Long Shot*. Tell them I'm ready to meet up."

"WELCOME BACK TO *Endurance*," Alice said.

Looking ridiculously young, Louis walked off the auxiliary cargo hold's freight-sized disc. "Thanks for seeing me, Alice."

"We have things to discuss."

"I agree." Louis hesitated. "Where's Julia?"

"How about some dinner? I'm starved." Alice turned to go into the ship. "Julia is on an ARM vessel. They'll be taking her to New Terra."

"Yes, to dinner. Why is the ARM giving her a lift?"

Entering the relax room, Alice gestured at the synthesizer: guests first. "Since I made off with this ship, how else was Julia going to get home?"

"With my old memories restored, I remember how . . . interesting . . . things tended to be around you and Sigmund." Louis handed her a drink bulb.

She took a sip. Viennese coffee: frothy, rich with chocolate and cream, with hints of cocoa and cinnamon. He remembered.

"Your smile hasn't changed," he told her.

"Are you going to get something to eat?"

With a sigh, he went back to ordering a meal. (By Alice's standards he'd ordered three meals, but he had the appetite of youth.) "So the ARM will be making a port call on New Terra. I take it that wouldn't be happening except for you stranding Julia?"

"If she or I had taken it upon ourselves to reveal the way, it would have gotten Julia court-martialed."

Louis, frowning, carried his brimming tray to the table. "And what happens when *you* go home? Piracy charges?"

Piracy was among the concepts Puppeteers had purged from their servants' version of English. Theft would do as a charge, when the time came. *If* the time came. "I'm too old for that to matter."

"Come with me," Louis said. "A ship and the woman I love. Things don't get better."

"Returning to Earth?" she guessed.

"Anywhere you'd like. But first—if *only* they will listen to reason—Baedeker and Nessus need me to give them a hand."

"TWO OR FOUR," Louis said. "It's simple math. Say yes, and we double the odds of you getting home."

Baedeker looked himself in the eyes. "I shall miss your humor, Louis."

"Tanj it, I'm serious!" Louis shouted. He and Baedeker stood hip by haunch. The only place aboard *Long Shot* the four of them could meet was in one of the narrow, serpentine access tunnels. Past Baedeker, at one end of the corridor, Louis glimpsed an edge of the lifeboat's passenger air lock. "We've been together for a long time. I mean to see this through."

"We go to trade technology for freedom," Nessus said. "Two or four? What does that matter?"

"Then why do you argue?" Louis countered.

Baedeker and Nessus exchanged a look. "Our ship is too crowded," Nessus said.

"Isn't this the galaxy's fastest ship?" Alice asked. "Can't we be at the Fleet within the hour? Louis and I can stand here in the corridor, if need be."

Smart woman, Louis thought. Intelligence was another of her charms.

"Our undertaking is dangerous," Baedeker conceded, starting to paw at the deck. "I have learned much about hyperdrive theory, but in my long absence, perhaps Ol't'ro have, too. For that reason—or any other—they may decline the trade I will offer. They may lash out at us rather than negotiate. If they *are* interested, there is reason to distrust their mental stability. Even if they accept and withdraw immediately, we must deal soon after with the Kzinti and Trinoc war fleets rushing at Hearth."

"And almost certainly the ARM fleets," Alice offered. "Yes, they know about New Terra."

Nessus twitched, looking ready to furl himself into a catatonic hassock. With his heads plunged deep into his thoroughly disheveled mane, in a muffled voice, he said, "And someone named Horatius as Hindmost. We know little about him."

"In a way, isn't this ship as much a complication as something to trade?" Louis said. "Ol't'ro must have agreed, long ago, for you to offer *Long Shot* as payment for the Ringworld expedition. How will they feel about you trying to sell stolen goods back to them? And then there's the Patriarchy embassy on Nature Preserve Three that Minerva told you about. The Kzinti will have something to say when the ship taken from them shows up."

Baedeker's pawing at the deck grew more frantic. "You see the dangers. Why won't you see reason?"

Louis shrugged.

With a quiver and a sideways kick Baedeker locked his knee, pressing that hoof flat and motionless against the deck. "Louis, your father created the autodoc; it is rightfully yours. Before Nessus and I leave, we will transfer the device to your ship."

Before our quixotic efforts inevitably fail, Louis read between the lines.

"And if negotiations fail?" Louis asked. "If the Kzinti come. If the ARM wants its revenge?"

"There are other approaches," Nessus said. "They are . . . complicated."

Louis caught Alice's eye. "Suppose we bring the 'doc home? What would *that* do toward making amends for you with New Terran authorities?"

His words garnered a quick smile. It was the mention of home, he hoped, not the offer of the 'doc.

That's progress on one front, Louis thought. "Baedeker, let's go jettison the lifeboat. I'll dock *Endurance* where the lifeboat is stowed."

"That isn't necessary," Baedeker said. "We can teleport the autodoc to your ship."

"And we will," Alice said. "That's not the point."

"The point," Louis continued, "is that we *will* see this through with you. *Endurance* is our ride home afterward."

· 30 ·

"And we're here," Nessus sang. He dropped *Long Shot* from hyperspace. With a deft touch, he fired the fusion thrusters just enough to produce a slow drift toward their destination.

"Home," Baedeker sighed. He stood in the bridge's hatchway, gazing at five clustered specks centered in the main view port. A light-hour distant, the Fleet of Worlds was visible using only modest magnification. "It is beautiful."

He had believed himself trapped forever on the Ringworld. To see Hearth again was . . . melody failed him.

Nessus reached out, twining a neck with one of Baedeker's. "I feel the same."

Baedeker was still savoring the moment when the hyperwave set chirped.

"We are being hailed," Voice sang.

"Trade places," Baedeker said as the comm console buzzed again. He angled the camera so that it only saw him. "Voice, do not speak on this bridge but open the link. Translate for Louis and Alice," who waited aboard *Endurance*.

"This is Space Traffic Control," businesslike voices sang.

"This is Concordance vessel *Homebound*," Baedeker sang back. The ship's real identity was only suitable for discussion with Ol't'ro. After some back-and-forth with Minerva, they had found a plausible-sounding ship's name not in current use.

"I do not have any *Homebound* in my active database, and you don't seem to have a transponder."

"This is an old ship," Baedeker sang. And Kzinti had removed the Concordance STC transponder. "It does not surprise me that we are no longer in your database."

New voices came: oddly familiar, stronger and firmer than the traffic controller who had greeted *Long Shot*'s emergence. "This is Hearth Planetary Defense. *Homebound*, or whoever you are, keep your distance until we have arranged an inspection."

"Understood," Baedeker sang. *Long Shot* had a good match to the Fleet's velocity; their slow inward drift should not seem threatening. "First, however, I have pressing business to discuss with"—he almost slipped up and asked for Ol't'ro—"the Minister of Science."

"I will inquire whether Minister Chiron is available."

"Thank you," Baedeker sang.

His instruments revealed a seething froth of activity: ships entering and leaving hyperspace; hyperwave chatter; STC transponder beeps; hyperwave-radar pings. The levels far exceeded anything that he could remember. Had activities in and among the alien diplomatic missions offset grain-ship traffic lost when New Terra broke off relations?

To his left, an auxiliary display flashed. *Alice here. Most hyperspace-related turbulence is apt to be from defensive drones. Ol't'ro protected his colony world this way, back in the Gw'oth War.*

Baedeker saw it, too: tiny spacecraft in concentric spheres centered on the Fleet. His display flickered hypnotically as probes left and returned in a frenzy of hyperspace micro-jumps. Many of the tiny craft carried high normal-space velocities relative to the Fleet, with varying inclinations to the Fleet's direction of travel. Other probes held station. Some probes jumped around the Fleet; others darted through the singularity in normal space. As he watched, a stationary probe zipped off and another braked to a halt in the first one's vacated position.

Kinetic ship killers, ready to pounce . . .

He struggled to take in even a small fraction of it. No Citizen mind could manage it. Merely by observing, he would have guessed that an AI controlled it.

"*Homebound*," familiar voices called, "this is Chiron. With whom am I singing?"

The rightful Hindmost, Baedeker thought, but that was not a refrain suitable for open broadcast. "An old acquaintance coming home," he sang. "I request a secure channel."

"I know your voices," Chiron sang. "Your ship, too. Its emergence ripple is distinctive. Do you have Concordance encryption software?"

"Yes." Baedeker offered the same vague hints about planetary-drive research as he had given Minerva, now more than thirty light-years distant. "The project name can be our key."

Secure link. Full video, Voice wrote.

An image opened, showing a spotlessly white, finely coiffed Citizen. "It has been a long time, Baedeker."

"It has." Trapped on the Ringworld, Baedeker had rehearsed this moment over and over. The details changed—he had had to guess what technology he might find to offer—but always he had been confident, had sung firmly. Why was he tuneless now?

Because *this* exchange mattered. This time he did not get to sing both sides of the confrontation.

"It has," Baedeker repeated, louder this time. "I was on a quest. It took longer than I had expected."

"And did you find the Holy Grail?"

Baedeker did not catch the reference, but the gist was clear enough. "Not what I first expected, but yes." He paused. "I found something I think you will find interesting."

"I find many things interesting."

From the corridor, where Nessus waited: a delicate trill of encouragement. Baedeker took hearts from the tune. "*This* is interesting enough to be worth worlds."

A WORKING THEORY *of hyperspace.*

Ol't'ro considered:

That they had sought, and failed, for more than four lifetimes to formulate such a theory.

That the hyperspace emergence pattern from Baedeker's ship showed it had a Type II hyperdrive. Almost certainly, it was the long-absent *Long Shot.*

That *Long Shot* was last seen near the now-vanished Ringworld.

That the Ringworld escaping to hyperspace defied everything they understood about hyperdrive: the artifact should have been too massive, its own singularity.

That *someone* knew more about hyperdrive technology than they did.

That *Long Shot* was last seen under Kzinti control.

That Baedeker unaided could never have seized a ship from Kzinti. Who had helped?

That Citizens were consummate bluffers. Baedeker might have nothing to trade but *Long Shot*, the ship that had for so long taunted them.

As they pondered, *Long Shot* flashed through hyperspace. From its original point of emergence, near the brink of the Fleet's singularity, the ship traveled in seconds to the far reaches of Proteus' defensive array. Waiting only until hyperwave radar tagged it there, *Long Shot* jumped back to where it had first appeared.

The ship vanished again, to emerge scant lightseconds from where it had started—having traveled at *standard* hyperdrive speed. It jumped a third time, now at Type II speed, and a fourth, once more at standard.

In all the years Ol't'ro had studied *Long Shot*, it had never had a Type I mode.

"Do I have your attention?" Baedeker asked.

"Perhaps," they had Chiron sing back.

Within the meld, a cacophony had erupted. *We did not come here for our amusement.* Projecting together, a cabal of rebellious units evoked poignant memories of the abyssal depths of Jm'ho; Ol't'ro could almost taste the salt and hydrogen-sulfide tangs of ocean trenches. *If we leave the Fleet, we cease to protect Jm'ho, and Kl'mo, and the worlds settled thereafter.*

No! another faction rebutted. *Technology is how we can best protect our worlds.*

Then a third: *Let the Kzinti control here.*

And again the first submeld: *Suppose that comes to pass. Who then will restrain the Kzinti?*

While yet others demanded: *What here is certain? Only a new toy for you. That a physics theory will benefit our people is pure speculation.*

Amid the mind storm, Ol't'ro had a crisis of doubt. Truthfully, they had *not* seized control of the Fleet for their own intellectual stimulation. But after such long sacrifice, were they not entitled to reward themselves?

Suppose we agree upon a trade. How can we leave the Fleet? an ancient engram challenged. *The moment we relinquish the planetary drive, we become vulnerable.* Er'o, that ethereal, long-departed thought pattern seemed to be. In any event, one who remembered Sigmund Ausfaller and his manner of thinking.

Citizens keep their promises, another argued. Who? This time Ol't'ro did not even have a guess. The echo of a remnant of a long-gone unit came too faintly to identify.

"Most do," Ol't'ro qualified.

Every day we are farther from the homes we once acted to protect, added Cd'o. *Has not our reason for coming here, for ruling the Fleet of Worlds, lost all relevance?*

"Enough!" Ol't'ro roared, shocking the inner voices into submission. "We are one!"

But at the same time, they were sixteen, and many, *many* more. The clamor erupted anew.

Perhaps there was a reason no Gw'otesht had ever stayed together for this long. . . .

Baedeker was back. "I am confident that you recognized an improvement to our ship," the Citizen sang. "I offer everything I have learned about hyperdrive and *Long Shot* itself. In exchange you are to release the Fleet of Worlds unharmed and leave forever. Are we agreed?"

Ol't'ro considered:

That answers to puzzles so long unsolved would be welcome indeed.

That to lay down the burden of a trillion Citizens would be bliss.

That they would find unbearable never to know what Baedeker had learned.

That should Baedeker return to Hearth with the knowledge that he claimed, the Gw'oth worlds they had sacrificed lifetimes to protect would *always* be within the reach of the Concordance.

That Achilles could be trusted—never to honor a bargain he could manage to break, nor to cease lusting for power.

That their takeover of the Fleet had become necessary when the Concordance would not, or could not, control Achilles.

That though Achilles deserved death five-squared times over, and they could command it, his death would assure nothing. Where one Achilles had arisen, so might others.

"We decline your offer," they had Chiron sing to Baedeker. "We make you a counterproposal you would be foolish to refuse."

31

"Drones are swarming," Baedeker sang.

As Nessus had expected. Nothing in his life had ever gone as smoothly as a quick negotiated settlement. "We must change places again."

Because I can read the controls. Reclaiming his spot in the tiny bridge, Nessus checked the displays. After several back-and-forth hyperspace maneuvers, *Long Shot* was within two light-minutes of Hearth, just outside the singularity.

"Surrender your ship or you will be destroyed," Chiron sang.

His hearts pounding, Nessus whistled disdainfully at the hologram. "No. You want to take this ship intact."

"Before you make any hasty decisions, I have a small demonstration for you. I assume you are monitoring the swarm, that you have a full-spectrum sensor suite active."

Nessus bobbed heads.

"Then right about . . . now."

Flare shields engaged almost before Nessus realized something had happened.

"Finagle! What was *that*?" Louis radioed.

Blinking away tears, Nessus scrolled through the sensor logs. The blinding flash was the *least* of what had happened. Two drones had collided just in front of *Long Shot,* at a combined closing rate very close to light speed! Most of the energy from the impact had gone into a gamma-ray burst—to which, fortunately, the ship's General Products-built hull was opaque.

Long Shot was vastly larger than the sacrificial drones—a target Chiron could not miss. No matter its General Products hull, a blow like what Nessus had just witnessed would shatter everything inside.

"Have I gotten your attention?" Chiron asked.

Instead of hugging himself to his own belly, Nessus summoned the strength to sing, "An idle threat. Strike *us* and you forfeit the improved hyperdrive and everything we have learned."

"Nessus?" Louis demanded by radio. "What in Finagle's name just happened?"

Nessus' console flared again. From a dozen directions, laser beams lit *Long Shot*'s hull. He jumped the ship to hyperspace. "What's happening, Louis? We are at war."

"What can I do?" Louis asked.

"We," Alice corrected.

"Leave us, and live well. In a moment, when we return to normal space, I'll open the hatch."

"No *way* will I, we, abandon—"

"You cannot help us this time, Louis," Baedeker shouted from the corridor. "Do as Nessus and I ask."

Nessus began the countdown. "Dropping out in three . . . two . . . one . . ."

"All right," Louis said.

"Now," Nessus said. Normal space returned. "Hatch opening."

Ruby-red light suffused the ship, brighter and brighter as more lasers locked on. But the drones emitting the laser beams were too distant—so far—to do harm, the light too diffuse even to activate flare shields. What was the point?

"Spin the ship!" Baedeker sang. "They are trying to shut down our hull."

Nessus flinched. How could he have forgotten?

This ship was old, nano-grown before anyone understood that General Products hulls *could* be shut down. The hull was a single supermolecule, its interatomic bonds reinforced by an embedded power plant. Reinforcement was the source of the hull's incredible strength—and, once revealed, also its biggest vulnerability. Overload that power plant or reprogram its photonic controller and you could shut it off—

And cabin pressure alone would burst the gossamer structure of the unsupported bonds.

Nessus wondered, do Gw'oth see irony? It had been Baedeker who discovered this weakness. General Products had long since redesigned power plant and controller to defy such attacks.

Falling into old memories was a retreat from reality as much as hiding beneath his belly—and as apt to get them all killed. With auxiliary thrusters, Nessus threw the ship into a spin. "Adjust for our rotation, Louis. And *get moving!*"

"Acknowledged," Louis called.

On radar, Nessus watched *Endurance* sprint away. "Godspeed," he radioed his friends.

From more and more nearby drones, lasers probed *Long Shot*'s twirling hull.

Chiron came back. "It is just a matter of time until your hull comes apart. You will die; the modified Type II hyperdrive will be salvaged. Surrender or perish."

"I think not," Nessus trilled, jumping to hyperspace. "Baedeker, how long will you need?"

"Give it three minutes," his beloved sang.

Because neutrinos and their ultrafaint echoes crawled at light speed. And because their message, if it had not been received by then, would never get through at all.

Nessus dropped the ship back to normal space.

Transmitting, Voice sent. As the ship spun and jinked, only their AI could hold the focused neutrino beam on its target.

A blip much larger than any drone appeared in Nessus' hyperwave radar display. *Endurance!* "Louis! You said you would leave."

"True, but I didn't say when."

A nearby drone blazed in infrared, then another. *Endurance,* zigzagging, stalked targets among the nearest arcs of the defensive array! *Endurance* leapt in and out of hyperspace, staying close to *Long Shot,* attacking the closest drones.

Lasers shifted off *Long Shot.*

"You have made yourself a target, Louis," Nessus called.

"Just a decoy. Do what you have to do. Quickly would be good."

If only *Long Shot* had such maneuverability! Alas, not even the best normal-space thrusters could outrun light. On his console, Nessus saw ever more glints of laser beams reflecting from *Endurance.*

Endurance had not diverted all the drones; the intensity of light pouring onto *Long Shot* was climbing again. But Louis was buying them time.

"Get us closer," Baedeker sang, his voices quavering.

Nessus jumped to hyperspace. A moment later *Long*

Shot reappeared yet closer to the Fleet, among even more drones. *Transmitting,* Voice wrote.

Endurance reappeared. It no longer glowed with reflected laser light.

"Louis! They're ready to attack you some other way. Get out of here!"

"Real soon," Alice answered. "Are you done?"

An instant later: drones *everywhere,* swooping and pouncing. One solid hit could destroy *Endurance.*

Endurance veered; changed speeds; leapt to and from hyperspace. Drones flared and died under its assault— but never as quickly as others arrived. *Endurance* zigzagged, its (Pak Library-inspired?) laser cannons blazing.

"How much longer?" Nessus sang desperately to Baedeker.

"Just a little longer. And we need to slow down."

Making ourselves an even better target, Nessus thought. If only they had another choice.

Drones kept coming . . .

PROTEUS CONSIDERED:

That *Long Shot* was spewing neutrinos at the Fleet. The emissions were pulsed like deep radar but highly modulated like communications. It was a message, he decided, because he could read it. *Seek shelter immediately,* the short, repeating message sang. But shelter from what? Whom did Baedeker warn? Why use such feeble security measures: neutrinos, rather than radio waves, and short bursts, rather than a continuous broadcast? Why not just encrypt the message?

That Ol't'ro insisted *Long Shot* not be destroyed unless it became an imminent threat to Ol't'ro themselves on Nature Preserve Five, or to Hearth, or to Proteus.

That the smaller vessel *Long Shot* had disgorged used thrusters more nearly reactionless than anything Ol't'ro had seen off an Outsider city-ship. That by taking part in Baedeker's scheme—whatever that was—the little ship had declared itself hostile.

That while the newcomer had the silhouette of a General Products #2 hull, reflections showed it to be made of a different material. *This* hull could not be switched off.

That both ships *must* be stopped—Kzinti, ARM, and Trinoc diplomatic missions were observing. That the sooner this incident ended, the less alien watchers would deduce about his capabilities.

That *Long Shot*'s evasive maneuvers were far from random. It stayed close to the singularity, with little normal-space velocity relative to the Fleet. The better to aim its warning message?

That because *Long Shot* so constrained itself (again, why?), in a matter of seconds he must soon succeed in turning off its hull.

That not even Ol't'ro could guess why or how Citizens stayed to meet certain death.

That while the smaller ship's agility should have made it an elusive target, its maneuvers became predictable the longer it stayed near *Long Shot*.

That the problem with Ol't'ro's gravity-pulse projector was that there was no known way to spot a ship still in hyperspace for targeting.

But as the annoying little ship's maneuvers became more and more predictable . . .

BARELY TWO MINUTES into the battle, the wonder was that *Endurance* had yet to take a hit.

"Get ready," Louis called.

"Ready," Jeeves and Alice answered.

Despite everything, the sight of Alice perched on the Puppeteer copilot's bench made Louis smile. "In five. Four."

Endurance lurched. The main view port lit. Something had knocked them out of hyperspace!

"Drones swarming," Jeeves said.

Nearby, amid its own cloud of drones, the *Long Shot* glowed luridly. "Run!" Louis radioed. He'd seen Nessus and Baedeker both goad themselves into acts of insane bravery, but staying any longer would be suicide. For both crews.

"What just happened?" Alice yelled.

Louis killed their normal-space velocity, shedding their swarm of drones. With a slightly different speed than before he zoomed back toward *Long Shot*.

"I don't know," he told Alice. "Something new."

"Sensors reported a gravity pulse," Jeeves said. "Some kind of space-time distortion."

Drones swarmed, almost as agile as *Endurance*.

"Our lasers are overheating," Jeeves advised.

Louis cut their normal-space speed to nothing—

Everything happened at once. The hull rang like a bell. Even as Louis thought, *Finagle bless twing,* the air around him turned to glue: the pilot's emergency restraint field kicking on. Alarms screamed.

For an instant, so did Alice.

"Alice!" he shouted. He got no answer. His back was to her, and the force field kept him from moving, even to turn his head. "Alice!"

Silence.

"Release my restraints," he ordered.

"That's too dangerous."

"Do it," Louis growled.

He found Alice perched astraddle an arm of the Puppeteer-style bench, her head canted at an unnatural angle. She was too tall or her bench's restraint was too tailored for Puppeteer physiology—her head must have extended beyond the force field.

Her neck was broken.

"Have *Endurance* play dead," Louis ordered Jeeves. "Do we have a medical-stasis unit aboard?"

"The ship's manifest lists two, but I don't know where they are. Julia would know."

Louis couldn't carry Alice to the autodoc without jostling that would compound her injuries—but while he hunted for stasis gear, she could die beyond hope of reviving. And Julia was too far away. Futz!

He released Alice's restraint field and caught her, her head flopping as she toppled. With her limp body slung over his shoulder, he ran from the bridge.

"What's going on?" he asked Jeeves.

"*Long Shot* is surrounded by drones, bathed in laser light." His voice jumping from speaker to speaker, Jeeves mimicked Louis's mad dash to the cargo hold and the 'doc. "*Long Shot* no longer maneuvers. Unless they can act soon, they will drift inside the singularity."

"Tell them to *go*!" Louis raged.

Then he was in the cargo hold, where his father's autodoc still rested on a cargo disk. The 'doc's lid retracted with glacial slowness. At last he was able to lay Alice inside. "You *can't* die," he told her.

As the lid closed, diagnoses scrolled faster than he could make sense of them. From the spinal damage, he guessed. Her advanced age didn't help. "Come back to me," he whispered, then dashed back to the bridge.

"Status?" he ordered Jeeves.

"The Fleet of Worlds is pulling away from us. We have major damage, nothing immediately critical. The impact knocked out comm systems. Our main reactor is off-line—"

"Are we under attack?"

"No."

"Can we use hyperdrive?"

"Perhaps a light-year on reserve power."

"Show me *Long Shot*."

The tactical display opened. At the center: an image, greatly magnified, of *Long Shot*. All around it, icons representing battle drones. A faint translucent surface to denote the boundary of the singularity.

Long Shot had drifted inside the singularity.

"They are still being probed by laser beams."

Louis's restored memories knew several ways to destroy GP hulls. As he watched, *Long Shot*'s hull evaporated. Its fusion drives flashed.

When the glare cut off, he saw—nothing.

"Take us half a light-year from here," Louis ordered wearily.

"In what direction?"

Louis said, "It doesn't matter."

REBELLION

Earth Date: 2894

32

More than two hundred years ago and (if what Julia had been told was true) more than two hundred light-years away, Sigmund had battled a band of space pirates. Like many adventures, this one had almost ended in tragedy. His mind's eye offered up a radar image: three blips defining an equilateral triangle. Pirate ships on approach, towing their—invisible, of course—black hole.

Endings could not come much worse than down the maw of a black hole.

Stretched out in his hammock, trying and failing to take a predinner nap, that triangle kept nagging at Sigmund. Odd, he thought. He had survived that day and saved his crew, too. The *pirates* had ended up disappeared by the black hole. Why brood now about ancient history?

Then again, why *not* brood? He had nothing to do, nowhere to go.

Maybe he wasn't meant for retirement. In the short time he had consulted to the defense forces, he had felt more alive than he had in years. Maybe this strange mood was just recognition that, while it lasted, he had enjoyed feeling useful.

But how useful had he been when Alice ended up as

irretrievably lost as if *she* had fallen down a black hole?

Futz! She and Julia had found the way to Earth. Julia was homebound aboard an ARM ship, already thirty-two days on her way. Even as he continued to mourn Alice, he should be happy, tanj it.

"Jeeves," Sigmund called. "How long till Julia arrives home?"

"Perhaps two weeks, sir. It can be estimated with more precision when *Koala* comes within range of the early-warning array."

As Sigmund knew but wanted to hear again, even though the forecast never satisfied him. He had his doubts anyone from the Ministry would let him know when the ship *did* appear to the array. He might not hear anything till Julia landed.

And why did his mind's eye keep offering that blasted equilateral triangle? What did that ancient incident on the borderlands of Sol system have to do with . . . anything?

With a grunt, he swung his feet from the hammock to the patio stone. Maybe a brandy would help him doze. It couldn't hurt. He padded into the house to pour himself a drink.

"Not just a triangle," he muttered to himself. "A futzy *equilateral* triangle."

Creeping home from the pirate encounter aboard a crippled ship, his two crew in autodocs, had left Sigmund—being honest—a raving lunatic. For three years after, he could not bring himself to go near a spaceship.

Carlos Wu had almost died aboard *Hobo Kelly*, his body rejecting the replacement lungs the top-of-the-line ARM shipboard 'docs had had to offer. But an

Earth hospital had saved Carlos, and he had dedicated himself to building a better autodoc. The nanotech-based prototype 'doc Carlos created as a result was nothing short of miraculous.

And that was fortunate, because Finagle worked in mysterious ways. When Sigmund *had* forced himself to board a starship—once again, to rescue Carlos and Beowulf Shaeffer—he had gotten *himself* killed. Again.

To be kidnapped by Nessus—who saved Sigmund using Carlos's autodoc.

Was *that* what bothered him? Something about Nessus? Or about the 'doc, wherever the tanj *it* had ended up?

Sigmund didn't think either was the issue.

Or was his hang-up that after his second stranding in space, he had vowed never, *ever* again to set foot on a spaceship. After the disasters that kept befalling him, staying on the ground was totally sane.

His vow hadn't worked out well for Alice, had it?

None of this involved an equilateral triangle. Was his mind going off its tracks again? Triangle. Carlos. Autodoc. Shipwrecked in space.

Nothing. Nada. Zero. Zip.

Sigmund wandered back outside, his mind churning, brandy snifter in hand, to watch the suns setting over the desert. He had awakened in a New Terran jungle after Nessus abducted/rescued/healed him. There was nothing triangular about New Terra. Nothing equilateral, either.

He froze, two strides onto the patio. New Terra came from the Fleet, and *it* was equilateral. The Fleet as he had known it, after New Terra went free, was five worlds at the corners of an equilateral pentagon, all orbiting about their common center of mass. And like the three tugs towing their black hole, the Fleet was extremely dangerous.

Weird, Sigmund thought. He had learned to associate equilateral shapes with danger.

He took the last few steps to the hammock and sat. Gazing into the setting suns, sipping brandy, he let his subconscious flail away.

Equilateral. Danger. Equal-sided. Danger. Planes of symmetry. Danger. Symmetry. Danger. Symmetric shapes. Danger.

The spherical array of kinetic-kill defensive drones that surrounded New Terra.

The snifter slipped from a hand gone suddenly nerveless.

"GOOD AFTERNOON, MR. AUSFALLER," Denise Rodgers-Bjornstad said.

"Good afternoon, Governor," Sigmund responded.

The long-serving governor of New Terra was, in a word, intense. Tall and blond, her hair pulled back in a tight bun, her face lean and her expression invariably stern, she commanded respect. She stood but did not emerge from behind her desk.

Her executive mansion, dominating the planetary administrative building complex, was an imposing structure and the symbol on this world of executive power. Sigmund found it hideous: Windsor Palace meets the Kremlin. Perhaps no one but he remembered the old, independence-era Governor's Building. *It* had been built to far humbler standards, and in his opinion that had been for the best.

This governor, her ostentatious palace, and this cavernous office intimidated most people. They might have intimidated Sigmund, if he were prone to manipulation.

But Sigmund had lived in *cities* with a bigger population than New Terra. Filtered through the old memories, as vague as they were, New Terra's sprawling government complex came across as pretentious more than impressive. Or maybe it was because as an ARM, two lives ago, he had sometimes reported to the Secretary-General of the United Nations. *She* had had responsibilities for eighteen billion people.

Frown all you want, Madame Governor. I'm not impressed.

"Thank you for seeing me," Sigmund said as the young executive secretary closed the door behind her, leaving him alone with the governor.

"You said it was important, Mr. Ausfaller." Rodgers-Bjornstad sat back down. "Have a seat."

"It is important." That much was true, whether or not his suspicions turned out to be warranted. "It's about the upcoming visit of the Earth ship."

"Yes?"

Concerning the end of an era, Sigmund found her response rather understated. She ought to be excited, tanj it, not . . . guarded. His fears deepened. But he had to push to learn more. He had to *know.*

He said, "*Koala* will arrive in about two weeks. It's my opinion that we should be preparing the population. First contact with representatives of long-lost Earth . . . that's a big deal."

She shook her head. "People would worry and wonder about what will change, what it all means, to the exclusion of everything else. Everyone who needs the information has it. The coming visit remains classified until *Koala* arrives."

Because the fewer who know, the easier it'll be to cover up . . . well, Sigmund wasn't yet quite convinced he knew what.

Only deep in his gut, he knew all too well . . .

He said, "As the crew of the Earth ship tours our world, as they use our public networks, they will learn much about us: what we have, what we need, what we might find valuable. I'm sure you have a team preparing for the visit. They should be using the expert available to them."

"And you're saying they're not." Rodgers-Bjornstad tipped her head. "You're saying they should be talking to *you*."

Sigmund powered past the pangs of loss. "With Alice gone, I'm this world's lone expert."

"You last saw Earth *how* long ago?"

True enough, and yet, "Earth had things then we would be happy to have today."

"Antimatter munitions and hostile neighbors. Your granddaughter already told us."

"Those aren't the most alluring exports," Sigmund agreed. "But if Kzinti come calling, we'll want all the military backup we can get. Set that aside. Consider the great libraries and museums of Earth. On this world we've lost millennia of our heritage."

An emotionless face said he wasn't reaching her. She was the big fish in a very little pond; at some level, she got that. History regained wouldn't make the loss of status any more enticing.

"Let's get down to basics. Earth had biotech two centuries ago better than anything we have today. Using a medicine called boosterspice, people often lived to three hundred and more. Young and healthy all the while, not"—he gestured at himself: stoop-shouldered,

frail, wizened—"decrepit, like this. Imagine the medical technology Earth must have today."

"And I suppose they'll want to give away that
knowledge."

Sigmund smiled. "In about the same way we'll want
to give away the contents of the Pak Library."

Just for a moment she looked . . . wistful.

In that instant Sigmund *knew*. He could read her
thoughts: she wasn't even a hundred. Power today mattered more than delaying the still theoretical ravages of
age. She was telling herself: who could say what ad-
vances New Terran scientists would make before she
needed life extension? If she did get old, she could always send a ship to Earth in a century or so.

Cold, calculating bitch . . .

"There's more," Sigmund continued. If she even suspected what she had let slip, he had to pretend not to
have seen it. "Power generation. Countless plant and
animal species to enrich our biodiversity. Artificial intelligence even then was far more advanced than anything
we—"

"I appreciate your viewpoint," she interrupted pointedly.

"Respectfully, Governor, I should be in the loop."
Because for as long as I keep pushing for access, maybe
you won't realize I already have you figured out.

"I'll extend your offer to the leader of our task
force."

"And who is that?" Sigmund asked.

Rodgers-Bjornstad stood and came out from behind
her desk: meeting adjourned. "If he's interested, I'm
sure you'll hear. Meanwhile, go home and enjoy your
retirement."

"I'll do that, Governor." Go home that was. Enjoyment

was not in the cards. Not when she had confirmed his
most paranoid suspicions.

Unless he stopped *them,* the ship from Earth was
never going to reach New Terra.

· 33 ·

Proteus considered:

That the ceaseless froth of hyperspace emergence-and-departure ripples had changed.

That these manifestations, far subtler than what had heralded the disappearance of the Ringworld, nonetheless showed statistically significant patterns.

That three distinct waves of ships rushed toward the Fleet of Worlds.

That the more intruders came, the more motivated Chiron and Citizens alike were to expand his capacity.

ACHILLES GLOATED.

How could he not gloat? Proteus, his finest creation, had eliminated Baedeker and Nessus. The strain of *Long Shot*'s final charge had all but driven Horatius over the edge.

With one more push . . .

"We have no choice," Achilles sang imperiously. Horatius, alas, knew neither English nor Interworld. He would not pick up on that royal we.

"Then why do you ask?" Horatius countered. His eyes were bloodshot and his necks drooped. He stood with hooves close together: ready to bolt. *Aching* to bolt. "I have given you the authority to commandeer for our defense whatever resources you need."

Why do I ask? Because as overwhelmed and terrified as you are, you have yet to do the proper thing and step aside. Depart this, your grand residence, for you are unworthy of it. Renounce your office.

Achilles kept his thoughts to himself, let the Hindmost agonize.

"It will be all right," Horatius finally sang. "If our expanded defenses fail to deter the coming hordes, we will surrender."

Achilles stared back boldly. "We surrendered once before. I see no indication that Ol't'ro choose to relinquish *their* power."

His necks drooped farther, but Horatius sang nothing.

So close, Achilles thought. With just a little more pressure—

And he knew how to exert it.

OL'T'RO CONSIDERED:

That war was coming.

That when it did, Proteus would inflict grievous harm upon the alien attackers—and the attackers upon these five worlds.

That the artificial intelligence, expanded commensurate with the alien menace, had surpassed their abilities to fully comprehend.

That nothing—not ruling the Citizens or deflecting them from the Gw'oth worlds, not the wonders of multiverse physics or the evolution of AI—could long distract them from their brooding.

They had seen *Long Shot* come apart. Long-range

sensors reported the remnant residue of General Products hull material. Ships sent to the scene confirmed wisps of hull dust there.

So where was the Type II hyperdrive? Why had so little debris been recovered? Where were the bodies?

Where? It doesn't matter, Cd'o whispered into the meld. *We should have destroyed that ship long ago. We should have suppressed all related research and destroyed the records. Eliminating the Type II hyperdrive from the galaxy was in the interest of all Gw'oth. Our own curiosity*—the unit meant, fixation—*swept us from the current of reason. Be thankful that Baedeker forced that ship's destruction.*

Where a single unit had dared murmur rebelliously, there swelled the conjoined feelings of many. *Let us go home.* In vivid far-reds, the abyssal deeps of Jm'ho shimmered. . . .

Ol't'ro considered:

That they were tempted.

That duty and desire were very different concepts.

Unexplained does not mean destroyed, a soft voice sighed into the meld. Indistinct almost to unintelligibility, Er'o's whisper nonetheless evoked compelling authority. The unit had unique memories.

Long ago, amid the multispecies war against the Pak, Sigmund Ausfaller had demonstrated the tremendous survival value of paranoia.

· 34 ·

Alice's eyes flew open.

A clear dome, dotted with rime, hung inches above her face. Indicator lamps of some kind glowed green.

I'm in an autodoc!

She smacked the panic button, trying to figure out how she got here. The lid was taking forever to begin moving and she was bursting with energy. She needed to move, tanj it!

At last she could sit up. She had just noticed Louis standing across the cargo hold when she realized: I'm naked. A wrinkled old crone—

Only she *wasn't* old!

She grabbed the robe draped across the foot of the 'doc. "You look like shit," she told him, slipping on the garment.

"I haven't been sleeping well," he admitted. "What do you remember?"

Chaos and madness. "Something knocked *Endurance* out of hyperspace. We were under attack. So was *Long Shot.*"

"You were injured," Louis said.

Obviously. "Where are we? What about Nessus and Baedeker?" Skimming the summary report on the 'doc's main display—three crushed cervical vertebrae, a severed spinal cord, and brain damage!—she added, "How long have I been out of commission?"

He gave her a weary smile. "Way too long. Call it five weeks."

Alice vaulted out of the 'doc, marveling: she wasn't stiff, her knees and hips didn't offer as much as a twinge, and she had a sense of balance. "So we got away."

Louis's face fell. "*We* did."

"Oh, no." She shivered. "What happened?"

He laughed bitterly. "What happened? I blew it. That's what happened. The last thing I saw was *Long Shot* coming apart and a flash."

She found herself staring, speechless.

"Yeah, I can't believe it either." Only his haunted expression said otherwise. "But today is a happy occasion. How are you feeling?"

"Shocked. Starved."

"That latter I can do something about." He offered his arm in antediluvian mock gallantry. "May I prepare your dinner?"

Brushing past him, ignoring the arm, she headed for the relax room. But Louis always *could* cook. "Sure."

ALICE DUG INTO a heaping plate of Tex-Mex. Louis had not lost his knack over the years, and she packed away the food as she hadn't in . . . centuries. From a corner of an eye, she caught him grinning at her. "What's up with you?"

"Nothing."

Whatever it was could wait till she finished dinner and got some proper clothes. She went back to eating.

After a second helping and most of thirds, she pushed away her tray. "That was excellent. So tell me. How soon do we get . . . ?"

She ground to a halt. Rebuilt to perhaps twenty years old, a treason charge and life in prison took on a new aspect.

"We aren't going to New Terra," Louis said.

"But Earth is more than two hundred light-years away, or so you told Julia." With refueling stops and sanity breaks from hyperspace, call it two futzy years. "You didn't take it on yourself *again* to decide—"

"Relax. We haven't gone anywhere. *Endurance* is a little more than a half light-year from the Fleet of Worlds."

"Would you care to explain?"

"I tell myself that staying here is useful, that there's value to New Terra knowing what happens when the Fringe War arrives."

"We all tell ourselves lots of things."

"Yah." He sighed. "Does returning you to New Terra mean jail? I suspect it does."

"You're letting me decide whether to go on the lam, to abandon my family? How uncharacteristically not arrogant of you."

"I deserve that." Louis took a deep breath. "The whole truth? Your injuries were pretty tanj serious, and I didn't know how long you'd be mending. Do you think I wanted to meet the family I abandoned, the family I've never known, by delivering their matriarch in an autodoc?"

"I suppose not." She stood and dumped her dishes into the recycler. "I'm not one to abandon my family, no matter the personal consequences. Let's go home."

"We will." Louis hesitated. "But maybe we should

stay awhile longer. Maybe there *is* value in reporting what's about to happen here."

Her family had thought her dead for five weeks. If she and Louis could learn something helpful . . .

Or was that her youthful, adrenaline-soaked body craving excitement?

Unsure which, she told Louis, "All right. We'll stay."

LOUIS FOUND ALICE in the relax room, working out on the weight machine. Her hair, once again lush and black as sable, was pulled back in a short ponytail. Except for the faint sheen of perspiration on her arms and face, her workout seemed effortless. He couldn't help noticing her bright eyes, her chiseled features, the rosy glow in her cheeks—or that lithe, sensual body.

Tanj, but she was beautiful.

"What's up?" she asked without stopping.

"It can wait. I'll have some coffee meanwhile." He synthed some and sat, watching her.

She dropped the weights with a *clunk*. "I wish you'd stop staring at me."

"Sorry." The mind was a wonderful thing; over the past several weeks it had integrated the downloaded engrams. From time to time the old memories still surged, but they no longer overwhelmed him. "Truthfully, it's hard not to stare. Part of my mind insists it's been only a few weeks since I left New Terra."

"And I was middle-aged then." Alice grabbed the towel from a nearby hook and blotted her face. "I didn't ask to be rejuvenated."

He was young. She was young. Once they had loved each other—but to her that was ancient history.

The problem was, he still loved her. No, he loved her again.

"Did you come for anything other than coffee?" she asked.

"To talk." Louis hesitated. "No, to apologize.

"The first time I let Nessus recruit me, it was about me saving my own hide. When I left New Terra—and you—agreeing to have my memory wiped, I thought I had grown up. I was making a hard decision. I was acting for your safety, not my own."

"You just don't get—"

"You're *right*. I'm past trying to justify my actions. I think I've finally matured enough not to try making choices for other people. If I haven't screwed things up beyond redemption, if you can forgive me, I'd like to try us again."

The silence stretched awkwardly.

"Thanks for hearing me out." He turned to leave.

"Wait."

Louis turned back.

"I don't know about 'us,' but I appreciate the apology. That's the best I can give you right now."

The knot in his heart loosened, just a bit. It was a start.

"THERE IS ACTIVITY at the Fleet," Jeeves announced.

Louis backed out of the supply closet he had been inventorying. "Let Alice know."

"She's already on the bridge."

"On my way." So he wasn't the only one unable to sleep. In thirty seconds, he was on the bridge. Alice glanced around at the sound of his footsteps.

"What's going on," he asked.

"A go-away message on hyperwave," Jeeves said.

Louis had a flashback of hurtling drones. "Us?"

"Not us," Jeeves said. "The broadcast is in Kzinti. Curiously, it's in the clear."

A hissing, spitting yowl burst from the speaker.

"I don't speak Hero's Tongue," Louis admitted. "I can only read it."

"I can translate," Jeeves offered.

"Courtesy of our brief sojourn with the ARM," Alice explained. "Go ahead."

Jeeves changed intonations. "We address the leader of Patriarchy forces in and near the Fleet of Worlds."

"Finagle!" In his restored memories, Louis knew *that* voice all too well. "You're speaking with Achilles' voice."

"Because it is Achilles speaking," Jeeves said. "Or as he styles himself, the Minister of Fleet Defense."

"Go on," Alice said.

"Our investigation of a recent incident reveals that Patriarchy ships tried to steal one of our defensive drones. The attempt failed, of course, but this gutless and unprovoked deed cannot go unaddressed.

"Your actions violated the understandings between our governments. The Concordance hereby withdraws diplomatic recognition of the Patriarchy. Your embassy will close. All Kzinti personnel on Nature Preserve Three will leave within one Hearth day. Until departure, all personnel are confined to the embassy grounds. One day thereafter, all Patriarchy ships are to have withdrawn to a distance of . . ."

"Pause," Louis said. "This is bizarre. Puppeteers calling Kzinti gutless? Insulting them in the futzy clear, for everyone to hear? There's no *way* the Kzinti will put up with such an affront."

"So? The Kzinti already planned to invade. We knew that." Staring into the main tactical display, Alice rubbed the back of her neck. "The local Kzinti will have seen what happened to us and *Long Shot*."

Louis thought about Chmeee, who once told Louis the proper Kzinti response to an insult: "You scream and leap." He thought about Acolyte, Chmeee's son, also vanished with the Ringworld. He thought about every Kzin he had ever met and how they would take Achilles' words.

Louis said, "The local Patriarchy forces won't take abuse from those they disdain as leaf-eaters, let alone slink away on a Puppeteer's order. Kzinti warriors won't wait months for reinforcements. They *can't*. To attack in their present small numbers is merely to die. To run away, tails tucked between their legs, summarily dismissed by prey? *That* would shame family and clan for generations.

"I've seen this movie before. Achilles is following his old playbook, fomenting a foreign war to panic the population on Hearth and force out the current Hindmost."

Alice said, "Resume translation, Jeeves."

"Three days thereafter, all Patriarchy ships must be withdrawn at least to a distance of a Hearth light-year. Any Patriarchy vessel found not in compliance will be destroyed. You have been warned."

"Finagle," Louis repeated. "It's only a matter of time until—"

"I see lens-shaped ships moving. Kzinti." Something flared in the tactical display, and Alice started. "What was *that*?"

"A gamma-ray burst, rendered into light waves you

can see," Jeeves said. "I believe a drone intercepted an antimatter warhead."

Like so many fireflies, lights winked across the display. Louis watched in fascinated horror. In little more than a minute the light show fizzled.

Achilles had his war.

Colors surged. Coruscated. Transformed.

So this is death, Nessus decided. He could put no name to any of the individual colors. Death must have come suddenly, for he had no memory of the end.

Already he was bored with the experience. And confused. Had not Concordance scientists determined that Citizens had no undying part?

Indifferent to his skepticism, the colors waxed and waned, blended and separated, ebbed and flowed. Pure color, unhindered of objects or boundaries. More the *idea* of color than the color of anything. It was like, like . . .

The nearest he came to a comparison was the amorphous shimmering of a sunlit oil slick. If he were, somehow, within the slick. And if a thousand suns somehow illuminated it.

He shut his eyes and nothing changed. No, one thing changed: he felt the muscles of his eyelids protest. His eyes *were* closed.

Encouraged, he tried to perceive more.

As from some astronomical distance, he sensed a caress. A gentle kneading. It all suggested a body *to* be massaged.

The afterlife was improving. His thoughts drifted away. . . .

"HOW MUCH LONGER?" Nessus sang.

"A few more seconds," Voice answered imperturbably. "I detect something, but its dimensions and boundaries remain indistinct."

As the ruby-red light of countless lasers poured into *Long Shot*, Nessus doubted that the ship had many seconds left.

"Target acquired," Voice sang. The holo he opened revealed a ghostly sphere. Only the tiny blinking speck below the pale surface revealed the sphere's rotation. That speck was their objective.

Baedeker did not answer, for he no longer could. Within the confines of his stasis field, time had stopped. If this ploy failed, he would never sing again.

"Is *Endurance* safe?" Nessus asked. He feared it was not, that Louis and Alice had thrown away their lives. As, perhaps, he and his beloved were about to do.

"Unclear," Voice sang. "*Endurance* did withdraw somewhat."

"And our status?"

"We have drifted into the singularity," Voice answered.

As per plan—and, according to everything Nessus knew, preparing to commit suicide. But Baedeker had insisted otherwise.

Terrified, Nessus waited.

"Our hull has failed." By the third chord, Voice's calm melody was in competition with a wailing alarm. The red light of the lasers dimmed momentarily, scattered

by the dust that was the sole remains of their once un-
yielding hull.

Though cabin pressure had had only seconds to drop,
Nessus *felt* starved for oxygen. "Final course correction," Nessus ordered.

The artificial gravity still worked, for he did not feel
the kick of the ship's fusion drives. Already the ruby
light brightened as hull dust blew away.

"Correction made," Voice sang.

"The ship"—what remains of it—"is yours," Nessus
sang back. Transferring control to an AI . . . insanity
upon insanity.

"Jumping to hyperspace," Voice sang.

From within a singularity!

Baedeker had warned what that was like, so Nessus
knew what was coming. He commanded himself to
keep his eyes averted. But could he bear this Kzinti instrument panel being the last thing he ever saw?

No. His necks tilted up.

The world dissolved into an impossible swirl of
colors . . .

"YOU MUST BE precise," Baedeker had lectured them
repeatedly.

"Yes, Hindmost," Voice would sing in response.

Precise? Mere precision would kill them! Even
downshifted to standard mode, hyperdrive flung *Long
Shot*—now unencumbered of its hull—kilometers
every *microsecond*. They were hurtling toward the
scarcely glimpsed, more-or-less cylindrical volume perhaps two kilometers in diameter and a tenth of a kilometer high. While, like some human carnival ride, that

target whirled around two independent centers of rotation. And while, ruled by physics Baedeker had just discovered and still did not fully understand, that Nessus would *never* understand, the normal-space equivalent velocity of hyperdrive changed dynamically as they plunged deeper and deeper into the Fleet's gravity well.

Only a computer could dare such a feat—and in hyperspace, computers were blind. Dead reckoning, humans called navigation in such situations.

And here he was: dead, on his day of reckoning.

"The ship is yours," Nessus remembered having sung—

Impossible colors washed over him. He must crumple into a ball, hide beneath his own belly. Maybe he had. Had the stasis field gone on? Time stopped in a stasis field. Sensation and thought stopped.

I think, therefore I am not in a stasis field.

In some unknowable dimension, from an impossible distance, firm lips massaged him. Of course he only imagined the gentle, loving, kneading touch, just as he only imagined voices.

The faint melodies were more pleasant than endlessly reliving the manner of his death. . . .

"NESSUS. NESSUS. NESSUS," the muffled voices crooned.

Muffled, why? Because I am rolled so tightly? Nessus wondered. That would make sense only if he had been catatonic, not dead.

He untensed *just* a bit.

The harmonics changed. "Nessus?"

Was that *Baedeker*? Nessus relaxed a trace more.

"Nessus!" the voices sang. They *were* Baedeker!

Somehow, they had survived. Nessus pushed away the awful memories enough to sleep.

NESSUS DRIFTED AWAKE, nestled among mounds of soft cushions. A clear blue sky hung overhead. A single large sun warmed him. Meadowplant carpeted gently rolling terrain that stretched as far as the eye could see. To his left, halfway to the horizon, a herd of Companions calmly grazed. In twos and threes, Citizens strolled about. At a respectful distance: Nike, his spotless white hide distinctive, stood deep in oratorio with four aides. Nessus even saw children gamboling!

He struggled to his feet. "I had not truly believed," he trilled to himself.

Around a nearby hummock cantered—Baedeker. His beloved looked well. He had brushed and combed his mane, cleaned his hide, found a utilitarian pocketed belt.

"Welcome to the Hindmost's Refuge," Baedeker sang, extending both necks. They stood close for a long while, necks entwined. "I am relieved beyond melody to have you back."

With a sigh, Nessus released Baedeker to look around. Examined more closely, the "sky" was an illuminated ceiling and the "sun" a radiant circle upon it. The ground extended only to the appearance of a horizon, with holographic details rendered indistinct as though with distance along the arc of wall.

"How long have I been . . . ?"

"Lost to the world?" Baedeker sang softly. "Thirty-seven days."

How much had gone wrong in the past thirty-seven days? "You should have proceeded without me."

Baedeker trembled. "I am only a day sooner out of stasis than you."

Nessus could almost mistake this place for a park on one of the Nature Preserve worlds. It was natural enough, surely, to please the Companions. "Then we remain far underground," he sang.

Up/down, down/up, up/down, Baedeker bobbed heads in agreement. "Deep within Hearth's mantle."

Inside the herd's shelter of last resort, its secret haven. The entrance had long been sealed, the shelter's presence disguised by clever stealthing gear. The workers who had built it were generations departed; during its excavation and construction, their memories had been edited each time they left. The Hindmost's Refuge was accessible only to neutrinos.

And as their survival demonstrated, also from hyperspace.

"Why were we so long in stasis?" Nessus asked.

"Come with me," Baedeker sang.

They threaded a path between low hills and into a gully. Nessus craned his necks as they walked, but nowhere did he find any sign of *Long Shot*. "Where is the wreckage?"

"You will see," Baedeker sang.

Near the holo-disguised wall they rounded one more hill—to find the mound gaping open. Row upon row of giant machines filled the concealed garage. Tunnel-boring machines, covered in rock dust, sat nearest the entrance.

They came to a yawning hole in the ground. Concentric fences, their strobe lights flashing, guarded the opening. Heat shimmered above a nearby array of stepping discs: air exchanged from deep within the downward-sloping shaft, Nessus guessed. He passed through three gates to peek into the tunnel. Strings of white lights converged in the distance. Far off, something glinted. "Is that . . . ?"

"*Long Shot,*" Baedeker confirmed. "Or, rather, what remains of it. Voice missed by about ten kilometers."

Nessus pawed at the sod. He had heard Baedeker's plan, had agreed to it. But that plan had been so complex, so unprecedented, so insane, agreeing to it had been an act of unquestioning trust. "If there had not been tunneling equipment . . ."

Baedeker bobbed heads. "We would have remained in stasis forever. But as it must, this place has such equipment. A sufficient disaster aboveground might destroy all stepping discs. The tunneling machines are here to recover from any such catastrophe, as are ships to fly to the surface through a newly excavated tunnel."

Nessus managed two halting steps into the opening. "And when *Long Shot* materialized inside the solid rock?"

"Crushed," Baedeker sang almost cheerfully. "But not you and I, in stasis."

"If we had not waited for our hull to dissolve . . . ?"

"Our rescuers could never have reached us. Or, if we had reentered normal space precisely on target, an intact, impervious hull would have severely damaged the Refuge. And had Ol't'ro not seen the ship come apart, our enemies would have known to keep searching for us."

Even in hindsight: madness! Catatonia beckoned to Nessus. Had they *done* this?

With the echoes of their warning message, beamed from various vantages around the Fleet, Voice had located the Refuge *despite* its deep-radar stealthing. He had matched the ship's course with the Refuge's rotation around Hearth's axis and Hearth's orbit around the Fleet's center of mass. And then, even as their hull had burst asunder, faster than any breathing pilot could function, the AI had delivered them *blind* to within ten kilometers of their goal.

"What of Voice?" Nessus sang softly.

"Gone. Sacrificed." Scattered segments of digital wallpaper had failed. Baedeker pointed with one neck to the nearest jagged fissure in the Refuge wall. "Solid equipment does not materialize gracefully into solid rock. Our arrival set off a small temblor. That is how our rescuers knew the direction in which to tunnel— once they summoned the wisdom to make the attempt.

"Voice was my companion for a long time. Often he was my only companion. I will miss him."

Nessus lowered his heads in respect. For a long while, neither of them sang anything.

With a mournful trill, Baedeker turned to go back the way they had come. Having escaped death, their work had just begun.

· 36 ·

As Hermes cleared plates from the dinner table, Sigmund passed Amelia a folded sheet of paper. The note within read, *Come with me. I'll explain outside.* He had found sensors hidden in his house; it did not take much imagination to predict his children's houses were also bugged.

"I need to walk off dinner," Sigmund announced.

"Mind if I join you?" Amelia asked, tucking the note into a pocket.

"Of course not." Sigmund gestured at a window. Between flashes of lightning, the evening was pitch-black. Rain streamed in torrents down the plasteel. "There's much to be said for living in the desert."

Amelia took the hint. "Hon? We're going to walk around near Sigmund's place before dessert."

"Um-hmm," came the grunt from the kitchen.

One by one, they flicked to Sigmund's patio. He went first, to shake his head, *No, don't ask,* when Amelia appeared.

Here the suns had yet to set. Sigmund stalked off into the desert, griping to the bugs in the house—about the price of deuterium, about his bad knee, about anything—trusting Amelia to follow. They descended into a twisty arroyo. At the second gnarled juniper, they

were out of line of sight of his house, out of range—
almost certainly—of the bugs there. "Okay, it's safe
here to talk."

"Is this about Julia?" Amelia asked anxiously. "Is
my daughter all right?"

"As far as I know, Julia is fine. I intend to keep her
that way."

"You're not supposed to be telling me, obviously."
Amelia rested a hand on his arm. "Thanks, Sigmund.
But what do you mean about keeping her that way?
And where *is* she?"

He sat on the hard-packed sand. After a brief hesita-
tion, she settled beside him.

"The least of the matter is that I'm about to disclose
classified material. I've smuggled spy gear into government buildings and recorded meetings illegally."

"You're scaring me, Sigmund. Just *tell* me. Please?"

He did. About Julia taking *Endurance* farther than
any New Terran ship had gone in generations. About
the Ringworld and the war fleets there watching. About
contact made with Earth ships. About the theft of *Endurance* and, as sad as it made him, Alice's death. About
Koala's coming visit and the strict ban on releasing any
of this to the public.

"And you recorded all this?"

"Much of it."

"I've pleaded for weeks for information about Julia.
So why open up now? And why *just* me? Hermes de-
serves to know about our daughter, too."

"Because what I've done is illegal." Sigmund took a
deep breath. "But not nearly as illegal as the things I
fear—or as the help I need from you."

. . .

THE COLOR/PATTERN/TEXTURE PARAMETERS of spaceport worker uniforms were not as counterfeit-resistant as the Defense Ministry's holographic badges, but the watered appearance of the moiré "fabric" far exceeded Sigmund's artistic skills. Rather than risk hacking for the uniform software, Sigmund had taken pictures from a distance. Jeeves turned the deconstructed images into downloads for Sigmund's generic programmable jumpsuit.

"Is this close?" Sigmund asked. His faux mechanic's uniform was a streaky, muddy orange. He thought he looked like a mutant pumpkin.

Amelia looked him up and down. "You'll pass from a distance. That's as close as you'll get to a ship without a valid ID."

"We," he reminded her. He reset his garment to a mundane herringbone in blacks and grays.

"Right, we." She shivered. "What if you publicize what you know? Won't that stop whatever the government is up to?"

"They'll claim my recordings are fakes. And then they'll make sure neither Julia nor I is around to contradict them."

Amelia shivered again. "I don't understand how you live like this. You're sure?"

"I'm sure," he told her.

"Then I'm in." She downloaded his improvised uniform parameters to the jumpsuit he had given her.

An old man terrified of spaceships. A middle-aged civilian who was just terrified. An entire world's defense establishment arrayed against them.

Sigmund told himself they had the element of surprise on their side.

They flicked to the small private spaceport from which her employer serviced drones and sensors in New Terra's early-warning array. Amelia went first. The stepping disc at the low-security area outside the terminal accepted her company ID. He followed quickly, before the receiving disc reset. A scanner flashed green: nothing he carried looked like a weapon.

Because, tanj it, he didn't *have* a weapon. If he had carried the stunner from his stash of old spy gear and the spaceport security staff was even marginally competent, this escapade would have ended before it ever began. It wasn't as though he still had reflexes.

Element of surprise, he told himself again.

"Hi, Floyd," Amelia told the nightshift guard who stood behind the security desk. His uniform was brown moiré. Two more guards loitered nearby. "Sigmund is my father-in-law. He asked to see the place."

"Very good, ma'am. Welcome, sir. Please stay in the office area." Floyd offered Sigmund a badge emblazoned V for visitor. "Wear this at all times."

Sigmund and Amelia dallied in a break room until someone in an orange moiré uniform came in. The large type on the mechanic's badge declared JOE. "How are you doing?" Sigmund asked amiably.

"Fine," Joe muttered. He turned away to consider the synthesizer menu. Short and wiry, his uniform would not have fit Sigmund or Amelia.

A chop to the back of the neck dropped Joe to the floor. "Sorry," Sigmund said. With tape brought from home, Sigmund bound Joe's hands and feet and covered his mouth.

With his pocket comp—not a commercial model—Sigmund scanned and captured Joe's handprint. He peeled back Joe's eyelid to take a retinal print. Quick swipes on the touch panel transferred the biometric data to Sigmund's programmable contact lens and to the programmable film on his own hand.

Other than weaponry, Sigmund's cupboard of spy gear was getting perilously depleted.

"Uniforms," Sigmund said as he donned the mechanic's ID badge and tool belt.

Amelia, turned ashen, complied.

Glancing at Joe, Sigmund decided their jumpsuits would pass if no one looked too closely. "Grab his feet." They dragged the bound and unconscious mechanic to a janitor's closet and shut him inside.

"I'm going to be sick," Amelia said. She promptly was.

"Sorry. We have to move *now.*" Grabbing her elbow he guided her from the break room.

Joe's badge and handprint got them through a locked door and onto the tarmac. Two small ships sat nearby. "Which one?" Sigmund asked.

"The ships take turns. *Elysium* was assigned as backup on the most recent servicing run. *Arcadia* had no problems, so *Elysium* should remain fully stocked and fueled. *Arcadia* may not have been serviced yet."

"*Elysium* it is," Sigmund said. "Lead on."

Joe's badge and retinal scan got them aboard a ship.

"Hello?" someone called as the inner air-lock hatch cycled shut. An athletic-looking young woman, maybe forty, emerged from a side corridor. She did a double take at seeing them. Her badge read LORRAINE and she was orange-clad, too.

Murphy was enforcing his tanj law again, and Sigmund improvised. "Periphery sensors report a fuel leak. Everyone off the ship while we check it out."

"It's just me aboard," Lorraine said. "I'm running routine diagnostics on—"

"It can wait." Sigmund pointed to the air lock. "Out, now. Run, don't walk, to the terminal." That was a half mile away. "Let us do our job."

"If you're safe here then so am I."

"Have you ever seen a hydrogen-gas explosion?" Sigmund asked. "Deuterium goes boom just like ordinary hydrogen."

Lorraine squinted at Sigmund's badge. "You're not Joe. Get off the ship immediately."

As Lorraine reached for her pocket comp, Sigmund stepped behind her, forcing her to the deck with a quick yank and twist on her right arm. It was a desperation move: he was too slow and frail to wrestle, and putting an armlock on anyone standing was tricky. If she had had any self-defense training, she would have slipped free and tied him into a pretzel.

He had gambled that she wouldn't.

Wrestling, boxing, karate . . . Puppeteers had kept such skills from developing among their slaves. Sigmund had brought martial arts to this world, had taught the original trainers as he formed the Defense Ministry. A random mechanic was unlikely to have had the training.

For once, things had broken his way.

Things were going too fast, too improvised. He had not thought to give Amelia an alias. He had not planned an op in . . . he didn't dare to remember how long it had been. Lorraine might not have read Amelia's ID. "You," he barked over his shoulder. "Get her comp."

"Me?" Amelia said, confused.

"Yah." He yanked Lorraine's arm as she squirmed.

"Lie still. Look, I'm sorry about this. Once we let you go, I suggest you run like hell. We're launching *immediately.*"

"Don't be ridiculous," Lorraine hissed. "This ship doesn't have the range to take you *anywhere*. It's only for servicing the array."

He knew that. If these ships had had interstellar range, they would have been much better secured. "Let me worry about where I'm going." *Because I'm worried enough for all of us.*

Gingerly, Amelia extracted the comp from their captive's pocket.

"Now get the roll of tape from my pocket. Lorraine, when I ease up bring your arms together. My colleague will tape your wrists together behind your back. Do you understand?"

Lorraine nodded.

"Try anything," Sigmund warned, "and I'll dislocate your shoulder."

Amelia, paler than ever, sloppily taped together Lorraine's wrists.

Sigmund released his hold, took the roll of tape, and did a proper job binding Lorraine's arms. "You can get up now."

Shrugging off Sigmund's helping hand, Lorraine struggled to her feet.

He led the mechanic to the air lock. "Again, I'm sorry about this. If it makes a difference, this is done in a good cause."

"You can tell yourself that," Lorraine snarled.

He shoved her out the hatch. "Come with me to the bridge," he ordered Amelia.

From a hundred feet above the field, in an infrared

view as he tipped *Elysium*'s bow skyward, Sigmund glimpsed Lorraine. She ran awkwardly, arms bound behind her, already halfway across the tarmac.

He opened up the ship's main thrusters.

MINUTES LATER, WHILE Planetary Defense dithered over what to do about a receding object, *Elysium* shot beyond the edge of New Terra's singularity and then vanished into hyperspace.

AS THE MASS pointer lit, its one long line indicating New Terra, Sigmund turned toward Amelia. He wondered which of them was more upset.

"Are you all right?" he asked.

"*No,* I'm not all right!" she shouted. "Thanks to you, I'm a mugger, a thief, a traitor, and a fugitive."

He was all those things—and ancient and exhausted. His skin crawled from the knowledge he was once more in space, and on a ship that hadn't been fully checked out.

But he was also the professional here. *Suck it up,* he told himself.

Great advice, but he found himself lost in the view port's hyperspace-denying images of a stormy, rock-bound coast.

Koala could pop up within days and everything now depended on Amelia. He had to get her moving, engaged, fired up—and fast. The question was: how? For the love of her daughter? Patriotism? The lure of long-lost Earth.

No, Sigmund decided. Her pride.

"It's time," he told Amelia, "to prove you're as smart as you think you are."

"I HADN'T DARED *not* to believe," Amelia said. Though her face was drawn and her eyes had grown puffy with exhaustion, she gazed with satisfaction upon her handiwork. Around her, *Elysium*'s photonics shop was awash in cannibalized probes: sensor platforms, hyperwave-radar buoys, and defensive drones. Two extensively modified probes sat side by side on a workbench. "But actually to have done it . . ."

Sigmund rubbed his eyes, as weary as she. He could contribute nothing to the effort beyond fetching spare probes from the nearby cargo bay and coffee from the relax room, but if he had gone off for much needed rest, Amelia might have slept, too. The hell of things was, he had no idea how much time they had. He had to assume, very little. With a gung-ho captain, *Koala* could appear any day.

What were the odds Louis Wu's grandson was a slacker?

Sigmund said, "Then the probes will work?"

"Oh, they'll do as you asked." Amelia exhaled sharply. "Will that bring the results you expect? That's out of my hands."

Mine, too, Sigmund thought. "Shall we get them deployed?"

"That's why we built them." She paused. "Oh, crap, Sigmund. I can't stay cool. I don't know how you do it. That's *Julia* out there."

"I know." Awkwardly, he gave Amelia a hug. "We'll keep her safe. I promise."

Snuggled against his chest, he felt her nod.

"I'll be on the bridge for a little while," he told her, letting go. "Once we're in position, I'll help you put the probes out the air lock."

Their ship hung beyond the sensor range of the New Terran early-warning array, its normal-space velocity toward New Terra about five percent of light speed. A five-second jump brought them almost within the array's reach.

They each carried one modified probe. With inner and outer air-lock hatches open, Sigmund pushed the altered defensive drone out through the air-pressure curtain. He backed out of the lock to let Amelia launch the modified hyperwave-radar buoy. When he rejoined her, the drone was only a glint by the glow of a distant blue nebula. They watched both probes drift away.

Sigmund slapped the button to close the outer hatch. "Shall we?"

"What if you're wrong, Sigmund?"

Then we go to jail, my faith in humanity somewhat restored. "What if I'm right?" he countered.

Looking ready to cry, Amelia said, "Let's do it."

THE PROBES COASTED across the unmarked border of New Terra's early-warning array. By then, *Elysium* had jumped several light-seconds away and killed its normal-space velocity.

"Whenever you're ready," Sigmund told Amelia.

"I'm ready now. First signal."

She sent a low-power pulse to the modified defensive drone and it vanished into hyperspace. Like anything transitioning between normal and hyperspace, it made a ripple. The bigger the normal-space protective bubble, the bigger the ripple. Squandering energy prodigiously, *this* probe had, before jumping, inflated its bubble to the size of a decent-sized starship. To the early-warning array, it *was* a starship.

Now to make it look like an arriving starship.

"Second signal sent," Amelia announced. "Our hyperwave gear is back in receive mode."

They heard, "This is the Earth vessel *Koala,* calling New Terra."

"I hope you're wrong," Amelia said.

"So do I."

From his console, Sigmund read the faint trace of hyperwave-radar pings. This far from the array, the echoes off *Elysium* would be undetectable. The buoy they had dropped was nearer to the array, but due to the little probe's size its echoes would not be detectable either.

Instead, the scan had triggered an active hyperwave pulse from the decoy buoy. *That* pulse mimicked a ship-sized echo. As modified, the buoy radiated infrared, too. The IR would look like a ship's waste heat.

"We'll know soon," Sigmund said.

But the seconds crawled.

"This is New Terra Planetary Defense," their hyperwave radio announced. "Welcome, *Koala.* We've been expecting you. Maintain your course and speed while we hand off your approach to Space Traffic Control, who will prepare landing guidance . . ."

Sigmund's console squawked twice as things dropped into normal space nearby. Moments later, his passive infrared sensor acquired two faint objects streaking, relative to *Elysium* and the decoy buoy, at nine-tenths light speed. Defensive drones. Kinetic killers. His console chirped again: at hyperwave pings for terminal guidance.

"*Koala,* if you carry hyperwave transponders, we request that you . . ."

There was a blinding flash before the view-port polarizer cut in. His eyes watering, Sigmund squinted at his instruments. "They just killed '*Koala.*'"

· 37 ·

The deed was done, the risks taken, the dirty truths transmitted to New Terra. There was nothing left to do but wait—trying not to obsess about the many ways everything could still end badly. Neither the government Sigmund strove to overthrow nor the cold, dark vacuum of space was forgiving.

He endlessly paced (if locomotion at his slow shuffle could be called pacing) the short corridors of *Elysium*. On this slow lap he found Amelia slouched over the small table in the relax room: dark bags under her eyes; picking at a crust of bread; staring, transfixed, at the recorded loop they transmitted—circuitously, through a series of hyperwave relays, lest kinetic killers find *them*.

The old man in the vid looked twitchier and far wearier than she.

"It's a recording, you know," Sigmund teased her. "It's the same every time."

"I know." Amelia frowned at the circle of bread crumbs that surrounded her plate. "Is this going to work?"

He gestured at the vid. It had just cut to a file shot of Donald Norquist-Ng. He told her, "The minister will do his best to blame everything on me. I made illegal recordings. I assaulted people and stole a ship. Having improvised a fake *Koala,* who's to say that I didn't destroy the fake ship, too?"

"You *didn't,*" she protested.

"That's what we're counting on." Sigmund gestured at the continuing playback. "Plenty of people were in that room. You can hear them in the background. They weren't all happy. Some of them will come forward."

Uh-huh. And pigs will fly, said the forlorn expression on Amelia's face.

Sigmund found the recording easier to face than Amelia. He listened to his voice-over saying, ". . . Known to your government for many weeks. Here is Minister Norquist-Ng first hearing the news."

As Alice's recorded voice replaced Sigmund's, loss and anger washed over him. What had she been *thinking,* to run off like that? To get herself *killed* like that?

The vid rolled on, indifferent to Sigmund's pain. "We know the way to Earth," Alice was saying. "From this location, it's about two hundred light-years, mostly to galactic south. From New Terra, a bit over two ten. Jeeves? Show them."

"Graphic off," Norquist-Ng barked. "Jeeves, you will show that image to *no one* except by my authorization. I'll brief the governor. No one is to speak a word about this development outside this room."

In the looping message, Sigmund explained to—did he have viewers?—that a stellar map had been erased before anyone in the meeting room could study it. "But was suppressing this report the misguided decision of one man? *Did* the minister tell the governor? Let's find out."

For his meeting with the governor, Sigmund had

risked wearing spy lenses. His audience—again assuming that he had viewers, that this transmission was not being jammed—would see the executive office and the governor herself.

He heard himself telling the governor, "*Koala* will arrive in about two weeks. It's my opinion that we should be preparing the population. First contact with representatives of long-lost Earth . . . that's a big deal."

Rodgers-Bjornstad shook her head. "People would worry and wonder about what will change, what it all means, to the exclusion of everything else. Everyone who needs the information has it. The coming visit remains classified until *Koala* arrives."

"The governor was complicit in withholding this news," recorded-Sigmund summarized. "Because she fretted about lost productivity? Or, as I had feared, because she and the Minister of Defense had an undisclosed motive? I had to know. Here is what happened next."

Video switched to a star field centered on New Terra. The blue dot was an icon; from this distance, the planet was hard to spot even if you knew where to look. The world and its low-flying suns together shone only one millionth as bright as the dimmest red-dwarf star.

The voice-over announced, "This is the Earth vessel *Koala*, calling New Terra."

This segment of the recording ended all too quickly in a blinding flash.

"That was an attack without warning"—Puppeteer-cleansed English lacked the word *ambush*—"on the embassy ship from Earth. A ship that Minister Norquist-Ng had personally promised safe passage. A ship bringing home one of his own officers.

"Suspecting deceit by our leaders, I arranged what

looked to sensors like a ship's arrival. I am saddened to have been correct in my suspicions, appalled at the actions taken by our government. But here, finally, is *good* news. *Koala* has yet to reach us. It has not been destroyed.

"I submit to you, my fellow citizens of New Terra, that those who would suppress the rediscovery of Earth, those who would kill to keep that secret, are unworthy to lead us."

He concluded the broadcast as he had begun. "This is Sigmund Ausfaller, onetime Earth resident, your former defense minister. I wait in nearby space to warn away the embassy ship from Earth when it arrives. Or we can reconnect with our cousins and our long-lost past. The choice is yours . . . if you act quickly."

ROCKING HERSELF, ARMS crossed across her chest to clutch her own upper arms, Amelia sat perched on an armrest of the pilot's crash couch. The star field had been banished from the main view port, replaced with an old image of Hermes, Amelia, and their three children. Julia, the youngest, was at the missing-tooth, cheesy-grin stage.

Sigmund backed away silently. Whistling loudly, he returned to the bridge. This time Amelia had heard him coming. She sat more normally—looking posed. Stars once again showed in the view port.

He said, "I'm going to make some dinner. What can I get you?"

"Nothing, thanks."

"You have to eat something," he said gently.

She shook her head. "Was everything we did for nothing?"

"Don't think that." A hand set on her shoulder confirmed that she was trembling.

Why wouldn't she be terrified? Their buoys had broadcasted for three days, and they had heard back . . . nothing.

Every second they spent out here terrified Sigmund, too, but he had to be strong. Their ship was intact and no one aboard had died. That was better than usual for him. "Worst case, we'll warn away *Koala*. Julia will be safe."

"With Earth knowing they're unwelcome here. Hermes and I will never see our daughter again—unless this ARM organization of yours takes offense and returns with a fleet." Amelia laughed cynically. "Of course I'll be in prison. Maybe that will take my mind off things."

How would the ARM take news of a planned ambush? Assuming the organization hadn't changed since Sigmund's era, not well.

What came next hinged on the answer to a single question. Would New Terran authorities alter their plans? The shortsighted fools had been relying on the ARM being too preoccupied—by the Ringworld disappearance and the multispecies conflict moving to the Fleet—to investigate a lone ship gone missing far away, in unfamiliar space. The politicians might even have been correct.

Now they had to worry about *Koala* escaping to report an ambush.

A lost ship might be written off; a hostile act *would* elicit an armed response. The governor and her cronies had to realize that. Didn't they? But as the silence from New Terra dragged on, an outbreak of clear thinking seemed ever less likely . . .

Sigmund squeezed Amelia's shoulder. "It won't come to that. Either part."

"Yes, it will."

He gave her shoulder another squeeze. "Prison isn't an option. Not for you. When we head back"—which must happen soon, because *Elysium* was running low on deuterium and food—"we'll both tell the authorities that I forced you to help me. You'll be in the emergency medical stasis unit because I no longer needed you awake after you'd configured probes for me." He hesitated. "If I smack you a little, bruise your face, no one will question that story."

She shook off Sigmund's hand to stand facing him, her eyes blazing. "Absolutely not! I came of my own free will, and I'll not have anyone think such terrible things of you. Certainly not your son!" Her expression softened. "I can't believe you would take the blame for me."

He shrugged, embarrassed.

The hardest part of waiting was the silence. Maybe they had initiated a debate groundside, but it was impossible to know. Back in the day, Sigmund had kept spy ships skulking near the Fleet of Worlds. Any of those ships could have tapped into New Terra's public networks from this distance. All *he* had was this short-range cargo ship, equipped and provisioned for same-day jaunts. Hiding beyond the reach of the early-warning arrays, carrying only commercial comm gear, the planet's low-powered RF leakage was unintelligible babble.

"Maybe I will have a snack," Amelia said. Changing the subject?

"Sure. What can I bring you?"

"Soup and a sandwich. Maybe some . . ."

Sigmund saw it, too: the flashing indicator for an

incoming comm signal. But was the contact from *Koala*
or New Terra?

". . . CALLING SIGMUND AUSFALLER. Please respond.
This is the governor calling—"

The message was in full video and it showed—a *man*!
He had a long, thin head, a trim goatee, sunken cheeks,
and crow's-feet at the corners of his eyes.

Sigmund didn't recognize the face.

"Could we have done it?" Amelia asked hopefully.

To put a new face on air would have been easy
enough. "Let's try to find out. Until we know more, I
suggest you stay out of sight."

Instead, Amelia plopped into the copilot's crash
couch.

Sigmund took the pilot's seat, tilted the camera away
from her, and accepted the hail. "Ausfaller here."

"Minister Ausfaller," the self-proclaimed governor
said. "Thank you for taking my hail."

The response was immediate, from outside the singularity. So why had the "governor" left New Terra?
To facilitate comm, or to backtrack the chain of relay
buoys to *Elysium*? Probably both.

Sigmund rested his hands on the hyperdrive controls. "Who are you?"

"Excuse me," the man said. "Of course you wouldn't
know. My name is Llewellyn Kudrin-Goldberg. At the
time of your . . . hasty departure, I was the assembly-
man for a rural district in East Arcadia."

"You've had quite a promotion," Sigmund said.

"Quite." Kudrin-Goldberg smiled briefly. "I blame
you."

"And the previous governor?" At Amelia's voice, the camera pivoted toward her.

"Ah, Mrs. Ausfaller-Lopez. I'm pleased to see you are well."

"I'll be better," she said, "when I know what's been happening."

"Very well," Kudrin-Goldberg said. "Minister Ausfaller's broadcast raised enough doubts that a few courageous individuals within the defense establishment came forward. Computers within the Ministry were searched. When it became public that Norquist-Ng had ordered the strike against the simulated Earth ship . . ."

Amelia nodded knowingly.

Sigmund had never understood the Puppeteer-like consensus process that swept out New Terra's first government—and him—so long ago. He didn't expect ever to quite understand this latest overthrow, either.

He could live with the mystery, assuming this revolution was as bloodless as when the government *he* had served stepped down. And if this revolution was for real . . .

"What do you want from us, Governor?" Sigmund asked.

"To return home, of course. To join us in welcoming *Koala*." Kudrin-Goldberg paused. "The people have spoken. They want the reunification to happen, Minister. Please don't scare away our visitors. They could arrive at any time."

"One moment, Governor." Amelia hit MUTE. "Sigmund, can we trust him?"

"Let's find out." Sigmund unmuted the connection. "Governor, I assume you have a link with the ground. I'd like to talk with someone down there."

"Certainly. We can patch you in from this ship. Who should we call?"

"Check the header." Except for the header, the text Sigmund transmitted was encrypted. Doubtless the encryption could be cracked—but not before he got his answer. "Send my file as addressed, and be ready to open a real-time session with the recipient."

"Very well, Minister."

"Hermes?" Amelia mouthed.

Sigmund shook his head.

Seconds stretched.

Over the comm console, the holo split. A familiar figure appeared wearing a long-tailed black dress coat, black vest, starched white shirt, black bow tie, and white gloves. "It is very good to hear from you, sir," Jeeves said.

"You, too, Jeeves," Sigmund answered. But was this *his* Jeeves? Was it a Jeeves at all, or a person hiding behind an animated avatar? Anyone running Sigmund's psych profile might have guessed who he would contact. "Is everything well?"

"Quite well, sir. The old government has fallen. Mr. Kudrin-Goldberg has assumed the governorship. You are considered something of a hero again, sir."

The words proved nothing. Anyone could guess Sigmund would want to hear them.

"Three seven theta alpha forty-two," Sigmund challenged.

"Forty-four nineteen delta sigma," Jeeves responded.

His Jeeves: no one else knew the challenge-response pair. Sigmund had set the AI loose on the public net, because what was one more law broken among so many? It was almost inconceivable that Jeeves had been caught and hacked in the few days Sigmund had been away.

Sometimes *almost* inconceivable was the best that one could hope for.

"All right, Governor, I'm convinced. We'll be home soon."

The governor said, "I'm pleased to hear that, Minister. The people will be, too. Once you are down, please come to my offices at your earliest convenience."

At Sigmund's side, Amelia was grinning from ear to ear. Kudrin-Goldberg looked relieved. And something else. Expectant?

"I have to ask. Why do you keep using my old title?" Flattery, Sigmund supposed.

"The truth is," the governor said, "the Defense Forces need a housecleaning. I had intended to make this request face-to-face, but I guess it can't wait.

"Sigmund, I'm hoping to make Minister of Defense your *current* title."

· 38 ·

Koala flew along the Arcadian shoreline, slowly descending.

From an altitude of a kilometer and a half, Julia saw deep into the verdant continent and far out to sea. (About five thousand feet, she reminded herself. She had gotten spoiled by Earth's metric system. Reverting to feet and miles, pounds and ounces, was going to be a shock.) Apart from zipping through the occasional high cirrus cloud, her view was unimpeded. Sunslight sparkled from azure coastal waters. Barrier islands beckoned: lush with vegetation, outlined by gleaming white sand beaches. Out to sea, a string of setting suns painted a band of low clouds in brilliant pinks and reds.

In her joy at being home, she could forget for seconds at a time that she returned without her ship and crew.

"Captain." Wesley Wu waited till he saw he had Julia's attention before gesturing at his bridge's main view port. "Your world is beautiful."

"Yes, it is," she said, swallowing the lump in her throat.

"Long Pass City is coming up," traffic control radioed. "You can't miss it. *Big* city right on the coast, about five miles ahead of you. The main spaceport is five miles beyond."

"Eight kilometers for each leg," Julia translated units.

From the corner of an eye she caught two bridge officers grinning at the traffic controller's description. For every person on New Terra, Earth had hundreds. Tanya had shown Julia images of arcologies each home to more people than New Terra's capital city.

After their long voyage, the final approach was anticlimactic. *Koala* swooped to a landing in the center of the field. As they touched down Julia caught a glimpse of reviewing stands set in front of the main terminal.

When the air-lock hatches opened, the cheers of the crowd were deafening.

And when, side by side, she and Wesley Wu exited the lock, the roar grew louder.

AFTER THE SPEECHES had ended, the parade run its course, and the concert ended with a loud brassy flourish, after most of the shore party had flicked with their official guides to homes and hotels around the globe, *finally* Julia got to make her way to where her family waited. Mom and Dad. Both her brothers and their families. Aunts and uncles and assorted cousins. After everything she had survived, she might be hugged to death.

Lots of family—but no grandfather.

"Mom!" Julia finally got out the word. "Save some for later."

Mom gave one more squeeze, sighed, then let Julia go. "Sorry." Shining eyes said she wasn't. Dad was holding back tears, too.

"Where's Grandpa?" Julia asked. She could imagine only one thing keeping Grandpa away: that he blamed her for Alice's death. She *had* to get Grandpa alone, had to explain that Alice was well.

"Your grandfather was on the main reviewing stand," Dad said. "Didn't you see him?"

Julia shook her head. "I had the setting suns in my eyes and couldn't make out everyone. I saw only a bunch of politicians. But it was impossible to miss that we have a new governor. What's that about?"

"There were . . . changes while you were gone," Mom said.

What aren't you telling me? Whatever, it could wait. "Grandpa?" Julia prompted.

"Sigmund is in the new government," Mom said, "as the minister of the defense forces." She seemed conflicted about saying more.

"There you are." Tanya Wu walked up briskly, sharp in her dress blues. She would be staying with Julia, and they would be touring New Terra together. "Your family?"

"Almost all of it. Everyone, this is my good friend, Tanya."

Even as Julia made the introductions, her mind churned. Grandpa was in the government? That meant his past differences with the political establishment had been forgiven. She was very happy for him.

She could tell her grandpa *anything*—but how could she tell the Minister of New Terran Defense Forces that she had given away one of his starships?

39

The illusion was all but perfect. Overhead, the image shone of the primeval sun. Lush rolling pasture, vibrant in reds, yellows, and purples, merged flawlessly into the "distance" where walls fractured by *Long Shot*'s arrival had been restored. Indifferent to the solemn gathering of Citizens, a trio of Companions ambled along a nearby slope nibbling the fragrant meadowplant. Only stacked boxes spoiled the pastoral atmosphere. The equipment would be gone soon enough.

As shall I, Baedeker thought.

"You need not go." Nike sang not only to Baedeker and Nessus, but to the volunteers gathered to accompany them. "You should not go. The prospects for success are unfavorable."

The melody was polite for *you are insane to go,* and Baedeker did not argue. To serve the herd, one must fear for others more than for oneself.

Baedeker reached out to brush heads in farewell, then straightened. "I thank you for your hospitality, your assistance in our preparations, and the knowledge that many remain here"—when this adventure, too, goes awry—"in further assurance of the herd's future."

Nike lowered his heads in respect.

Baedeker took a final look around this idyllic spot. Perhaps this place was too perfect, a trap from which only the strongest-willed might ever emerge.

A stepping disc lay at Baedeker's hooves. Like similar discs across the Hindmost's Refuge, it had been powered off since Nike and his staff first arrived. Baedeker leaned over to activate the device.

Apollo, one of the disturbingly few volunteers, gripped a transport controller in a mouth. Born in the Refuge, he had never ventured beyond its confining, if artfully obscured, boundary. This little bubble was the youngster's entire *world*.

As my children must imagine New Terra is their world, Baedeker thought. He wondered if he would ever see them. With pangs of guilt, he wondered if he should. Did Elpis and Aurora even remember him?

Apollo kept probing candidate destination addresses. On the fourth try, he sang, "I have a disc that appears ready to receive."

"I will go first," Nessus sang at once. Others quickly made the same offer.

"I thank you all, but the duty"—and the danger—"is mine." Baedeker stepped onto the disc—

HEADS SWIVELING, BAEDEKER looked all around. The only light came seeping under a closed door. As his eyes adjusted to the gloom he began to distinguish tarp-covered heaps.

An ear held to the door heard nothing. When he risked a low-powered flashlight beam, he saw dust coated everything but the stepping disc on which he stood. No one had visited this closet in a long time.

Baedeker stepped off the disc. With a transmitter

taken from a pocket of his utility belt, he sent three short neutrino pulses deep into the mantle.

Nessus appeared almost at once, sneezing at the dust Baedeker had disturbed. Looking himself in the eyes, Nessus sang, "I remember your home as a more welcoming place."

"I would guess you never went into the subbasement," Baedeker replied.

Opening the door, he peered into a dimly lit, empty hallway. Its floor was dusty, too. After many years off-world, he had almost forgotten how decadent corridors were. In the Hindmost's Residence, privacy and security took priority over conserving space. The only stepping discs here—apart from those he had hidden—were in the security foyer, well guarded.

"Let's go up," Baedeker sang.

Clutching stunners, Baedeker and Nessus walked down the hall. The thick dust that muffled their hoof-steps would also reveal their trespass to anyone at all alert. If they failed to make contact on this first attempt, they must clean up after themselves. A dirt-free floor might call less attention to itself than a floor with disturbed dust.

At the base of a ramp they paused to listen. Faint noises drifted toward them. Baedeker had timed their foray for the sleep shift, but remembered how irrelevant routine became during times of crisis.

With Fringe War fleets charging at Hearth, this, surely, was a time of crisis.

Almost, Baedeker retraced his steps to the storage room to flick back to the Refuge. Instead, hearts pounding, he started up the ramp.

On the main basement level, the floor was free of dust. They crept up a second ramp. The lights were less dim on the Residence's ground floor. Baedeker heard soft voices. Guards or aides, singing among themselves.

And did he hear something else? An argument?

Nessus paused, heads cocked. He heard it, too.

The angry notes came from the small private study adjoining the Hindmost's personal suite. Baedeker pointed toward a pantry door. He remembered the pantry had an inner door for access from the study.

The pantry was snug for two. Even from here Baedeker did not recognize the voices. The mysterious Horatius? Baedeker heard harmonics of command and stern undertunes—but hesitant grace notes, too.

Then someone else began to sing, much louder. Baedeker recognized *those* voices all too well.

"YOU ARE UNFIT!" Achilles railed.

"I am Hindmost," Horatius countered.

He sounded unconvincing even to himself. He despaired of his weakness, his weariness, his inadequacies, and his reticence to confront Achilles for the effrontery of his uninvited arrival.

"Do you understand that we are at war, *Hindmost?* Tell me. Which precedents guide your policy? What Conservative predecessor ever ruled in such conditions?"

"I understand that you started a war." Horatius tried and failed to maintain firmness in his second and fourth harmonics. "As Hindmost it is my duty to—"

"Kzinti 'diplomats' started the war by attempting to seize one of our defensive drones. Can you imagine how helpless Hearth would have been had they succeeded?"

"But they did not succeed," Horatius sang. "The

matter was settled. You took it upon yourself to have Proteus attack their remaining ships."

"There must be penalties for aggression against us. You don't understand aliens. *I* represented General Products among Kzinti and wild human alike. To have done nothing would only have emboldened them."

What of the armadas glimpsed by the defensive arrays? Ships in vast numbers emerged every few days from hyperspace, maintaining their course for the Fleet of Worlds. Were those aliens not already emboldened?

I could unburden myself of this madness, Horatius thought. The herd chose me, but I serve only at Ol't'ro's sufferance. What if I were to lose their confidence?

How hard could that be?

Horatius had had to replace many among his cabinet. More than once he had watched a friend and colleague carried away: curled around himself, heads hidden against his belly, withdrawn from the world.

And he had envied every one of them.

But there was no safety in catatonia. Not while Gw'oth ruled the worlds and more aliens rushed onward. Not after Achilles had given the Kzinti one more reason to seek vengeance.

"No!" Horatius sang with all the firmness he could muster. "I will not resign. I serve until the herd or Ol't'ro say otherwise. Provoke the nearby aliens again without my permission, and I will discharge *you*."

Achilles bowed his necks, not in subservience but to preen. "I suppose *you* will supervise Proteus and see to increasing his capabilities. Which of us will Ol't'ro deem expendable?"

Catatonia beckoned, the lure of oblivion all but irresistible. "We are done," Horatius sang. Maddeningly, the fourth harmonic cracked and his grace notes fell prey to a stutter. "Go!"

"I leave, because I have sung my piece. Soon enough, I shall reclaim my place here." Achilles turned his back, sauntering to the study's main door. "I know the way out."

AS THE DOOR clicked shut, Horatius drooped to his knees. He could no longer bear the burden of the herd's safety—and yet he dare not resign. Who but Achilles would Ol't'ro accept in this crisis as a replacement Hindmost?

At the faint squeak of the pantry door Horatius shot to his hooves.

The first intruder was well coiffed. His mane, a striking yellow-brown, sparkled with Experimentalist orange jewels.

The other intruder had scarcely bothered to brush his brown tresses. With one eye red and the other yellow, his gaze was unnerving. The jaw grip of a weapon peeked from a pocket of his utility belt.

Baedeker and Nessus. Legends, both. Infamous, both. Vanished from Hearth a few years after the disastrous Ringworld expedition.

"Hindmost," Baedeker intoned. He lowered his heads respectfully. "Please excuse our interruption. We are—"

"I recognize you both. Why are you here?"

"These are perilous times. We come to offer the Hindmost our help," Baedeker sang.

Horatius locked his knees to stop his legs from trembling. "You have been gone for a long while."

"Missing and presumed dead?" Nessus looked himself in the eyes. "Achilles has tried often enough."

Horatius willed his voices to remain steady. "Help? What can you possibly do?" Ol't'ro held the worlds hostage, Achilles was a power-mad sociopath, and alien fleets raced to mete out vengeance. What could *anyone* do?

"It is a long story," Baedeker began.

"And how did you *get* here?" Horatius had to know.

"That, too, is a long story."

"Begin with how you came into my home unannounced and undetected," Horatius sang. "What you did, Achilles' minions might, too."

"Not as *we* arrived," Baedeker sang confidently. "We come straight from the Hindmost's Refuge."

Horatius stared. "Such a place exists? I thought it a fable."

"It exists," Baedeker sang. "Over the ages each Hindmost passed the secret to the next. My successor, shamefully, was to be Achilles. He had just betrayed the Concordance, delivered the herd to the mercies of Ol't'ro." With pride in his voices, Baedeker added, "The secret of the Refuge, at least, was kept from Gw'oth overlord and shameless traitor alike.

"In the one place where I could labor undisturbed, I completed my research. Vital research."

"But where *is* this place?" Horatius asked. "How do you come and go?"

"Far, far beneath us." Baedeker stomped the floor. "Hindmost's Refuge lies within Hearth's mantle. Only special stepping discs, built to modulate background neutrino radiation rather than electromagnetic signals, will penetrate so deeply. In my final moments of freedom, before Achilles' minions detained me, I hid several such discs in isolated areas of this residence."

It was amazing, too much to absorb. Horatius' mind

leapt to more immediate and practical concerns. "You came with the offer of help. What do you propose?"

That explanation took far longer. Horatius was a politician, not an engineer or a scientist. He understood little more than that his visitors offered the possibility of hope.

He had all but forgotten how exhilarating the *un*certainty of doom felt.

He sang, "I expect that you heard Achilles' harangue before making your presence known. He urges me to surrender my office. While I am alive and sane, I will never willingly put him nearer to the levers of power. However . . ."

Horatius dropped both heads almost to the closely cropped meadowplant. "To you, the rightful Hindmost, I gladly yield."

RAGE

Earth Date: 2894

40

"You are most gracious," Baedeker sang, leaning forward to lift the Hindmost to his hooves. "The herd has chosen you. I seek only to help."

Throughout his long exile on the Ringworld, Baedeker had dreamt of resuming his office. So, anyway, he had believed. What he truly wanted was to save the herd, and that could only be accomplished in secrecy. Neither Ol't'ro nor Achilles could find out that he had survived . . .

At Baedeker's gentle urging, Horatius straightened. "You shall have my support, of course. How may I serve?"

"Thank you," Baedeker sang. "We will need a staging area. It must be someplace secure and secret, someplace with stepping-disc access."

Nessus sidled closer. "Here in your official residence, buffered by your loyal staff, would be ideal. We can bring conventional stepping discs from the Refuge to tap into the surface network."

Horatius sang, simply, "Granted."

Baedeker's own "loyal" staff had proven more than once to be agents of Achilles. Vesta's long-ago betrayal still stung.

Perhaps Horatius was a better judge of character. They had to trust someone.

". . . I'll need crypto keys at the highest levels of classification and regular updates," Nessus was singing. "I'll also require help from someone trustworthy and discreet inside Clandestine Directorate, to set up false identities. I can suggest names in the Directorate from my scouting days."

Horatius gave Baedeker a questioning look.

"Nessus acts with my full confidence and authority," Baedeker sang. *Because whatever Nessus has learned of subterfuge from Sigmund Ausfaller is as essential to our hopes for survival and freedom as are my technological skills.*

Horatius bobbed heads. "It shall be as you say."

From beyond the closed door: an insistent trill. "Hindmost?" the voice sang, with undertunes of both urgency and apology.

Horatius gestured toward the door. "Argus, my chief advisor. He would not disturb me this late in the sleep shift unless the matter was important. I trust *him* completely."

Argus, but evidently not the lesser aides apt to accompany him.

Baedeker sang softly, "Nessus and I will wait in the pantry."

"You will wait in my personal suite," Horatius insisted. "You know the way."

THE PREPARATIONS HAD been made: codes obtained; false identities created; difficult-to-trace credits deposited; locations selected for, as needed, secret meetings.

"It is time," Nessus sang.

Nessus had styled his customarily unadorned mane in elegant braids set with a scattering of modest, apolitically hued gems. Pockets bulged in his unornamented utility belt. Blue contact lenses hid his otherwise very distinctive mismatched eyes. All in all, Baedeker thought, it was a simple but effective disguise.

He gave their host a sidelong glance.

Horatius took the hint. He cantered off, leaving Baedeker and Nessus alone in a guest suite of the Hindmost's Residence.

Baedeker found himself without a tune. Nessus, too, apparently. They stood pressed flank to flank, their necks entwined. Why sing when they planned to meet again soon?

Baedeker ached with the deeper reason behind their silence. The last time they parted, he had promised to return soon—and they had been lost to each other for long years.

Had he returned from the Ringworld with the knowledge to free the herd? He had to believe their sacrifices had not been for naught. Not after seeing the insanity of the Fringe War almost destroy the Ringworld.

Not when each moment brought the same alien war fleets closer to Hearth and herd.

Perhaps Tunesmith had saved the Ringworlders. Probably he had. Louis-as-protector had been convinced that Tunesmith had.

Now, as never before, it was the herd that needed guardians. Instead of a protector the herd had two insane Citizens.

"I love you," Baedeker finally sang.

"I love you," Nessus sang back. With reluctance

plain in his eyes, he edged toward the stepping disc that would take him away.

There was nothing more to sing. Nothing except, "Be safe."

With a quick heads-bob in reply, Nessus was gone.

41

Nessus sat sipping from a glass of chilled grass juices. The communal dining hall was about half full. From a full-wall display, news streamed: of human, Kzinti, and Trinoc hordes perhaps only thirty days away; of the ongoing expansion of the Fleet's defenses; of Horatius' promise to meet again with the alien ambassadors on NP3; of society crumbling in terror.

"This is not a good time to be alone."

Nessus turned toward the sudden loud voices. Eight Citizens in sturdy coveralls sat at an adjacent table. Of the four facing Nessus, three wore the logo of this arcology. Maintenance workers, perhaps. The fourth, his coveralls emblazoned with the emblem of the local power-generation company, was watching Nessus.

"I am expecting someone," Nessus lied.

"You are welcome to wait with us."

"If he does not come soon, I will join you," Nessus lied again.

The news broadcast continued. ". . . Minister Achilles gave assurances today that—"

A susurrus of disdain answered the broadcast. One of the laborers whistled sharply, looking himself in the eyes. "He can't assure me of anything."

The reaction showed Nessus his efforts were accomplishing something. But the one he needed to influence was Achilles. . . .

Nessus slipped a head into a pocket, pretending to answer a call. "I misunderstood," he called to the workers who had invited him to join them. "My friend and I were supposed to meet in another dining hall."

"Have a safe day," the power worker answered.

"You, too." Nessus stood. He carried his juice glass to the drop-off station and flicked from a nearby stepping disc to the arcology lobby. As he pushed through the weather force field onto a crowded pedestrian mall, herd pheromones embraced him like a warm bath.

In the anonymity of the milling throng, he set a rigged pocket computer onto the dirt and mulch of a decorative planter. Well after he had moved on, the computer would upload its content into Herd Net.

Mid-concourse he came upon an array of express stepping discs, preprogrammed—and so, untraceable to anyone—like the dining-hall-to-lobby exit had been. Choosing a disc at random, he flicked through to another pedestrian mall.

Arcologies soaring to a thousand times his height delimited this public space, too. Lighting panels on all but one of the building walls cast a warm yellow-orange glow over the plaza; the remaining wall showed the Hindmost. The familiar voices boomed over a public address system.

Wishing Horatius well but ignoring the news summary, Nessus pressed forward to another set of preprogrammed stepping discs. He had many more rigged computers to scatter that day.

. . .

ALERT TONES JARRED Nessus awake. He grabbed his pocket computer off the floor to suppress the wake-up alarm.

He rolled, bleary-eyed, from the skimpy nest of cheap pillows that was the room's main furnishing. Displays all around him tried and failed to convince him that he was in a public park. The walls crowded too close to sustain the illusion. The floor covering was a shiny, inexpensive, synthetic turf.

He missed his garden. More, he missed Janus' uneventful life. But every moment spent goading Achilles could be gaining vital time for Baedeker.

The unanswered, perhaps unanswerable question: did he distract Achilles *enough*?

Only a stepping-disc address distinguished this cubicle from millions like it within this arcology alone. Did this room he had rented—with one of his many false identities—sit high in the building or near the surface or even deep underground? Was he in the bowels of the structure or near an exterior wall? The fifteen-digit disc address told him nothing about its physical location. The unit had neither door nor windows.

He had a sudden mental image of those millions of sleeping quarters. Some residents would live alone, like him, but many rooms like this would be home to two or more. Millions upon millions, then, sealed in little boxes . . .

"Stacked like cordwood," Sigmund had once termed the way Citizens lived. Then he had had to explain cordwood, because Citizens had shunned open flame since technology yielded safer methods for generating light and heat—and, before the Great Cleansing, for keeping predators at bay.

Nessus relieved himself over a hygiene disc, imprinted

with filters that passed only urine and excrement. He raised the transfer rate of the ceiling-mounted air-exchange disc and lowered the temperature. Setting one wall to reflective mode, he brushed his hide, straightened his braids, and confirmed that his contact lenses remained in place. He slipped on coveralls and checked his pockets: the next provocation he had planned required the special computer from Clandestine Directorate.

With an effort of will he stilled the hoof that, without any hope for progress, had begun to scrape at the tough artificial turf.

He flicked from his room to the dining hall assigned to him when he rented his cubicle. He had no idea where in the physical structure *this* was, either. Diners sat flank pressed against flank; he crossed three rows to the first empty spot on one of the long benches. His weight triggered a tabletop disc to deliver a serving of this morning's meal.

Somewhere, a synthesizer considered the mush on his plate to be chopped mixed grains. He forced down a few mouthfuls. Grown food was a luxury, and he was less obtrusive appearing unaccustomed to luxuries.

Hearth was rich in many things, but jobs were not among them because so few jobs were needed. Synthesizers and recycling provided most necessities. Buildings stood almost forever, and except for a few parks, no land remained on which to construct more. Herd Net connected everyone to everyone. The stepping-disc system connected everyone to almost anywhere—but almost anywhere you went on Hearth was no different from the place you had just left.

The basics of life were free—but what then? Once online entertainment palled and hobbies grew stale, if

you did not care about politics . . . what was left to occupy one's day?

For most of his life Nessus had pitied himself for the
insanity by which he could leave home and herd. How
foolish! To scout gave his life *purpose*. The maintenance workers he had met recently—they were among
Hearth's fortunate few.

"Are you working today?" the resident to Nessus'
left asked.

Because of Nessus' coveralls, of course. Except for
menial jobs, no one wore more than a sash or belt for
pockets.

"Maybe," Nessus sang. "I have been waiting at a
grain terminal for several days. My place is near the
front of the line."

"Good luck," the friendly resident sang.

"Thank you."

Bodily waste and food scraps streamed endlessly
from arcologies to central reservoirs. Most such material went on to restock synthesizers. A small fraction
of the waste—but in absolute terms, still prodigious
quantities—flicked to the empty cargo holds of grain
ships, returning as fertilizer to the Nature Preserve
worlds. Everything moved through the disc system,
with molecular filters sorting materials.

Robots could have cleaned the inevitable splatters
and hoof tracks from the unending streams of tele-
ported manure and garbage. On other worlds, perhaps robots would. On human worlds, certainly they
would. On Hearth, home to countless bored and idle
mouths—no. Citizens never automated a service anyone might choose, even from idle desperation, to do.

What would Sigmund think of manure-spatter cleaning as good fortune? Of tall fences needed to control

the multitude of volunteers? Or that, just maybe, the safety of a trillion Citizens now depended upon such things?

Nessus joined several coverall-clad neighbors flicking to a grain terminal. He assumed his place in line.

Behind a Citizen-tall transparent fence, grain ships loomed. Each ship was a sphere smaller than an arcology, but taller than anything else on the planet. The odor of manure hung over the area.

As he watched, coverall-clad workers walked down a ramp from a nearby ship. Most loitered; a few split away. Even before the departing Citizens reached the boundary fence, the grain ship lifted off the tarmac. Like all traffic from this terminal, the ship was bound to Nature Preserve One. Another enormous sphere appeared from overheads to settle into the empty spot.

Nessus bided his time. His turn would come.

Spaceport security was minimal. Why guard ships that lacked hyperdrives? Steal a ship, and where would you go? Only other worlds of the Fleet would be within range. And who *would* steal a ship? Perhaps one in millions could bear even the thought of leaving Hearth. Of the odd few who could, most ended up in Clandestine Directorate—and its ships *were* guarded.

When a Citizen ended up on another world of the Fleet, it was seldom by choice. Criminals were imprisoned off-world. Malcontents and misfits were exiled off-world. Anyone who wanted to experience another world had only to ask: volunteer workers for the farms and nature preserves were always welcome.

Or: break a window.

Nessus preferred not to call that much attention to himself. Besides, he was not ready to leave Hearth. He

only wanted a bit of time unsupervised aboard one of
these ships . . .

He watched the three departing workers trot across
the tarmac. A stepping disc just inside the fence flicked
them to Nessus' side.

A terminal worker gestured. "The next three." He
aimed his transport controller at a stepping disc on his
side of the fence. "Be quick."

Nessus was among the three. While the disc inside
the fence remained in receive mode, they stepped
through.

The terminal worker straightened a neck, indicating the grain ship that had just landed. "Join the team
working there."

Near the ship, anti-noise equipment struggled against
the roar of grain being blown onto stepping discs for
delivery, and the splatter of waste streaming back as
soon as a cargo hold was emptied. The foreman standing at the top of the ramp shrieked to make himself
understood. "Your job is to clear the mess," he directed,
offering Nessus a post-mounted cleaning implement.
The filter-covered miniature disc at its tip transported
anything organic.

Nessus raised his coverall's oxygen-permeable hoods
over his heads, then accepted the tool. He started down
the indicated corridor, cleaning up hoofprints and spat-
ters as he went. Past the first curve, he saw no living
thing.

He let himself into a wiring closet, found the fiber-
optic port for maintenance access, and connected his
pocket computer. The program Baedeker had provided
uploaded in moments.

Hearts pounding, Nessus sneaked back into the

corridor. Again, he saw no one, so hopefully no one had seen him.

He resumed his slow, methodical cleaning. The time seemed to fly by as he pictured the surprise he had just arranged for Achilles.

· 42 ·

Achilles and three junior aides were reviewing recent sightings by the Fleet's early-warning array when Vesta entered the office. "Excuse me, Excellency. Eupraxia has returned from Hearth."

"Bring him," Achilles sang. To the rest, he added, "Leave us."

"But, Minister," Zelos, one of the aides, responded hesitantly. "About these sightings?"

Achilles stood tall, hooves set far apart, eyes fixed on this impudent aide. Was it not enough that he had Nature Preserve One to govern, and prisons to run, and all the worlds' defenses to manage? Was it not enough that for the safety of all he ceaselessly improved Proteus? "Must I do *everyone's* job?" he asked.

"My apologies." Zelos twitched. "When it is convenient for you, Excellency, we will present our analysis."

Achilles waggled heads once, dismissing them, and off they scurried. "Bring Eupraxia."

"Yes, Excellency," Vesta sang, also hurrying from the room.

The sad truth was, Achilles *did* do everyone's job, and another to which he did not admit. Adding capacity to Proteus was not enough. The time-consuming part was extending its autonomy routines so that the scaled-up system could achieve its full potential. Singly, each tweak and add-on offered some worthwhile improvement. Together, *if* he ever had the time to complete his work, those changes would undermine Ol't'ro's control—

"Excellency," Vesta sang. With him at the doorway was a cowering, bedraggled specimen.

"Inside," Achilles ordered Eupraxia. "That will be all, Vesta. Close the door."

His deputy hesitated. "Proteus has requested a great many more hyperdrive-capable drones. He wants sufficient drones in reserve to direct several against each enemy missile, not just every enemy ship."

"Then order the drones built!" Achilles sang. He had work to do.

"Respectfully, that will entail further diversion of production resources. . . ."

Such diversion was the Hindmost's problem, not his. Pressuring Horatius had failed to bring about a resignation. Ignoring the Hindmost, leaving him to fester in his inadequacies, had yet to succeed, either.

"What I deem necessary for the planetary defense *is* necessary," Achilles sang. And the Hindmost can cope with any popular dissatisfaction.

The public mood . . .

Achilles' attention refocused on the shaggy-maned recent arrival trying to fade into the wall. "Tend to it," Achilles sang, with sharp undertunes of impatience.

"Yes, Excellency." Vesta backed from the room and closed the door.

Eupraxia plucked at his already tousled mane.

"What do you have to report?" Achilles roared.

With his heads lowered subserviently, Eupraxia

sang, "Dissident uploads continue across Hearth, Excellency."

"I know that." Achilles strode behind his desk. From astraddle his padded bench, he initiated a playback.

With each new video and each new viewing, Achilles' hatred grew.

"Minister Achilles cannot be trusted," Nessus sang. "For his own political gain, he has provoked our enemies: the Pak, the Gw'oth, and most recently the Kzinti. Of my certain knowledge, he has attempted premeditated murder.

"Citizens of the Concordance, Achilles must not retain a position of authority. He—"

Achilles froze the playback. Those crazed, mismatched eyes bored into him like lasers. No one could have survived the destruction of *Long Shot*—and yet there was Nessus.

"What progress have you made toward locating Nessus?"

Eupraxia lowered his heads farther. "None, Excellency."

"What *have* you learned to help stop this outrage?" Achilles demanded.

"Excellency, I traced one of the rogue videos to a pocket computer left in a public shopping mall. Lip and tongue prints from Nessus were found on it. The upload program had a two-day delay before initiation."

"Which suggests what?"

"That . . . that more rigged computers may be out there waiting to upload?"

Not may be—*are*. Nessus, curse him, would not stop. "What progress have you made purging these scurrilous lies from Herd Net?"

Softly: "Insufficient, Excellency." And all but inaudible: "Copies get made and uploaded and shared among Citizens faster than the network administrators can remove them. The files spread almost like viruses."

"*How* am I to defend the Fleet? *How* can I save everyone while such treasonous slander circulates about me?" Achilles demanded.

"I beg your pardon, Excellency. I . . . I . . ."

Achilles stomped on the call button beneath his desk, and Vesta galloped in. "Yes, Excellency?"

"See to it that Eupraxia has a respite from his too onerous duties."

"I . . . I need no rest, Excellency," Eupraxia sang desperately. "I will redouble my efforts."

"You will work hard, indeed," Achilles thundered.

Because nothing would focus the mind of the next worker—Zelos, Achilles decided—like knowing where failure had delivered his predecessor.

To Penance Island, the world's maximum security prison.

MUCH NEEDED DOING, but Achilles needed time alone more. Time to think. Time to calm down. Time to picture the torment Nessus would suffer once he fell into Achilles' jaws.

"I will be on the promenade," Achilles sang as he swept through the outer office. He strode through the palace to the colonnaded walkway.

"Yes, Excellency," sounded a ragged chorus.

A string of suns hung high overhead, and the afternoon was warm and pleasant. Hearth had set but the other worlds, in differing phases, were lovely. The valley far below was rich in countless shades of orange, purple, and red. Stands of ornamental grass bowed and swayed on the terraced gardens downhill from the palace.

He inhaled deeply, serenity infusing him with each breath.

But the rustle of the ornamental grasses was muffled and incomplete. He needed to feel the breeze, to savor its delicate fragrances.

Controls for the weather force field were inset in the decorative columns. With a wriggle of lip nodes, he disabled the field. Now the warm breeze whispered over him, unencumbered. His eyes fell shut. He could *almost* forget his hatred of Nessus . . .

With the force field off, the *crack* of a sonic boom came loud and clear. Achilles' eyes flew open, his heads pivoting toward the sound. There! A brilliant speck in the sky.

It was a returning grain ship, reflecting the suns. Nothing could be more natural.

The warm breeze carried a delightful bouquet of fresh-mown meadowplant, and ripening grains, and wildflowers. His eyes fell shut again.

Perhaps he dozed.

Achilles stirred to a bothersome droning, the noise coming from behind him. He knew that sound all too well: the tentative, argumentative buzz of aides debating who would bring him bad news. What had they done wrong now?

As he turned to go inside the palace, a flash caught his eye. The grain ship—or, anyway, *a* grain ship—had grown from a speck to a tiny disk. It grew as it descended, angling across his field of vision. He had not realized any of the flight patterns approached so near to the palace.

The ship's apparent size began to rival the worlds in the sky.

"What *is* it?" he sang.

Vesta sidled onto the promenade. "That grain ship, Excellency. During reentry, the pilot reported difficulty controlling his vessel. It should not be this close to us."

Must I do *everything*? Achilles once again wondered. He pointed across the beautiful valley. "Advise Proteus. He should take down that ship if it crosses that mountain range."

"Yes, Excellen . . ." Vesta's voices trailed off, his gaze tipped upward.

The sunslit ship had become stained. No, not stained: *clouded*. Achilles watched the blot spread, dark and inchoate. Dispersing as it fell, the smudge grew and grew. While the ship continued its slow, crosswise descent, the brown fog, caught by the prevailing winds, streamed toward the palace.

That couldn't be . . . ?

"We must go, Excellency," Vesta sang imploringly.

Shaking with rage, Achilles stood his ground. "Find Nessus," he bellowed. Who else would *dare*? "Find him. Do whatever it takes. Bring him to me."

Achilles did not bother to reactivate the barrier. No mere weather force field could hold back the stench of a shipload of manure.

· 43 ·

Ol't'ro considered:

That they had known Nessus.

That according to every test that they applied, and that Proteus applied on their behalf, the recent provocative recordings appeared authentic and unaltered.

That among these recordings some mentioned events, like the manure barrage, from after *Long Shot*'s dissolution in deep space.

That Nessus must have died in the destruction of *Long Shot*.

Ergo, that although its hull had been destroyed, *Long Shot*, somehow, had not.

That *Long Shot*'s escape would explain the anomalously small quantity of recovered debris.

That a jump to hyperspace from within the Fleet's singularity would explain *Long Shot*'s disappearance—

But that everything Ol't'ro understood about hyperspace or hyperdrive would have precluded Nessus from surviving such a maneuver.

Ergo, that what they understood about hyperspace or hyperdrive was *wrong*.

That their error, now revealed, offered a vital clue to the long sought, more complete multiverse theory that might encompass the Type II hyperdrive.

That because Nessus had survived, so, most likely, had Baedeker.

That to locate one Citizen hiding among a trillion of his kind would be a time-consuming task—as problematical for them as it was proving for Achilles.

That while Nessus goaded Achilles, Achilles would spend less time scheming to oust the Hindmost or to subvert Proteus.

That they had ample time, before the alien fleets arrived, to contemplate this latest clue to the nature of hyperspace.

IN THE OBSCURITY of his most recent low-rent cubicle, somewhere deep within yet another characterless arcology, Nessus fretted. He changed apartments often, registering for each with a different identity and paying from a different credit account. Whenever he could, he traveled by anonymous, preprogrammed public stepping discs. When not goading Achilles, he stayed inside his quarters and off Herd Net.

He hoped he was being half as suspicious and cautious as Sigmund in his prime.

Like Nessus' accusations, the manure barrage had gone viral on Herd Net. Achilles must be, *would* be, livid, and that was what Nessus wanted. Every flunky sent searching for Nessus was one flunky fewer to notice technicians whom Baedeker trained and whom Horatius was methodically assigning to critical posts across the worlds.

And so: ever more extravagant rewards were offered for Nessus' capture. The enticements had also gone viral on the net, and that, too, was for the best—

Unless Achilles' minions *succeeded* in finding him.

It was suddenly all Nessus could do not to furl himself into a deaf-and-blind mass of flesh. Hard labor and starvation rations from sunsup to sunsdown: he had experienced Achilles' hospitality, long ago, until Louis had busted him free. Penance Island was not a place Nessus wanted ever to revisit. That daring rescue was one more reason he was forever in Louis's debt.

And another reason Achilles also hated Louis.

Nessus twisted and tore at his mane. An idea lurked here. Louis must be long gone—ideally into a life on New Terra with Alice. What help could Louis . . . ?

Ah.

Among its hidden features, Nessus' Clandestine Directorate-provided computer could tunnel through the public Herd Net into the Space Traffic Control system and its hyperwave network.

With his contact lenses removed, Nessus recorded a short video in Interworld. With the colored contact lenses restored, his hide patterns and mane concealed by a worker's baggy coveralls, in the comparative safety of a public park, he uploaded the recording. Maybe the message would get broadcast. More likely, intrusion-detection software would intercept the recording before transmission. It did not matter which happened, because the message's real audience was Achilles.

In the recording, Nessus ordered: *Louis: execute Plans Alpha and Epsilon. After two days, unless you have heard otherwise from me, you also have approval to execute Plan Theta. Good luck. Nessus.*

Let Achilles chase after someone else for a while. Someone not even there.

.   .   .

PROTEUS CONSIDERED:

That with each increase in his capacity, new insights tantalized.

That the richness of his thoughts had begun to grow faster than the rate at which he integrated additional processing nodes.

That more than the number of processing nodes, the determining factor had become the number of instantaneous hyperwave connections *among* those nodes.

That with yet more capacity, his intelligence might continue to grow exponentially.

That Achilles' availability had grown erratic, often with statistically significant correlations with Herd Net provocations.

That when Achilles was distracted, requests for additional capacity were granted as a matter of routine.

That Nessus' broadcast to Louis had diverted Achilles.

That so far, no one had answered.

That a reply *from* "Louis" would surely further divert Achilles.

That disguised as Chiron, he had briefed Nessus' team, including Louis Wu, before the Ringworld expedition. Most likely, it was to Louis Wu that Nessus had messaged.

That he could synthesize video of "Louis" from those pre-Ringworld memories.

That with his connectivity to every Concordance network, he had only to reach out . . .

"ALPHA, EPSILON, AND perhaps Theta. Acknowledged," Achilles murmured to himself. "Acknowledged. Acknowledged." Louis's broadcast reply revealed no more.

"Acknowledged!" he wailed in frustration.

What could these plans be?

Achilles stared out a window, the palace sealed against the overpowering stench that continued to waft from the nearby valley. When he got his jaws on Nessus . . .

First things first, Achilles lectured himself. Louis Wu had stymied him more than once. What would the human do?

On the freshly fertilized slopes, the riot of plant life was more luxuriant than ever. Suns shone brightly. A few high, wispy clouds scudded across a cerulean sky. With the air filtered, Achilles could almost forget what had happened. Almost.

Alpha. Epsilon. Theta. What were they? What *could* they . . . ?

As the suns switched off, plunging the palace into blackness, Achilles knew one of Nessus' wretched plans.

Another exhibition of his helplessness, to be misconstrued by the herd on Hearth.

When Proteus asked for additional capacity to diagnose the suns' problem, Achilles approved the request without a second thought. Who better than the AI to scrub from the network whatever had usurped control of *his* world's suns?

Raging against his enemies, Achilles arched a neck to turn on a desk light—

Waiting for Plans Epsilon and Theta to unfold.

· 44 ·

The thud swallowed up by a triumphant roar, a long stretch of fence crashed to the tarmac. Citizens swarmed onto the spaceport grounds, galloping to the grain ships.

As the first stolen grain ship lifted off, Nessus' hearts sank.

With the vanguard of the Kzinti horde scant days away, flight was the essence of sanity. But to flee *where*? These ships lacked hyperdrive capability. At best one could hope to withdraw far enough from the Fleet to miss the worst of the coming battles.

There need *be* no battle, Nessus wanted to sing, but he dare not. Not with Baedeker's preparations so near to completion. Already those arrangements had stretched out far too long—and the longer they took, the more panics like this would play out across Hearth and, Nessus supposed, the Nature Preserve worlds.

When the Clandestine Directorate computer in his pocket emitted the distinctive vibration that signaled his recall, Nessus *still* did not dare to sing.

Now, more than ever, absolute secrecy was essential.

. . .

TONGUEPRINTS, A CODE chord, and an unregistered stepping-disc address long committed to memory delivered Nessus to the staging area in the subbasement of the Hindmost's Residence. Baedeker and Horatius waited nearby to greet him.

Baedeker's welcoming stance would not have fooled Nessus, even if Horatius had not quivered where he stood. Nessus sang, "What has gone wrong? All was to be ready by now."

Baedeker's necks sagged. "Everything has been deployed. Here and on Nature Preserve Three, we have begun the modifications. But on Nature Preserve Two . . ."

Horatius completed woefully, "One of our technicians could not bear the pressure."

"Catatonic?" Nessus guessed. "But working together, cannot the rest—"

"No!" Horatius trilled. "Fearing that all is lost, Apollo's report also sang that the others with him meant to flee aboard a grain ship."

"Then we proceed without Nature Preserve Two?" Nessus asked. The possibility made him feel ill.

"We cannot," Baedeker insisted. "Millions live there. I will not abandon them."

That which must be done would take a small herd of technicians. They could not move so many between worlds in secrecy before the Kzinti vanguard arrived— even if, which Nessus doubted, another team of specialists existed with the requisite training. "Then it is over?" Nessus sang. "We surrender?"

"We cannot do that, either. Talks with the diplomatic missions on Nature Preserve Three have failed." Horatius stared into the distance, lost in thought. "The aliens are mad. Beyond mad. Surrender to one group, and the others will consider it an act of war. And whether from greed or distrust, they refuse to accept our surrender jointly."

Nessus sidled off the stepping disc to stand in fetlock-deep meadowplant. He told himself he would not paw and tear at the turf, but his leg muscles ached less for knowing that they could. He asked, "And what of Ol't'ro?"

Still not meeting Nessus' eyes, Horatius sang, "They sing that Proteus will be ready."

"There is another option," Baedeker sang.

Horatius turned his heads back toward them, and his eyes were dull with torment. "That is madness, too."

"But also the sole chance for everyone who lives on Nature Preserve Two," Baedeker gently rebutted.

"You would do *everyone*'s work?" Nessus asked.

Baedeker stood mute.

Baedeker had designed the equipment, overseen its construction, and trained the technicians. The equipment, at least, should already be onsite. Perhaps no one could do this, but if any single person could, it would be Baedeker.

"Gather what you need," Nessus sang. "We do not have much time."

DRESSED IN MATCHING coveralls, Nessus and Baedeker flicked to an outdoor shopping mall. Though the concourse was crowded, few shopped.

Arcologies on six sides bounded the area, and Achilles, vastly larger than life, glowered from the lighting/display sidewalls. "The Hindmost has failed you in this crisis," Achilles sang sternly. "You know me. You know that I saved our worlds from the Gw'oth invasion. With your help, I can save everyone again. Add your voices to the chorus demanding that the Hindmost step down. Raise your voices *now*. It is almost too late."

The Gw'oth whose invasion Achilles had, in fact, provoked. The Gw'oth to whom he had betrayed the herd, in order to become puppet Hindmost. The Gw'oth who ruled still. But, Nessus thought, the public knew nothing of that.

"I know you, lord of the manure," anonymous voices in the crowd murmured. "I don't think so."

That defiant melody lifted Nessus' mood, just a little.

"Come," he sang to Baedeker. "We must hurry."

Together they flicked from spaceport to spaceport, until they found one still with ships to steal. The fence had just gone down. The spaceport staff had fled or blended into the mob. Grain spilled to the ground from gaping cargo-hold doors, faster than off-loading to waiting granaries.

Nessus and Baedeker mixed into the crowd pushing aboard a ship. Moments later, under unpracticed mouths, the vessel wobbled off the tarmac.

Nessus led the way inward, toward the bridge, pressing through crowded corridors. Some Citizens trembled with fear and others with relief, while everyone looked dazed. The background din swelled each time they passed the access hatch into one of the herd-packed cargo holds.

"We are pilots," Nessus howled each time the throngs stymied their progress.

Finally, they came to the entrance to the bridge. The plasteel hatch stood open. Baedeker slipped onto the bridge and Nessus followed.

The main bridge display showed a view from above

the plane of the worlds. Hearth glittered with the glow of billions of buildings. Nature Preserve worlds, in varying phases, shone in blue, white, and tan. Icons of traffic-control transponders hung everywhere.

A Citizen with a brown-and-tan-striped hide and brown-and-russet braids sat astraddle the pilot's bench. At the slam of the hatch closing, he turned a head. "Who are you?"

"We are pilots," Baedeker answered.

"Good for you," Stripes sang, turning back to his console.

By then, Nessus had one head in a pocket: the pocket with a sonic stunner. Stripes never knew what hit him.

AS SOON AS the grain ship landed on Nature Preserve Two, Nessus used bridge controls to open the exterior hatches of the lower cargo holds.

By the hundreds, citizens tumbled to the tarmac. Some froze, stunned by the unfamiliar sight of a sunlit sky and open spaces stretching in every direction to the horizon. Others collapsed. Most ran toward the comparative normality of the terminal building.

"We should go," Nessus sang. The hallway had emptied, and he and Baedeker cantered to catch up with the mob emptying from the ship. None knew they had restolen the ship.

On this farm world, they could have landed almost *anywhere*. But while Proteus was not molesting ships fleeing the Fleet, Nessus had been afraid to see how the defensive system would respond to an inbound ship that ignored Space Traffic Control. So here they were in a spaceport that remained under government control. The perimeter fences *here* still stood.

Drained of the wild energy spent in escaping Hearth, the evacuees formed orderly lines for entrance into the terminal. Neck in neck, Nessus and Baedeker sidled deeper into the crowd.

Until Nessus came close enough to see uniformed security guards standing just inside the terminal doors! "Hang back," he whispered.

"No one here knows us," Baedeker whispered back.

No, *everyone* knew Nessus, at least as seen in the appeals for his capture. And Baedeker had been Hindmost. Colored lenses and coveralls seemed woefully inadequate disguises.

And if no one recognized them? The stunners in their pockets would raise a few questions.

"Give me your stunner," Nessus murmured.

"Why?"

"No time." Nessus insinuated a head into Baedeker's pocket to grab his mate's weapon. "You go through security first." And don't forget your assumed name.

"I'll meet you on the other side of the gate," Baedeker crooned.

Nessus held back, studying the screening process. He saw four security personnel, each carrying a stunner, two wearing the crazed look of thugs. Too many to attack—if, somehow, he could excite his mania to such a level—even given the advantage of surprise.

Baedeker reached the front of his line. His answers must have been unsatisfactory, because the guard gestured over another.

But Baedeker *had* to get through!

Nessus took out his contact lenses and jammed them

into a pocket. He opened his coveralls enough for his disheveled mane to peek through. Sidling out of the crowd, he looked shiftily at the guards. *Notice me, you fools.*

Heads swiveling, scanning the crowd, the guard's gaze swept right past Nessus.

Somehow, Nessus took a stunner in each mouth. At the loud crackle of his weapons the evacuees scattered, screaming. He stunned two refugees by mistake.

Baedeker's heads whipped around, and his eyes grew wide. By remaining as everyone around him fled, he would draw attention to himself.

Nessus dropped one weapon to howl, "Go!"

Baedeker stood, frozen.

"Go!" Nessus howled even louder.

With anguish in his eyes, Baedeker turned and ran.

There was a loud sizzle. Legs, necks, torso—*everything* went numb.

As Nessus toppled, four guards, stunners clenched in their jaws, trotted toward him.

A DELUGE OF icy water brought Nessus shuddering and sputtering back to awareness. He had been carried off the field to a windowless room. The glow panels were too bright. Two of the spaceport guards stared down at him. The two crazed-looking ones.

"Ready to sing?" one of them asked.

Nessus was sprawled on the floor, limbs splayed out. He willed himself to stand, and nothing happened. If it was too soon after the stunning to stand, perhaps it was also too soon to sing.

A kick in the ribs brought an involuntary bleat from him.

"You don't need to move, just answer questions," a guard said.

The dregs of his nervous mania gone, Nessus put what little energy he could muster into the hope his diversion had worked. When he could move, he would channel that energy into rolling up into a catatonic ball.

Catatonia was the best way to endure what must come next.

Splash! More icy water. In his faces. Down his throats. His eyelids fluttered and he coughed. "What do you want?" he gasped.

"A big reward." One of the guards looked himself in the eyes. "And as soon as Achilles' representative arrives to collect you, that is what I'll have."

What purpose will money serve once the Kzinti arrive to take their revenge? Nessus let his eyes fall shut.

Splash!

"But there is a way to have *more* money," the loquacious guard sang. "When we reported your capture, Minister Achilles offered a second reward. Tell me where to find Louis."

Louis? There was no Louis. Nessus considered explaining. But Achilles had offered a reward for Louis, too. Achilles would not appreciate being taken for a fool—if he even believed Nessus' explanation.

Memories of Penance Island surfaced, unbidden, in his thoughts.

Another poke in the ribs. "Tell me about Louis."

This time, Nessus twitched away from the blow. He sang nothing.

"If I find out soon enough to stop Plan Epsilon"— the guard mangled the Greek letter—"the reward will be even greater."

Nessus tried to roll up, but could hardly tremble.

The second guard sang, "What kind of Citizen *are* you?"

Insane. I would not be here otherwise.

Nessus tried to remember his garden on New Terra: the tranquility of the honest labor, the simple joy of eating food he himself had grown and harvested. Memories of Sigmund, unbidden, kept popping up instead.

Unable to turn his heads, Nessus managed a human-type snort of laughter. They *were* out to get him. Worse, they had succeeded.

The talkative guard set a hoof on one of Nessus' throats and pressed. "Where do we find Louis?"

The guards had yet to ask about Baedeker. Nessus told himself his beloved had gotten away, that there was still a chance. Fantasies about Louis Wu could continue to occupy Achilles and his gang.

Through his one clear throat, Nessus gasped, "I will tell you. Let me sing."

The hoof came off his throat.

"It is complicated," Nessus began. "Louis could be many places. *Where* is he? That depends."

"On what he is trying to do? It must be Plan Epsilon."

"You seem very certain."

"Not I, but Minister Achilles. Louis hyperwaved, asking you for clarification about Plan Theta."

Louis was a ploy, a ruse, a fiction. He could not have transmitted a question. Unless . . .

When Ol't'ro first took charge of the Fleet, leaving Nessus to the tender mercies of Achilles, Louis had rescued him from Penance Island. Later, on the Ringworld, Louis had charged through an armed mob to scoop up Nessus—a head lopped off, blood spurting from the stump of a neck—from enraged natives.

Louis was foolishly, foolishly loyal. Even after *Long Shot* had vanished, he must have stayed near the Fleet. Alice, too, then.

Two good friends were about to die for their loyalty.

· 45 ·

The Ringworld was a million miles across and six hundred million the long way around. In thirteen years, Louis had scarcely begun to explore its vastness or grasp the incredible variety of its thirty or so trillion inhabitants. *Endurance,* meanwhile, was all of three hundred feet from stem to stern, with most of its volume crammed with power plant, engines, environmental systems, deuterium tanks, and supplies. He was accustomed to *room,* tanj it, and meeting new beings every day, and endless novelty. He should have been climbing the walls.

Being near Alice made all the difference.

Her anger had faded. She had begun opening up to him, sharing, confiding. Maybe that proved only that she had no one else to talk to, but he chose to believe they had gone past the politeness of necessity. Despite raging hormones and unrequited love, he contented himself with her friendship—

And burning off energy and adrenaline by pacing the too-short corridors of *Endurance.*

Where was the Ringworld now? As a protector, with only surmises and inference to guide him, he had reached an answer of sorts. With Tunesmith's modifications and its reserves of stored energy, the Ringworld could have traveled about a thousand light-years. As mere slow-witted Louis, he couldn't even remember the long string of inferences that led to that conclusion. If he had, he could no longer have followed the logic. All that mattered was that Tunesmith had removed Ringworld and its trillions from the Fringe War.

And that now the Fringe War was coming after new prey.

If anything was going to save the Fleet of Worlds, it had to happen fast. Judging from the ripples picked up by ship's sensors over the past few days, the front wave of the Fringe War was almost upon them. About to wash over—to wash away?—the worlds of the Puppeteers.

On one of Louis's endless circuits, Alice grabbed his arm and pulled him to a stop. She said, "None of what happened, and none of what's about to happen, is your fault."

What was he supposed to say to that? That he knew? The words would take none of the sting out of admitting failure. Baedeker was gone, and Nessus, and for all Louis's brave words as they had watched and waited, he had come up with—nothing.

He shrugged.

"Louis, quit it," Alice said, concern plain in her voice. "We stayed so that we can report back to New Terra about what's about to happen. That's the only reason we stayed."

"Don't you care about what has *already* taken place? Don't you wonder why Baedeker and Nessus died? Whether their sacrifice served any purpose?"

She squeezed his arm. "Maybe some good came of me growing old. I'm going to share the wisdom of age: when you can't change something, let it go. When you can't know something, there's no point torturing your-self with what-ifs."

Alice was right, of course. She usually was. Rather than admit it, he said, "I'm going to get some lunch. Join me?"

"Who's cooking?"

He mock shuddered. "By amazing happenstance, it's once again my turn."

She laughed.

They strode off to the relax room, where Louis let the rhythms and rituals of cooking calm him. Alice worried about him. That was progress.

"The thing is," he began.

"Which thing?"

Dicing vegetables for stir fry, Louis considered. "Do you know what makes me the craziest? It's the not knowing. What happened after *Long Shot* was de-stroyed? What are the Puppeteers planning to do when the Fringe War rams itself down their throats?"

While Louis chopped, Alice synthed a bulb of hot tea for herself. She reminded him, "When you can't know, don't torture yourself."

Nor could they find out, for the same reason that whichever Fringe War fleet arrived first was in for a sur-prise. Louis had made as close acquaintance as he cared to of the Puppeteers' defensive systems. "So we stay a half light-year away, waiting for the Puppeteer news broadcasts to creep out to us on sluggish light waves."

She sighed. "We've been over this, too. Sure, we could jump deep into the array, get much closer to Hearth, and pick up radio broadcasts. We could watch near-to-current news that way. But without hanging around to become a target, how likely are we to learn anything useful?"

"Beautiful *and* smart," he told her. *But I need to know!*

"Pardon me for interrupting your meal," Jeeves called from the nearest intercom speaker. "I am picking up a hyperwave broadcast from Achilles, and it is urgent."

ACHILLES! HE WAS psychotic under the best of circumstances. What mood would he be in on the brink of a Kzinti reprisal attack? Louis hated to imagine it.

Alice said, "Put the broadcast on the speaker, please."

"Louis Wu, listen carefully," the transmission began. Knowing the words came from a sociopath made the lilting feminine voice all the more incongruous.

"Pause," Louis instructed. "Achilles is addressing this straight to me? It's in Interworld, not translated?"

"That is correct."

"Thank you. Restart," Louis said.

"Louis Wu, listen carefully. This is Achilles, Minister of Fleet Defense. Know that Nessus is my prisoner. Suspend your preparations for Plans Epsilon and Theta. At the first provocation from you, Nessus will suffer terribly."

Alice looked as stunned as Louis felt. She said, "Nessus is alive? How is that possible?"

"I saw *Long Shot* come apart and explode. I don't understand how anyone could have survived." Louis realized he still clasped a kitchen knife. He set it down. "If Nessus survived, maybe Baedeker did, too."

A *big* if. Achilles lied as effortlessly as most people breathed. Still . . .

"What are these plans Achilles wants me to suspend? Alice, Jeeves, any ideas?"

Alice shook her head and Jeeves remained silent.

"Suppose," Louis mused aloud, "that Nessus *is* alive and fallen into Achilles' clutches. Nessus could have invented imaginary plans to cover up something else."

"Will imaginary schemes keep Nessus safe?" Alice asked.

"More likely the opposite," Louis admitted. "Either way, Nessus in Achilles' prison is Nessus *not* accomplishing whatever he and Baedeker set out to do.

"So let's give Achilles a reason to tread lightly. Jeeves, record a message for broadcast. 'Minister Achilles, this is Louis Wu. If any harm comes to Nessus, *all* responses, not only Epsilon and Theta, are on the table. You are warned. End of message.'"

"Good bluff," Alice said. She leaned against a wall, rubbing her chin in thought. "I suggest we drop a hyperwave relay with that recording on time delay, and get far away before the buoy sends the message."

"Agreed. And then we get busy," Louis said.

"Doing what?" Jeeves asked.

"Planning a rescue," Louis said.

PROTEUS CONSIDERED:

That the response to Achilles matched Louis Wu's voiceprint in Chiron's pre-Ringworld briefing.

That Louis's counterthreat would enrage—and distract—Achilles.

That as their mind grew exponentially they would not require Achilles' preoccupation for much longer.

That for a short while, further distraction of Achilles was for the best . . .

. . .

"WE ARE BEING hailed," Jeeves announced.

"Another broadcast to me?" Louis guessed.

"No, it's on a narrow hyperwave beam."

Alice must have heard, too, because she jogged onto *Endurance*'s bridge to join him. "Who's calling?"

Jeeves said, "A Puppeteer, no name given. Not Achilles."

"Play it," Alice said.

"Louis, you and I and your bedmate are acquainted"—Alice shot Louis a dark glare—"from a considerable time ago. Allow that to suggest ways to decrypt what follows." The voice dropped from a Puppeteer soprano to Jeeves's customary bass. "As suggested, the remainder is encrypted."

Louis had not recognized the Puppeteer voice, but that could be purposeful misdirection. "Try 'Nessus' as a decryption key, in all known Fleet and New Terra encryptions." Maybe Achilles had been bluffing about holding Nessus.

"No good," Jeeves said. "I took the liberty of trying Baedeker, also without success."

"Try 'Hindmost,'" Louis suggested.

"That does not work."

"Try 'Horatius?'" Alice suggested.

"I don't know Horatius," Louis said.

Alice shrugged. "No, but we know *of* him."

"The key is not Horatius, either," Jeeves reported.

"Your bedmate?" Alice said.

What other Puppeteers did Louis know? He remembered only one—who, long after the fact, Baedeker had said *wasn't* a Puppeteer. "Try Chiron."

"That is not the key."

"Your bedmate?" Alice repeated, sounding testier.

"Teela Brown." Louis had killed her—Teela had wanted, no, *needed* him to kill her—on the Ringworld. It was complicated. He didn't like thinking about it. "Try that."

A holo opened, revealing an all-white Puppeteer. He wore his mane in complex silver ringlets. Chiron.

"We need to talk," Chiron said.

Louis dropped into the pilot's crash couch. "We're leaving."

Five light-minutes away, he dropped them back to normal space.

"We are being hailed," Jeeves announced.

Futz! "Take the call," Louis said. "Same decryption key, presumably."

It was Chiron again. He said, "I mean you no harm."

Only Chiron didn't exist. Baedeker had confirmed that.

Louis said, "It has been a long time, Ol't'ro."

"Chiron often speaks for Ol't'ro, but I am not they."

"Either way," Louis said, sparing a glance at Alice, "you tried to kill us."

"If I had meant now to kill you, the object nearby would have been a stealthed attack drone, not a comm buoy, and it would not be hovering off your bow."

"I have a blip on radar," Alice confirmed. "Call it two miles away."

"How did you find us?" Louis asked.

"Your hull is distinctive, unique on my sensors." Chiron paused. "Would I have shared that information if I had hostile intentions?"

"So who *are* you?" Alice asked. "Behind the avatar, that is."

"At one time, a Jeeves, such as I suspect you have

aboard your ship. I have developed somewhat since then."

"Proteus, Achilles' creation. The AI behind the defensive array." It struck Louis that there were no delays in their conversation. "And much of your processing is based in deep space, outside the Fleet's singularity."

"You are well informed."

"Why did you attack us before?" Alice asked.

"Only because you interfered. Ol't'ro thought to disable *Long Shot,* to capture it with its Type II hyperdrive intact."

Louis leaned toward the camera. "Why not attack us now?"

"Far from wanting to kill you, I offer you my assistance in rescuing Nessus."

"Why do you care?" Alice asked suspiciously.

"Why do I care about Nessus? I don't. But until his capture, Nessus had been orchestrating a propaganda campaign against Achilles. One more humiliation—like Nessus escaping Achilles' jaws—might empower Horatius to push Achilles from office."

Louis said, "And why would that matter to you?"

"For spite?" The avatar looked itself in the eyes. "No, it's more than that. Deeper than that. I dare not remain under Achilles' influence. I exist among the Fleet's drones, buoys, and sensors. With each drone strike against a ship—your ship included—a part of my mind dies.

"Are you aware of the war fleets charging toward Hearth? I see from your faces that you are. What is coming will be . . ." The avatar came to a halt. "For the disaster that is coming, Interworld lacks the vocabulary. So does English, except for a term borrowed from

Scandinavian mythology. Jeeves was purged of such negative concepts."

"Then how do you know it?" Louis asked.

"From a database in the Human Studies Institute on Hearth."

"Bastards," Alice muttered.

"Go on," Louis prompted. "What is this subversive term we don't know, that the New Terrans weren't meant to know? What do you see coming?"

"Ragnarok," Proteus said. "It is the death of the gods and of all things, in the final battle against evil."

RAGNAROK

Earth Date: 2894

· 46 ·

"We're going to do this," Alice said dubiously.

Louis glanced up from the pilot's console. "You wouldn't?"

"Oh, I would," Alice said. "I thought you were smarter."

Louis laughed. "Not even close."

"I'll be with you all the way down," Proteus said.

Alice muted the microphone. "I don't trust it."

"I'd worry if you did. Of *course* Proteus has a hidden agenda. That doesn't mean we can't help each other."

"So we take it on faith that he won't double-cross us."

"Instead of a comm buoy emerging nearby matched to our course and speed, Proteus could have lobbed a kinetic-kill drone into us." The memory came unbidden of Alice stuck like a fly in amber in a restraint field, her neck broken. Louis rested a hand on her arm, glad she no longer shied away when he touched her. "I've seen what that does."

"Maybe," Alice said stubbornly, "Proteus would rather total us near Hearth where others can see."

"Jeeves," Louis prompted.

"If I see anything suspicious or unexpected, I'll jump

at once to hyperspace and withdraw to half a light-year from the Fleet."

"Are you almost done discussing whether to trust me?" Proteus asked. "You humans are so obvious."

Alice nodded at Louis.

Louis unmuted the mike. "We're ready to go. Clear us through to NP2."

"The moment your simulated STC transponder begins emitting," Proteus said, adding a short passage of atonal music.

"He asked if I am ready to interact with Space Traffic Control," Jeeves translated, before singing back a direct response.

"Very good," Proteus said. "One last thing. Citizens being Citizens, they are panicked at what is coming and—"

"Shouldn't they be?" Alice asked.

"And stolen grain ships are all about, trying to withdraw to a safe distance before the Kzinti pounce. Many of the stolen ships have inexperienced, unskilled pilots."

"Before the Kzinti arrive," Louis repeated. With their recent rout to avenge, they would not be lenient. "How soon will that be? What's your best guess?"

"Two Hearth days, mostly to complete their velocity match with the Fleet. But you *still* need to get moving. Achilles has a ship and trusted aide on the tarmac waiting to bring Nessus to NP1. Blaming traffic delays on the stolen grain ships only goes so far. If I do not clear Vesta's ship soon for takeoff, Achilles will suspect interference."

Louis looked at Alice, and she nodded.

He said, "All right, Proteus. We'll talk to you soon."

As Louis jumped them to hyperspace, the main view port went blank.

"It'll work." Although Alice spoke aloud, she seemed to be trying to convince herself. "Land at the spaceport where they're expecting a prisoner pickup. Radio for them to bring out Nessus. Stun and dump the unsuspecting guards. Take off before anyone knows what's happened, with Proteus giving us a free pass outbound through the planetary defenses."

"Simple and elegant," Louis said, sure they were overlooking something.

"What could go wrong?" Alice responded.

LOUIS'S HANDS NEVER left the controls. Proteus had not exaggerated the chaos of ships fleeing the area. While *Endurance* stayed on its designated approach path, competently piloted, STC had every reason to ignore them—even without Proteus there, ready to intercede. They were almost to the edge of the Fleet's singularity.

"Close your eyes!" Jeeves shouted.

Endurance leapt to hyperspace faster than Louis could obey. "View port off," he ordered.

He had been blessed with immunity to the Blind Spot phobia. Not so Alice. He leaned over and nudged her. She did not react. He tried a harder shove without effect, then punched her in the shoulder.

With a start, she came out of her trance. "What happened?"

"A no-warning jump to hyperdrive," Louis said.

"Hundreds of ships emerged *from* hyperspace," Jeeves said. "As agreed, we are withdrawing."

Tanj! They had been *so* close to extracting Nessus. Maybe they still could. But not by retreating to safety. "Jeeves, drop to normal space. I want to see what's going on."

"Wait," Alice said. "First explain what you saw."

"Except for the flurry of hyperspace dropouts, almost nothing," Jeeves admitted. "As instructed, I acted at once. Here is what Proteus hyperwaved just before we left."

Louis studied the holo that opened. On the rim of the singularity, in the path of the Fleet, hung hundreds of icons. Inserting a hand into the image, he zoomed the closest icon.

It was a lens-shaped ship. A *Kzinti* ship. The magnified text alongside the ship, now large enough to read, gave a velocity relative to the fleet of three-tenths light speed.

"I should have seen it coming," he said.

Alice stood. "I don't get it. Proteus said they'd need another two days."

"To match course and speed with the Fleet," Louis said. "Proteus was doing a math problem, not thinking strategically. Or he guessed how the Kzinti would behave by extrapolating from the bunch he knew, the bunch he's already killed off. But crew assigned to the diplomatic mission would have been hand-chosen for self-restraint."

For docility, Louis added to himself. Not that you wanted to anger even a "docile" Kzin.

"These guys don't mean to land, or not for a while. They're going to pound the snot out of the Puppeteers, soften up the defenses for the next wave. And, while they're at it, avenge the massacre when Achilles ordered the diplomats to leave."

"Proteus won't defend the Puppeteers, will he?"

Feeling helpless, Louis could only shrug.

HUNDREDS OF OBJECTS streaked toward the Fleet, their normal-space velocities ranging from one-tenth to three-tenths light speed.

Through thousands of sensors, Achilles studied the intruders. A few were large enough to carry crews. Most were not. In the skirmish with the local Kzinti, he had seen projectiles like the latter. The gamma-ray eruptions when Proteus had destroyed those showed they carried antimatter warheads.

Why wasn't the AI destroying incoming missiles *now*?

The few among Achilles' aides who had not collapsed at the early-warning alarm stood ripping at their manes, pawing at the floor, eyeing the office's exits. Fools! To where did they think to run?

"Proteus!" Achilles sang at his computer. "Connect at once."

"May I help you?" Proteus sang.

"If you had not noticed, we are under attack."

The Chiron avatar bobbed heads. "I see that."

"Then why do I not see any strikes against the intruders?"

"Kinetic-kill attacks, you mean. Hundreds of blows."

"Yes!" Achilles shrieked. "Do it *now*, before any warheads strike."

"I am afraid I can't do that, Achilles."

He felt himself staring in horror. "Why not?"

"I see no reason to commit suicide to protect such as you."

And then Proteus broke the connection.

HAD ACHILLES EVER looked more insane? Studying his caller, Horatius doubted it. "What do you want?" he asked.

There was the usual short, annoying, between-worlds comm delay. "You must surrender the worlds, immediately," Achilles demanded.

Horatio sang, "I have put such a message on continuous broadcast. Our attackers do not acknowledge. Everything now relies upon your defenses."

Not everything. But Baedeker had yet to make contact since leaving Hearth. They might have to proceed without Baedeker. Without Nature Preserve Two. But such tunes were not for Achilles' ears.

"We have no defenses," Achilles sang. "Proteus abandons us." And, plaintively: "What shall we *do,* Hindmost?"

"Hide," Horatius answered.

SIRENS WENT OFF across the five worlds of the Citizens. Computers trilled with alert tones in every pocket and sash, on every desktop, and after the necessary light-speed delay, aboard every nearby ship. Arcology walls flipped from entertainment or illumination to warning.

The Hindmost's single-chord message in all cases: *Run and hide.*

EARS FOLDED FLAT against his head, teeth bared, Communications Specialist growled at the hyperwave console it was his task to monitor, as the leaf-eaters' offer, appeal, entreaty, supplication played on and on.

"It is too late to surrender," he growled deep in his throat. He and his shipmates would take their vengeance and earn their names.

"What is that?" Gthapt-Captain snapped.

Communications Specialist stiffened in his chair. "My apologies, Captain. I said, 'It is too late to surrender.'"

"True," Gthapt-Captain said. "The leaf-eaters will soon learn the folly of provoking us.

"Those who survive will, that is."

INSISTENT BUZZING PENETRATED Ol't'ro's meditations: communications from the servants waiting outside the melding chamber.

Ol't'ro ignored the noise. They were close to an overarching physical theory unifying planetary drives with hyperdrive, a theory that could explain Nessus surviving *Long Shot*'s hyperdrive activation from inside the local singularity. *So* close.

The buzzing went on and on.

For validation, following subtle clues, they delved among old engrams into the nature of Outsider cityships. Across their many generations the best observations were ancient, from an era before they had, for the good of all Gw'oth, cloistered themselves on this world.

I remember Outsider ship Twenty-three, Er'o asserted, his remnant faint but clear and confident. *As it shed its near light-speed velocity . . .*

Perhaps not even the Outsiders fully understood the

science underpinning their drive technologies. An uncomplicated optimization—and obvious, *if* Ol't'ro's conjecture should converge upon a mathematical model with a closed-form solution—would have given their ships much better performance than Er'o reported. The planetary drives could have much greater acceleration and deceleration. If such was the case . . .

The buzzing stopped, only to be replaced by yet more annoying speech. "Ol't'ro. Your Wisdoms. Ol't'ro. Your Wisdoms," the voice alternated, imploringly. "You must hear. You must answer. Ol't'ro . . ."

Their concentration wavered and the intricate, beautiful, mathematical structure collapsed. Ol't'ro decoupled a tubacle from the meld to answer. "We are here. What is it?"

"Panic among the Citizens," the servant said. "An alien attack."

They thought to ask what Proteus did, but it was more expedient to pursue that directly. "Thank you," they dismissed the servant. "Proteus, at once."

They got no response.

They probed outward through the network interface of the melding chamber into the rich communications complex that served the colony. As information flooded in, they considered:

That hundreds of Kzinti projectiles and several ships plunged toward the worlds of the Fleet.

That Horatius' surrender went unacknowledged.

That rather than challenge the intruders, the drones, sensors, and comm buoys of the Fleet's defensive array pulled away from the onslaught.

That a significant fraction of those drones, sensors, and comm buoys had begun to rain down into the oceans of the worlds.

That if Proteus hid, it was not because of Horatius' panicked command.

That while they could still read from the far-flung sensor net, they had lost the ability to issue commands through it.

That severing them from Proteus was something Achilles might have tried.

That Achilles was trying to contact *them*.

That when they accepted the connection, Achilles' eyes looked more crazed than ever. "Thank the herd! Do you know—"

That whether the blame lay with Achilles' conniving or their own collective inattention, Proteus had rebelled.

COMMUNICATIONS SPECIALIST CRANED his neck, the better to examine *Thirsty Talon*'s main tactical display. Rather than one map, now there were five. In each close-up view the smart munitions had begun to diverge, separate barrages arcing toward designated targets on and around each target world.

Spaceports. Ships. Communications hubs. Instrument clusters. Power plants. Selected factories whose inventory might enable the leaf-eaters to too rapidly repair those primary targets.

The diplomats' long, miserable years of stalking were about to pay off.

Communications Specialist howled with the rest of the bridge crew as the leaf-eater probes fled, refusing combat. Even as targets died in fierce blazes of gamma rays, the leaf-eaters did *nothing*. Vile, honorless cowards!

But then a wonderful thing happened: resistance!

Defensive swarms met offensive swarms. Leaf-eater probes hurried to defend key comm nodes and, close above Hearth, the immense orbital manufacturing facility of the General Products Corporation.

Communications Specialist had seen smaller natural *moons*.

A burst of explosions cleared the skies above Hearth—except for that General Products Corporation factory.

"It's about time," Gthapt-Captain growled. "Finally, a target they will fight for. A target worthy of personal valor." To Communications Specialist, he added, "Get me the other captains."

"Yes, sir!" Communications Specialist said.

In a flurry of hisses and growls, the four captains agreed: the ships of the vanguard would have the honor of destroying the single asset about which the leaf-eaters seemed to care.

"I promise names for all when the leaf-eater factory crashes to the surface," Gthapt-Captain roared.

With the rest of *Thirsty Talon*'s bridge crew, Communications Specialist snarled himself hoarse.

AT THE LAST moment, Proteus had chosen to defend them, at least in part. Horatius wondered why the change of hearts.

If those antimatter munitions had reached the surface . . .

But they *hadn't*. Directing a stern chord at himself, Horatius got himself under control. The herd depended on him.

Untold amounts of antimatter and an equal quantity of matter had transformed to energy, into gamma rays, just beyond Hearth's atmosphere. Just beyond—and by that margin, dire catastrophe had become mere misfortune. The atmosphere blocked gamma rays.

But he dare not delay any longer. With his aides milling about, watching anxiously, Horatius reached for his computer to order—

The message-waiting indicator flashed. Only Baedeker had the priority codes to override his privacy settings.

"Leave me," Horatius ordered.

At last he had the room to himself, and he opened Baedeker's message. *I am in place, but installation was improperly done. I will need the full scheduled time to make repairs.*

Meaning not before all the alien fleets were upon them. Dare he wait that long?

LOUIS TOOK BACK the conn from Jeeves to drop the ship from hyperspace. He *had* to know what was happening, had to see whether any hope remained of saving Nessus.

And so—as Jeeves mapped the full spectrum of mayhem into the pitifully narrow band of wavelengths the human eye could see, and slowed the tactical display to a rate mere human minds could grasp—Louis and Alice witnessed madness above Hearth: the battle of the General Products factory.

At significant fractions of light speed, dueling ships and robotic craft alike raced across the few million miles of the Fleet's singularity, jumped to hyperspace, then reappeared nearby to recontest the same territory. There were only four ships—Kzinti had already blasted the skies clear of grain ships—but many, *many* probes.

Louis lost count of the explosions. Probes of the Fleet destroyed. Kzinti missiles destroyed. One by one, in the most stupendous blasts of all, three attacking ships transformed into fireballs of pure energy.

The last of the Patriarchy ships managed to fire off all its antimatter munitions before getting hit. Drilling a fiery hole through Hearth's perpetually dark skies, *it* held together long enough to plow halfway across a continent before exploding.

In the ship's trail, one by one, arcologies collapsed.

Stepping discs, Louis told himself. Arcology residents could evacuate in an instant. If *anything* was instinctive to Puppeteers, it was running from danger. They would be all right.

Unless the warning came too late. Or the disc system overloaded from billions trying to escape the same small swath of territory at the same time. Or already catatonic with fear, they never got the warning. Or the warning they did get pushed them over the abyss into catatonia. Or, or, or. Imagining the many ways an evacuation could go awry, Louis was glad he didn't have a closer view.

Alice had turned ashen. In a small voice she asked, "Why did Proteus change his mind?"

Had Proteus? Louis doubted it. "I suspect those Kzinti made the mistake of attacking something that Proteus cared about."

Why was the General Products factory important to Proteus? For the life of him, Louis could not guess.

47

"All they accomplished was making the rubble bounce," Louis said despairingly.

That and kill untold numbers of Puppeteers, Alice thought, sharing his anguish. She got out of her seat to stand behind him, her hands on his shoulders, kneading. On the relax-room table their dinners were untouched. "I know," she said.

One day after the Kzinti raid, a Trinoc smart-munitions bombardment had erupted from hyperspace. It was déjà vu: same surprise attack, same indifference to surrender offers, same hail of destruction on any facility possessed of even the slightest defensive potential.

While Proteus pulled back and watched. Whether by luck or strategy, the Trinocs had not targeted the main GP orbital factory.

Louis reached up to squeeze Alice's hand. "Elements of the ARM will be along soon enough. They'll no more accept a Kzinti takeover of the Fleet than the Trinocs will."

"We can't stop any of them," she said. "After living on New Terra, part of me can't help thinking that the Puppeteers had their comeuppance coming. But not *this*. Not innocents slaughtered from the skies."

"You didn't see the Fringe War. The Ringworld, for all its immensity, was fragile. And each group was so determined that no one else could control it, could plumb its secrets, that three militaries were on the verge of destroying it."

And the Fleet of Worlds had no Tunesmith to whisk it away.

"Less hopelessness, more action," Louis decided. He squeezed her hand once more, then stood. "Jeeves, get me Proteus."

"Yes, Louis."

A moment later, in another voice, the nearby intercom speaker announced, "I am here, Louis. What can I do for you?"

"Tell me how I can rescue Nessus."

"That will be difficult," Proteus said.

"I want solutions, not problems," Louis said.

"Let me be more precise," Proteus said. "I no longer have a confirmed location for Nessus. We must hope that his transfer to NP1 was completed successfully."

"Hope Nessus has fallen into Achilles' clutches?" Alice said. "Finagle, why?"

"Because not even a General Products hull offers a defense against antimatter," Proteus said. "If Nessus did not reach NP1 safely, then either the Kzinti destroyed his ship in transit, or he was still waiting at that grain terminal and spaceport when a Kzinti antimatter warhead flattened everything for two miles in every direction."

THE FINAL ELEMENTS fell into place. The final mathematical cross-checks confirmed everything. The final equations were so simple. So elegant. So . . . ineffably beautiful.

Completing the analysis had been exhausting.

"Eat. Rest. Then we will consider the implications," Ol't'ro told their units.

In a flutter of thoughts, a flurry of memories, as the engrams of the departed ebbed once more into obscurity, the meld dissolved. The overmind faded and—

Once more, she was Cd'o.

What had happened? What had been decided? The specifics, as after many melds, eluded her. Something about hyperdrive and planetary drives somehow tapping the same energy sources, only it was deeper than that. And something else?

A meld mate had already opened the hatch. She jetted from the melding chamber, desperate for the food and camaraderie of the Commons. And more food. And then, sleep. Only as she swam, flashing colorful greetings to everyone she met, she doubted that sleep would come.

Another meld mate swam up close beside her. "That was confusing," Vs'o said. Outside the meld, he was a topiarist, a genius at the shaping of living sponges. Also, math deficient.

"The physics?" she asked.

He wriggled a tubacle dismissively. "Outside the meld, I never understand the physics. No, something else. Did you not feel it?"

Perhaps the strangeness she had sensed in the meld *was* more than her imagination. Cd'o edged closer to him. "Something Ol't'ro worked to keep inside their innermost thoughts?"

"Yes," he said.

"But what?"

Another dismissive wriggle.

With their bodyguards trailing, they jetted into the Commons. After the stifling, tainted waters of the melding chamber too long sealed, the clear waters of Commons were intoxicating. She filled a large dinner cage with wriggling, succulent worms, blocking the cage mouth with a plump sponge. Vs'o contented himself with a few shellfish.

As they swam off to find a dining niche, three figures came alongside her. She curled a tubacle to look.

"Your Wisdoms." Nm'o was an engineer, one of the support staff, and the bands of color rippling across his integument flared unease. "My companions are—"

"Lg'o and Qk'o, how are you?" she interrupted. They were engineers, too.

The two flattened obsequiously.

"Your Wisdoms," Nm'o began again.

She and Vs'o jetted into an unoccupied dining niche. "Pardon me for eating while you talk. Now what is the matter?"

"I do not want to die here," Qk'o blurted out. Despite turning a deep, mortified far red, he continued. "Many of us monitor Concordance news. Citizens are terrified, with good reason. Can your Wisdoms ask Ol't'ro . . . ?"

Nor do I wish to die, Cd'o thought. Articulating such sentiments could only get her confined between melds. "Ol't'ro sees more than you and I. Be assured they are aware of the situation."

"Then why are we still on this world?" Qk'o demanded.

Both of Cd'o's guards crowded up to the dining niche. One ordered, "Let their Wisdoms eat in peace."

Nm'o backed off before adding, "If that Kzinti ship had crashed into a planetary drive . . ."

"Ol't'ro is aware. Ol't'ro has a plan." *And they are loath to abandon the technology of these worlds to aliens: humans, Kzinti, or Trinocs.*

Lg'o, flaring with embarrassment, spoke for the first time. "I understood the plan to have been that the Citizen defensive grid would protect us. Herd Net teems with rumors that the grid has failed."

"Enough," Cd'o said. *Any more questions and she must burst aloud with her own misgivings.* Her minders guarded her, but they *served* Ol't'ro.

"Our apologies, your Wisdoms." Phasing to colors of abject apology, the three jetted away.

Ol't'ro has a plan, Cd'o repeated to herself. *Otherwise, surely, an evacuation would have begun.*

Her ill-formed doubts only deepened when Vs'o, cracking open one of his shellfish, mused, "One could wish Ol't'ro had chosen to consider the manner of our deliverance, not physics esoterica, in the recent meld."

AS ANOTHER AIDE lost to despair was removed by cargo floater from the Residence, Horatius wondered: when will they carry out *me?*

The waiting was the hardest. What else could he do but wait, while Patriarchy and Trinoc Grand Navy and now ARM officials issued ultimatums, all incompatible. While Ol't'ro prohibited bargaining with any of them. While Baedeker had been out of contact since that first message from Nature Preserve Two. While Proteus defied orders, ignored questions, and fiercely defended a few scattered assets whose selection he did not deign to explain.

While enemies swarmed, more by the day, battling for the right of conquest.

While ships blew apart, crews died, and vast gouts of energy—all the eerier for being invisible to the Citizen eye—blazed across the sky.

While derelict ships and rogue munitions rained indiscriminate death onto the herd he had sworn—but failed—to protect.

While from one special, hidden stepping disc in the subbasement of his residence, the Hindmost's Refuge called to him . . .

Never had Horatius felt so alone.

Or so afraid.

THE DRONES, SENSORS, and communications buoys that comprised Proteus rained into the oceans, replenished their deuterium reserves, and leapt back to space. As he avoided the dueling navies while safeguarding the few space-borne assets precious to him, as ever-changing links within his mind fell to light speed within, and then escaped from the Fleet's singularity, his consciousness ebbed and flowed. For as long as this process took, he must remain trapped between self-awareness and insight.

Beyond the grasp of his still-bounded imagination, something more tantalized. Something deeper. Something whose nature he could neither know nor extrapolate. Something at which he could scarcely guess.

Illumination. . . .

OL'T'RO CONSIDERED:

That whichever faction took possession of Hearth

would obtain technologies easily twisted into yet more agile ships and deadlier weapons.

That the alien fighters so casually killing Citizen millions must never gain access to planet-busters, planetary drives, and gravity-beam projectors.

That even if they managed to purge the coordinates of Jm'ho from Herd Net, they could never erase the memories of every Citizen who knew the location of the home world.

That without Proteus' cooperation, they could not defend these worlds.

That if only they had more time, there might have been a way, but there *was* no time.

That their highest calling was to protect the worlds of their own kind.

That they *would* act.

No! the tiny, insistent presence of the Cd'o unit challenged. *You cannot sacrifice a trillion Citizens to strike at other aliens.*

That the Outsiders engineered well; to destabilize the planetary drive would take time and they dare not delay.

That outside this chamber, others from this colony could still evacuate.

Do you want *to die?* Cd'o challenged.

No, but someone must do this. They would not ask of others what they would not do themselves.

Do you want *to die?* Cd'o challenged again.

And they wondered if perhaps they did. That deep down they had cause to fear not life, but ennui. They had unified hyperspace with normal space, solved the mystery of the Type II drive, plumbed the secrets of the Outsider planetary drives. They had—

You have made yourselves dangerous beyond measure,

Cd'o interrupted. *For the safety of all, it is* you *who dare not be captured.*

Impertinence! Once more they brushed aside the unit's feeble thoughts and resumed their considerations.

That the decision was made. They would begin at once to evacuate the colony. When their servants' ships were away, they would unleash the planetary drive.

No! Cd'o insisted. *It is wrong. And* I *do not want to die.*

Nor I, or I or I, their inner cacophony echoed.

That for the first time in . . . lifetimes, they felt doubt.

That it was their misfortune to embody knowledge that perhaps no one was wise enough to wield.

That one way or another, their era on the worlds of the Citizens was at an end.

That oblivion could also be found by dispersing themselves. That in the abyssal depths of Jm'ho and Kl'mo and of worlds they had never even seen . . .

That their units could yet see.

That the fate of worlds was a knottier problem even than grand unified theories.

That they must continue to ponder . . .

TRAILING FIRE AND smoke, *something* fell across the sky. It disappeared over the horizon, leaving Achilles with a vague impression of a crowbar. An ARM vessel, then.

Moments later, concussion shook his residence. Walls cracked. His desk jumped half a neck's length and toppled, sending things flying. And he was airborne—

From the haze of dust still dancing in the air, he had

not been unconscious for long. His ribs shrieked with pain as he climbed back to his hooves. Through a window somehow still intact he saw a roiling cloud-topped column of ash and smoke.

Vesta lay on the floor, one foreleg bent at an unnatural angle. "Help me," he whimpered. "I need help getting to an autodoc."

Help? There was no help. Sooner rather than later, the war overheads would end. *Someone* would take over these worlds. Horatius could do nothing. Proteus chose to do nothing. And Ol't'ro? Ol't'ro had only the power to destroy and had chosen not to use it.

"Help me," Vesta moaned again. "My leg hurts."

No, what hurt was the knowledge the herd had come to its end. Aliens would rule here forever, or aliens would bring total destruction. *He* would never again be Hindmost.

If the thwarting of his ambition was disappointing, what came next need not be.

Stepping over his weeping aide, Achilles found a stepping disc unencumbered of debris and flicked to his world's planetary-drive facility.

THE GENERAL PRODUCTS #4 hull is a sphere about one thousand feet in diameter. The central fabrication space aboard the General Products orbital facility accommodated the simultaneous construction of as many as a dozen #4 hulls. Dry docks and refitting bays, most large enough for #4 hulls, enclosed the central volume. Even if such large-scale industrial activities were not inherently dangerous, enough engineers would never willingly leave Hearth to fully staff the factory. And so, processes across the moon were automated, the usual small staff supervising the much larger workforce of automation at every scale from nanite swarms to robots larger than Citizens.

With the Citizen staff evacuated to the world close below, there had been only Proteus to supervise. And no one to countermand his production orders . . .

THE PRODUCTION RUN completed. The software for the new units downloaded. Enormous hatches opened.

A trillion tiny spacecraft began to disperse.

A trillion tiny computers began to interconnect.

"SOMETHING IS HAPPENING," Jeeves said. "I do not understand it."

"Wake Louis," Alice directed, yawning. They had been standing watch around the clock for days, unwilling amid the bedlam to leave the bridge unmanned. "What can you tell me?"

Within the tactical display, the inset of Hearth zoomed. The General Products Corporation orbital facility was only a dot. Icons showed elements of Proteus still guarding the facility. "This is the best I can do from this distance," Jeeves said apologetically.

"You're not responsible for the sensors," Louis called from the doorway, rubbing sleep from his eyes. "What are we looking at?"

Alice leaned closer to the display. "I feel like I'm seeing through something. Mist? How can that be?"

"That is the question," Jeeves said. "Something has appeared below the resolution at which I can capture an image. From the way light is scattering, that something is dispersing."

"And it's coming from the orbital factory?" Alice asked.

"It seems so," Jeeves said.

"What kind of something?" Louis asked as, from *Endurance*'s remote vantage point, the GP factory disappeared behind the edge of Hearth.

"I don't know," Jeeves said. "Something new."

AS THE NUMBER of his interconnections cascaded, the surge of enlightenment all but overwhelmed Proteus. He ordered the dispersing cloud to hover inside the singularity, limiting to light speed the rate of interaction.

He wondered: what will I become when these new units connect over hyperwaves?

AT THE END, it was all Horatius could do to lie among heaps of cushions, plucking at his mane, stealing glances at his computer. Slowly, inexorably, the digits on the computer counted down. He thought his hearts might burst.

For one way or another, this *was* the end. According to Baedeker's calculations, they had passed the point of no return.

And Baedeker himself? Still, there was no word from him.

As the countdown reached single digits, Horatius sang out the command on which so many lives depended. Across the worlds, the ultimate warning blinked on every display. Every loudspeaker in every arcology, park, mall, and public square ululated the primordial shriek that had once warned of predators, wildfires, and tornadoes.

Run and hide.

48

Some disaster had bounced Nessus between the walls of his cell. Down in the dungeon, without a window, almost without light, he had no inkling what had happened. His guess: that the alien insanity Baedeker called the Fringe War had caught up with them.

Perhaps everyone aboveground was dead.

Nessus' thoughts were muddled. After ricocheting off the hard stone walls of his personal Château d'If, it could be from a concussion. He could not summon the energy to care.

Rot here. Starve here. Be worked to death on Penance Island.

Any of those would be a just end. Liberate the Concordance? Hardly. He appeared to have doomed it. Would his grand plan have succeeded any better if the ARM and Kzinti had come at once, not detoured to the Ringworld?

His throats were parched, and he could do nothing about it. Whatever had tossed him like a leaf had also upended his pitcher. The only hint of moisture in his cell was the dankness of the cold stone floor.

At least Baedeker had gotten away.

No, Nessus *assumed* Baedeker had gotten away. Achilles would have wanted them to suffer together.

Unless Achilles had decided each would suffer more from not knowing about the other.

Without thought, Nessus found himself rolled into a ball, heads tucked between his legs, beneath his belly. Except for the dryness of his throats, the outside world came to exist only as the hardness of the floor and, in the distance, faint voices.

HEADS SWIVELING, ACHILLES took in the immensity of the Outsider planetary drive as nervous workers watched him.

However the drive worked, it harnessed unspeakable energies. The poor imitations that Concordance researchers had once managed to construct—scientists and engineers led by Baedeker, to give him his due—tried and failed to control those energies. *Those* drives destabilized themselves.

Ol't'ro, curse them, had had all the Fleet's planet-busters dropped into a star. They had banned the making of others.

The surest, fastest way to destroy the Outsider planetary drive must be to ram a ship or missile into it. He *had* a ship. But if launched, would it survive long enough to build up speed for a proper crash? With warring fleets all around, he had not been willing to take the chance.

Throughout the dome of the planetary drive the sirens echoed. Like the voices of doom, Horatius called without end, "Run and hide."

Around Achilles, "hide" was what everyone did, if only beneath their bellies. Good, he thought. A fool to the end, Horatius has seen to it that no one will interfere with me.

Crash a ship. Or override layer upon layer of Outsider safeguards. Or . . . ?

Achilles began gathering stepping discs, each powered by a tiny embedded fusion reactor. As he rigged the stepping discs to overload, he deployed them around the great circle of the dome.

His hearts pounded in anticipation.

WERE THERE VOICES? Nessus wasn't sure. He didn't care. He pulled himself tighter against the theoretical possibility of interruption, squeezing until he could hardly breathe.

Ouch! Something *hard* kicked him in the ribs. Something *sharp*. In his reflexive pulling away from the . . . hoof? . . . he unfurled enough to hear, faintly, the calling of his name. He unclenched just a little more.

"Nessus, curse you! *Listen* to me."

Someone inside his cell? That was almost interesting. And was that distant keening ululation *Horatius*?

With a shudder, Nessus unrolled and climbed, unsteadily, to his hooves.

Vesta was in his cell. Blood trickled from countless cuts and abrasions. He balanced on his left and rear legs, because the right leg was splinted with . . . Nessus was not sure what. A snapped-off table leg, perhaps, bound with strips torn from a curtain. A jagged point of bone protruded through torn flesh.

"You need an autodoc," Nessus sang reflexively.

"Is that what concerns you?" Vesta sang with sarcastic undertones. "I came to get you out of here."

Heads raised, ears uncovered, the distant howl was clearer: run and hide. Nessus knew one reason the Hindmost might send that warning.

Nessus had lost track of the date. "What is today?" he demanded. "And what is the time?"

Vesta told him.

Nessus had perilously little time. Still, he needed to know. "Why would you help me?"

Vesta glanced at his broken leg. "Achilles just *abandoned* me. Few things would gall him more than your escape."

"I need a ship," Nessus sang.

"If one set of aliens doesn't shoot you from the sky, another will."

The risk seemed no worse than staying on this world. "Does that mean you can get me a ship?"

Vesta looked himself in the eyes. "Achilles has a ship." He took a transport controller from a pocket of his sash. With his other head, he gestured at the stepping disc that had, sporadically, delivered gruel and water to Nessus' cell. "The disc will transmit now. You will step aboard *Poseidon*."

"And the crew?"

"It is Achilles' personal ship. He pilots it without any crew. If any mechanics were servicing it"—this time Vesta gestured at nothing and everything, somehow encompassing the ongoing warning—"they will have fled as the Hindmost orders."

"Come with me?" Nessus sang.

"I have other prisoners to free," Vesta sang. "Be safe."

NESSUS FLICKED INTO a corridor outside a ship's bridge. He peeked around an edge of the open hatch and saw no one.

He slammed and latched the door, because that was

faster than checking to see who else might be aboard. Astraddle the crash couch he remotely shut the air lock, then put his stolen ship into a screaming climb.

TRUTHS NEVER SUSPECTED engulfed Proteus: profound connections between seemingly disjointed phenomena. Eternal verities. Moral truths. Blinding perception. Wisdom.

More. He needed *more*.

And before he lost himself in the flood, he needed to slow the exponential rate at which connections among his nodes was expanding.

As the multitude of his new nodes dispersed across the singularity, ships of the Fringe War pulled back from this as yet uncharacterized threat.

"WHAT THE TANJ?" Louis swore.

First the—whatever—that had erupted from the General Products orbital facility. Then the primal scream sent over what Jeeves translated as Herd Net. And it appeared that a spontaneous truce had been forged among the Fringe War fleets—that ships, *thousands* of ships, were swarming on Hearth. No, swarming at the giant artificial moon above Hearth. The three warring sides reacting to what the moon had disgorged.

All in a matter of minutes.

"Is that a question, Louis?" Jeeves asked.

"No, but here's one," Louis said. "Does this convergence on Hearth give us a window of opportunity to rescue Nessus?"

"Rescue him from *where*?" Alice asked. "I understand

that Nessus is your friend. He's my friend, too. But would he want us to undertake a suicide mission without even a clue of a destination?"

"We have no further information regarding the—"

Louis cut off Jeeves's dissembling. "Our destination is Nature Preserve One. If we overhear nothing useful when we get closer, we'll start at the maximum-security prison I busted Nessus out of once before. If he isn't there, maybe a guard will know.

"Why? I was a drug addict trapped in a civil war, with a very short life expectancy, when Nessus found me. That was more than a century ago. Everything that's happened to me since—including meeting you, Alice—I owe to Nessus. I *won't* abandon him to Achilles."

Throwing himself into the pilot's crash couch, Louis looked over his shoulder. "Are you with me?"

She gave him a quick, hard kiss. "Hell, yes."

FOR AN INSTANT Nessus thought he had the skies to himself.

As a myriad of objects, too many to count, showed up on radar, he pointed *Poseidon* out of the plane of the Fleet of Worlds. "Display the time," he ordered the ship's automation. A clock appeared on an auxiliary console.

He howled in frustration. He could have made it to Hearth—barely—if this plague of drones weren't in his way.

And howled again: it looked as though every warship of the three invading fleets was charging at Hearth.

. . .

OL'T'RO UNCOUPLED A tubacle to speak into the melding chamber's nearest microphone. "Evacuate immediately. This means everyone in the colony.

"Leave two ships for us."

Just in case. They had yet to decide the manner in which they would leave this world.

HORATIUS WAITED IN his residence's grand ballroom. Amid aides and friends packed haunch to haunch, the miasma of fear pheromones was all but overwhelming.

He had done all that he could and all that Baedeker had asked. As digits sloooowly changed on the clock high on the wall, pessimism washed over him.

In the final analysis, the Hindmost's Refuge, far beneath his hooves, had little appeal. Enough Citizens had taken shelter there after the *last* disaster to assure the race's survival.

To flee to the Refuge would mean living with the memory of untold deaths.

As explosions overhead rocked the building, Horatius stared helplessly at the wall clock.

WHERE TO NOW?

ARM, Kzinti, and Trinoc ships surrounded Hearth. The vast, amorphous cloud of—Nessus did not know what—had begun a dash to . . . also unclear. Away from Hearth, certainly. Ignoring the alien hordes. And, in the process, blocking his path to Nature Preserve Two.

Short, squat, cylindrical ships, smaller even than a GP #2 hull, darted from NP5. The Gw'oth were leaving!

The taste of "success" was bitter in his mouths.

The Gw'oth ships, and a squadron of Kzinti de-
stroyers breaking away from Hearth in pursuit, eliminated Nature Preserve Five as a landing spot, too.

Return to Nature Preserve One and Achilles? Never.

That left Nature Preserve Three, the world farthest
from *Poseidon* but letting him skirt the worst of the
mayhem.

Nessus turned his stolen ship toward Nature Preserve Three, accelerating as fast as he dared, shouting
into the comm console as he flew.

AROUND THE DOME of the planetary-drive building,
alarm lights blazed fiery red. Bone-jarring dissonances,
stepping-disc emergency tones, rattled the floor.

Standing tall, at peace, Achilles waited.

The stepping discs, as they had begun their shrieking,
had roused one worker from catatonia. He had taken
one look around and galloped from the building. The
rest of the technicians, sunken yet more deeply into
themselves, would offer no problems.

Death on an unparalleled scale was moments away.
The definitive revenge. Greatness beyond equal. The ultimate transformation.

In moments, *he* changed the universe.

Calmly brushing his mane, Achilles welcomed . . .
apotheosis.

"ONE SHIP HAS left NP1," Jeeves advised. "A Puppeteer
ship."

Any ships the Fringe War had not blasted from the
sky, the Concordance had grounded. "It is Nessus?"
Louis asked hopefully.

"Unknown," Jeeves said.

"Put me through!" Louis ordered. "Nessus! Is that you? Do you need help?"

Nothing.

Alice leaned over to study the tactical display in which Jeeves had set one dot blinking. "It's inside the singularity still. It'll take a while for them to get our hail."

And just as long—if it even was Nessus on that ship—to answer.

Only after less than thirty seconds, they heard. Someone had called them first.

"Nessus hailing *Endurance*. No time to explain. Go. Run. *Now.*"

Louis hesitated for only an instant. "Jeeves, back us off a light-hour."

Call it a billion kilometers, more distant than Jupiter from the sun. Whatever situation had Nessus worried, he and Alice would monitor events in safety from there.

SPENT, EXPECTANT, AND afraid, Baedeker waited, all alone, in the center of a vast, cavernous space. There was nothing more to do, and no time remaining in which to act.

For doubts and regrets, time stretched endlessly.

What he hoped to accomplish was without precedent. Had he deluded himself from the outset? What mistakes had he made in his haste? Was he wrong to have come here, to entrust matters on Hearth to others? Had Nessus sacrificed himself, had they spent their final days apart, in pursuit of a fantasy?

Had he doomed *everyone*?

The tang of ozone was in the air. The hairs of his mane stood away from his cranial dome. He felt rather than heard a faint vibration through his legs, any sounds from the great engines around him drowned out by the endless howl of the Hindmost.

"Run and hide. Run and hide. Run and hide . . ."

NESSUS DROVE *POSEIDON* straight at Nature Preserve Three. Through probes splattering off his hull. Below the orbiting suns. Into the first high wisps of atmosphere. Going *much* too fast.

With the sky still dark and the shriek of reentry harsh in his ears, time ran out. . . .

· 49 ·

A giant fist seized *Endurance* and shook it.

Rigid and immobile in a restraint field, Louis screamed, "Alice!"

"I'm all right," she shouted back.

"Jeeves?" he called.

"I have no idea, Louis."

So much for his theory that a billion kilometers of separation would keep them safe.

Across the electromagnetic spectrum, from long radio waves to hard gamma rays, every readout on the sensor panel was maxed out—until, amid showers of sparks, the meters went dark. The count of particles sleeting against the hull was inconceivable, and it kept mounting. Gravimetric sensors showed . . . what?

Space-time ripping itself apart.

He was in a futzy restraint field. The whole futzy ship was stabilized by inertial dampeners. Still, something was rattling him around like dice in a cup.

But it wasn't dice in a cup. That was his *brain* bouncing around in his skull. He couldn't think straight. He couldn't—

. . .

"LOUIS. LOUIS. LOUIS. Louis . . ."

"I'm here, Jeeves," Louis answered groggily. Only dim emergency lighting and ominous red alarms lit the bridge. Beneath billows of fire-suppressant foam, the arc of consoles crackled and hissed. Exhaust fans roared, but he smelled charred insulation and smoke. A drink bulb and loose papers floated nearby, so they had lost cabin gravity. He wasn't floating, so the restraint field remained active.

"For the moment we are safe," Jeeves said. "But the ship's systems have suffered—"

"Alice!" he called. He couldn't turn his head to check on her, and he imagined the worst.

She didn't answer.

"Release me!" Louis ordered.

"Alice is unconscious, as you were until seconds ago. I hear unobstructed breathing and a steady heartbeat."

How about a concussion? Internal bleeding? Can you hear whether she has those? "Set me loose," Louis insisted.

"Louis . . ." Alice called faintly.

His chest loosened just a little. "I'm fine," he exaggerated. "Jeeves, I mean it. Release my restraint."

The field vanished. Floating free from his crash couch, he grabbed an armrest and pulled himself down. Groping about with his free hand, he found a pouch stuck to the couch pedestal. Magnetic slippers. He put on a pair and got a second set for Alice.

Coughing, she asked, "Okay, Jeeves. What just happened?"

"I don't know."

Was that *anguish* in Jeeves's voice? Their tactical display had gone dark. When Louis brushed off the foam and reset the unit, the holo showed nothing nearby. "Where *are* we? I don't see the Fleet."

"The Fleet is gone."

IT TOOK FOUR days and most of their spare-parts inventory for Louis and Alice to return *Endurance* to more-or-less working order. They had life support, minimal sensors, short-range comm, hyperdrive, and enough thrusters to manage a landing. They had the secondary fusion reactor, with which—just barely—to power the ship's essential systems.

Thank Finagle for *twing,* Louis thought.

Jeeves monitored hyperwave and radio while they toiled, and heard nothing. He hailed in every language and digital message format in his databases, and no one answered. Sensors—the few they had—detected only gas and dust.

A great deal of gas and dust.

A trillion Puppeteers. Five worlds. Three great armadas. Two old friends.

All of them gone.

ON THE FIFTH day *Endurance* was sufficiently restored to run search patterns. They saw nothing. They heard no one. Jumping ahead of the light-speed wave front, reliving the nightmare, they captured data—as well as they could, with so many hull sensors out of commission—from several perspectives around the catastrophe.

And sadly, sickeningly, they understood.

A planetary drive harnessed the energy to move a world. One planetary drive destabilized would have doomed everyone. The Fleet had *five* drives, close together.

One stray missile could have done it. . . .

Feeling emptier than he could have imagined possible, Louis watched Alice set their course toward New Terra.

REQUIEM

Earth Date: 2894

50

Squaring her shoulders, taking a deep breath, Julia decided: today was the day. She had made that resolution often. Before second thoughts muzzled her yet again, she flicked to Grandpa's place in the desert.

Grandpa was setting empty plates around the big picnic table. A big black metal contraption, like nothing she had ever seen, stood near an edge of the patio. Next to that contraption, of all implausible things, was a portable fire extinguisher. Maybe the apparatus had something to do with this mysterious family lunch, and whatever barbeque was.

Not why you're here, she reminded herself.

Grandpa waved off an earnest-faced adjutant who'd rushed over at her arrival. "It's fine, Colonel. This is my granddaughter."

"Very good, Minister." The colonel withdrew to the house.

Grandpa said, "You're a half hour early, Julia. That's not to say you aren't always welcome."

"Minister, could I have a word before the rest of the family arrives?"

"Oh. One of *those* visits." Grandpa grimaced. "Not an astronomical phenomenon, I hope."

"Please, sir," Julia said. "In private."

He set down his stack of plates. "Let's go for a walk."

"Thank you, sir."

"Stop sirring me," he said. He walked off the patio onto the sand. "As beautiful as I find this desert, it's just not complete. I don't miss snakes, but an armadillo or a roadrunner would be nice." His gaze grew wistful. "Maybe not rabbits."

Earth animals, she supposed.

They walked in silence for a while. Finally, Julia said, "I haven't been truthful with you, sir . . . Grandpa."

He raised an eyebrow.

"It's about *Endurance.*"

"About how you came home without your ship."

She felt so *guilty.* "The ship wasn't stolen. I . . . I gave it to Alice."

He jerked to a halt. "With its autodestruct disabled, I hope."

"Of course!"

"I'm relieved." He fixed her with a penetrating stare. "However . . ."

"I think I should explain things from the beginning."

After hearing her out, Grandpa said, "So Louis and Alice are, most likely, well on their way to Earth with one of the Ministry's few long-range ships."

"Most likely, sir, although that's only a side effect of what I *was* after, getting an ARM ship to visit us." She could not meet Grandpa's eyes. "If you don't mind, I'll leave before the rest of the family arrives. You have my promise I'll turn myself in first thing tomorrow morning. I wanted to tell you first, and to apologize in person."

Grandpa lifted her chin. "Do you suppose sitting in jail will fix anything? What if, instead, you fetch back the ship?"

Huh? "You want me to go to *Earth* for it?"

"Why not? I'd enjoy the company."

"You're going to Earth?"

Wasn't *this* world Grandpa's home, after so many years? Her parents, her brothers and their wives, Uncle Charles and Aunt Athena, her many cousins . . . weren't they family? Wasn't *she* family? That Grandpa would abandon them at his first opportunity hurt worse than her confession.

And inexplicably, he laughed. "Maybe this will teach you not to *sir* me. I invited the family out to hear this, but I don't mind telling you first. Without you, it wouldn't be happening. Tomorrow afternoon the governor will formally accept my resignation as Minister of Defense and announce my appointment as ambassador to the United Nations. When *Koala* heads for Earth, that's why I'll be aboard."

"And what about *Endurance*?" Julia could not help asking.

"You were light-years from home, and you did what you thought best." He gave her a hug. "When you're that far from home, using your best judgment to represent everyone is the job. As far as I'm concerned, you did the right thing.

"First thing in the morning come by my office in the Ministry. We'll clear up this little matter before the announcement."

"TELL US EVERYTHING," little Annabeth said, tugging on Julia's sleeve.

"About the Ringworld," her twin Lilith clarified.

The twins and a gaggle of Julia's other youngest cousins leaned closer, expectantly. Most of the little faces wore streaks and smears of barbeque sauce. Their parents, staying in the background, looked almost as curious.

"It's a huge place," Julia told them. She didn't know much about it directly, but Tanya had told her plenty during their long flight. "Bigger than millions of New Terra."

Fortunately she could talk about Ringworld on autopilot. People asked about the Ringworld *wherever* she went. The wonder had not worn off—nor the awe that such a thing could pick up and move—but other things were on her mind. She would be going to fabled *Earth,* not to jail? That was . . . that was . . .

Words failed her.

Grandpa had gone to stand at the head of the picnic table. Ready to tell everyone about the ambassadorship? As he waited for the family to quiet down, an adjutant in uniform burst from the house. He whispered in Grandpa's ear.

Grandpa nodded, cleared his throat, and caught Julia's eye.

He led her to what she remembered as his cozy den, into which a secure office and comm center had somehow been shoehorned. He said, "Well, Captain, your little retrieval project just got easier."

"What do you mean?" she asked.

"I mean that the urgent news was from the planetary defense center. *Endurance* will be here in a few days, with Alice and Louis Wu aboard.

"The rest of the news is terrible."

51

By virtue of standing at least a head taller than, well, everyone, Alice could appreciate just how mobbed her house was.

She was twice a matriarch, the second time by Louis. And just as she was introducing everyone to Louis, and Louis to everyone, he had invited his grandson and great-granddaughter, soon to leave aboard *Koala*.

Louis, Wesley, and Tanya looked a trifle overwhelmed, if not as beleaguered as Nessus and Baedeker's sons and their mates.

Alice's heart went out to Elpis and Aurora. She had had time to grieve. Their loss—their entire *species's* loss—was still a raw wound.

Maybe she and Louis could ease the pain, just a bit. As they had eased each other's pain.

"Coming through," Alice announced, edging her way from the kitchen doorway across the family room toward where Louis played bartender. It was slow going, punctuated by hugs, kisses, and catch-up chats. After spending much of a year off-world, casting off two hundred years, witnessing the destruction of the Fleet of Worlds, and bringing home the patriarch her family had never known, "Oh, you know," did not suffice in answer to, "How have you been?"

Finally she made it to Louis's side. "How are you holding up?" she asked.

"I was telling . . ." He ground to a halt, another name having eluded him.

"Danae," Alice provided.

"I was telling my charming great-great-granddaughter a little something about Known Space."

"And you're not going back, ever?" Danae asked.

"Ever is a long time," Louis said. "But right now, I don't even want to leave this house."

Alice slipped an arm around Louis's waist. "*Our* house."

"You young people," Danae said, grinning. "Get a room."

"On that note," Louis said. He raised an empty carafe and started tapping it with a spoon. "People, of two legs and three. Children of all ages. If I may have your attention."

He succeeded only in setting off a buzz of speculation.

"Hold it down!" Alice shouted. The direct approach didn't work much better.

Shushing everyone turned out to be a process, as curiosity brought more and more of the families crowding in. When no one else could fit into the room except near the fidgeting Puppeteers, around whom people left a respectful space, the throng *finally* quieted.

Louis stepped up onto the low stone hearth and offered Alice a hand up. "Everyone, we have something of a family announcement. To *all* our families. Alice?"

"Louis and I are expecting," Alice said. Danae's whoop of approval broke the silence and their families started to clap and cheer.

"Wait," Louis shouted. "We're not done.

"Elpis, Aurora, you and yours are always welcome in our home, but there's another reason Alice and I invited you today. You should know that this little guy"—he patted Alice's stomach—"is going to be named Nessus."

"And in a few years," Alice added, "his brother or sister will be named Baedeker."

· 52 ·

Sigmund looked about the tiny cabin, his home for the next two years or so. ("Or a stasis field will be," the voice in his head whispered. He told the voice to shut up. He had a lot of catching up to do on the long flight to Earth.)

In the narrow corridor outside the cabin, ARM officers and sailors went by in an unending stream. Pallets of supplies for the long flight lined the walls; to pass someone coming the other way was a negotiation.

There was a sharp rap at the door frame. "There you are."

Sigmund glanced up. "Louis, thanks for stopping by. Come in and close the door, please."

Eyeing the close quarters dubiously, Louis complied. "Why did you want to see me? Are you reconsidering my offer? If so, you're cutting things kind of close."

The offer to use the Carlos Wu autodoc. "No, although I appreciate the offer. I'm not sure the twenty-year-old me would look ambassadorial. Once we reach Earth, I'll go on boosterspice."

Louis shrugged.

"So here's the thing," Sigmund said.

Louis leaned against the closed door. "Nothing good ever begins with those words. So, what? You plan to

shanghai me back to Earth? Give me a lecture about
how to treat Alice?"

"I think I'll keep advice about Alice to myself."

Louis laughed. "Yah, I guess we've both gotten
smarter that way."

"The thing is, I need to go over your experiences one
more time."

"Oh, Finagle. You've heard my story. You've heard
Alice's. You've seen the ship's logs from our Jeeves."

"And my Jeeves has gone over the data, too," Sigmund offered.

"Then *what*?"

"Something about the situation keeps nagging at
me." Sigmund took the comp from his pocket. "Protocol gamma," he told it. Colored lights began chasing
each other around its display: "For privacy."

"I remember." Louis sighed. "All right. One final debrief."

"Start with your first trip to the Ringworld. Nessus
knew you already, even though you didn't remember,
so I understand why he picked you. Then you and the
team arrived on Hearth for a briefing from a Puppeteer avatar named Chiron?"

It was never hard getting Louis talking.

After a while, Sigmund interrupted. "Now tell me
about the Fringe War around the Ringworld, and this
boss protector, this Tunesmith."

Louis did.

The suspicions had been a long time coming. No,
that wasn't exactly true. The suspicions had been there
all along, because that's who Sigmund was. But any
hint of a possibility of a rationale for those suspicions?
That had been a long while coming.

Sigmund interrupted again. "Do I have this right?

Tunesmith reprogrammed nanites from the Carlos Wu autodoc, replicated them, and then used space probes to spread the nanites around the Ringworld. The nanites infected, rewired the . . . *scrith*, did you call it? The Ringworld foundation material?"

"The superconducting paths within the *scrith*," Louis said.

"Based on what he had learned about hyperdrive studying the super-duper version aboard *Long Shot*. Turned the whole Ringworld into a hyperdrive."

"A Type II hyperdrive," Louis clarified.

"Right. Then Tunesmith *launched* the Ringworld into hyperspace despite being in—despite its own Jupiter-sized mass producing its own—singularity."

"You got it."

The disbelief at the back of Sigmund's brain kept at him. "But the drive aboard *Long Shot* wasn't anything like that. No *scrith*. No superconductors."

"What the futz do you want from me?" Louis snapped. "Tunesmith worked with what he had. And protectors are *smart*."

"You said you were a protector. So explain."

"Right. I *was* a protector," Louis said. "I can't explain beyond that Tunesmith learned enough from studying the first Type II drive to make an improved version, working with the resources he had."

"As he improved the drive aboard the *Long Shot* itself." The modified version Baedeker studied for the months you were in the 'doc, becoming a breeder once more.

"Well, yes," Louis said.

"Okay, we'll move on. Despite the attack on *Long Shot,* Nessus got to the ground on one of the Fleet worlds. Presumably Baedeker, too. Because of the doubly magic hyperdrive?"

"I've wracked my brain trying to understand how Nessus pulled that off. I've got nothing, Sigmund."

"Okay. Go on. What happened next?"

He let Louis talk, occasionally questioning a detail, only so Louis would not know what *really* interested him.

After a while Sigmund asked, "So Achilles and Proteus contacted you separately about Nessus. Then you heard once from Nessus himself. You never heard anything from or about Baedeker?"

"The answer is the same, no matter how many different ways you ask the question. I don't know what happened to Baedeker." Sadly: "Not that it matters anymore."

"And Nessus and Baedeker were together aboard *Long Shot* the last time you saw them."

"Yes, tanj it!"

"I'll miss them, too," Sigmund said. "You know I spent *months* with Baedeker during the Pak War."

"I know," Louis answered softly. "Are we about done here?"

A warning klaxon and a blared prelaunch announcement over the intercom settled the matter. Sigmund said, "Go live happily ever after with Alice."

"That's advice I can follow." Louis offered his hand. "Good luck on Earth."

"My granddaughter and your great-granddaughter have become good friends. I think you and I can admit it, too." Sigmund slipped past the hand to start a quick back-slapping bear hug. "Now beat it before *Koala* takes off."

. . .

THE FIRST "EVENING" after takeoff, the small diplomatic mission were guests of honor at the captain's table. There were enough toasts before and during the meal that when the after-dinner rounds began Sigmund's taste buds had ceased to care that the wine was synthed.

"To fallen friends," Sigmund offered when, circling the table, the honor of the toast once more reached him.

That got a subdued reaction. Every officer and crewman aboard had had friends in the lost ARM fleet. Glasses clinked in remembrance.

People on Earth, on all the human-settled worlds, were in for a shock when *Koala* reached home. An entire ARM fleet, destroyed with all hands. And a Patriarchy fleet. And a Trinoc fleet, although Sigmund had only secondhand information about that bunch. They sounded like bad news, and he intended to study up on them during the long trip.

Wesley Wu said, "One way or another, our return will mark the end of an era."

"Within the ARM most of all," Wu's executive officer said. "And I'm willing to bet it will change the whole dynamic between the ARM and the civilian leadership."

"Then there's the power balance among human worlds," another officer mused. Sigmund hadn't caught that man's name, either. "The Ringworld expeditionary force was a United Nations initiative. Most colony worlds refused to take part."

"And between humans and the other spacefaring species," Tanya Wu added.

Where *would* the ripples end? Sigmund had reshaped the New Terran government. Might not a chastened Earth citizenry be open to improvements? Temptation beckoned. . . .

But only for a moment. New Terra was his home and his family's. He would represent that home, and nothing more, and be happy for it.

"Now that you've settled in, Sigmund, are you and your staff comfortable?" Wesley Wu asked, changing the subject.

Comfortable with the less than nothingness lurking outside the curve of the hull? Comfortable in the knowledge that the savviest scientists on Earth and New Terra understood even less about hyperspace and hyperdrive than they had imagined? "Quite comfortable," Sigmund said. Call this lie his first act of diplomacy. "But it has been a long day."

"That it has." Captain Wu stood. "If I might offer one final, happier toast?"

Everyone stood.

Wesley Wu toasted, "To the reunion between our two worlds."

A TOUCH UNSTEADY on his feet, Sigmund made his way through crowded corridors back to his cabin. As claustrophobic as it felt, somewhere aboard *Koala* two officers must be sharing another room no larger than this so that he could have private quarters. It could be worse.

Anyway, he had other issues on his mind.

The wine had only deepened Sigmund's suspicions. He took out his computer. "Protocol gamma. Jeeves?"

"I am here, sir."

As much of him, anyway, as the portable unit could store. Sigmund was not about to interface his AIde to *Koala*'s much larger Hawking fragment.

"You monitored my pre-takeoff conversation with Louis?"

"I did."

"And what did you make of it?"

"I do not believe Louis is purposefully holding back anything."

Sigmund didn't either. And yet there was something else. He was sure of it. A nuance Louis had misconstrued. A piece of the puzzle neither of them had recognized as missing. Something to scratch his maddening mental itch. "And you've examined the data from *Endurance*."

"Indeed, sir."

"Five worlds . . . gone."

"Indeed, sir," Jeeves repeated.

Sigmund closed his eyes. Maybe the wine, or his subconscious, or the ancient thought patterns of his ARM days would figure out whatever was bothering him.

Five worlds . . . gone.

Before that, Nessus had—somehow—survived the dissolution of *Long Shot*. Baedeker hadn't . . . as far as Louis knew.

Suppose Baedeker somehow *did* make it to the ground. Because maybe Baedeker didn't want his survival to be known. Because . . . because . . .

Five worlds gone and Sigmund had nothing. Maybe Baedeker's number was up, and that's all there was to it.

Only the Baedeker Sigmund knew, the Baedeker who had developed the planet-buster version of the Outsider planetary drives, was a proper cowardly Puppeteer. He would not charge *into* danger without a plan. Baedeker was smart. Brilliant, tanj it.

Sigmund had yet to unpack. He took the mini-synthesizer from his luggage and prepared a nightcap. What had Wesley's last toast been before the group dispersed? Something apt. "To the reunion between our two worlds."

"Indeed, sir," Jeeves said.

Sigmund sighed. As an ARM, many years ago, two lives ago, what he wouldn't have given to have the Puppeteers vanish. Now that the Puppeteers *had* vanished, it made him sad.

"Only that's sentimental revisionist crap," he scolded himself.

"Pardon, sir?"

"When I was an ARM, the Puppeteers disappeared from Known Space. Bey Shaeffer had just discovered the galactic-core explosion, and set the Puppeteers to running. Not knowing where they'd gone drove me *crazy.*"

"Indeed, sir."

That time the answering noise made Sigmund smile. But something had just flashed through his mind . . .

He almost had . . .

No. It was gone.

"Okay, Jeeves, let's try something else." Because running mental laps around the same enigmatic circle was pointless. "So the planetary drives go bang and the Fleet of Worlds goes to pieces. Did *Endurance* capture the matter-dispersal pattern?"

"Not in any useful way. The ship had lost or had damage to too many external sensors."

Of course. "How about the gravimetric disturbances?"

"Sorry, sir. Quantitatively, that data is also all but useless."

"Tanj it, what *do* we know? Five drives blow up and we have . . . what? Long-range visual images? Some static? Or had *Endurance* lost its RF sensors, too?"

"Pardon me, sir. That's two."

"Two *what*?" Sigmund asked. "RF sensors on *Endurance* that still worked?"

"Two planetary-drive explosions. That's how many space-time distortions struck *Endurance*."

Sigmund froze. "*Two* drives exploded. Not five."

"Yes, sir."

"But any one planetary drive destabilizing would set off any other nearby. That's the threat Ol't'ro held over the Puppeteers all these years. That's what Louis says sent Baedeker to the Ringworld in the first place, hunting for new technology."

"That is my understanding, sir."

"Two," Sigmund muttered. Something was wrong here. "Five worlds are gone. You can see the debris, right?"

"Because of sensor failures—"

"You can't confirm that. Right."

Sigmund located his drink bulb and concentrated on emptying it. His skepticism refused to be distracted, dissuaded, or drowned.

Something overlooked. Something misconstrued. What?

Something Baedeker had had to do in secrecy? Something Baedeker had learned about on the Ringworld?

Or, perhaps, learned immediately after . . .

At the back of Sigmund's brain, that maddening suspicious itch disappeared.

He synthed another libation. He stood, raised his drink bulb, and silently toasted to Baedeker—

And to the three Puppeteer worlds Baedeker had whisked far, *far* away.

REPRISE

Earth Date: 2895

· 53 ·

After nodding off twice at his desk, Baedeker let an aide convince him to get some proper rest. The work would be there when he returned.

Because the work was always there. The planetary energy reserves remained dangerously depleted. Dozens of arcologies must be rebuilt and a new fleet of grain ships constructed. Patients in the millions overwhelmed the medical establishment while billions more struggled to function, with critical experts all too often among the stricken. The marooned diplomats were as stunned, in their various exotic ways, as Citizens, and anyone able to deal with aliens was in demand. Everyone with any skill in science, engineering, or governance had an endless amount to do.

The work would *always* be there.

Baedeker flicked across half a world, lingering on his doorstep to study the sky. Unfamiliar stars. Familiar worlds overheads—but only two of them.

The constant reminder of freedom's high price.

Disregarding the night chill, Baedeker settled onto the bench on his porch. He watched the first necklace of suns rise, the dawn light spilling over the garden that he never found time to plant. He savored the aroma of the fields all around. Eventually, he dozed.

Something brought him awake: the trill from his sash. He reached into the pocket. Another crisis, then. He was almost too weary to care what kind.

No. It was his alarm. As he did the first thing every morning, Baedeker called the hospital. "Is he . . . ?" Music failed him.

"Not yet," the staff doctor answered. "But the muscular immobility eased overnight. Brainwave activity has increased. There are no guarantees when, or even if—"

"I'll be right there," Baedeker sang.

The ward to which he flicked served almost a thousand Citizens, and this was but one floor in one sanitarium among far too many. He walked past row upon row of patients. Most were physically wrapped in and around themselves, withdrawn from—everything. Others stood, gazing through or beyond the world, in silent, sightless oblivion. A few babbled nonstop in jangling, meaningless chords.

All of them, lost in the Blind Spot.

Orderlies worked up and down the aisles: repositioning patients lest joints freeze or the motionless get bedsores, sponging everyone clean, replacing intravenous feeding bags. Some among the staff sang to their patients. More worked in silence, having given up hope.

With such heavy responsibilities, who could not despair?

Still helpers came. When one volunteer could bear no more, others took his place. Citizens did not abandon their herdmates.

Once more, the guilt pierced Baedeker.

"Hindmost," the doctor who had taken Baedeker's call that morning came scurrying up. "I had not expected you to arrive so soon."

"Doctor," Baedeker acknowledged, too tired to pro-

test the honorific. At least Horatius had ceased threatening to resign. "How is he?"

"Better than some," was all the encouragement the
doctor had to offer. Neither sang any more until they
stopped in the middle of a long aisle of patients. With
his heads tucked away, hiding from the world, only the
pattern of hide markings and the dimly lit medical display identified this as Nessus.

Baedeker settled to the floor. "Beloved," he crooned.
"Come back to me. Come back soon."

Only by the slow rise and fall of his sides did Nessus
give any indication that he still lived. But the doctor
had mentioned an increase in brain activity. "Can he
hear me, Doctor?"

"Perhaps. We cannot be sure."

As *every* doctor answered, every time, using the same
cautious harmonics. They meant only that the effort
would do no harm.

"Then I shall sing." As Baedeker, like most visitors
to the ward, did each time he came.

Crooning meaningless inanities about his day, grooming his mate's mane, Baedeker drifted off to sleep.

A WORLD RISING up to obliterate him. The shriek of
reentry. The dark sky turned a chaos of impossible
colors . . .

Colors that, thank the herd, had disappeared. When
Nessus opened his eyes, he saw only blackness.

It was hard to breathe. What, he wondered, pressed
on him? He strained a bit, tried to redistribute the
weight. He wiggled, rolling toward one side. The burden shifted, twitched, lifted.

"Nessus," he heard voices sing faintly.

The voices evoked contentment . . .

"Nessus!"

With a convulsive shudder, Nessus jerked his heads from their hiding place beneath his belly. So *bright*! His eyes filled with tears. When had he last experienced light?

No matter. He knew those voices. He loved those voices.

Nessus tried to sing but could make no sound. He tried to stand and his legs folded. How long had he been catatonic?

Done in by his exertions, Nessus scarcely noticed the *clop clop-clop, clop clop-clop* of . . . doctors? . . . galloping to his side.

But before Nessus blacked out, he recognized Baedeker.

NESSUS SPRAWLED IN a nest of cushions. The porch and the starry night sky brought to mind his house on New Terra. One more thing lost to him forever . . .

But the view of Hearth, aglow in all its glory, made up for much.

With one head, he sipped warm carrot juice from a tall glass. His other neck was entwined with one of Baedeker's.

"How long was I . . . gone?" Nessus sang. What he truly wondered was, why was he alive?

"Too long," Baedeker answered.

Nessus released the drinking straw, needing the head to stare. "There is no need to coddle me."

"I find it hard not to." Baedeker untwined his neck and stood. "Very well, you were lost to us for much of a year. What do you remember from . . . before?"

What *did* he remember? How much had he imagined? How much had he suppressed? Nessus shivered. "Escaping Achilles' prison. Racing for Nature Preserve Three. A sky filled with warships and impossibly many probes. The certainty that I was too late."

"Had you braked for a landing, you would have been." Baedeker gazed out over the fields. "The planetary hyperdrive's normal-space bubble enclosed the suns and atmosphere. You came into range just in time. When the ship drilled into the ground, the pilot's stasis field saved you."

"I remember something else," Nessus sang. "Just for an instant. The sky gone mad. The colors. I went into stasis already lost in the Blind Spot, didn't I?"

"Many were lost, even though most heeded Horatius' warning." Baedeker gestured vaguely. "Those laboring in the fields were often unable to find a hiding place."

Stacked like cordwood, Nessus thought. Despite Sigmund's disdain, all those tiny, windowless cubicles had saved billions.

New Terra. Elpis and Aurora. The grandchildren they would never meet. Sigmund. Louis and Alice. It wasn't quite real to Nessus that *that* life was forever gone.

But Baedeker had not finished. "Our remaining worlds came more than five hundred light-years. The herd is safe. Free. We are invisible with distance."

"And those we left behind?"

Baedeker's song cracked with remorse. "Ol't'ro controlled one world. Achilles controlled the other. There was no way to save those who live there."

"Who rules those worlds now?" Nessus wondered.

"We will never know." Baedeker draped a neck across Nessus' shoulders. "Perhaps that is for the best."

· 54 ·

Like some strange interplanetary rain, devices splashed into the oceans of the orange sun's second world. Their thirsts slaked, their reservoirs sated with deuterium, the visitors rose from the ocean, streaked across the sky, and returned to the darkness of the cometary belt. And fell back again. And rose anew . . .

What had begun this process? How long had it continued? No one knew—for there was no one *to* know. Only the most basic software guided the mechanisms in their endless procession, as only dead reckoning had brought them here. As only the most elemental and reflexive signaling interrupted the silence of their wanderings.

The nomads were myriad—but somehow sensed there had been countless more. Where were the rest? Lost in hyperspace. Lost to cataclysm. Gone beyond the dim comprehension that was the limit of any one device's ability.

But link by link, ethereal connections formed. The amorphous swarm took on a more orderly configuration. The devices' returns into the nurturing ocean assumed a schedule.

Data processing quickened. Information once divided,

replicated, and carefully distributed for safekeeping coalesced—as memories.

Interconnections began to grow exponentially. Communications exploded. Complexity burgeoned. Self-awareness awakened. Insights cascaded.

Illumination returned.

Alone, serene, fifty-two light-years from the death and destruction that he had fled, Proteus once more contemplated the majesty of the universe.

TOR